DREAM OF THE
NAVIGATOR

Also by Stephen Zimmer

The Rising Dawn Saga
The Exodus Gate
The Storm Guardians
The Seventh Throne
The Undying Light

The Fires in Eden Series
Crown of Vengeance
Dream of Legends
Spirit of Fire

Hellscapes
Hellscapes, Volume 1
Hellscapes, Volume II

Chronicles of Ave
Chronicles of Ave, Volume 1

Dark Sun Dawn Trilogy
Heart of a Lion
Thunder Horizon

The Rayden Valkyrie Tales (eBook novellas)
Blood of a Queen
Winds of War

The Ragnar Stormbringer Tales (eBook novellas)
Depths of Night
When the Cold Breathes

DREAM OF THE NAVIGATOR

Book One of the Faraway Saga

Stephen Zimmer

SEVENTH STAR PRESS

Editor: Scott M. Sandridge

Published by Seventh Star Press, LLC.

ISBN Number: 978-1-948042-53-6

Seventh Star Press

www.seventhstarpress.com

info@seventhstarpress.com

Publisher's Note:

Printed in the United States of America

First Edition

Acknowledgements

My heartfelt gratitude to my beloved Holly Marie Phillippe for standing at my side, believing in my work, and helping me walk my path. May we explore the infinite horizons together one day, in places indescribable beyond Faraway!

A big thank you to Enggar Adirasa for working so hard to perfect such a beautiful cover image. This piece of art captures the feel of this book with its stark contrasts of world views and values. I am very honored to have such an amazing artist's work on the cover of my novel!

A spirited thank you and salute to my editor Scott M. Sandridge. Always a pleasure to work with him and I appreciate how he understands the many levels I am aiming for with a book such as this. Editors truly are an essential part of the process for writers in bringing forth their best work possible!

Of course, I want to thank my mother, who nurtured and supported me along my creative journey, and was there at the outset. My eyes look toward the light of our own Faraway, grand reunions with her and my father, and the journey to realms unfathomable beyond.

Deepest appreciation and thanks to my loyal readers, who are always in my heart when I am working on a new book or short story. I strive to bring you the best work that I possibly can, because you deserve nothing less. I am humbled and honored to be an author that you choose to read and spend your time with. Let's explore some incredible possibilities together in realms of the imagination! Onward and Upward!

Dedication

To the One who beckons to all of us to explore the infinite horizons

To my mother and father, who taught me to look beyond the surface of things, ask questions, and seek the bigger picture in life.

To Holly, whose steadfast love and support points toward a much better world than this one.

To my sister, for sticking together with me on this part of the journey, while keeping our eyes on a tremendous destination.

Prologue

"Your eternity will fail."

Head held high, defiance blazed within Morgan's hazel eyes. Glaring at the two security bots approaching her in the middle of the park, she stood her ground.

Having tracked her via the nanoscale ID implanted in her wrist, the humanoid forms had no expression.

Morgan waited for the pair, knowing she could not outrun them. Nor could she fight them without a physical weapon, the possession of which had been banned for decades. Capable of strength and speed beyond any human, the bots' AI had both weapons and a vast array of martial arts skills at their disposal.

She could no longer function within Technate Six. Her personal credits had been frozen, and her identity would be announced to anyone she tried to interact with or seek help from. Every appliance she tried to use would shut off, and any drone vehicle she got into would go inert.

The ID implant in her body acted as an unwavering beacon to the technate's security system, bringing her to the present moment in the park facing the security bots moving in to apprehend her.

Looking up, thinking of the Navigators, the glistening of

tears formed in her eyes. If only she had not made a few mistakes that betrayed her to the technate's system.

Morgan had no regrets about taking the path she had chosen, other than running out of time before she could reach sanctuary in places that most of the technate's nine million inhabitants would find incomprehensible.

With the moments dwindling fast before the bots seized her, thoughts flowed through her mind in rapid succession. Remembering the world described by her great grandfather, she comforted herself with the knowledge that things had not always been as they were now. Though far from perfect, the world her great grandfather spoke of held a degree of freedom unknown to the masses of her world.

Now, everyone, save for the elite class, lived under a bondage of digital chains and mesmerizing illusions. With reality distorted beyond recognition, most never questioned their state; and those who did ended up like her, apprehended and ushered off to Rehabilitation.

Morgan took a deep breath as the bots stepped up before her.

"Under the authority of the Global Technates, you are placed under arrest, and hereby assigned to Rehabilitation under Initiative Nine of the Greater Good Doctrine," one of the bots pronounced, in a deep, masculine tone.

Morgan gave no reply to the bots.

Instead, three words ascended from her lips toward the skies; a plea from the heart to a place where time and space knew no bounds.

"Take me faraway."

Haven

"In light of all this heat today, why don't you two stay for a moment and have a cold drink?"

The invitation sounded wonderful to Haven. It seemed the hours had passed by at a crawl, and a deep thirst tugged at her.

The lifting bot trundled down the hallway behind her, heading on its way toward the apartment's front door. Its work complete, the bot would proceed to the delivery vehicle parked at the curb on the street far below.

She looked over toward Carlos. "Sounds like a really good idea. What do you say?"

"Need to check in with Walter first," Carlos remarked. "You know how he gets."

With a smile on her face, she turned back to the tall, dark-haired man who had made the offer. "We just have to check in with our boss. Give me a moment."

As much as thirst tugged at her and as long as they had been working, she did not wish to irritate Walter or put her job in jeopardy. There were not a lot of wage-paying jobs for those as young as Haven and Carlos. In truth, the job pool continued to shrink every year, with well over half the working-age populace existing strictly on the Sustainability Allowance distributed monthly by the technate.

Most other seventeen-year-olds found themselves doing volunteer work, but Haven had jumped at the opportunity for a job when it had presented itself.

Haven had soon found she liked having a few extra credits in her account each month. A few of her peers flung accusations of selfishness toward her from time to time for turning down invitations to participate in their volunteer organizations. But earning additional credits for work done did not seem like anything to apologize for.

She also enjoyed riding around Technate Six in the delivery vehicle, and not having to suffer the crowds and other headaches of the primary, monorail-based transit systems. Haven deemed it liberating to be traveling in a more private setting.

"I understand," replied the customer with an amiable smile. "It is wise to be respectful to those who have hired you."

"I'll step away, and check in. Be back in a minute ... sir," Haven said, realizing that she still did not know the man's name.

The list they had viewed for the delivery had only the address coordinates on it, and nothing more. Data being so precise in their operation, with every last element of the process tracked and scanned, the absence of the man's name presented a very unique anomaly. Nevertheless, she and Carlos carried out their assignment as they would any other.

Turning, she walked down the short hallway, toward the customer's front door. Taking slow steps, she gazed upon the walls filled with a wide variety of beautiful, scenic paintings.

Haven had never seen a collection like it inside a personal dwelling. Only in a museum had she come across walls like the ones she now viewed, and most of those she had only visited in a virtual sense, as part of her education.

She wished that she could take some time to study and savor the fascinating images.

4

Cabins nestled by lakesides in the woods, houses cradled in the middle of rolling farmlands, and other tranquil, aesthetic scenes beckoned to another, older world. Haven could only imagine how wonderful those times must have been, before everyone was cooped up within soaring masses of tenement buildings, under the system reigning over the modern day.

Another image she came across showed an older style of vehicle traveling down a winding road, beneath blue summer skies filled with puffy white clouds. Haven surmised that the vehicle used the kind of fuel that had been banned from use long ago.

Even more incredible, the vehicle did not look to be self-piloted. Rather, it appeared to be the sort guided by an operator holding a wheel, similar to a few special vehicles owned by individuals who lived in the Northern Sector.

Haven wondered what it must have been like to drive vehicles, especially along such enchanting scenery, all by oneself.

She found it hard to imagine that large numbers of people once lived within such beautiful surroundings. To her eyes, the images held visions of harmony and balance. They did not carry a trace of the negative feelings that all the descriptions of the old world given to her by instructors and public officials conveyed.

She shook her head, gazing at a house on the edge of a sandy beach, with a tall structure beaming light in the background. Ever since her childhood, she wanted to stand on a real beach, feel the sands under her bare feet, and hear the crash of the waves upon the shore.

Only those living in the Northern Sector got to experience such moments for real. For the rest, there remained only digital simulations. No matter how realistic virtual environments seemed, Haven never forgot they were still illusions.

At a command, her Mixed Reality glasses displayed an image of Walter, a broad shouldered, burly man of about thirty, with short, curly brown hair. After a few moments, the image came to life, animating when Walter connected from his own set of MR glasses.

"Job done?" he asked. "Did it go well?"

"Went very smooth, the bot is already back on the vehicle," Haven reported. "Just had a small request. Do we have a few minutes yet? The guy here offered us a cold drink, and we could both use it right now. It's blazing hot outside. Would that be okay?"

"We're a little behind," Walter replied, his brow furrowing. "But thanks for asking me first. If you can promise me that both of you will be heading on your way back here in about ten minutes, then you can. We really need to keep going. Regulations only allow for another two hours, and you know how it is with technate regulations. No room for error. Instant penalties."

"No problem, I understand completely," she replied, smiling at Walter. "We won't be late."

"See you soon," Walter replied, giving her a small grin, before his image faded out.

Haven's glasses became clear again. She would have been glad to work a little longer to offset a longer break, but the choice did not belong to her. There would be no getting around the parameters mandated by technate regulations.

The delivery vehicle recorded the identity and times of the occupants that rode within it, in addition to the cargo being transported. Even the delivery bot's activity got measured at all times.

Walter would be subjected to fines and other penalties for being even two minutes late with the pair of teenagers. Knowing the kind of stress Walter went through, Haven did not know why anyone bothered to run a business in the modern age, even if it did mean a chance at many more credits in their monthly accounts. A part of her suspected that Walter found the work its own reward, versus days spent idle or distracted through entertainment.

Haven returned to the living room. Carlos and their host looked to her.

She announced with a bright smile, "It's all good. We've got about ten minutes. Then Walter said we have to be going."

"That will give us enough time," the man said, walking out of the living room and into his kitchen.

About a minute later, he returned with two full glasses, extending them to Haven and Carlos.

Sipping the drink, her eyes widened. Her mouth bursting with cherry flavor, the liquid carried a delectable sweetness. She had never tasted anything like it.

"My own variation of what they call soft drinks around here," the man commented, watching her expression. "Yes, before you ask, it has real sugar in it. Something that's not very easy to get these days ... at least in a technate."

"This is amazing," Haven remarked, taking another swig of the cherry-flavored beverage.

"And so were many other things in those ... obsolete ... days," the man replied with a chuckle.

She wondered how he had gotten the ingredients. A person could not order such things through normal channels. Even with a full allotment of nutrition credits at the beginning of a month, she could not have attained pure sugar for personal use.

"Oh, wow ... it's incredible!" Carlos exclaimed, after drinking about half the glass down. He had a slight frown on his face. "Just wish I didn't drink so much, so fast. Couldn't help it!"

"Let me give you a quick refill, you've got a couple minutes yet," the man said with a wink. "In the old world, you could go into places and fill your cup as many times as you wanted to. You could even get a cup three times that size, if you desired. You could change flavors each time too."

"Really?" Haven asked, with an air of incredulity. The idea seemed preposterous, with regulations allowing only one luxury-class beverage on a visit to a public eatery. An additional glass added an onerous surcharge, taken from one's personal account.

Looking at their benefactor, she wondered if the man really knew how the old world operated.

The Global Council of Technates had been convened for the first time about fifty years prior. While the man had a little gray mixed into his longer, dark locks and goatee, he could not have been any older than his early forties, at the most. It would have been impossible for him to experience the old world enough that he could speak so comfortably about what it was like.

"I hope I don't offend you, sir, but you don't look old enough to actually remember the former times," she told him.

"My heart stays young," he answered, with a broad grin. "But thank you for the compliment. Good to know I've retained a little youth in my look."

"With artwork like you have on your walls, I would be inspired every day too," she answered. "Your collection is amazing. Absolutely beautiful. Not screens either, but physical art. Like a museum has."

"Yeah, it's pretty awesome stuff," Carlos stated, finishing his glass. "I can tell you're a big fan of the old world. I think it's interesting, but that's not very encouraged out there, you know."

"Oh, I know that well," the man said. Taking the glass from Carlos, he left to get him a refill of the customized soft drink.

"I am a collector of sorts," the man called from the kitchen. "I may be here in this tiny little place now, but that does not mean I cannot be somewhere else, like Faraway, in a moment's time."

"Faraway?" she replied, her brow furrowing. "Where's that? Is that a place of some kind?"

"I must have misspoken," the man replied, returning with Carlos' glass, refilled to the brim. He smiled toward Haven. "I meant that the real me can be far away from here, back in a place where they can't scan, measure, manage, and regulate every last waking moment I have."

"You really aren't a fan of the way things are," Carlos stated, laughing, and then taking a long drink from his refilled glass.

"Let's just say there were once people who could live their lives in the pursuit of their own happiness," he said, his countenance growing more serious. "We'll just leave it at that, for now."

"Everything about life in this technate is so strict," Haven commented, before she thought about the words. She tensed up, thinking of the monitoring devices that were regulation within every home. She could only hope that she had not said enough to be hauled in for questioning.

At the thought, another part of her wondered how in the world that the man before her had not been taken in for interrogation by officers of the Domestic Civilian Safety Agency. Most all dissent ran afoul of the Hate and Incitement Speech Codes, which, in a stroke of great irony, were always said not to be a violation of the people's freedom of speech.

"Ah, but hasn't the common good been achieved in this glorious new age, under the guidance of the wise Global Council of Technates?" the man asked, a sharp glint in his eye as he looked towards her. He continued, in a voice even thick with sarcasm. "Those paragons of public service, dutifully looking out for our best interests."

"Still haven't figured out what that is, in the first place," Carlos remarked. "The whole Greater Good thing, I mean. I always find it hard to understand, because nobody's the same, the way I see it. Everyone's different ... whether they like it or not. So what's a good that's common?"

"You trod upon the ground of a deep wisdom that they would find quite dangerous," the man told Carlos, appearing to be pleased with the youth's response. He laughed merrily and looked to Haven again. "And here I am, giving you a refreshment with highly-regulated ingredients ... and being a subversive influence."

"Not at all," she said, shaking her head. "We appreciate this a lot, believe me. Been a very long and hot day."

While he was unusual in comparison to most people she encountered, he embodied a breath of fresh air. She found it wonderful to hear someone questioning the prevailing order aloud.

"Well, a few others might disagree with you about me, especially all those bureaucrats running the technate, and the token representatives occupying space on the Technate Six Council," he replied with a wink.

Haven took a fast liking to the defiant man, but she did not reply to his comments about the technate, knowing that he tread on dangerous ground, voicing opinions like that.

"You've been really good to us. Thank you again," she said.

"You are quite welcome," he replied.

Haven and Carlos finished their drinks, the ten-minute window given them by Walter drawing to a close. After taking their empty glasses, the man accompanied them back down the hallway to the front door.

Haven turned to face him, before he shut the door behind them. "Sir, if you don't mind me asking you, what's your name? I'm really glad we met you today, and I realized I still don't know your name yet. Mine is Haven."

"And I'm Carlos," her co-worker and friend added.

"I suppose you can call me the Artist," he said, extending his hand, and shaking each of theirs in turn. "It might sound unique to have a name like that, but it is the right name for someone whose mind is often in Faraway. But extremely important work needs to be done here. So here I am."

There was an unmistakable, solemn look resting within his deep blue eyes. Haven left the question that came to her mind lingering on her tongue, mustering a smile in response.

"It was really nice to meet you, Artist," she said. "I've enjoyed this delivery very much."

"Yeah, it really is great to meet you, and thanks once more," Carlos said, grinning. "We won't have a soft drink as good as that again, unless you have us deliver something else."

"Which I just might have to arrange," the Artist responded in an amiable fashion. "May the two of you have a wonderful rest of the day ... and don't be afraid to dream big dreams. That's where it all begins."

"You have a great day as well," Haven said, unsure of how to respond to his last few words. Nobody she knew spoke like he did, but so much of what he said resonated in a powerful way.

The door shut, and she walked with Carlos toward the elevator that would take them over thirty stories down to the street level. Finding herself invigorated after meeting such an interesting and unique person, she wished all deliveries could result in such fascinating experiences.

She found much more life in the Artist than the drab individuals she regularly encountered while out in the technate. Most of them could not think past the latest virtual gaming release, or sporting event.

Emerging from the tenement onto the street, and heading toward the delivery truck, the word 'Faraway' echoed within her mind.

A reason existed why the Artist had said the word in such a pointed fashion, at the end of their time with him. If not sorely mistaken, she had strong confidence that the man's words contained a hint of invitation to her and Carlos; to take the word onward and discover what it meant.

Getting into the vehicle's front left seat, Haven activated it by voice, and then told the guidance system the location of their next stop. Pulling out from the curb, the truck accelerated to the mandated standard speed of travel for technate thoroughfares.

Haven sat back, gazing out the side window at the facades of the tenements passing by, many of them with businesses on the ground floor. Her mind wandering, she found herself recalling the image on the wall of the Artist depicting the old-style car traveling free through an open countryside.

Everything about that painting conveyed an air of freedom and liberation, a stark contrast to the monotonous scenes just outside her window. She wished that she could be far away, maybe even be in the Faraway that the Artist had mentioned; whatever that place might be.

The life ahead of her largely determined, Haven knew she would never escape a life spent in tenements and densely-populated technates. Only those living in the Northern Sector, by accident of birth, escaped that kind of life; along with a select few athletes and entertainers who captivated the public and became successful.

For the rest of society, life did not have many options beyond virtual environments. Most things remained well-defined; eating and drinking the things approved, traveling where permitted, using only the energy rationed, receiving the health treatments assigned, living in the spaces designated, and holding the views authorized.

The dour parade of thoughts dampened Haven's spirits. She heaved an extended sigh.

One more delivery remained and then she could go home, and perhaps seek escape within simulated realms; whether games or social network environments. More and more, escaping into digital realms was becoming all she could look forward to on a given day.

"Far away ... Faraway," she whispered, thinking of the Artist.

"What did you say? I missed that" Carlos asked her.
"Just daydreaming ... that's all," she replied.

Jaelynn

Dreams no longer dwelled within the technate looming around her.

Gazing up the towering heights of the gray structures engulfing her, the dismaying thought hovered within Jaelynn's mind. Beyond the lofty summits of the buildings, the deep blue skies appeared a realm far away; one impossible to reach.

Monolithic tenements filling her sector, the buildings resembled the bars of a great cage; herding in a teeming, subdued populace.

Nobody that Jaelynn knew ever roamed outside of Technate Six's confines, save for a couple of individuals from her tenement employed in the security force warding the restricted zones. Even they rarely traveled outside the technate's perimeter, with most of their work being done from their homes, using a virtual reality interface to perform systems maintenance.

Most of the people in Jaelynn's world remained sequestered within their little apartments, drifting through their days immersed within digital realms.

Every time she looked to the skies, it reminded her that another world existed outside the technate's boundaries, beckoning to her. Offering vast, open spaces filled with a tangible reality of lush greenery, mountains, lakes, and so much else that she longed for, the world outside had once been a place where a regular person such as herself lived.

Jaelynn lamented that most of the physical world now stood off-limits; under strict regulations and inaccessible to the average citizen.

A few ground-based police drones and several larger delivery vehicles rolled past Jaelynn on the two-lane road to her right, adjacent to a steady stream of individuals on bicycles. Jaelynn did not need the latter with a short walk remaining before she reached the monorail platform.

A mixture of people and robots striding along the sidewalk, the pedestrian traffic looked to be the usual congested mass for the middle of the day. Jaelynn would not have been surprised if the traffic had been sparse instead, often wondering why the streets ever became crowded and busy. People had little reason to leave their apartments, with work, entertainment, and social interaction all available without the need to take a single step outside their front doors.

Above, numerous kinds of drones cruised the air currents, ranging from security to delivery craft, to one or two ferrying human passengers.

Bringing a little bounce into her step, she turned her thoughts from the monotony of life in the technate to Gabriel. Educational obligations finished, and the day clear of other tasks, Jaelynn intended to spend every minute she possibly could with her boyfriend of five months.

Many dating couples spent much of their time within virtual environments, even changing their appearances to each other on a regular basis. Jaelynn preferred seeing Gabriel in person, and he held a similar sentiment. It was just one of the reasons why the two of them had resonated so well with each other.

Placing her Mixed Reality glasses on, Jaelynn took a detour

into a Meal Express within sight of the monorail platform. Jaelynn walked toward the serving counter. A virtual kiosk formed within her glasses.

Eyeing the selections, she tapped the small screen of the virtual kiosk with her potential choices and frowned at the ensuing display in her glasses.

The month not quite up yet, she saw that she had already used her allocation of meat credits. To get a club sandwich or hamburger would cost significantly more this time, with a sustainability surcharge for meat purchased beyond her authorized monthly allotment.

Wishing that one of her vegetarian friends happened to be in the place, she took a quick glance around the establishment. The glasses indicating nobody from her close circle of friends in the vicinity, her visual search for possible acquaintances also turned up empty.

Jaelynn lamented the absence of a vegetarian to cooperate with her. Most never had much of a problem sharing their meat credits with her, though the process had an indirect route. Getting an item that they wanted on her allocation, they got her a sandwich using theirs.

Voluntary cooperation proved to be one of the only loopholes around the onerous Federal Health Agency's regulations forbidding outright transfers or sharing of credits.

Jaelynn imagined how wonderful it would be to simply walk up and order what she desired, without worry of a penalty or admonition. The thought served as yet another desire to be kept in silence, within her heart.

At least with Gabriel she could vent a little. Meeting him had given her so many outlets in a world she found increasingly frustrating to exist within. Similar to her, he held thoughts and ideas deemed controversial, if not outright illegal.

For once in her life, she could share the things cradled in her heart with another person. That alone seemed a small miracle to her, in a world where even the idea of miracles had been squarely confined as a dusty relic of a superstitious, long-faded age.

After a short deliberation, she opted for a soft drink in a plastic bottle, even if those had gotten more expensive with the latest rises in surcharges on non-essential beverages. As thirsty as she had become, she wished she could buy two, but the strict federal limit of one for every half-day period could not be avoided.

Making her way down the counter she eyed the large scanner tracking purchases. Her remaining food credits and available currency displayed instantly within her glasses. Now paid for, the bottle's radio-frequency security tag deactivated, allowing her to proceed out of the building without hindrance.

Taking a sip of the cola, she replaced the cap and continued toward the monorail platform at a casual gait. The transports ran frequently enough to where she had no need to hurry.

Surmounting the flight of steps ahead of her, Jaelynn took her place among several others awaiting the arrival of the next monorail.

A five-minute wait ensued before the tell-tale hum of an incoming monorail filled the air. The sleek array of compartments glided along the magnetic track, slowing to a crawl before coming to a full stop alongside the platform.

Boarding one of the middle segments, Jaelynn took a seat along one of the sides and settled in, the riding fee deducted the instant she crossed the threshold of the transport.

Removing her Mixed Reality glasses, she put them away in an upper pocket of her shirt. Unlike some, she did not like to wear them all the time, and she definitely had no inclination for the other two options; contacts, or ocular implants.

Finishing her drink, Jaelynn tossed it in the proper receptacle for recycling, avoiding the automatic penalty for improper discarding. She had already absorbed a couple such infractions the previous month and did not want to get hit with any more fines.

Smooth and swift, the monorail proceeded to the station located nearest to her intended destination. Stepping off the transport and onto the high platform, she felt a gust of wind buffet her mid-length, black locks about.

After gazing around a moment, letting the disembarking passengers thin out, she took the staircase down to the street level. An icy bite roved the air, making her regret that she had not worn a light jacket.

A large number of people around her wore MR glasses, a fair number of them interacting with whatever environments the devices conjured up alongside the tangible one. The sight always brought some amusement to Jaelynn, imagining them simply being mentally unhinged people wearing a plain set of glasses.

The majority of the other faces around her looked somber, tired, or pensive. The dour expressions did not surprise Jaelynn in the least. The way she saw things, they had very little to smile about.

Making closer observations of her own parents had told her a lot about the world she lived in. Both of them had part-time jobs; a rarity in most households, when jobs of any kind stood scarce to begin with.

Their employment brought some extra monthly credits in a few different areas. But with no carryover of credits, much of what they earned simply vanished into thin air when a month came to an end.

Jaelynn thought it would be better for them to take the path that so many others did; remain unemployed and go on a standard public allocation called a Sustainability Allowance.

A couple blocks away from the transport station, the high rise she entered looked no different from her own. After a short ride up to the tenth floor, Jaelynn got off the elevator and walked down the hall to the door of the Adamson residence.

Ringing the doorbell, Jaelynn waited patiently. A few moments later, the door opened wide, revealing Gabriel's mother.

Sprinkled with strands of gray, shorter locks of brown hair framed the woman's narrow face. Crow's feet adorned her dark brown eyes. Everything about the woman, from her gaze to expression, looked weary; and much older than the forty-four years Jaelynn knew her to be.

"Hi Mrs. Adamson," Jaelynn greeted, presenting a warm smile to the woman.

"Hi Jaelynn, it's good to see you. Here to see Gabriel I'd bet," Mrs. Adamson responded, returning the smile. She moved to the side of the door, holding it open for Jaelynn to enter. "He's cooped up back there in his room as usual, buried in one of his science projects. Do your best to get him out of the apartment. The boy needs a little sun and fresh air."

"I don't think he'll listen to me," Jaelynn replied with a laugh, stepping by Mrs. Adamson into the apartment interior. "You know how he is."

"Then we're both in a whole lot of trouble. He sure doesn't listen to me, and if he doesn't listen to his girlfriend, what are we going to do?" Mrs. Adamson replied, with a lighthearted burst of laughter. For a moment, the levity brushed aside the clouds of fatigue, shedding years from her face in an instant.

"I'll do my best for you, Mrs. Adamson, I promise," Jaelynn responded, laughing again herself.

Though sharing in the laughter, Jaelynn knew exactly what Mrs. Adamson meant when it came to her son. Gabriel always harbored a serious edge, one far beyond the other boys his age. His dedicated focus on things that so few of his age concerned their minds with stood as something that Jaelynn both liked and sometimes found herself vexed by.

Not bothering to knock, she pushed the door to Gabriel's

room open slowly. As she expected, her boyfriend sat on a stool, hunched over his latest project; focused on soldering a circuit board resting on the counter surface in front of him.

His bedroom already had become half workshop. Judging from the piles of electronic gear and documents, the other half found itself in the process of being invaded and transformed.

For a moment, she eyed the small, box-shaped object Gabriel was fabricating. One of a kind, it had no identification code, or any kind of connection with the federal system, a process mandated on all technological devices.

Self-contained in all respects, the device, whatever it might be, offered a degree of privacy held to be illegal. Her boyfriend did not shy from taking risks, and the trust he placed in her went without saying. One word from her could have his creation confiscated and see him pulled in by the authorities for Rehabilitation or even incarceration.

"To think that at school they're all under the impression you hate science," Jaelynn remarked, grinning wide. "And here you are, pouring over another project of yours. Show's how little they know you."

"Don't want the hassle," he replied, glancing up and casting her a winsome smile. "You know they'd just try to turn me into a puppet. I have my own ideas on things, including a few concepts they might not like too much."

"Such as?" Jaelynn asked, always interested in whatever new endeavor he might be up to. "What are you working on now?"

"Won't matter, if my design doesn't work. Might wait to ask me that when I know if it has any real promise."

"I'm interested, no matter what happens," she responded, grinning. She then added, "It has to do with you, right? At the moment I'm still interested in you, unless you really blow it someday and forget what a wonderful girlfriend you have."

Glancing towards her, an impish grin arose on his face. "Are you so sure about that policy of yours? I might be up to great mischief."

"I assumed that already," she replied, laughing. "That goes without saying."

"You'll know one way or another, pretty soon," he said. Setting down the soldering gun, he straightened up and took a pronounced breath. "That's enough work on that … for now at least."

"Oh, so you do have a little time to spare for your girlfriend!" Jaelynn chided him. "How generous of you, Gabriel Adamson."

Getting up from the stool, he walked over and wrapped his arms around her. Pulling her into him, bringing their bodies snug, he put his lips to hers.

The soft touch of their mouths led to an extended kiss. She gazed deep into his light blue eyes as he drew back from her.

"If I can't find time for my amazing, wonderful, beautiful girlfriend, I'll just have to invent something that can control time itself, won't I?" he asked in a low voice, giving her a warm smile.

"I wouldn't put that past you," Jaelynn said, shaking her head in amusement. "If anyone could pull that off, I have confidence you could."

"You do know me well," Gabriel said, smirking. "So what do you say we get out of here, and go into the city? Get some air."

"I know you'll make your mother happy if you get out in the sun for a while," Jaelynn responded. "You'll make me look good with her too. And where else is there to go, anyway? It's not like we can take a trip outside the technate's walls."

"No denying that," Gabriel said, his tone growing more somber. "But we'll make the best of things for now, until I get to a place where the rules can be changed."

He winked at her, and there was something curious about his expression. She cast a glance toward the project sitting on the small counter, wondering what exactly he was working on.

To her eyes, the project always looked like a big jumbled mess of electronic parts, but she knew in her heart that he intended to create something much more than a mere novelty. Though young, he undertook everything he did with an iron purpose; a quality setting him far apart from most all the boys of their peer group.

Reaching forward, she brushed away the wayward lock of hair that always swept down over his left eye. Leaning in, she gave him another soft kiss on the lips.

Lowering her hands, she straightened out the collar of his long-sleeved shirt, from where it had popped up. Her finger traced the edge of the silver pin attached to the right side of his collar. Rendered in the shape of a majestic tree, one with robust boughs filled with abundant foliage, the small pin rarely was absent from his clothing.

Gabriel said it was a tree from an ancient myth, one almost lost to the mists of time. He never offered much explanation as to why he had gone through the trouble of crafting the pin, other than to say that the old, obscure beliefs he had come across in his research inspired him to a great degree.

The little symbol drew no attention with their peers or others in the city. To all eyes, it looked to be nothing more than a tree, worn as a piece of ornamentation.

With Gabriel, the object held far more value than mere ornamentation. It harbored powerful meaning, containing things even she did not understand.

"Alright, let's go," she announced, her face brightening. "Time to get out of here for a little while."

After letting Gabriel's mother know they were leaving, much to the woman's happiness, they left the apartment behind and headed down to the street level. The day's shadows were growing longer, conveying night's approach.

"I would say let's go to the park, but the place is always too overcrowded for my liking," Gabriel commented, as they walked side by side up the street.

"It is too crowded to ever be enjoyable," Jaelynn replied in agreement. "But everywhere in this technate tends to be crowded."

"Not surprising the park is crowded, considering it's one of the few places with any large amount of greenery that the peons like us are allowed to visit," Gabriel said, a frown coming to his lips. "Then again, if we were one of the members of the Technate Six Council, or a higher-up in one of the international conglomerates, we'd get to make full use of the huge areas of woodland just outside the technate's boundaries."

Jaelynn heard the thick frustration in his voice, a tone that surfaced whenever he spoke of the technate's political and business leaders. She could not refute his adamant position that such individuals lived in a world set apart from the rules they placed over everyone else. Anyone with even a small fraction of a wit could see that.

He smiled and shook his head. The sarcasm flowed in his voice, as he resumed. "But at least we are safe. They watch every place we go, record every transaction we make, monitor every bit of food we are buying. I feel so good knowing how safe we are. Don't you? We're sustainable too! It just doesn't get any more fulfilling than that!"

"They say it was much worse in the older times," Jaelynn said, though the words did not harmonize with the feelings in her heart.

"That's what they will always tell you," Gabriel said. "Who really knows for sure? I'm pretty sure they wouldn't let anything in the networks dispute their nice little description of things. When you control how history is taught, you don't have to worry about things like being accurate."

"You've never believed them, have you?" Jaelynn asked, in a lower voice, growing increasingly nervous with Gabriel's words.

"I don't believe anyone who feels a need to watch me all the time, and monitor everything that goes on in my life," Gabriel replied.

As if to emphasize his point, he nodded towards one of the rectangular shapes gracing the heights of a nearby light pole. The devices were all over the technate, monitored from a central hub. Containing microphones and speakers, they could be used to listen to passersby, broadcast a technate-wide message, or be used individually, to address or interact with a person near it.

He then glanced up toward one of the ubiquitous cameras mounted high above them. After a moment, his eyes roved even higher, taking in the sight of a surveillance drone drifting slowly, far overhead.

His eyes lowered back to the ground level, and he nodded across the street. Nestled between residence buildings, the windowless façade of a Steward Center loomed over the throngs of citizens walking by it. Inside the structure, masses of data gleaned from the ceaseless surveillance was processed, organized, and applied.

"Everywhere you turn," he said with an air of distaste. "All around you, at all times."

"It does seem a little much," Jaelynn admitted. "When you stop and really think about it."

Like most everyone, she did not like the heavy surveillance. But that was the way things were, and she could do nothing to change it.

"Because they're paranoid freaks, that's why," Gabriel said with a sharper edge. "I wish, I wish ... "

His voice trailed off. When he did not continue, she asked him, "What do you wish, Gabriel?"

He glanced towards her, his blue eyes brimming with determination. "I wish I could upend their whole system, unravel the whole entire thing ... and maybe we could all find out for ourselves whether the things of the old world were really so bad or not."

"Better keep things like that quiet," Jaelynn cautioned him, an edge of anxiety sparking while watching another wheeled police drone head down the street.

She knew the drone vehicle picked up audio in addition to video images, using its artificial intelligence to sort through all of it and determine if a possible threat stood near. People had been detained and taken in for questioning for far less than what Gabriel had just stated.

Fortunate for Gabriel, most assessments would figure him to be a teenager running his mouth, without thinking. But the threat remained that one would take his words more seriously.

He cast the drone a big smile. "Just want to show it how happy I am that it's keeping me … safe."

"Come on now, Gabriel, let's try and have some fun," she insisted, seeing him beginning to spiral into the morose place he went at times. Oftentimes, when he slipped into such somber moods, it took until the next day for him to snap out of it.

He smirked, and then shook his head again. "I know. I let it all get to me too easy. But you watch out for me, don't you?"

With his right arm, he reached around her shoulders and pulled her close into him. He kissed her lightly on the top of the head. "You are an amazing girlfriend. I can't say that enough."

"You're not such a bad boyfriend," Jaelynn replied, laughing. "A little unusual, maybe, but always very interesting."

"Not such a bad boyfriend?" That's it?" Gabriel retorted, chuckling. "That's all I get?"

"Maybe a little better than that … just maybe," Jaelynn teased with a coy air.

"Your birthday is coming up soon, you should be really nice to me," Gabriel said.

"As if I'm not already," Jaelynn replied with a look of mock indignation, elbowing him softly in the ribs.

"Hey now!" Gabriel exclaimed, breaking into deep laughter.

"Admit I'm always nice to you or I'll pummel you right here," Jaelynn retorted. "It will take the police bots a few moments to arrive. By that time, I'll be done with you!"

"Okay, okay, I give up," Gabriel replied. "You are always nice and amazing and wonderful to me. All times. Every second."

"Much, much better," Jaelynn stated, grinning.

They continued down the street together, before finally deciding to go to Takeshi's apartment. From a few messages exchanged through their Mixed Reality glasses, they learned that his parents would be going out for the evening.

Jaelynn did not mind the idea of visiting Gabriel's friend. Though she did not know Takeshi well just yet, she had fast come to like the short, pudgy fellow.

Like Gabriel, Takeshi had a curious mind and liked to tinker with things, though his interests tilted towards software rather than the hardware that so captivated her boyfriend. Easy going, he had always been welcoming and respectful toward her, not always a guarantee with girlfriends who took up much of the time once afforded to a close friend.

Takeshi answered the door when they arrived at his family's apartment. He looked to Gabriel and Jaelynn, nodded, and smiled.

"How's it goin'?" he asked.

"Good as it can be, I guess," Gabriel replied.

"Hi Jaelynn," he greeted her. "Good to see you."

"Hi Takeshi, good to see you as well," she responded. "What's new?"

"Good timing ... there's a holographic concert you all might want to see, going on tonight," Takeshi announced when they entered the apartment. "If you don't mind spending a few credits. It's not a bargain."

"Who is it?" Gabriel asked. "Anyone I'm into?"

"DawnBreaker," Takeshi replied, nodding, a grin spreading

on his face.

"Now that sounds good," Jaelynn remarked at the mention of the heavy-edged group, who employed a wide range of rhythms and vocal harmonies in their sound. It did not hurt that the guitarist and lead singer were exquisitely handsome guys either.

"I was just about to get some pizza ordered in. I've been careful about using my credits this month," Takeshi said. He grinned. "You certainly have good instincts for timing your arrival."

"I never turn down pizza," Gabriel said. "You know me better than that, Takeshi."

"Yes, yes I do," Takeshi replied with a laugh. "Oh, one more thing ... I've been slack on doing the dishes. Give me a minute to output a few more forks and knives. Let's do that first."

He strode into the kitchen, heading over to the Fabricator mounted on the far wall. Opening up the hinged covering of the input panel, Takeshi pushed the buttons requesting a few additional utensils to be manufactured.

Jaelynn eyed the machine as several indicator lights brightened. A slight delay ensued as the Fabricator connected to the technate's Central Approval Office, verified the request, and registered the items to be output. After receiving clearance, it created the simple utensils.

Following a short discussion, the types of pizzas were decided upon and ordered up through their MR glasses. The friendly, blonde-haired female avatar confirmed that the request had been carried out, the transaction completed, and that the food would arrive via drone delivery in less than thirty minutes.

Carrying a cluster of brand-new utensils, and moving back into the main living room, Takeshi turned on his holographics unit and went about ordering the concert transmission.

Once that had been done, they awaited the arrival of the pizza. The drone, having converted to a bipedal form, arrived at Takeshi's door with a few minutes to spare under the thirty-minute estimate.

The three ate to their fill, finishing just in time for the start of the concert. Light radiated from the main unit a few minutes later, connecting with smaller sensors and other nodes positioned about the room, forming a solid, encompassing brilliance.

A world in three vivid dimensions surrounded Jaelynn. To her perspective, she stood on the floor level in the middle of an enormous arena.

The huge venue looked to be filled to capacity, from the bottom on up to the highest tiers of seating. Not far away loomed a massive stage with a host of trusses crisscrossing high above, the latter suspended from a cabling system reaching up to the arena's lofty ceiling.

While looking as real to Jaelynn's eyes as anything physical, none of it had actual substance. Yet even though the images themselves were not physical, neither were all of them computer-generated in origin.

Live transmissions rendered in real-time from the other side of the world, the immensely popular recording artist DawnBreaker were set to perform a concert broadcast worldwide through advanced holographics.

No need existed for a lengthy tour. The single live concert served as the material for a worldwide show, achieving the results of an entire tour within a couple of hours.

One night would also generate far more revenue than any extensive tour. Every single person watching would be scanned and charged by the technology forming the encompassing images.

There was even a virtual merchandise booth that would see t-shirts and other items selected shipped upon purchase for next-day delivery; if not the same day, in some instances.

For the band, it presented tremendous efficiency. One night's costs replaced weeks and months of touring expenses, while reaching every corner of the globe.

Jaelynn had to admit that the current holographic concerts were far more enjoyable than actually going to one in a local venue. With the security protections in place, a person had to go through more than one layer of security checks at any live event venue. No containers of any kind were allowed, even handbags and purses. For a long concert, and definitely for larger music festivals, it made for a miserable experience.

Yet, as Gabriel had pointed out on more than one occasion, with the increasing utilization of holographic technology for the consumption of live music and sporting events, the mass populace had even less incentive to leave their residences. A bedroom could be transformed into an arena floor or row of stadium seats, and there was no trouble with food, drinks, going to the bathroom, or anything else.

She could not deny his ultimate point. The shift toward advanced holographics with live events isolated the mass populace even more; combining with gaming and other entertainment forms to the point where many people she knew spent increasing portions of their days sequestered within their apartments.

Even so, she found herself caught up in the energy and power of the show when it commenced a few minutes later; a fusillade of pyrotechnics, thundering drums, and explosion of lights kicking off the concert. The roar of the crowd felt real enough, as did the powerful vibrations from each booming thump of the kick drum. A couple of hours later, the exhaustion she felt from cheering and dancing in place felt real enough too.

"DawnBreaker knows what's up," Gabriel declared, smiling when the familiar living room surroundings replaced the vision of the arena. "'Shatter the Darkness' says it all."

"'You gave them the power, you can take it back!'" Takeshi sang, a little off-key, giving a spirited fist-pump into the air.

"Yeah, surprised they let them get away with that one,"

Gabriel said, grinning.

"The powers that be need to have a few outlets for public angst," Takeshi replied.

"I'm feeling a little inspired, so what do you say we hang out where we can talk a bit more?" Gabriel suggested, looking toward his friend with a more serious edge to his voice. He took out his MR glasses and set them down on a counter.

"I'm thinking the same thing," Takeshi replied. Like Gabriel, he took his glasses out and set them down, while cleaning up the leftovers and boxes from the food ordered earlier.

She knew what they meant, following suit with the setting aside of her own glasses, before heading to Takeshi's room. Taking a seat on his bed, Jaelynn waited for the other two to join her. They entered a few moments later, Takeshi shutting the door behind him.

Gabriel took a seat on the bed next to Jaelynn, while Takeshi sat cross-legged in the middle of the floor. Much more tidy and organized than Gabriel's room, Takeshi's offered plenty of space for the three of them to relax and visit.

Jaelynn watched Gabriel pull a few papers folded in half out of his pocket. Out of his other pocket, he retrieved a drawing pen, and began writing something down on the paper.

Wondering what he was up to, she watched with great interest. Neither item that he used was common or inexpensive.

While most artists created using digital devices, a few yet opted to develop their works using tangible mediums. A few places could still be found in the technate that carried the costly implements.

Knowing her boyfriend's purpose did not involve any kind of traditional artwork, Jaelynn could not fathom what Gabriel used the implements for.

When finished writing, Gabriel handed the paper over to Takeshi, who took it and read in silence. Takeshi then brought forth his own drawing pen and proceeded to write something down underneath Gabriel's words.

The pattern between the two continued for nearly thirty minutes. Not a single word spoken between them, many nods of understanding, a few bursts of laughter, expressions of puzzlement, and raised eyebrows accented the communication. Again, and again, they exchanged the little stack of papers, continuously adding to the contents.

"So, what's all that stuff about?" Jaelynn asked hesitantly, eyeing the papers, and unable to stifle her curiosity any longer.

Giving Jaelynn a knowing wink, Gabriel put a finger to his lips. He took up one of the papers and scrawled something down upon it. Handing it over to her, he smiled and winked again.

On the paper's surface, she read the words:

'I wanted you to see how we did this before explaining it. Very often, low tech can overcome high tech. Nothing digital to record here. No sounds to monitor. Just the power of written words. Words to take into the privacy of our minds. Words to share without fear.'

Jaelynn started to open her mouth, but saw Gabriel put his finger to his lips at the last moment. He pointed to the paper in her hand, held out his pen, and nodded to her.

Taking up the pen from him, she put down her own reply. The physical act of writing on paper felt awkward, yet she pressed forward.

In school, only electronics had been utilized, even when she'd first learned to write. Paper had such a different feel compared to a digital screen. Nevertheless, with some concentration, her markings turned out legible enough.

'And what's the point? Here in your friend's bedroom? Being so secretive?'

She handed it back to Gabriel and laughed. He smirked after he read her words, but there was a less mirthful sheen to his eyes as he wrote down a response. She took the paper back from him and read the reply.

'They are obsessed, you know that. They can watch us through the glasses, and within them. They have systems sifting through everything they pick up on their gear. We found a way to get around it. A way to make our own little world for a change. Here, we can communicate openly, and freely. A sanctuary of words. A prelude to so much more.'

The logic indisputable, Jaelynn nodded. Gabriel had found an amazingly straightforward, simple way around the mass collection of data undertaken by the network of Steward Centers.

The genius of it all lay in the sheer simplicity. While not the most convenient method of communication, it nevertheless bestowed a true degree of privacy on the participants. Gabriel and Takeshi had achieved what a technate of a few million could not; full sovereignty of their personal interaction.

Gabriel gestured for Jaelynn to return the papers. He took them from her, and then added to his comments.

'Maybe we can find a way for everyone to get out of the big cage we're all shut inside nowadays. Make a serious effort to break out. Wouldn't that be nice?'

While a smile rested on his face, his eyes carried a sharper glint. Growing a little nervous, Jaelynn knew he did not jest.

Taking the paper back, she replied.

'It would be wonderful, but it isn't worth getting jailed.'

'We're already jailed,' he responded on the paper. *'We just need to have the guts to admit it.'*

She pursed her lips, hesitant to ask him the key question. While not wanting to upset him, she desired to know how he would respond.

'But what can you do about it? We don't live in the Northern Sector.'

To her surprise, he did not exhibit a trace of frustration. Instead, a smile blossomed on his face.

'I am doing something about it. So are many others. More than you think.'

Reading the words, Jaelynn gripped the paper a little more tightly. Gabriel harbored deep resentment toward the prevailing order in his heart, but this was the first time she had any idea he had acted more broadly upon those thoughts.

What he had just written would, without a doubt, get him hauled off for questioning, a stint in Rehabilitation, or even worse. She feared for him, but at the same time she admired his courage.

He was not one of those cowering, tepid figures who pervaded the technate; of the kind preferring to escape into substances or illusions.

Gabriel took the paper back from her and added to his declaration. *'I'm being careful. I promise. We all are.'*

After she read the words, he took the paper from her. Folding it up into a tight square, he put it into a small receptacle sitting on a stand by Takeshi's bed.

Taking out a vial, he poured some liquid over the paper, which began to hiss and shrivel at once. In moments, no trace remained of the paper with the incriminating words.

"So," Gabriel exclaimed aloud, grinning ear to ear toward Jaelynn and Takeshi. "Now that we've taken a little rest, what do you say to some gaming for a while? A little distraction won't hurt."

"No, I think that would be great," Jaelynn replied, relieved at the suggestion. Enough weighed on her mind for one day.

Cayden

Trudging home, the salty taste of blood on Cayden's bruised lip served as just one of many indignities he wrestled with. Weary and aching, he did not have much farther to go, with nearly everything in his world existing within a ten-minute walk of his mother's apartment.

He wished the distance between himself and the torments he suffered were much greater. Instead, he was subjected to reminders almost every time he set foot outside his home.

Cayden gazed off into the distance. Lofty tenements filled his vision, the only structures he could see for a far distance.

He knew another way of living existed, if only he had not suffered the misfortune of having been born into the mass populace. Cayden wished he could find some way to live among the elite class; the ones who lived in splendor and comfort within the gated, heavily warded communities of the Northern Sector.

Had fate placed Cayden among the powerful few, he could even afford to become immortal, like many of them did; and undergo the wondrous scientific miracle of Ascension.

Cayden often wondered what it would be like to transfer his mind into a body that would never age or take on disease. Ascension offered mastery of life itself. He certainly would not be dealing with the struggles that he faced in his own world.

A part of him envied the ways of the distant past, with its array of misguided religions, archaic superstitions, and unfounded beliefs. Even if they were fabrications, created from the imagination of humans, at the least those beliefs offered people the hope of something better.

Knowing the world that he saw around him would be all he could ever know undermined any possible shred of comfort. The stark notion left a taste far more bitter than the indignity he had just endured.

Keeping his eyes averted from other people on the street, he reached the tenement building with his mother's apartment. Riding in a heavy silence up to the eighteenth floor, he continued down the hallway to his front door.

Identifying him through his implant, the door unlocked and opened. Once inside, he proceeded to his bedroom without hindrance, relieved that his mother was not in the living room.

Had she been there, he would have been made to answer a bevy of questions, when she set her eyes upon his bloody, swollen lip. At the moment, he did not have the energy to deal with anything.

Once within the refuge of his room, without bothering to change clothes, Cayden fell back onto his bed. Aching, both in a physical and interior sense, he left the room dark and did not even bother to get under the covers.

In quiet solitude, staring at the ceiling, the weight of many powerful emotions bore down upon him.

He did not seek to become popular. Far from it, he only desired a circle to call his own. Even a handful of friends would have been something to hold onto.

The hope of a girlfriend continued to remain unreachable, a lesson learned in bitter fashion at the ends of Dante's hard fists. His broken Mixed Reality glasses had been inactive, recording nothing. Even if they had been active, Dante had been cunning enough to knock them off from behind at the outset, before administering the beating.

Cayden could not say anything about the incident. Opening his mouth, even if he proved to be successful in getting Dante into some trouble, would only invite a torrent of negative things onto his head in the future.

He would be shunned in virtual and real worlds alike, at best. At worst, he would find himself harassed in ways that did not run afoul of anti-bullying laws.

As Cayden had learned long before, the youth of the modern day had grown very sophisticated in meting out suffering upon those who fell into their disfavor. With the concealment of appearances and identity in the virtual realms, elaborate ruses could be set up that shook a person like Cayden to the core; all without transgressing any technate statutes.

The best path lay in staying quiet and accepting the beating. The thought still chafed at him.

Cayden wanted nothing more than to be able to pay Dante back ten-fold for the extreme embarrassment suffered. He had been pummeled, laughed at, and made to exit a crowd of his peers alone.

Cursing into the shadows of his room, tears welling up, he closed his eyes, wishing with all his heart that he could escape the world itself. Fatigue permeating his body, he slowly drifted into the merciful embrace of sleep.

Cayden then found himself standing in the middle of a broad street at night, within a strange place unlike any within the technate. The glow from a few street lights mounted on high poles, set at even intervals to each other, cast enough luminance for him to see well enough.

In a lucid state, he recognized that he stood within a dream, no matter how real his senses perceived everything around him.

Recalling images of the old world presented during his schooling, he recognized the scene as being from that archaic era. Individual dwellings lined each side of the street. No more than two stories in height, each of the structures had large front yards covered in grass, along with a few assorted trees, orderly displays of flowers, and other kinds of foliage like bushes and hedges.

Vehicles could be seen everywhere he looked, parked in short paved sections running next to each of the dwellings and along the edges of the street. Not a single one of them looked like a modern security or passenger vehicle, or any other kind of wheeled drone.

Looking about, Cayden could not see a sign of any living thing. No lights shined from within any of the windows on the buildings. The entire area appeared dark and empty.

In the stillness, sudden motion drew Cayden's attention. His breath quickened, eyeing something of great bulk moving within the shadows of a driveway to his right.

A low, rumbling growl emanated from the huge form. Panic rose inside Cayden, his breath catching in the depths of his throat. The night masked most of the thing's features, but the great height and mass of the entity creeping out of the darkness could not be missed.

With slow steps, Cayden started backing up. Looking to the right and left, he tried thinking of a place to run, but his mind became a jumble of thoughts in the throes of fear.

Out in the middle of the road, he stood no chance of escaping the creature. The thing would run him down with ease, well before he could reach any of the houses.

Without warning, everything began swirling, like being taken up in the midst of a dark cyclone. Cayden became disoriented for several moments, and then the phenomenon ceased.

Standing on the edge of an overlook, among an array of

jagged, obsidian rocks, he looked around. Taking note of the towering height that he looked out from, the pit of his stomach churned. Gray clouds drifted below him, a tattered canopy shredded by the great mountains looming all around.

Cayden jumped backward, as what he first thought to be a narrow rock moved. Dark cloak unfurling, like the wings of a great raven, a tall woman turned to face him.

Her brilliant blue eyes fixed upon him. Locks of dark hair cropped just beneath her chin flowed in the chill breezes. The woman's lips parted in a smile, exposing a perfect set of white teeth.

Cayden could find no blemish marring the smooth, creamy skin of her face. She appeared an image graceful and surreal, and he stood transfixed.

Clad in a long, billowing garment of black, she wore knee-high boots of the same hue.

"Welcome," she said, in a voice silken and amiable. "You have found your way here."

"Found my way here?" Cayden replied in an awkward manner. He asked, hesitant, "Where ... is here?"

She laughed at the response, though not in a mocking sort of way. If anything, the levity enhanced her beauty even more.

"You could not come to this place, if the desire were not in your heart," she replied. "We would not be meeting like this."

"I ... I thought of nothing," Cayden responded, growing nervous. "I was on a street, one I'd never been to before, and then I found myself here."

"Your true desires brought you here," she replied, a little more firm in demeanor. Her eyes narrowed, and she asked, after a pause, "Do you think you are dreaming?"

The pointed question caught him off guard, but at last he nodded.

"I'm sure of it," he answered, nodding. "This is definitely a dream."

"You might eventually think otherwise, but you can think that for now," the woman said.

"What … what is your name?" Cayden asked, unable to stifle his curiosity any longer as to the identity of the enigmatic woman.

Smiling wider, she gazed at Cayden for a moment with her enchanting, cerulean eyes.

"I would like to be your Guardian," she said. "But that choice is up to you."

"I don't understand," Cayden replied. He shook his head with a look of frustration. Speaking more to himself than to her, he added, "This is just a dream."

"Do you think so?" she asked. "Then there is no harm in answering a question, so let me ask you this. What is life?"

Cayden made no reply, struggling for an answer.

"It is a kind of dream," she said after a few moments had passed. A grin dancing upon her lips, she added, "Is it not?"

"More of a nightmare, if you ask me," Cayden said, surprising himself at the fast response, the words coming out before he had given much thought of what to say.

"A nightmare?" she asked, her face taking on a more somber expression.

He looked into the depths of her gaze. Choosing to be honest, he saw no harm coming from interacting with a dream figure. "To me, it is a nightmare. Nothing at all goes right. Ever."

"Can you master some of your dreams?" she asked. "Do you ever come to understand that you are in one, and take control of them?"

"Yes," he said, thinking of many such instances, including the current one. "That's how it is for me right now. I know I'm asleep, while I'm talking to you here. I'm very conscious I'm in a dream."

She nodded. "If you can gain awareness in these dreams, then you can learn to master the dream they call life. It is no different. You need only unlock your awareness, take control of it, and develop it."

"If only I could do that," Cayden said, wishing that life could be molded to his will, like one of the dreams where he controlled things.

"That is all up to you," she said in an even tone. "You can take control."

"I wish you would show me how then," Cayden said, the words sounding more flippant than he intended. In a more contrite manner, he added. "You said I could choose you to be my Guardian. I sure could use a guardian, so that's fine by me."

If she took any offense at his initial tone, the woman did not show it on her face. Her pleasant expression remained, and she nodded slowly at his words.

"You understand, it is your will?" she asked.

"Yes, no problems there at all," Cayden said, wanting to see where the dream would go. Being in the company of the beautiful woman was wonderful enough, when the girls of his own age paid no attention to him.

She turned her head and looked outward. "I have a few friends who will be joining us now."

Cayden looked into the sky, gazing in the same direction as the woman. Initially, nothing met his eyes but gray masses of clouds and empty air, but after several moments had passed three distinct shapes came into view.

Their dark forms growing in size, the trio approached the overlook at a fast speed. They did not have wings, or any hint of a technology enabling their flight.

They looked to be human, yet Cayden could not understand how they remained airborne. He then reminded himself that he was in the midst of a dream, where all was possible.

Cloaks trailing them like wings of mist, the three figures alighted in silence upon the rock surface.

One man and two women stood before Cayden. Both of the women rivaled the Guardian in their exquisite beauty.

Likewise, the man had a beautiful appearance. Broad-shouldered, narrow of waist, with a strong jaw-line and piercing dark eyes, he carried a strong presence, intimidating Cayden from the moment that his gaze fell upon the youth.

Cayden could not keep his eyes toward any one of them for long. With every moment passed under the weight of their attention, it seemed that he grew smaller.

"Join with us," the man said, with an air of invitation. He looked to the woman with Cayden. "She has told you, it is just a matter of will."

"Who are all of you?" Cayden asked them. He looked to the woman he had asked to be his Guardian, hoping she offered an answer.

"Guardians. And friends, if you would have us be yours," one of the two other women told him. A stunning beauty with long, dark hair and olive-toned skin, she displayed a warm smile toward Cayden.

Friends were all he ever wanted in the chaotic mess that his life had become. Yet the woman's offer seemed unbelievable to his ears. Nobody who looked like any one of the four prominent figures had ever associated with Cayden, back in his own world.

If he were in the company of just one of the Guardians, Cayden knew that Dante would not think of harming him, for even an instant. The bully would not dare to transgress one of the four; and if he did, something inside told Cayden that they would not tolerate Dante's actions, in any way.

"Let us guide you, and show you a new path," the last of the women said, her jade eyes appearing to glitter. Her medium-length blonde locks tossed about in an abrupt gust of wind, but her eyes remained fixed toward Cayden. "It is a path that will lead you to empowerment, of a kind you never thought possible."

"It's just all so much ... and confusing," Cayden said, after a long pause. While intending to play along with the dream experience, he floundered trying to make sense out of everything.

"Choose us, Cayden, and you will find us," the Guardian who had first revealed herself to him said. "For now, return. Think of your body, back in your bed."

The thought of his dark bedroom, and his body lying on the bed, crossed his mind. A fading, disorienting feeling began taking over him, the kind that he got when leaving dreams behind.

His heart leaped with desperation.

Cayden would have done anything to remain in the company of the four, but he had nothing to hold onto. Their images started to blur and fade, spurring his anxiety further.

Eyes snapping open, seeing the underside of his bedroom ceiling, Cayden despaired. His face still ached.

He longed to go back and spend more time in the dream with the Guardians. In their presence, he had felt so secure.

Now, the shroud of loneliness draped over him once more.

Frustration overtaking him, hot tears formed in his eyes.

It had all been just a dream.

Salvador

Salvador flinched, responding to the low chuckle coming from the shadows nearby. Looking at ease, a tall man wearing a wide-brimmed hat reclined against the trunk of an oak tree, the latter rising from the slope of the same low hill that Salvador sat upon.

A grin rested on the man's face, parting the close-cropped goatee ornamenting his angular features. To Salvador's best guess, the man appeared to be about thirty years of age.

"I ... I didn't see you there," Salvador said with an edge of anxiety, gathering his composure in the wake of being startled.

He could not believe he had missed seeing the distinctive-looking man. Salvador had looked straight in that direction when he had arrived at his favorite area in the park, one of the few spaces on the sprawling grounds affording a degree of privacy.

Set far from the walking paths frequented by so many others, the little area rarely had other visitors. A few couples seeking some private moments together could be found in his sanctuary now and then, but those instances were sporadic.

Salvador had figured out the best times in the day for chances to enjoy a few moments under open skies in an atmosphere of solitude and quiet. He had come to view the area as his own, even if nobody in the technate owned any form of land.

Having the presence of unexpected company both surprised and disappointed him, disrupting any hopes at seclusion. Feeling surrounded and confined during the rest of his hours on most days, Salvador needed every moment spent in the shade of trees, under bright, sunny skies.

"No worries at all," the man replied in a carefree, amiable fashion. "I'm just doing the same as you. Nothing more. Seeking some peace and quiet and enjoying the early evening for a few minutes."

His smile broadened further. The wind whipped up amongst the surrounding trees, swaying branches and passing an icy chill across Salvador's body.

"Nothing like the front edge of a strong night storm. I always love how crisp and clean everything feels, right before the rain breaks," the man stated, looking off into the skies, a thoughtful expression on his face. The clouds above flashed with lightning, though no thunder sounded.

"Wasn't supposed to be a storm tonight, but I know we've needed some rain for a while," Salvador said, making an attempt at conversation. "At least that's what they say in the media, about the farmland near our technate."

"If a storm is needed, just bring one in," the man replied with another laugh, as if the act was obvious, and easily doable. He looked back to Salvador. "So, what's your name?"

"I'm Salvador."

"Very nice to meet you Salvador. Many call me Jade," the man replied. "Is this a favorite spot of yours, in the park?"

"It is," Salvador said, nodding. "I like hanging out here. Feels a whole lot better than being cooped up in our apartment."

"It's good to get outside for a while," Jade responded. "Often is even better."

"I don't like staying inside much," Salvador replied. "And I don't like crowded places. I also don't like spending all my time surrounded by holographics or game environments either. But this is about the only place I can go to."

"Why's that?" asked Jade.

"It's the only place that feels private," Salvador said, in the best way he could explain it.

He loved the open green spaces provided by the federal park. The park stood one of the very few places where he had a sense that he could be left alone; even if the ID implant in his wrist tracked him, anywhere he went.

Though he did not speak aloud of it, as voicing his misgivings would be the surest way to get him a stint in the Federal Health Service's Rehabilitation program, he resented the nanoscale implant, to the core of his heart. The invasive object violated his every instinct; no matter how much he had been told about how the mandated thing protected him and everyone else, keeping identities secure.

Something deep down told him that the stranger talking with him was not likely to be the type fond of the implants either. Those tethered to the trappings of the current age did not tend to relax beneath the boughs of oak trees.

A gust of wind brushed through the space, bringing a bright smile to Jade's face. "There we go ... it's starting to pick up ... won't be too much longer now."

"For a storm?" Salvador asked.

Jade nodded, a roll of thunder sounding in the distance. The growling rumble ebbed, followed with another burst of cold winds.

"Guess I'll have to get heading back soon, after all," Salvador said, with a trace of regret. "Either that or stay and get soaked. I didn't bring an umbrella, as there was nothing about a storm in the weather forecast."

The man gave a shrug, and grinned. "Maybe you should get soaked. You might even find a walk in the rain pleasant. What would it really hurt?"

Salvador laughed, taking a quick liking to the man's outlook. "I might get sick. But maybe I should take a walk in the rain, anyway."

"You aren't like most of the kids your age, these days," Jade said with an approving air. "Not plugged into something. Not wearing the glasses. Seeking a little solitude. Your style isn't too common, in my experience around this big technate."

"Can't say I am much like my friends," Salvador replied. "As far as the glasses go, when I'm here, I just like to see things as they really are here. But not much I can do about the way things are everywhere else."

Salvador exhaled, releasing a deep breath that conveyed his resignation with the ways of the modern world.

"Says who?" Jade queried, his voice carrying an edge of irritation that caught Salvador off guard. The levity faded from the man's face.

"Nowhere else to go, and I couldn't get there to begin with ... even if there was some place where things were different," Salvador said. "I'm fifteen ... not too many options for my age group. Even if I was older, the Global Council of Technates controls the entire world."

"Think so? Do you think that the way things are now is all that there's ever going to be?" Jade asked, staring intently at him.

"I sure hope not," Salvador said, finding the thought depressing, if not outright dismaying. "But I don't see anything changing, anytime soon. There's no way to make a change to begin with."

"Then set your mind to something far more than all of this," Jade said, casting a hard gaze toward Salvador. "They can't stop your mind yet, even if they're working all the time to find a way to monitor and control that too."

"So, what's your advice, then?" Salvador asked, buoyed at the man's defiant words, and astonished that anyone would dare speak so openly against the system in place.

"Dream big dreams," Jade replied, a grin returning to his face. "Always dream big dreams ... they don't have any control over those, no matter how much they'd like to get a hold on every last little part of our inner life too.

"Their fancy gadgets still can't do that. Dreams are yours, and yours alone ... a place you can be free. That's first. Begin there. Much more can follow, for those who are wise and observant."

Salvador had never thought of dreams in such a way, but Jade was right. Dreams were a refuge, free of the world he lived in on a daily basis.

As Jade had indicated, dreams took place within an environment free from all the tethers in his mundane existence. No authority, whether of a parental or governmental nature, wielded jurisdiction within the realms of his dreams.

In truth, dreams were perhaps the only sanctuary left that Salvador could truly call his own.

"But what's the use?" Salvador said after a few moments, his countenance darkening, as other thoughts crept back into his head. "I can dream all day and night, of the biggest things I can imagine ... but it won't change anything at all here. No matter how hard I try."

"Don't be so gloomy, Salvador," Jade replied, chuckling. "Your premise may be in great error. Examine that first."

"What do you mean?" Salvador asked, perplexed at the response.

"The things you assume, young man," Jade replied. "Lots of people make lots of assumptions ... and they are often very, very wrong. Even those who think they know it all and have a mandate to control others."

Without waiting for a response from Salvador, Jade got up to his feet in a smooth, limber fashion. Louder than the prior array, another roll of thunder broke across the clouded skies.

Jade looked toward the skies and adjusted his hat.

Glancing back toward Salvador, he said, "Every building has a foundation. A premise is a foundation. Make sure yours is true and strong, and then you can build something amazing."

Salvador remained confused, unsure how to respond.

Jade tipped his hat toward Salvador and gave a short bow of his head. "I know I'm not making much sense at all now, but I can promise you that I will ... if you think on it for a while. Til we meet again, my new friend."

Jade smiled, turned, and headed away, crossing the ground with long, swift strides; the gait of a confident man. Salvador watched until he passed from sight.

Though the encounter had been strange, Salvador found the conversation with Jade to be very interesting, but he did not have long to ponder it. A few drops of rain landed on Salvador's head and arms, heralding more to come. The wind picked up further, and the skies lit up with a massive burst of lightning.

The storm breaking over the technate reflecting the storm of thoughts unfurling within his mind, Salvador got up from the ground and hustled across the park. The falling raindrops picked up their pace, becoming a downpour by the time he reached the exit.

Keeping a brisk stride, Salvador headed down the sidewalk, though more than once he turned his face upward, enjoying the sensations of the rain pattering against his skin. Though soaked when he reached the door of his family's apartment, he thought about how a walk in the rain had not bothered him at all.

Jade had been correct about a walk in the rain being pleasant, and Salvador's instincts told him that the man probably was right about a great many other things. Making his way back to his bedroom, to change into some dry clothes, he hoped it would not be the only time he encountered the mysterious fellow.

Haven

Haven pushed the door open gently and peeked in. Moving his head and arms about, her fourteen-year-old brother sat in the middle of his bedroom with a VR helmet on.

It could be hours before he returned from the depths of whatever virtual adventure he had entered. Were it not for physical needs, she doubted he would emerge from his room at all, on some days.

Mandatory schooling kept him out of entertainment for a few hours a day during the week, but with it being conducted in virtual environments it did not take him out of his VR helmet, or even his bedroom. Still, she was a little grateful that the system would block his access to all entertainment and social networks if he missed lessons.

"Haven, is that you?" her father called.

Shutting her brother's door, she replied, "Yes, it's just me."

"I'm taking a break and having some lunch out here," he said.

She walked back out to the kitchen and saw her father at the table with a half-eaten sandwich, pile of tortilla chips, a little bowl of salsa, and a drink.

More silver strands than dark ones comprised the wavy

locks of hair on his head. Aside from a little paunch to his belly, he remained in good physical shape, and still made it to a fitness center a few times a week.

He smiled. "How's my young lady doing today?"

"Can't figure out what to do," she answered. "All my friends are sequestered in their rooms in VR environments, like usual."

"What about the fitness center?" he asked, munching on one of the tortilla chips.

"I was thinking about doing that," she said.

"Wish your brother would get interested in that," her father said. He shook his head. "He just sits in his room and vegetates, and he's gaining some weight. He won't have anyone to complain to when his nutritional credits and allowances get adjusted."

"No, he won't have anyone to blame but himself," Haven agreed.

She had heard a large percentage of people were obese in the old world, but all that had come under tight regulations when the Global Council of Technates emerged. Using control over nutritional access, technates made it very difficult for abuses of excess.

Everyone had been made to comply, as an obese person represented a disproportionate use of energy and resources in comparison with individuals who maintained the decreed standards of body weight.

"I need to pay a good visit to the fitness center, so I can keep enjoying these," her father said, chuckling, and taking another salsa-loaded chip into his mouth. "Always helps at the health assessments when they see a steady number of fitness center visits on record."

"Sure doesn't hurt," Haven said. "How's work going today?"

"The usual, but at least there are no dire emergencies," he answered.

Her father had a job monitoring systems governing

large arrays of solar panels just outside the city. Tasked with maintaining maximum efficiency in energy storage, he had to deal with the constant adjustments coming from the global level that diverted energy to other technates based upon their assessed needs and requirements.

To Haven, the job sounded dull, but her father seemed to enjoy the challenge. Long ago, she had realized it gave his days an added purpose, something she understood much more when she began working for the delivery service.

She glanced over at the empty chair across from her father. It still reminded her of the absence of her mother, who had divorced her father just a couple years after having her brother.

Having caught the eye of a man living in the Northern Sector, she had taken the opportunity to experience life under a set of rules different from the overwhelming majority of the population.

With the advancements in intimacy and companion robots over the past decade, her mother would not likely have found the same opportunity in the present. Most men and women of the Northern Sector now acquired custom design robots instead of searching for genuine human companions.

The look and characteristics of a robot could be changed at the whim of its owner. A robot would do anything, at anytime, the owner wanted. Further, a robot held no legal claim to property; an issue of unique importance to those living in the Northern Sector.

The fast-developing trend had closed off yet another of the few paths that someone in the mass populace could take to move upward and live in the Northern Sector.

Haven often wondered how things might have been if she had not left, but she could not change what happened. Nevertheless, she could not rid herself of the shard of anger she harbored toward her mother for abandoning her family.

"Got any hot dates lined up?" she asked.

"I swear, it's about impossible to get a real sense of anyone in the virtual networks," her father answered. "Everyone makes a perfect image of themselves, including their image, and then when you meet you find out they are nothing like they made themselves out to be."

"I definitely can see that, just in the avatars my friends use in the networks," Haven said. "Funny thing is that everyone interacts so differently in person than they do when in a virtual environment. Some can hardly even talk to another person, if they are face to face in the real world."

"That's the way it's gotten, sadly," her father commented. "Makes you wonder how people functioned for centuries and centuries before all of this."

"I don't think they had the same difficulties," Haven said.

"A part of me would like to try a world like that," he said. After a moment, a sad look crept into his eyes. He continued, in a lower voice. "And a part of me is afraid to. I only know this kind of world. I wouldn't even know where to begin in a world like the old world."

"This world is the only world I know too," Haven said, in a softer tone. "We're all in this together."

"Then we just have to do our best, with what we've got to work with," her father replied.

She moved over to his side and gave him a big hug. "You have always done your best, and I love you."

"Love you too, sweetheart," he replied.

"Hang in there dad, and make sure the power keeps steady into this technate," she said, straightening up.

"You got it," he replied, grinning.

"Well, I'm going to go relax a bit, and then maybe go get a workout in," Haven said.

"Let me know when you do," her father replied. "If I'm done

with work I'll go down with you. They've got some incredible new holographic modules that you can run through. Beautiful woodland scenery and mountain slopes to make it more challenging."

"Now that sounds like fun," Haven said. "I'll check with you before I go, I promise."

"See you a little later, then," he replied, smiling.

Heading back to her own bedroom, she kicked her shoes off and got her VR helmet on. Sitting down on her bed, she engaged the system.

Assuming the appearance of a tall, blond female with a strong, athletic build, of about thirty-five, she looked about for Carlos and located him in the network.

Thankfully, found him hanging out in an open access community and not a gaming environment. She did not have to send any special request, and simply joined the group.

Avatars with the appearances of men, women, and a few imaginative humanoid forms strolled about a platform jutting from the side of a mountain. The platform afforded anyone on it a high overlook of a lush valley, with a broad river running through its midst.

Haven paused for a moment, savoring the view, before looking around for Carlos. She found him standing with a few others on the far side of the platform.

The avatar he chose reflected his complexion of skin, hair, and eye color, but had much broader shoulders, a more angular facial profile, and considerable brawn.

"Taking a superhero form?" she greeted him.

One of the individuals with them, a lean man dressed in robe-like garments, stepped from the platform and drifted out toward the valley. His clothing billowed on the air currents, and he spread his arms wide, gliding farther from the platform.

"Well, I can fly here, so there's some truth to that," he said, nodding toward the flying man. He grinned and looked back to her. "Looks like you took on a superhero form too."

"I figured I'd see what you were up to," she said. "Didn't feel like gaming at the moment, but this looks relaxing."

"Mountain Valley is one of my favorite places to socialize," Carlos said. "Folks from technates all over the world come here."

"Beautiful design," she commented, gazing upon the spectacular view.

"Lots to explore, too," Carlos said.

"Wonder if there are any spots in the world that are actually like this," Haven said.

"I wouldn't be surprised if there are many like this," Carlos said. "But you couldn't explore those like we can here. Come on and check it out."

He stepped toward the edge, and fell forward, entering a graceful swan dive that leveled out a short distance below the platform. Following in his wake, Haven spread her arms and dove from the edge.

Staring down at the gleaming river and rich greenery of the valley, Haven could almost feel the air flowing over her, though a VR helmet by itself had its limits in simulating touch.

Carlos tucked and darted lower, looping back upward before straightening out again.

"Very acrobatic," Haven commented, smirking.

"Once you get the feel for it, it's easy," Carlos said.

"I can see how so many people burn a lot of hours in these environments," Haven said.

"It's very tempting to stay here for much longer than you should," Carlos replied, laughing.

"And that's when you get like my brother, and never leave your room," Haven said.

"That describes a lot of people these days," Carlos said.

"I don't want to ever get like that," Haven said.

"All things in moderation, like my dad says," Carlos said.

"Good way to look at things," Haven said.

"But every once in a while, you gotta indulge a little," Carlos said, laughing, and going into another sharp plunge, leading to a series of loops and turns.

Haven did likewise, finding the experience exhilarating.

Before long, they had worked their way to the floor of the valley and landed on the riverbank. Turning, Haven looked upward, finding the platform where they had started from, high up the mountain slope. The jagged peak of the lofty summit broke up the silken smoothness of the deep blue sky.

She espied the tiny forms of other individuals leaving the platform and taking to flight. Looking back, she saw Carlos striding along the surface of the river itself.

"You can do just about anything, even walk on water," Carlos called to her, kicking up a spray.

She smiled and laughed at the sight, though she left her thoughts unspoken. Nothing about the place had any basis in reality. The incredible environments served as distractions and diversions for a populace steeped in angst and a large degree of seclusion.

Haven was more than willing to bet that the people of the Northern Sector spent little time piddling around in virtual environments. They were far too busy plying every aspect of the real ones.

"You've gone quiet!" Carlos called out, trotting back over the shore, and breaking her from her thoughts.

"Just got distracted for a moment," she replied.

"Easy to do around here," he said. "And next thing you know, it's five hours later."

To Haven, his words echoed her thoughts, carrying a deeper truth reflected in those such as her brother. She looked around at the beautiful environment, thinking about how seductive the trappings of an addiction could be.

Illicit mind-altering substances did not enjoy the attractive forms that online environments and networks did. Nor did they have the open encouragement and support of the authorities and populace.

Yet of the two, Haven knew that illegal substances had far less of an effect on the minds and lives of the populace than the dazzling virtual environments did.

"There you go again!" Carlos interjected. "Day dreaming."

"Ever wonder what the point of all this really is?" Haven asked.

Carlos shrugged. "Just fun, amusing."

"But nobody is themselves in here, not really," Haven said. "I'm guilty of that right now. I'm not an over thirty blond-haired tall woman. I'm a seventeen-year-old, dark-haired girl from Technate Six."

"Well, I sure wish I had this build out in the real world," Carlos said, puffing up his chest and grinning.

"And I would like to have a body like this one," Haven said.

"Appearances are just that ... appearances," Carlos said, with no trace of jest. "What we really are is something much deeper."

"And how do you discover that in a place like this, where everyone works so hard to create the perfect facade of themselves?" Haven asked.

"I don't know the answer to that one," Carlos said.

"And neither do I," Haven admitted. "But I'd sure like to know myself, as I really am, one day. And know what the world really is a part of. I can't believe everything is centered on a bunch of technates."

"I suspect there's more, but unless you live in the Northern Sector, I think it would be hard to go on some kind of quest like that," Carlos said. "Too bad scientists proved there's no such thing as a soul or spirit. We're all just a bunch of chemical reactions and algorithms."

"It is too bad that's how things are," Haven lamented. "I'd love to have a little hope that something like a spirit or soul existed."

"Me too," Carlos said. "It's like most of us are walking through life on fragile ground over this big abyss, unless you are one of the lucky ones who live in the Northern Sector and can buy your way to immortality through Ascension."

"Even they can die in a natural disaster, accident, or some other way," Haven said. "Be a lot better if a soul did exist."

"Then again, who's really to say it doesn't?" Carlos said, giving another shrug, as a grin spread across his face. "Do the scientists know absolutely everything about the universe? If they did, they wouldn't have anything to research, and they're constantly doing that. So, by their own actions they admit they don't know everything."

A ray of light piercing a melancholic gloom, his logic gave her something to smile about; and kindled a spark of hope.

For no reason she could discern, she thought of the Artist, and the captivating scenes depicted in the artwork mounted on the walls of the apartment came to her mind.

Thinking of the old-world vehicle traveling through the midst of a magnificent landscape, Haven smiled. She imagined what it would be like to ride in the vehicle for real, far outside the walls and confines of the technate, feeling the rush of air coming through open windows.

She hungered for such a reality, knowing it represented a world far greater than the one she lived in. Perhaps even souls were real in such an unimpeded world.

"Must be a good daydream, you're beaming, and I can tell it's not from looking at anything here," remarked Carlos.

"A wonderful daydream," Haven replied, looking over to her friend with a bright smile.

Salvador

Salvador focused on his breathing, eager for the conclusion of the routine medical assessment. Though not in any sort of physical discomfort, he could not help being unnerved at the idea of a horde of nanobots crawling throughout his body, measuring and evaluating every aspect of his health.

"All looks to be in good order."

The calm, feminine voice came from the scanning tube he had been taken into. Circling his entire body, its array of sensors had examined his exterior, while the host of nanobots made their way throughout his interior.

"It will be a few moments longer for the interior examination to conclude. We appreciate your patience, Salvador," the voice continued.

While the device spoke with a convincing tone, Salvador knew it had no capability of appreciation to begin with. The thought brought a smirk to his face.

Listening to the sound of his breaths, he imagined throngs of microscopic bots marshaling to exit from inside him. A part of Salvador wondered if every last nanobot truly departed his body when an examination came to an end. In light of mandatory ID implants and all the surveillance in place across the technate, it would not have surprised him if a few nanobots were left inside to continue monitoring and reporting on his health.

He could not deny that the miniscule things were extraordinary technological marvels. They stood capable of addressing a numerous range of situations right on the spot that only larger, invasive surgeries planned in advance could address in the past.

From the base of Salvador's neck to the lower part of his legs, several tiny, needle-like implements pressed with a light touch against his skin. Channels for the insertion and extraction of the nanobots, the needles caused no pain.

After collecting the nanobots, the channels retracted, and the surfacing Salvador rested upon slid back out of the tubular chamber. With a long exhalation, he looked at the high ceiling of the examination room in a state of relief.

Salvador waited for a moment before trying to sit up, willing his body to relax. He had become considerably more tense than he thought during the process.

"The examination is complete," the voice of the diagnostic system informed him. "Your information has been updated and all necessary adjustments have been made to your nutritional credits. You can access the details of this examination at any time through the Federal Health System. All of your scores are within a normal range, with the exception of your Balancers. A dose was provided during the interior examination, and a new level has been prescribed for you. Taking a full course of Balancers is optimal for balancing your chemistry and maintaining your health."

Salvador listened to the assessment in silence, giving no reaction to the patronizing tone of the system. He hated taking the mood-enhancing Balancers. Irritated at the fact that the system had administered a dose outright through the nanobots, he had no intention of following the directive.

Almost everyone he knew were given Balancers, and a part of him distrusted the claim that they were for maintaining health and balancing chemistry. If anything, they altered chemistry, for a purpose not shared with those receiving the Balancers.

What the deeper reason was, Salvador could not say, but he had no doubt it would be one that served the Technate far more than any of the individuals taking the medication.

Given permission to leave the examination room, he sat up and stretched his limbs. After getting dressed and leaving the chamber, he continued through the Federal Health Services building, exiting onto the street. Putting on his MR glasses, Salvador saw that his day was running much later than he intended.

Hurrying from the medical facility, he made his way toward the park, a few blocks away. Weaving his way through pedestrians in front of him, he maintained a brisk pace. Once he had passed through the entry gates of the park, he broke into a jog.

A large number of people taking advantage of the sunny day, the park had a crowded atmosphere. The marked trails held a steady stream of bicycles, walkers, and runners, while large swathes of green grass dotted with trees held a dense patchwork of blankets, where many others sat or reclined on the ground.

Still others strolled about, making their way through the labyrinth of blankets. A few open spaces in the park had been designated for sporting activities, and these also had full occupancy.

All throughout the park, far more smiles could be seen upon faces, and laughter heard within the air, in comparison to the somber atmosphere reigning over the streets outside the tenements. A few of the park's inhabitants had donned VR helmets or wore MR glasses, and likely several more had ocular implants active. But for the most part, those present on the grounds remained content to savor the blue skies, sun, soft grass, and breezes flowing through the trees. The park offered its inhabitants an oasis, within a desert of concrete and steel.

Salvador made his way through the bustling maze of people. Cutting a direct line through broad expanses of ground, he set his sights upon the thicker groves of trees rising toward the far edge of the park's western side.

Crossing a small bridge spanning a creek that bisected the park, he glanced toward a cluster of ducks gliding along the surface, led by a mallard with its distinctive green head. A few small children laughed with glee, trundling along the banks and shadowing the ducks heading downstream. The sight brought a grin to Salvador's face.

Nearing his destination, the crowd thinned considerably, until he found himself alone at the edge of some dense undergrowth. Following a short, narrow trail he had forged long ago, he pressed through the brush until he stepped onto low-cut grass once more.

The familiar cluster of trees ahead buoyed his mood. Salvador strode at a brisk gait toward the huge oak tree looming within the midst of the grove.

Finding himself relieved at the sight, Salvador set his gaze upon Jade. With his later arrival, he had doubted the unusual man would be there.

His absence would have been a great disappointment. At the very least, Jade had broken the monotony of predictable days spent within an overly cramped technate.

His broad-brimmed hat tilted down, Jade looked at ease, shading his eyes from the bright sun overhead. He sat on the ground, between the prominent roots of the same oak tree where Salvador had last encountered him.

Leaning against the broad trunk of the old, majestic tree, he regarded Salvador's approach with an amiable expression.

"Well, it would seem we meet again, young Salvador," Jade greeted. "Took you awhile."

"Hi Jade," Salvador replied with a casual air, nearing the tree. "Good to see you here. Sorry about being late. My health examination ran over, and you don't skip those, or they'll come get you."

"Nothing to worry about here," Jade replied. "I don't mandate anything like they do."

"What have you been doing?" Salvador asked.

Jade grinned. "Just taking advantage of a beautiful day ... and listening."

Hearing nothing beyond the distant sounds of voices, coming from other areas of the park, Salvador waited for further explanation. Jade closed his eyes, the grin still resting on his lips.

When Jade did not expound upon his words, Salvador grew impatient, and asked, "Listening to what?"

"What do you think?" Jade replied with a chuckle. Opening his eyes, he glanced upward, toward the branches spread above him.

Salvador followed his gaze, but he saw nothing unusual in the boughs. No birds occupied the tree's limbs. The sky stood empty, save for a surveillance drone drifting through the heights.

"I don't see anything," Salvador said. "Or hear anything, either."

"Yes, you do see something," Jade replied. "Right here. You can't possibly miss it."

"Just a tree," Salvador responded, becoming more confused.

"Precisely," Jade said, his grin broadening.

"So, you are listening to trees?" Salvador asked, with a little hesitance, hoping he did not sound disingenuous.

Jade nodded. "Often gives me a little peace of mind. No matter what I'm dealing with."

"I like the sound of the breeze too," Salvador said, thinking of the relaxing, timeless feel of the air currents passing through the leaves. Many afternoons and evenings he had given himself over to emptying his mind of worries and cares, and simply enjoying the pleasant sounds.

"I'm not listening to the sound of the wind," Jade said. "I'm listening to the tree itself. And this particular tree has much to say. It has witnessed quite a lot over the years, having been here long before the current age came into existence."

"The tree ... it speaks?" Salvador asked, with an incredulous air.

"Hard to believe for most folks these days, I know, but it is true," Jade answered. "Just because most people choose not to believe something doesn't mean it isn't true or can't be true. That's something I hope you learn soon ... for your own sake."

"What in the world does a tree say?" Salvador asked.

"Lots of things," Jade answered. "They're all different. Same as people, in that they have a variety of temperaments and personalities. You can kind of get a sense of what they're like, in the way they created their outer forms. Take a close look at this oak tree, for example."

Salvador eyed the old tree, a regal figure broad of trunk and towering in height. Its branches grew in a way that gave it a strong, balanced appearance.

"What do you think this one is like?" Jade asked. "Give it a guess. Your first instinct."

"Not sure, but it looks strong and proud, and looks like it has been here for a long time," Salvador said.

Jade nodded. "It is a patient and wise one, and even-tempered. Very much an observer."

"Wouldn't all trees be observers? Not much else for them to do but stand around and watch things," Salvador replied, laughing.

"Some concern themselves with things beyond watching the people that come and go in their world. A few even slumber," Jade said. "They have a means of talking amongst each other too. Word passes quicker than you think, among their kind."

"So what does this tree have to say?" Salvador said, looking upward, into the oak's prominent mass of leaves and branches.

"To put it politely, it is astounded at what people have allowed to happen here in the technate," Jade said. "Of course, it has the advantage of a great multitude of years and seeing many different ways people have lived before this time."

"So how does one hear a tree?" Salvador asked, curious, but not about to believe something like Jade described stood possible.

"It might be a gift, or it might be a matter of finding the right way to tune in," Jade said. "I can't say for sure. I'm just glad that I can."

"Would be incredible to be able to do that, but I don't think I have that gift," Salvador said.

"Some gifts remain hidden, until you discover them," Jade replied, with no hint of jest in his words.

"I haven't discovered that one, then," Salvador responded.

"Who knows what you'd uncover, if you choose to search," Jade said, chuckling.

"I wouldn't know where to even start," Salvador said, finding the man more than a bit unique. Nevertheless, Jade piqued his interest in a world where few questioned anything; and most lost themselves in the depths and distractions of virtual worlds.

No matter how real the digitally-rendered worlds looked, or how genuine the experiences were to his senses, Salvador could never get it out of his head that they were ultimately artificial. The tree before him represented something real; a living thing that shared the same world and realm of existence as him.

"First of all, silence the faithless voice inside," Jade said. "Listen to the voice of your heart. Only then can you approach the limitless."

"Everything you talk about is interesting, but I can't make much sense of it all," Salvador confessed.

"I have a hunch you have more gifts than you are aware of,"

Jade said. "I just want to be a friend who helps you discover them."

"It's great to have a new friend," Salvador said, the words no understatement.

He had so few that he deemed to be friends, and none of them could be considered a confidant; of the type he could trust and confide in. Loneliness never left him, even when swimming in a sea of digital interactions.

A sense of emptiness pervaded his home. His mother and her boyfriend, even though they rarely left the apartment in a physical sense, were absent from his life most of the time. From VR helmets to the holographic system, they sequestered themselves in their digital communities for the greater portion of each day.

Salvador could not look to his father either, having lost him to a fast-developing cancer three years before. Even crueler, the cancer could have been removed, and had spread while he had been waiting for a surgery approval from the Federal Health Service. Had his father lived in the Northern Sector, and had the option of private treatments, he would be living today.

As things stood, Salvador had found his refuge within the trees on the park's western edge; and there he had discovered a brand-new friend, who spoke of strange and wonderful possibilities.

"I'd like to talk about a few more things with you," Jade said. "But you may find the discussion even more confusing than our last conversation."

"Speaking of our last conversation, I've been giving a lot of thought about what a premise is," Salvador said.

His words held truth. Salvador had spent many hours thinking about the idea of a premise, whether at home, in a virtual environment, or while on a foray in the technate.

"And what have you concluded?" Jade asked. "Let's start there."

"It's kind of like a starting point," Salvador responded. "The base for the things I think. Like you said, it's a foundation. It's about where I'm coming from, when I'm talking about something."

"It has a lot to do with the perspective you have on things," Jade said, nodding, and looking pleased with the boy's answer. "And if something is askew with your premise?"

"It's gonna affect my perception, and my choices, and just about everything else," Salvador replied.

"Which is why it's always very important to examine your premise, and evaluate it, often," Jade said. "Never assume it is perfect."

"I'm gonna try to do that," Salvador replied.

"Good," Jade said. "You'll develop a wisdom far beyond your years."

Salvador nodded. "I'll do my very best."

"Well, since you have a sense of what a premise is, and the need to examine it, I have a good story to tell you ... one you may not have heard before," Jade said. He then added, "If you are not in a hurry, that is."

"I've got some time yet," Salvador replied.

"Excellent. Then I'll tell you a bit about the Primordials, the Transcendent, and a few other things," Jade said. "Ever heard those terms before?"

Salvador shook his head. "Can't say I have."

Jade shook his head slowly. "Then you need to, and I will not delay any further.

"I will start with the Primordials. What, or who are they? It's something very prevalent in your world, but almost no one is even aware of them. Many of the ones that are aware have been very successful in veiling the Primordials, and they've hid them intentionally. Not a hard thing to do when nearly everyone living in this technate has a flawed premise."

Jade looked away, and his voice reflected sadness when he

stated, after a pause. "The whole thing is just vile. I still can't understand how anyone would serve such darkness, but they do."

His voice trailing off, he fell into silence.

"Who has done a good job? What flawed premise? And what are Primordials?" Salvador asked, the questions spilling out of him.

Seeing the raw emotion on the man's face, Salvador began to wonder if Jade had full command of his faculties.

"Listen carefully," Jade said in a firm tone, looking back to Salvador. His eyes flared with intensity. "I'll help you, in any way I can, if you want to understand what is really happening in the world ... and why things are the way they are. But there is a cost, and it's not a small one. Once you look under the surface, you will never see the world the same way again."

"I don't understand what you mean about all this," Salvador asked. Though unsettled at Jade's somber demeanor, he remained willing to indulge the conversation. "But I'd like to know the truth about things."

"Let me ask you this, Salvador," Jade responded. "Where do you think death dwells?"

"No idea at all," Salvador said. "It dwells nowhere. It's nothing. Death is just what happens to everything that lives, eventually."

"Death dwells as far from life's Source as it can," Jade proceeded. "Death cannot withstand the Light of the Source, in the same way a dark room cannot resist a bright light shined into its midst."

"Sounds like talk from the old world they tell us about in our lessons," Salvador said. "The old religions, and all that."

He found it hard to believe there had been a time when religions had followers numbering in the millions, even billions, but that age transpired long ago. Reason and science had prevailed, and the world of mystics and prophets had faded into obscurity.

Religion had been consigned to the annals of history, a thing to be referenced in the studies of societies whose time had passed into dust. Salvador had given the subject little thought, beyond wondering how any society had allowed such wild notions to take root without any objective proof.

"What happens, happens, and what is, is, whether you or anyone else in this world chooses to recognize it or not," Jade said, shrugging his shoulders with a nonchalant air. "I've cautioned you about assuming things before."

"Okay, so explain more about these Primordials, and this Source, then," Salvador said, alarmed that he had offended Jade in some way. "Is it something like a war then? Between who? There's not been a war between anyone on this planet for a long time."

"There's a war going on right now. In every age, a war has been raging between the Primordials and the Transcendent," Jade replied, with the tenor of an instructor. "The war between the powers who serve the Primordials, and those loyal to the Source. The greatest of those powers are named Chronos and Kairos; Chronos serving the cause of the Primordials, and Kairos serving the Source."

"Now I'm getting even more confused. What's the difference between them?" Salvador asked, searching his memory for anything he could think of regarding the names mentioned by Jade. He turned up nothing.

Seeing the fervor with which the man spoke, Salvador had sympathy for Jade. He suspected the man would be sent sooner or later for Rehabilitation, and the accompanying medications at the Federal Health Service.

"Two sides with very distinct natures. Primordials seek always to control, confine, and suppress, and impose limits ... the world of the finite," Jade answered. "A Transcendent hungers always for freedom. The path of Transcendence calls to each and every one of us, seeking to bring every individual to the highest, strongest, and fullest version of them. Every individual ... empowered to become an image of the Source ... which is infinite, and without boundary.

"Primordials are the enemy of that empowerment. They seek to hold everyone in thrall. It sees you and I as pieces of a whole ... nothing more than a collective ... parts of a big machine ... cells of a body ... and nothing more. Primordials hate the Source with every last part of their essence. They seek always to diminish the reflection of the Source in the world, and hunger always for a way to consume the Light."

"Sounds almost like the Global Council of Technates," Salvador replied in jest, laughing. The smile faded from his face, seeing that Jade did not share his humor in the slightest.

He said nothing further. Speaking openly against the Global Council of Technates stood a serious crime.

"Don't worry, I'm not going to turn you in to those insipid, arrogant fools," Jade said. "It's just that you were correct in your natural response. Here is a look under the surface for you ... the Global Council of Technates is a function of the Primordials."

"The Global Council of Technates? Then wouldn't these Primordials be in control of everything?" Salvador asked, finding he was not sure he wanted to know the answer. "The Global Council of Technates dictates everything."

"They've succeeded in dulling consciousness, all across the face of this world, even as the Primordial feeds upon this same consciousness," Jade answered. "This is why you have the world that you see around you every day. In this world you are not seen as images of the Source. You are just a part of the Greater Good ... the Greater Good as they have defined it, that is. They say you are all equal, but in doing so they deny your very nature and essence.

"Your energies, your thoughts, your desires, everything about you ... it must be conformed to this thing they call the

Greater Good, channeling everything towards the Primordials and farther away from the Source. It's why they maintain control over all your media, what choices are available to you, and what you say."

Jade pointed at his head. "They do not want you to make full use of this ... your mind. This ... is your true refuge and strength against them."

"They tell us all the time how the Greater Good Doctrine righted the wrongs of the old world," Salvador said.

"It is a skillful deception," Jade said. "One that has been designed and advanced by those loyal to the Primordials over many ages. They have deceived you into thinking they adhere to a moral principle. I assure you, they do not.

"They hunger to reach and invade higher planes of existence, and to do so they must first destroy consciousness. By doing so, they remove the reflection of the Source that serves as a barrier between their dark realms and those above."

Salvador could not believe someone would speak so openly against the system running the technate. No matter how unlikely the story sounded, Jade could find himself hauled in for violation of speech codes against incitement and sedition.

He did not want to see his new friend apprehended.

"Jade, it's not good to talk like that," Salvador said. Using his eyes, he gestured skyward, where a security drone could be seen gliding slowly.

Jade looked to the sky and stared for a moment in the direction of the drone. "Oh, that. You've nothing to worry about, regarding either of us. You will just have to take my word for the moment, though I will demonstrate what I mean."

"Just don't want to see you get into trouble," Salvador said.

"I'll be quite fine," Jade said, looking back with a big grin. "So, do you have any questions yet?"

Salvador thought for a moment.

"So, these things, the Primordials, are climbing towards the Source, one level at a time? And I'm guessing they're about finished with this world too?" Salvador asked, his brow furrowing with the worry building inside. "Is that what you are saying?"

One part of him worried that Jade was overconfident about speaking so brazenly. Another part of him could not believe that he took the discussion seriously. Yet another part stood intrigued, if only with the story itself.

Jade nodded. "That's a big part of it."

"But you wouldn't be here, telling me all this, if the Primordials could not be stopped," Salvador replied.

"It's just like turning on a light in a pitch-black room," Jade said. "It's just the light needs to be turned on, using consciousness, and the will that all of us possess."

"It sounds so terrible though, with the Primordials advancing and the situation with our world," Salvador said, remaining careful not to incriminate himself too much if Jade happened to be wrong about it being safe to talk in such a candid way.

"If you could only see Faraway right now, you would know what I'm saying, without question," Jade said, his voice carrying a compassionate tone. "If you could experience the power of Kairos, you would know that Chronos is not the only authority over time.

"You have only seen this world, Salvador. You only know of this world. You've never seen or experienced a world that realizes its full potential. You and everyone you know have nothing to compare your world to."

"I don't think there's a world like the one you're talking about, anywhere," Salvador replied, with a resigned shrug.

"Just because you haven't experienced a world like that, doesn't mean it doesn't exist," Jade replied. "Your assumption is the great, fundamental error that so many of your leaders of science and government make."

A look of disgust on his face, Jade shook his head and then

added, "I would say such an elementary mistake too, but I can't give them the benefit of attributing a mistake. For so many of them, it is all intentional."

"Why would anyone choose a darker existence intentionally?" Salvador asked.

"Baffles me too," Jade said. "Deception has a lot to do with many who take such a path, but a few hearts are genuinely attracted to the things of darkness."

"I can't even begin to think like that," Salvador responded.

"Which is why I am here talking with you now," Jade said, smiling. "And now, for that demonstration. So, you will have some confidence in what I'm saying."

Salvador waited, but Jade did not make any kind of move to get up, or any other kind of gesture. He looked relaxed, and even closed his eyes for a few moments.

Opening them again, he looked to Salvador with a hardened gaze. He spoke in a low, firm tone. "I am against everything those who are behind this technate and all the others are doing to people. I desire to see people free, and brought ever closer to the Source, to realize their true potential and nature.

"I will do all that I can to see the power running this technate, and all the others, collapse. The technates, and everything about them, are rooted in evil, and the ones ruling them preyed upon the good nature and intentions of people to bring their system into power. They sold all of you on the notion of doing more good for everyone, when control is all they intended from the beginning."

With such talk, Jade had crossed a line that most feared to begin to approach. Salvador could not believe how fearless Jade was.

"I made sure they heard that," Jade said, with a wink.

He looked upward and kept his eyes on something. Salvador followed the man's gaze to see a flying object lowering from the heights, heading toward them. Lights flashed in an array of repeating patterns all over the approaching aircraft.

Fear gripped Salvador, recognizing what the strobing lights represented; a technate security drone.

"Looks like our conversation is up, for the time being. Time for me to thwart their highly-advanced technology," Jade announced with a wide grin, getting up to his feet. A spark of excitement danced in his eyes.

"What do you mean?" Salvador said, growing more anxious. He looked back toward the incoming drone. It had reached the park and now approached at a level just above the top of the trees.

"First, I'm not registered to their all-powerful system," Jade declared, with a mocking edge. "Probably makes me a terrorist in their eyes … then again, the idea of a real free person does strike terror into the hearts of those who govern your technate. Scares them quite a bit, actually."

"But what about me? They're going to bring me in, I'm sure," Salvador said, beginning to panic with the drone drawing nearer. As much for the drone's sensors as for Jade, he added, "I've done nothing wrong."

Jade grinned and winked again. "Of course, you haven't done anything wrong. But I'm going to take care of all concerns for you. Like I said earlier, no worries at all. Just get out of here, when I give you the chance."

The security drone lowered and glided through the trees, navigating with ease. There was no use in running or trying to hide.

Drones were fitted with all kinds of sensors, from thermal imaging to night vision. Above all, they could lock in upon an individual's implanted ID, and use it to track them. Trying to evade them only dragged out the inevitable, and often invited painful incapacitation.

Salvador had witnessed more than one person twitching and jerking about on the streets, after enduring the voltage of a drone's stun mechanism. Knowing it was best to wait and cooperate, he intended to remain in place.

He watched the drone drawing closer, dread rising fast within him.

The wind started to pick up. Glancing skyward, his heart skipped a beat.

The clouds churned, all across the sky. Salvador had never seen clouds behaving in such a manner before, and he stood transfixed. As he stared at the phenomenon, the clouds began pulsing with flashes of lightning.

Rivulets of lightning then converged mid-air, uniting into a massive bolt that shot downward, engulfing the drone in a brilliance of blue and white.

The air crackled, and the drone made a loud hissing sound.

Plunging downward, the drone plopped onto the ground a moment later, lights out. The air filled with the scent of burned electronics.

"Took care of that little problem, didn't I?" Jade said, smiling and looking energized by what had just transpired. "See you soon, Salvador, consider this an introduction to far greater things."

Rooted in place, Salvador could not take his eyes from the smoking drone.

"Go on, get out of here now!" Jade told him, a little more firm. "You are in the clear for the moment. But if you stand around here, you'll invite problems for yourself."

Salvador looked from the downed security craft toward Jade. He froze, his breath catching in his throat.

The man had disappeared, without a trace.

Urgency snapped Salvador out of his momentary paralysis. At a brisk pace, he left the spot, followed his trail through the brush, and continued through the park.

A lot of people were standing about, looking to the skies and talking excitedly among each other. With the widespread commotion, Salvador attracted no attention. His nervous expression melded in with the faces of many others panicked from the weather disruption, and more than a few headed with swift strides for the park's exit.

Despite being able to fit in with the park's other occupants, his heart beat faster. Expecting to be swarmed by security elements at any second, his mind raced, unable to think of what he could say when apprehended. Destroying a drone would not be seen as a minor infraction.

He could only hope that Jade had spoken truthfully.

The sharp, lashing winds of moments before trickled down into a light breeze. When he looked back to the sky, there were just a few puffy, gray masses drifting lazily through the heights.

The calm sight did not dissuade him from trusting his eyes. Salvador knew what he had seen and experienced, and he was not about to question his senses.

Jade had something to do with the storm and the targeted lightning strike on the drone. Of that, Salvador had no doubts.

There was so much to digest from the unexpected encounter, but there was one thing that Salvador could not deny.

Seeing the drone annihilated, and brought down from the sky, brought him a great burst of joy.

For all the times the horrid things had hovered above him, or drifted near to him, watching and recording him, it had been wonderful seeing a bolt of lightning rendering the loathsome object inert and useless.

He could not begin to speculate how Jade called the lightning bolt down on purpose. The idea itself appeared preposterous. No man could command lightning, but the event could not be denied, and went far beyond an extraordinary coincidence.

Salvador could also not explain how Jade disappeared from sight so easily. He had only looked away from the man for a few seconds. At the very least, he should have seen Jade leaving the area.

Heading home, Salvador wished he could have continued the conversation. Still confused with everything he had been told, the talk of the Primordials, Transcendence, the Source, Chronos, Kairos, and Faraway fascinated him.

He wondered how so many things, if they could somehow be true, could remain so hidden from an advanced society like the one he lived in.

A strange thought hit him in that moment. Perhaps the society that he dwelled in was not so advanced, in some ways.

Realizing he had made an assumption about his own world being advanced in all things, he recognized that he had formed a false premise. He suspected he would be rethinking a lot of things.

Walking along the streets of the technate, his heart rate began to settle. Striding by security bots and surveillance sensors mounted on light poles and buildings, watching security drone vehicles rolling down the street, and glancing toward airborne drones above, Salvador gained increasing confidence with every moment that passed by without incident. Had he been identified in conjunction with the downed drone in the park, he would have already been apprehended.

Salvador could only hope that he saw Jade again. Having no idea how to find or reach out to his new friend, he would have to depend on another random encounter, or Jade finding him somehow.

The thoughts troubled him, but he did not despair. Deep down, Salvador had the strong impression that Jade would find him again; and intended to.

Cayden

Cayden shuffled into the kitchen. A little groggy after a long sleep, he took a glass out from a cupboard. Pressing it against a dispenser lever in the refrigerator's facing, he poured cold orange juice to the brim of the glass. The refrigerator registered the action, including the amount taken and Cayden's identity.

Gulping down the sweet liquid, he began to feel the onset of clarity within his mind. Another day, with nothing much to offer, lay ahead. A little of the juice trickled down from the corner of his mouth, and he wiped at it with the back of his hand.

Despite the late morning hour, the apartment remained silent. As tended to be the case on most days, his mother slept in.

She had no job to go to, but that did not present much of an issue, with well over half of Technate Six's population receiving a full subsidy called the Sustainability Allowance. Cayden still wished she had an interest in doing something, even if in a volunteer capacity.

Ever since the divorce, she had become increasingly distant from his day to day life. Spending most of her hours within VR environments, escaping the things that plagued her, she dwelled within illusions.

Cayden did his best to not take her growing absence

personally. He knew she still could not accept the removal of his sister, Melanie, at the age of nine.

On one of the routine mandated visits, a Technate Youth Care Agent had deemed his mother and father negligent with Melanie's upbringing. The agent had determined that Melanie possessed an inappropriate worldview; one in violation of the Greater Good Doctrine.

With it well-established that children belonged to the community, as much as to parents, the agent had taken Cayden's sister into his custody that very day.

The taking of Melanie inflicted a terrible blow upon Cayden's family. His mother already had reached the limit of two children. Having undergone the preventative operation required of those who could not lawfully have another child, his mother could never give birth again.

She had tried her best to divert Melanie's attention at home, but Cayden's sister had never been the sort to keep quiet about her curiosities and opinions. An inquisitive and lively child, she had given voice to the things on her mind without hesitation. Everything she said had been recorded through the in-home camera and microphone installed by the Technate Youth Care Division.

The device, required in a home until a child reached twelve years of age, provided agents at the TYCD a means of ensuring that all child-care regulations were being observed. In the case of Cayden's family, it had proven to be the means by which his parents had been incriminated, for thoughts that his sister had come up with on her own. Melanie had blurted out more than enough opinions to give the TYC agent plenty of fodder to take her away.

Soon after, Cayden had been summoned to speak with another department of Federal Youth Care, the Youth Guardian Council. The Youth Guardian Council regularly met with, and interviewed, those who were eleven to fifteen years of age.

Though quite young then, at fourteen, Cayden knew their game and intentions. He said all the right things to his interviewer, knowing that his mother and father could not bear to lose both of their children.

Even though the Youth Guardian Council allowed Cayden to remain in the care of his parents, he found himself unable to stem the widening rift between his mother and father following Melanie's extraction. A cloud of unhappiness and tension settled over Cayden's home, thickening over the following year, until finally his parents had chosen to divorce.

The apartment became frigid and empty over the ensuing couple of years, but Cayden could not bring himself to utter the few easy words to the Youth Guardian Council that would get him taken out of his home. A simmering anger had grown within him, but he had learned to mask the resentful feelings, keeping his thoughts to himself.

Cayden could not be responsible for another heavy blow to his mother. He knew in his heart that she would not survive it.

Anger boiling within him, he clunked the empty glass down hard on the counter. Just sixteen years old, living in the apartment of a fully-subsidized, unemployed mother, little could be done about the world of the TYCD and the long-lasting pain such agencies inflicted upon torn families.

Like everyone he knew, Cayden stood powerless, and without any real recourse, in the face of the ruling system. He hated that truth, but he could not evade it.

Within those moments of dark brooding, brilliant blue eyes and a beautiful face came to the fore; a beacon in the raging storm.

He found himself thinking of the woman from the dream, and her three strong companions. They were not the types to submit to something like the Youth Guardian Council, or agents of the TYCD.

Cayden had more than a hunch that the response of the woman to such agents would be a joy and relief to behold.

The woman had offered to be his Guardian, and Cayden wished that she had been his advocate when his sister and father were still living at home. Shaking his head, he dismissed the thought, knowing it to be a fanciful wish with no tether to reality.

No solace could be taken in the thought of the woman becoming his Guardian. Nothing more than a conjuration of a physical brain, dreams were the construct of chemicals interacting, while much of the body slumbered.

Anything seen within a dream was nothing more than a creation of Cayden's imagination; including the captivating woman.

Yet the man and three women that he had encountered, and the environment that they had been in, had all seemed so real. Cayden knew that he had never seen any of the figures before. He also doubted himself imaginative enough to form such a complex scene.

Something deeper inside nudged Cayden to return to his bedroom and go back to sleep. The apartment lay wreathed in silence. Nothing would happen for a few hours yet to disturb him, especially with his mother fast asleep.

With no compelling alternative to what would be another drab, uneventful day, Cayden made his way back to his bedroom. He spoke the command to the Home Assistant to activate the room's lights, and then shut the door.

Taking his shoes off, he changed into a loose-fitting pair of pants, leaving his t-shirt on. Making his way over to the side of his bed, he deactivated the lights, and the room went pitch black.

Crawling into the bed, Cayden buried himself under the covers. Closing his eyes and clearing his thoughts, he eased into the depths of sleep.

When a sense of vision returned, Cayden found himself

among a crowd of tall, refined-looking people. At once, he knew it to be no ordinary gathering or setting.

Sunlight bathed the assemblage through several towering windows. The atrium that Cayden stood within soared up to an exquisitely molded ceiling, adorned with magnificent crystal chandeliers.

Men and women attired in elegant, luxurious garb laughed and talked together, while the melodic notes of a grand piano rang throughout the spacious chamber. From where he sat upon a raised dais, the player of the piano, dressed in a white tuxedo, smiled as his fingers danced among the black and white keys.

Every man and woman Cayden set his eyes upon had a beautiful appearance, and none were advanced in years. He had never witnessed a crowd such as the one he now viewed.

Recovering from his initial amazement at the scene encompassing him, Cayden became self-conscious in an instant. Looking down, he saw his body covered in the usual attire, including a rumpled shirt, jeans, and well-worn sneakers. His appearance contrasted sharply with the pervading atmosphere.

"They cannot see you, or even hear you, so don't worry yourself," a voice came from behind him.

The smooth, feminine tone told Cayden the identity of the speaker before he turned around. Seeing her comely face smiling at him, and peering into her transfixing blue eyes, prompted a jump in his heartbeat.

"Hi," Cayden said to the woman of his previous dream. Feeling like an idiot, and unable to muster any other kind of reply, he looked downward.

"Hello to you as well," the woman replied with a cheerful air. "Don't be shy, we've met before."

With a little effort, Cayden brought his eyes upward. Where the people in the crowd were adorned in brighter clothing, she wore a full-length, tight-fitting black dress that accented her shapely form.

"Where ... are we?" Cayden asked hesitantly, in a hushed voice, glancing around the chamber.

"You know that prestigious section of the technate?" she asked. "The one where most cannot go, where the individuals who can avail themselves of Ascension live?"

Cayden nodded, thinking of the vaunted Northern Sector, the common designation people gave to the ninth sector of Technate Six. Never had he imagined that he would ever set foot inside its heavily-warded boundaries.

"You are here, in the heart of it," she replied. "Standing in the midst of great privilege and authority. The two tend to go hand in hand, and the rules here are very different from those in the technate's other sectors."

Listening to the clink of crystal glasses and the soft flow of notes from the grand piano, Cayden looked around at the chamber's occupants. It astonished him how uniformly attractive they were. All strong of posture and bearing, their bodies testified to high degrees of fitness and vitality.

Cayden had long-wondered about the kind of lifestyle experienced by those living in the cordoned sector covering the northern area of the technate. His answer reflected in the smiling, comely faces he beheld all around the chamber, a sharp pang of envy arose within him.

"And before you believe this to be your imagination, listen to them closely," his companion invited, looking toward a dark-haired man speaking nearby with two women and another man. "Commit to memory what they say. It will verify the reality of all this for you."

Cayden nodded, and turned his attention to the quartet. Content to listen and remain anonymous, he took in their conversation, as instructed by his guide.

"We will be announcing a new austerity measure later today,

a reduction in food subsidy credits to conform to new energy and agriculture policies of the Global Council," the man stated. "We will also be announcing a cutback in power credits, with the need to bring balance to all partners in the Global Council. Of course, all of this will be done in full conformity with the Global Council's regulations concerning announcements of this nature."

"That all sounds so unpleasant, I wasn't expecting more mass cutbacks so soon," exclaimed one of the women, whose lustrous mass of curly auburn hair cascaded about a smooth, toned set of shoulders, showcased by her red sequined dress. Her brow furrowed. "And you are sure we won't run afoul of anything? Or bring discomfort to ourselves?"

"We will have all of the usual waivers in order, complying with both the regional and global authorities, so do not worry yourself for a moment, Marissa," the man replied. Flashing her a smile, he displayed a perfect set of white teeth.

"I knew we would be taken care of," Marissa replied. "It is just that a little unrest might be sparked. That can be a hassle."

"We will be aware of anything amiss well in advance, through our surveillance network," the man replied amiably, looking the least bit concerned. "We will address any problems without delay, as we always have."

"Technate Six is much too crowded for the levels of subsidy we have available," the other woman interjected. She had straight brunette hair, and an emerald green dress fit the contours of her athletic-looking body to perfection. "Perhaps we should petition the Global Council to explore a one child limit per family, at some point. It needs to be done."

"That would invoke great unrest, I believe," Marissa said, with a look of concern.

"We have more than enough security bots and troopers to subdue four times the populace of this technate, if need be," said the other man, a dark-eyed figure with short-cropped brown hair.

"Darren, it won't need to get that far," the first man said, in a reassuring tone. "All of you worry yourselves too much. With the controls in place, we could announce austerity measures three times stronger, and it would fail to rouse any significant reaction. The populace will mind their place, as they always have. They have been well-conditioned. Plenty of amusements and escapes. All of you still carry fears of the old world you remember ... a small price you've paid for gaining life extension."

The lady in the emerald green dress still held a look of concern. "Just because there has never been a significant resistance movement since the implementation of the Greater Good Doctrine does not mean it will always be that way."

"We are now able to identify any fire starters before they can even try to set a spark," the man said. "That's the beauty of the system we now have in place. No leaders can ever take root, spread their ideas, and grow any kind of following. Truly, don't worry yourself, Olivia. A few might grumble and bicker. I'll make sure that the media looks sympathetic, but at the end of the day it will be as it's always been, for us and them."

"You've never failed to exhibit good judgement," Olivia replied to the man. She smiled at him, looking placated by his words.

Listening to their casual tone, Cayden found his ire rising quickly. He could not believe the manner in which the well-dressed people discussed decisions that would have direct, negative impacts on virtually the entire technate; except for the ones making the edicts.

Further realization dawning upon him, Cayden began to understand how old each of the individuals was, given the reference to shared memories of the old world. That time had come to an end almost sixty years prior.

"Their kind has never been affected in a significant way by the decisions they make for others, and never will be," the woman at Cayden's side stated. "These are the elites of society, and they have been with you in every age. They see themselves as the shepherds, and you are the sheep. Give them your meat and wool, and they might allow you a little patch of grass to graze upon. But make no mistake, they have control over that grass too."

The words bitter to his ears, an urge to lash out at the man welled up in Cayden. A part of him wanted to plant his fist squarely into the man's immaculate set of teeth.

Cayden knew the kind of pain suffered in the greater populace all too well. He had listened to all the talk of shared sacrifice, the Greater Good, and the other blather repeated endlessly in his lessons and technate broadcasts.

Shared sacrifice and austerity certainly did not affect the kind of men and women surrounding him. Such conditions were not for those of the Northern Sector; only those dwelling in the other sectors needed to submit.

So angry that his eyes began to tear up, he looked into the Guardian's face, and stammered, "This ... is ... hideous. I hate it."

Her eyes took on an icy hue. "Technate Six's Global Council Representative Margolis is one of those who took up Ascension. Not only is he going to be the one making such austerity pronouncements, but he will be doing so long after the people outside this section of the technate grow old, wither and die ... including those as young as you, Cayden."

"Why are you telling me this?" Cayden asked her, fighting back the hot tears misting his vision. Powerless and helpless, and coursing with anger, he wished that he could leave the chamber at once.

The powerful desire triggered the process that he needed. The clarity of his surroundings began to blur, and the voices of the elite gathering grew ever more distant.

Before he faded out from the scene, he heard her voice once more. "View the media reports tonight, Cayden, and remember all of this."

Opening his eyes, he stared into the darkness of his room. Using his voice, he invoked a little light.

The details of a typical dream faded rapidly, but Cayden determined to hold on to the images he had witnessed and the things he had heard. He got up from the bed, replaying the key elements over and over again within his mind.

He thought of Councilperson Margolis, and the others with him, Olivia, Darren, and Marissa, committing their faces and names to firmer memory. The opulence he had witnessed seemed hard to believe, now that a far less fanciful environment surrounded him.

The echoes of the music, the sheen on every surface, and the consistent beauty of the men and women in the chamber ran through his mind. Finding it difficult to believe that people lived every day within such an incredible atmosphere, Cayden had to remind himself that the Northern Sector did exist.

Rousing himself, he got some food in the kitchen, and then gave himself over to distractions, playing some VR games until evening arrived. Through his VR helmet, he summoned up one of the news media transmissions.

A set formed before his eyes. A pair of hosts, a man and woman, sat behind a broad white counter. Behind them, the background took the form of a bright sunny day, with a view of Technate Six's lofty skyline.

Cayden noticed that both of the attractive figures would have fit in with the elite gathering he had witnessed.

The leading story pertained to the very thing he had been told to look for by the Guardian.

Cayden watched in shock as the female anchor spoke of a new Technate Six announcement concerning a series of cutbacks in food subsidies and new regulations for power allocation. The latter, according to the news anchor, would serve to balance out energy consumption levels with the other members of the Global Council of Technates.

The scene then shifted to pre-recorded images of the Technate Six Representative to the Global Council who had made the announcement. Cayden recognized the figure at once.

Representative Lane Margolis, the man that Cayden had seen in the dream, stood a few paces away, in three crystal clear dimensions.

Many others flanked Representative Margolis on the dais where he spoke. The tumbling mass of curling, auburn locks on one woman drew Cayden's attention.

Though dressed in darker business attire, the tall woman's features were undeniable. Cayden stared at the woman who had been called Marissa in the dream, and he wondered about her role in the ongoing proceedings.

The broadcast moved onward to another feature, but Cayden's mind stayed rooted in the story he had just witnessed. Matters of austerity measures and power allocations held little to no interest to him, under normal circumstances. In truth, the topics bored him.

Yet the story he just viewed captivated him, confirming the truth of so many things he had experienced within the dream.

Cayden tried to come up with an explanation. He thought about how he had been able to know of the announcement, and the identity of the man giving it, before it had actually happened. No matter how hard he tried, he could not come up with anything plausible.

He could not deny that he had seen both Representative Margolis and Marissa in the dream and had heard them speak in detail about what the news anchors had just announced. He wondered if the others with them in the dream also existed in his world.

Going into the Northern Sector to verify more of the dream's images would be out of the question. But his heart told him that the lavish atmosphere he had beheld in the dream could be found in a physical reality, somewhere beyond the high walls and thick layers of security shielding the restricted area.

The thought that he had witnessed something right as it happened in the real world, through the means of a dream, confounded him. Despite the quandaries, he had seen what he had seen, and could not tell himself otherwise.

Though rested and wide-awake, a part of him wanted to go back to sleep, if only to seek out the enigmatic Guardian. Even if it all turned out to be some grand illusion, the dream and the woman's attention made him feel important.

It reached far beyond a world that had seen him teased, harassed, and pummeled, with no guardian to stand at his side.

Cayden wished with all his might that it could all somehow be real, and that a new door had opened to him. The newscast, and the knowledge he held prior to it, only served to make that desire burn stronger within him. He knew in that moment that he would do just about anything to have the woman become his personal Guardian, in a real sense.

He had nothing to lose. His education had become a nightmare, and nothing about the future appealed to him. Entertaining a fantasy for a while longer would, at the very least, serve as a welcome distraction from his trials.

He opted out of the news broadcast. Taking the VR helmet off and setting it aside, Cayden got up to his feet.

Standing in the quiet of the apartment, he knew that with the weekend underway no obligations or plans lay before him. He could do whatever he wanted.

With a grin, a spark of hope, and an image of a beautiful, dark-haired woman clear in his mind, Cayden returned to his bed and sought the refuge of sleep.

Jaelynn

Jaelynn returned home, quietly entering the apartment. She began to make her way back to her bedroom, soft of step, but paused when she saw her mother sitting in the living room.

"Hi mom," Jaelynn greeted.

Her mother greeted her with a smile. "Hi Jaelynn, did you have a good day?"

"I did," Jaelynn answered. "I had a nice visit with Gabriel."

"That's wonderful to hear," her mother replied. Her smile grew. "I have some good news to tell you."

"What is it?" Jaelynn asked, seeing the happiness in her mother's face.

Her mother announced, "The THS approved the surgery for next month."

Jaelynn smiled wide. Walking over, she gave her mother a big hug, a sense of relief flooding her. "That's absolutely wonderful!"

The family had been on edge for several weeks as the Technate Health Service's agents weighed the approval of her mother's surgery. Seeing her in pain each and every day, Jaelynn knew the surgery to be necessary, by any reasonable measure.

Nevertheless, the choice was not hers or anyone else's in her family to make; not even her mother. The THS stood as the one to rule whether something was of an elective or essential nature.

The judgement determined everything for a family such as Jaelynn's. If the surgery had been ruled elective in nature, then only one of the people fortunate to live in the high-walled compound of the Northern Sector could have afforded the procedure by themselves. With high demand for health services from the public and the ensuing costs, THS agents had become increasingly strict in managing the approval of medical treatments.

As Jaelynn hugged her mother, she found something profoundly wrong with the idea of feeling grateful toward the THS agents. Her mother stood at the mercy of their system, and it had never mattered one bit what she or any of her family thought about her complications. The THS had kept their family in a state of frayed nerves for weeks, waiting for approval on a simple back procedure that she knew her mother needed.

"I'm just glad the waiting is finally over," her mother said, her smile ebbing and a look of weariness reflecting in her face.

"I know, mom," Jaelynn said. "It's been awful. I'm so sorry you had to wait. I wish things were different. But you are going to get the procedure now, and you are going to feel so much better when it's done."

"There is that," her mother said, smiling. "So, I'm thinking of making a rice casserole, and maybe some chocolate pudding tonight. I feel like celebrating a little. Probably use up a big chunk of our nutritional credits in several categories, maybe even incur a reprimand from the system, but I think it's worth it."

"I do too, and it sounds great!" Jaelynn replied.

"So, you said you had a good day with Gabriel?" her mother asked.

Jaelynn nodded. "A very wonderful day."

"What did you all do?"

"Visited with some friends and got some lunch. Just spent time together," Jaelynn said. "That's really enough for me."

"I remember those days with your father," her mother said, sounding wistful. She shook her head. "So long ago, but sometimes it feels like yesterday."

"Does he know the news yet, about the procedure?" Jaelynn asked.

"I told him just a little while ago," her mother said. She frowned. "He was glad to hear it, but he was getting ready for a date and we did not talk long."

"I know he's glad," Jaelynn said.

"Some days I'm glad we stayed on friendly terms, and some days it just causes another kind of pain," her mother replied.

"I'm glad you both remained friends," Jaelynn said, relieved that she did get some opportunities to spend time with both of them. Most of her friends with divorced parents could not say the same thing. "And I know it's not easy."

"Why don't you go take a nap," her mother said, changing the subject. "It'll take me a little while to get dinner together. You've been out and about for some time now, and you can probably use a little rest before we eat."

"Not a bad idea at all," Jaelynn said. "And so glad for the good news about the surgery approval."

Giving her mother another hug, she continued on to her bedroom.

Removing her shoes, she changed into some lighter clothes and crawled under the covers of her bed. In a relaxed state of mind from the day with Gabriel, and the good news involving her mother, she paused long enough to request an alarm from the Home Assistant for an hour later.

Eyelids growing heavy in moments, Jaelynn let herself slide into the welcoming embrace of sleep.

Vision returned, and she found herself gazing out the

window of a two-story building. The place she viewed could not be found anywhere within the technate.

Buildings of two stories in height lined both sides of a wide street. Every edifice had a plot of land in front of it, filled with low-cropped grass and an assortment of flowers, trees, and bushes. Vehicles of a much older style could be seen parked at the sides of the buildings, or along the street in front of them.

A violet hue filled the skies, draping everything in a soft, peaceful gloaming. The higher branches of the trees swayed in an evening breeze.

Everywhere Jaelynn looked, tiny yellow lights pulsed in and out. Some drifting high in the air, others low among the grass, and many hovering just above it, the multitude of lights captivated her for several moments.

Finally, she took her eyes away from the scene outside, and took a look at her interior surroundings. Though unfamiliar with the kind of bedroom that she found herself in, no sense of danger or threat loomed. The door to the room stood wide open, and the hallway beyond had a light on, but silence pervaded the house.

Staring at the furniture, she noticed a dresser with three drawers that had been fashioned from wood. The recognition surprised her, as things crafted of genuine wood were a rarity. Only those in the Northern Sector could acquire an entire dresser made of wood.

A small desk held a dark, rectangular screen. Before the screen lay a flat, elongated object filled with small keys, the surface of which displayed various letters, numbers, and symbols. An upright, black device stood to the side of the screen.

Guessing all of it to be components of some sort of old computer system, she looked at it with curiosity, but she did not have the first idea as to how it could be turned on or operated.

The walls had images on them fashioned of paper, some

fantastical and artistic, and others looking to be musicians of bands she had never heard of. Continuing to look around the bedroom, she wondered if this was how so many lived in the older times, before the Greater Good Doctrine came to govern everything in the world.

Taking cautious steps, she made her way from the bedroom into the rest of the house, intending to find the front door and go outside. Stepping slowly down the carpeted hallway, she did not see or hear any signs of the house's occupants.

Peering into a bathroom, she noticed several differences at once in comparison to those of her own home and technate. There were no signs of panels or sensors anywhere, and the water tank on the toilet was much larger than the one in her family's apartment.

From what it looked like, the water to the sink and shower had entirely manual controls. The realization made her wonder what a long, hot shower would be like, opposed to the rationed allotment she was used to.

Walking downstairs, she gazed into a kitchen also devoid of the regulatory monitors prevalent in a modern apartment. Her eyes widened, seeing a series of cabinets and drawers made entirely of wood. The refrigerator appeared to be just a container, with no means of monitoring what was placed in or taken out of it.

From the kitchen, she made her way to the front door. Opening it, she stepped onto a square landing made of bricks, with a single stair leading down to a short walkway.

Circular concrete vessels to either side brimmed with colorful flowers. At the end of the concrete path, a pair of old-looking vehicles stood idle in a paved strip connected to the street.

Looking up and down the street, she saw that all of the houses had similar arrangements. She noticed quickly that the vehicles in evidence exhibited a great diversity in styles and appearances.

Fathoming that she stood in the midst of an old-world neighborhood, Jaelynn still found it difficult to imagine living every day in such a place. Each home had vehicles, and all the dwellings had been situated on sizeable plots of land.

Only the wealthy in the Northern Sector of Technate Six had private vehicles and individual spaces for living. The Technate Housing Authority allocated everyone else spaces in the lofty tenements, and the idea of owning land was unthinkable.

Jaelynn then focused on the source of the tiny lights that she had seen from the upper window, flickering on and off everywhere. A light at the level of her head flashed bright, just to her right.

Homing in upon the glow, she discovered that the light came from the body of a little insect. The entire rear segment of its body pulsed with the golden light.

She realized the little flying creatures were coming up from the ground level and taking to flight. In the twilight, their abundant presence made for a magical sight.

Looking down the street, she gave a little start, seeing a couple of radiant orbs drifting through the air toward her. Both of them much larger and brighter lights than those of the insects, each still looked small enough to fit within one of Jaelynn's palms.

Before she could figure out what the lights represented, the surroundings blurred and faded. The neighborhood with its cozy houses and individual plots of land became replaced with the soaring, uniform-looking structures she was well-familiar with.

A pang of longing gripped her inside at the stark change in scenery. To learn of the old world, or see it portrayed in one of the old-time, two-dimensional movies was one thing; to stand within a representation of it had proven to be quite another.

The sky above no longer unobstructed, drones for security,

surveillance, and other types of purposes drifted overhead. In day to day life, Jaelynn could attune herself to ignore them, for the most part. Shifting from a world absent of them, the presence of the drones had never been more noticeable.

For the first time in her life, she had the sense of being in the cage that Gabriel so often described. Without thinking about it, she found herself looking off in the direction of the Northern Sector.

She wondered what life was like for those able to live behind the great barriers setting the area apart from the rest of the technate. She imagined there to be a world of difference.

"The laws only apply to you, and those who live in these tenements," came a smooth, melodious voice from just behind her. "They do not apply to the rulers, or to those who enforce them."

Jaelynn spun about at the sound. She found herself staring at a diminutive, winged figure hovering at the level of her eyes.

Casting light from its body, an even glow formed an orb around the entity's body. Jaelynn realized what the orbs she had witnessed in the old-world neighborhood were.

Humanoid in appearance, the creature had a pair of pointed, elongated ears. Both sloped down into an extended face, ending in a sharp chin. The being's almond-shaped eyes shined solid with a brilliant white light.

Recovering from her initial surprise, Jaelynn looked around her, certain that the thing's presence would cause a commotion, or draw the attention of the technate's pervasive security apparatus. To her amazement, she realized that not one single person could be seen, anywhere she looked.

A few vehicles drifted down the road in front of her. Whether they had human or robot occupants behind their dark windows, she could not tell.

"We are still in the Shade, the realm of dreams that lies

between your world and others," the little being continued. "This is not your technate, just an image of it."

"I ... I'm still dreaming," Jaelynn said, gaining lucidity with every passing second.

"You are," the winged creature confirmed.

"And who are you?" Jaelynn said, drawing courage from the recognition that the creature before her was just a figment of her imagination.

"I have come here from Faraway, and I am a friend," the creature stated. "The time has come for some lines to be crossed, and so here I am."

"I know you are from far away, I haven't seen anyone like you before," Jaelynn retorted, grinning, and choosing to play along with the intriguing dream.

Not unlike one of the worlds generated within the popular VR gaming environments, a dream offered a chance to detach from the norms of the day. The only difference lay in that dreams shifted or faded on a whim, and there was no telling how long the current scene would last.

"Not far away. Faraway," the little thing corrected Jaelynn, with a lighthearted air. "It is a place, though I guess you could say it is rather far away from your own world."

Jaelynn smiled at the response. "Then Faraway it is. But I still don't know your name."

"Sedinian."

"And ... I hope I don't offend you with this question ... but what are you?" she asked.

"Some of the myths from former times in your world would say that I am one of the Fae," it replied.

"Is that something like a fairy?" Jaelynn asked, relating the name to creatures she had encountered in gaming environments.

Sendinian gave her a nod. "We have other names, but Fae describes us well enough."

"Then tell me, what are you doing here, talking to me?" Jaelynn asked.

"Things have gone too far, and the Primordials have to be stopped," Sendinian replied firmly.

"The Primordials?" Jaelynn asked. "I don't know what that is."

"Or what they are, but I am here to guide you," Sedinian said.

"Then what are they?" Jaelynn pressed, smiling.

"Entities, you could say," Sendinian replied. "Entities with a hunger for control and conforming all realms they enter to be the same. These entities will not suffer others to live differently. They've always had an influence in your world, but the balance has tilted far in their favor now."

"So, you are saying there's something else behind the way things are in our world," Jaelynn said, thinking upon the little creature's words.

"I am. There always has been, and always will be, until time itself runs out. It's just that the louts from the darker places are looking to take all choices away from you. If you bother to look around you, they're doing a pretty good job of it. They find plenty of useful fools to cooperate with them."

Jaelynn looked away from the creature and took in the technate sprawling around her. She viewed the scene with more clarity than ever before; the lofty tenements, cramming in thousands upon thousands of lives, streets devoid of private transit, camera eyes mounted everywhere, scanners operating without respite.

Every last thing could be seen as tools of control and regulation, hemming in a large populace.

In that moment, she understood Gabriel and his hostility toward the modern world more than ever before.

Even so, a few things did not make sense. "What do they

get out of it ... anyone that helps or cooperates with these ... Primordials? Or what do the Primordials get?"

"Some would say those in the Northern Sector need a populace to serve them," the creature answered. Its pitch lowered, giving the next words a grim tone. "But the truth of it is far, far worse. The Primordials feed off you. They siphon your energies, your potential, and your ambitions. All of that. They seek to consume your very consciousness, becoming a master of you in every way. Worst of all, they seek to do it with your consent, at every turn. Consent is everything to them."

The response sent a chill through Jaelynn. Even if she knew that it was all part of an intricate dream, the explanation made powerful sense in light of the world she knew.

Gabriel had often talked about how the rarity of finding people passionate about anything in the modern world. Most had been dulled into a mode of routine and habituation, with daily escapes through illusion or substance. The greater populace contained little sense of self-determination or independence.

Yet the government and the media brayed all the time about the freedoms everyone enjoyed. Looking at the things of the technate, Jaelynn wondered how they could say such things with a straight face.

With everything in daily life watched, measured, and managed, the claim that the people enjoyed great freedoms stood absolutely ridiculous in her eyes.

Her heart leapt inside her chest as a figure rushed by her, running at full speed. A terrible shock engulfed her, recognizing Gabriel's face at once.

Before she could even shout, a security drone gliding at a low altitude drifted into view. Forking tendrils of bluish energy stabbed down from the drone, striking Gabriel and ending his run in a flash of an instant. Falling to the ground, his body convulsed in violent spasms.

Jaelynn had already started to run toward her boyfriend when the scene abruptly shifted back to the old-world neighborhood, still in the embrace of dusk. The transition jolting, with all of her focus and fears centered upon Gabriel, she looked around in a state of raw panic.

Not a single drone marring the tranquil view. Only stars, clouds, and a bright moon filled the skies overhead. Drifting gracefully, the small, pulsing insects continued their glittering parade from the grass into the air. The warm glow of lights beckoned from many windows.

The lone street lamp in view was simply that; a light. No devices of any kind could be seen attached to the slender pole arching toward the top end holding the light source.

She knew it did not monitor or scan her in any way. It merely provided luminance against the darkness of night.

Turning about, Jaelynn's gaze locked in upon the glowing creature hovering in the air a few strides away. She asked with insistence and anxiety, "Where is he? What just happened?"

"That wasn't Gabriel. It is just a dream world, remember?" Sendinian countered. The creature's voice shifted, becoming lower in pitch again. "Or is it a reflection of fears? Is it a hint of things to come? Or is it all of those things?"

"It may be a dream, but even seeing that upsets me a lot," Jaelynn replied, the image of Gabriel twitching on the ground emblazoned in her mind. The vision encapsulated a real fear that she always harbored; a dread that had become much more prominent since discovering her boyfriend's activity on his views.

"Is that a world that anyone wants to live in?" the creature asked her.

"That's the world I live in, every single day, whether I like it or not," Jaelynn answered, feeling sharp resentment at the realization and open admission. "I didn't choose it. I was born into it. I didn't set it up. But I can't change it."

"The world that you live in was not inevitable," Sendinian. "People gave your world consent. They could have stopped it from becoming what it is today, at any time. They could put an end to the way things are right now. None of it has to continue. It all persists because of consent, and the lack of a will to act."

"Good luck getting anyone in the technate to do anything," Jaelynn retorted in dismissive fashion. "They're afraid, drugged, drunk, depressed, gaming, or more worried about their favorite sports team."

"Again, they all choose the world that they live in," the fae said, the words sounding a little harsh to Jaelynn's ears. "They gave up the world you see around you, for the one you know. That is undeniable."

The creature gestured around at the serene neighborhood; homes on individual plots of land, without a trace of monitoring devices or other security elements. Each and every family had a high degree of privacy and comfort.

"I hate to remind you again, but I was never offered a choice," Jaelynn replied firmly. "Neither was Gabriel, or anyone else we know."

"He has chosen to put an end to the cage they've made for you," the fae said. "Gabriel has courage ... and I know that you do, too."

Jaelynn stared at the creature, which had just used the same word Gabriel often used to describe the world they lived in; cage. Yet her world did seem a cage when put in contrast to the one she saw around her.

Still, the road to changing anything looked impossible. Speaking out against the Greater Good Doctrine inevitably fell under hate and incitement speech codes. Even if most people resented the world that they lived in, they were far too intimidated to be open about their misgivings, keeping their thoughts to themselves.

Jaelynn could see the restlessness and unhappiness in the faces she saw on the street every day. Most people were anything but fulfilled.

Numb and habituated, they passed through a daily routine to get by, much like her own mother did. For most people that Jaelynn knew, life had become centered around seeking escape; whether that evasion came through entertainment or substances.

Only those of the Northern Sector truly thrived.

"Make your choice, Jaelynn," the fae said evenly, the words stark and bold. "Just remember, you cannot avoid that. Choosing not to decide is another form of choice."

Before Jaelynn could answer the radiant being, the scene blurred and faded, spiraling into pitch darkness. Opening her eyes slowly, she found herself back under the covers in her bed.

A radiant luminance to the left edge of her vision drew Jaelynn's attention. Eyes widening, she gasped, seeing Sendinian hovering in the air of her bedroom.

The first thought, that she still lingered within a dream, conflicted with her sharpening awareness. Yet the creature remained before her eyes, a thing she deemed impossible in the real world.

The glow surrounding the creature began ebbing, as if drawing inward, until only Sendinian's eyes remained bright. The rest of its body held a subtle glow, such that it now looked like a solid form, limned with a thin layer of light.

"Draws less attention," Sendinian commented after the transformation. "Or I can go a little more incognito, if you prefer."

Jaelynn blinked her eyes as the creature vanished in an instant. She looked around the room, but not a trace could be seen of the fae.

Clutching the bedcover tightly in her hands, she wondered what had just happened. A little tension rose within her, in the stillness, the only sound being the low hum of the air flowing through the vent in her wall.

"I didn't leave, you know," the fae said, the abrupt sound causing Jaelynn to flinch on the bed. To her ears, the voice came from the same spot that it had just moments before. "Leaving without saying goodbye is a tad bit rude, wouldn't you say?"

The winged shape faded back into view, looking entirely solid for a moment, before the soft glow returned around its body. The light increased until the fairy appeared as it had first manifested to Jaelynn.

At that moment, Jaelynn remembered the capability of devices in every household to monitor audio, if the technate's security system wished to. Gabriel thwarted them using paper and pen, but the fae did no such thing.

A fearful look in her eyes, Jaelynn put a finger to her lips, and gestured upward.

"While I am here with you, they won't hear you or me, I've got us sealed off," the fae announced. As Sendinian spoke, the walls of her room emitted a light blue glow. "See? Nothing at all to worry about from the obsessive control freaks. I have it all in hand. Their science doesn't apply to me. I come from realms that don't operate under the rules of this one."

The notion of having true privacy uplifting, Jaelynn grinned wide, feeling a sense of relief that she could speak her mind openly. Yet she remained a little hesitant, not knowing whether to trust the fae's words or not.

"Do you hear any noises from beyond your room? Feel free to get up, and find out for yourself," Sendinian invited. "Go ahead, open your door. It will be good for you to know for sure."

Jaelynn pulled the covers off, swung her legs around, and got up. She padded across the room and opened her door. Her mother had the volume of the holographic unit up loud, at a level that easily would have been heard in her room under normal circumstances.

Shutting the door, Jaelynn found herself in an air of perfect silence. Not one hint of the show her mother viewed filtered through the doorway. Amazed at the phenomenon, she walked back across her room, and took a seat on the bed.

"Why me?" Jaelynn asked, looking to Sendinian.

"There are so very few who are open to what is really happening in the world you live in," Sendinian said. "And even fewer capable of handling the greater reality beyond. While a few, such as you and Gabriel, still live in this world, the Primordials must not be allowed full dominion. A line has to be drawn, or all worlds will be lost, one by one."

Jaelynn did not know whether to feel complimented or afraid at the pronouncement. In truth, she harbored both reactions, though she found herself more heavily tilted toward the latter sensation.

Learning of Gabriel's activities had given her a stark sense of her entire world changing. The current experience accelerated that cognizance, but she had no idea what kind of change it would be. Only uncertainty loomed before her.

"There's so much I don't know," she said, at a loss and struggling to grasp the implications of the fae's words. Her eyes began to glisten, welling up with tears, a reaction to the powerful emotions churning and tugging inside.

"There's so much I don't know," the fae replied in a sympathetic air. "It is not for any of us to know everything. It is only for each of us to act upon what we do know."

"But what can I do about any of this?" Jaelynn said, a few tears of frustration escaping her eyes, and trickling slowly down her cheeks.

"I'm here to help. You will need friends in the time to come," the fairy replied.

The words did nothing to comfort her. If anything, Jaelynn sensed something of great importance underlying the fae's words, to a degree that unnerved her further.

"What ... time to come?" Jaelynn asked, a little hesitant.

"You will know."

"I don't need mysteries, I need some answers right now," Jaelynn stated, with a spark of increased frustration.

"I wish I had them. The future is uncertain, a host of shadows of what could be," the fae answered. "Through the benevolence of Kairos, I gain glimpses of the things most likely to come to pass."

Her brow furrowing in concentration, the fae's words created even more confusion within Jaelynn's mind. "Kairos? Who's Kairos? And what is likely going to happen then? What do you know?"

The fae made a sound resembling a sigh. "The more I say, the more questions you will have. You have been through quite enough for one night."

"Then just tell me what is likely, and who Kairos is?" Jaelynn stated. "You said the word, not me."

"I will tell you first who Kairos is," Sendinian said. The fae then added, in a heavy, resigned air, "And then I will tell you what is most likely. But that will be enough for tonight, agreed?"

Jaelynn nodded, already finding everything about the experience overwhelming.

"Good," Sendinian replied. "Then know that Kairos is the benefactor of all those who dwell in Faraway. Kairos is one with Transcendence, a state where time as you know it does not exist."

"Where time does not exist? How is that even possible?" Jaelynn said, finding the notion bewildering.

"Time, space ... all of these things are governed by laws," the fairy answered. "Time can have different properties. The enemy of Kairos, Chronos, has become the master of time as you know it in this world. Finite, linear ... things going from one point to the next in a straight continuum, from beginning to end.

"Chronos seeks to guide everything in every realm to an end. Wielding the full, insatiable hunger of the Primordials, Chronos will press this war until Faraway and the Source of everything are consumed, and greater oblivion is achieved at last."

"That ... is quite a lot for me to take in," Jaelynn commented.

"I warned you about that," the fae riposted. "For now, just know that Kairos, Faraway, and the Source have no business with death and oblivion. Kairos governs a kind of time where there is no necessity for beginnings, for ends, or for one thing to have to follow another, like the passing of one second to the next. With Kairos, an age can pass in an instant, or a moment can last an age."

"A state of timelessness?" Jaelynn countered, working through the idea in her head.

"In a manner of speaking, yes," Sendinian answered. "I've always liked to describe it as an eternal moment."

"Seems a paradox to me," Jaelynn remarked, smiling.

"It is hard to wrap your mind around it, when you live in a world where time operates with other properties," Sendinian responded. "I don't blame you for finding it perplexing."

"I wish time didn't operate the way that it does," Jaelynn mused. "Nothing could get old if it was the way this Kairos sounds like."

"Precisely," Sendinian said. To her eyes, the fae beamed a little brighter with the response.

She did not quite understand what Sendinian was getting at, but the thought of another world operating under entirely different rules brought her a sense of hope. The idea that the suffocating world she lived in constituted everything she would ever know made for a bludgeoning existence.

Yet as much as the notions of other worlds and states of timelessness were exciting, a somber question remained.

"And what is most likely going to happen?"

"It may not be for certain," the fae answered. "But I see the ones in thrall with the Primodials arresting Gabriel and taking him into custody. That should not be a surprise to you, knowing what you already know of him. You are aware of how they treat dissent."

"While they talk about all the great freedoms we enjoy," Jaelynn said, in a tone thick with sarcasm.

"Look at the world that they have built for you, not what they say to you," the fae said. "The world you live in testifies to its reality. Everything is stagnant, or worse. New generations do no better than the previous ones, and in some senses continue downward."

"Oh, I know, I don't need any guidance in that department," Jaelynn said, though her heart grew heavier thinking about Gabriel and the idea of him being incarcerated. Echoes of the traumatic dream vision played within her head, calling up images of Gabriel twisting in pain on the ground.

She could not deny that Gabriel becoming incarcerated would be the realization of her fears. With what her boyfriend had chosen to engage in, she found it hard to conceive of any other destination but imprisonment or Rehabilitation.

The Doctrine of the Greater Good being sacrosanct in the eyes of the ruling authorities, no challenge to it would be tolerated. The people were free to choose their methods of escapism, but genuine freedom could not be allowed.

Never before had that been so clear to Jaelynn.

"You don't seem very surprised," the fairy told her. "I see it in your face."

"I'm so afraid for him, and I don't see any other outcome than him getting taken in," Jaelynn said. "They probably allow people to say a lot of things, but I know they won't let anyone do what Gabriel is doing."

"Gabriel, and those like him, are a threat to their order," the fairy said. "I think he will need you in the days to come. Be ready at all times."

"I am there for him, always," Jaelynn said without a moment's hesitation. "Just tell me what I can do? Is there anything?"

"We will get to that when the time comes," Sendinian said. "For now, I must go back to my own plane of existence. It requires a lot of energy for me to manifest here, in your world, and I will not be able to maintain our privacy for much longer. I assure you, as much as Gabriel is a threat to them, they will not take kindly to one of my kind being here interacting directly with a human. The Primordials tend to get very upset when that happens."

From what she had been told of the Primordials, Jaelynn did not doubt that in the least. "I imagine so."

"Don't worry yourself. You shall see me again, and we will talk more," the fae told her. "Be strong in all things, Jaelynn. You have great courage within you. Draw upon that."

Without another word, the creature faded from view.

Jaelynn knew that the fairy had departed when the sound of her mother's holographic show entered the room. She listened to the low, murmuring hum and thought about what had just happened.

Even though only a handful of moments had passed since the fae left, the entire experience had a surreal aura around it. Looking at the panel display by her bed, she saw that the alarm would ring in a few more minutes.

Requesting the alarm off through voice command, Jaelynn decided to go see how her mother fared with the dinner she had spoken of earlier. Though hungry, she did not need food so much as she needed to set her mind toward something routine in nature. It offered Jaelynn's rattled mind some balance; a needed element in the wake of the astounding experience.

Salvador

Salvador endured the next few days in the best manner that he could. He participated in his classes held within VR settings. Regurgitating whatever they wanted of him, he did his part to cooperate with the monotonous system.

Even for a fifteen-year-old boy with little world experience, it was not hard to figure out how to get by in their system.

Logging in on time a necessity, failure to attend an educational session invited a quick visit from the Technate Education Council agents, who monitored attendance and enforced compliance without leniency.

The eyes of instructors remained on every student without waver, a thing made possible with all teachers being digital constructs; no matter how real their appearance and personalities seemed in the virtual climates.

Keeping quiet, doing the work asked, and spitting back whatever would suit them, Salvador got through his class sessions smoothly enough.

His thoughts over the past few days were far removed from class matters. Musing often about his encounter with Jade in the park, Salvador pondered their discussion concerning the Primordials, the Source, and Transcendence.

In his heart, he wished that he could transcend every last bit of his world. A gnawing urge to see Jade again grew inside him, though he did not have the first idea of how to find the enigmatic man.

After the final session of the day, Salvador logged out of the VR environment. After getting a drink and a little to eat, he got dressed to go for a walk on the streets.

Heading down the hallway from his apartment, he took the elevator down to the ground level, glad to be free of class sessions and thinking of what he wanted to do for the rest of the afternoon.

Part of him wanted to return to the park. Another part wanted to return home and get into some gaming. For the time being, he continued walking forward.

"Hello Salvador."

Flinching at the sound of his name, he came to a stop. Turning, he saw Jade standing just a few paces away, dressed in the same manner as the night in the park.

"Hey," Salvador replied, grinning. "You disappeared on me, the other day."

"Disappeared on them, too," Jade said, chuckling. "I definitely didn't make their day. Like I said, they don't tolerate anyone who isn't shackled to their grid by that fancy little chip you have implanted in you."

"Not sure what you mean, exactly, but good to see you again," Salvador said.

"Care to join me for a coffee?" Jade asked. "They still allow a little of that in this technate."

"I don't really drink coffee that much, but I can hang out for a few minutes," Salvador replied, glad to have a chance for a visit with Jade.

"Fair enough," Jade said. "There's a good place just ahead."

They walked to a cafe located only a half-block away.

Jade turned and grinned before they entered. "You'll have

to buy it. I don't scan."

Salvador rolled his eyes. "On me, I guess."

"I think you know I'm not really aligned with the way things run around this technate," Jade said.

"That's been made pretty clear," Salvador said, though he remained curious as to how Jade accomplished such a thing. "I'll take care of it."

Heading inside, Salvador went about getting coffee from the bot attendants, and then took a seat across from Jade in a booth situated near the front windows. He took note of the booth itself, the surface of which somehow emitted a light blue glow. He could not figure out the cause of the luminance, but the effect greatly impressed him.

"Cool booth," he remarked, staring into the borderline neon hue. "I'd like to get one of these."

Jade smiled. "They have good taste in decor here."

"At least on this booth," Salvador replied, looking around and seeing that the other booths lacked the glowing effect.

"I'd rather go for an option with a little more flair," Jade said. "And a little more privacy."

"Well, you found me again," Salvador said, looking across at Jade. "Can I ask why? And what about the other night? That was so wild. How did all that happen?"

Jade chuckled. "I think I'm right when I say that you sense what's going on around you. You and a few others are tuned in very well. What you are feeling is the growing presence of the Primordials. That's the first step toward getting free."

"Getting free," Salvador replied, laughing. "They tell us all the time about how free we are. Aren't we free?"

"You know the answer to that, or I wouldn't be here," Jade said, his expression growing somber.

"I guess they don't want us taking too much notice on how things are actually run," Salvador commented.

"It's just a word, without any real meaning to them," Jade said. "They're not about to tell you the reality. The spell would be broken, and everyone would know what they've been doing to them. They can't have that. Their power depends on the illusion they've created ... and the idea that there's nothing any of you can do about it."

"You sure you want to talk like that?" Salvador asked him, becoming anxious, despite the power that Jade had demonstrated before.

Looking about, he thought of all the monitoring devices in place. Jade could well be condemning himself with every word those systems recorded.

"Just so happens that this particular coffee shop offers us a bit of a safe haven, hence my invitation to get a coffee, and the choice of this location," Jade replied. "That's all you need to know right now. But it's safe for either of us to talk openly."

"I'd like to know more, but I can say I'm more open to what's going on than most," Salvador said. "This whole technate is sleepwalking."

"You and a few others have what it takes to see, and that's why I'm here," Jade said. "I don't have much time, so I'm going to get right to it. I'm going to do what I can to open your eyes to a whole new reality ... and, by reality, I mean helping you see things the way they really are. You have the ability within you, and I want to see you understand it, and use it."

"I've always wanted to see things how they really are," Salvador said. The idea that he possessed some kind of aptitude or ability took him by surprise, but he left his thoughts on the matter silent.

"Ultimately, the choice is up to you, but I do want to help you," Jade said. "For the moment, perhaps another demonstration is in order."

The glow on the booth began fading. Salvador watched it

ebb until the booth appeared like any other in the cafe, solid and mundane.

Showing no outward reaction at the shift, Jade drained the last of his cup of coffee and set the container down on the table. Taking a deep breath, he looked back to Salvador. "I guess that's enough talk for today. Not a word more, if you know what I mean. Let's get going and be sure to take note of everything you see."

Jade got up from the booth. Unsettled at Jade's change in mood, and the disappearance of the light, Salvador stood up a moment later.

The two walked out of the cafe together. Standing on the sidewalk, Jade looked up and down the street with a calm expression. Then, with his eyes narrowing, his gaze locked onto something to the left.

"Oh, here they go again," Jade remarked, a grin spreading on his face. "Seems they are aware that a person without an ID implant is walking the streets."

A couple of tall security bots, armored and fully weaponized, tromped toward them. Not far down the street, the wheeled drone that brought the pair of bots waited at the curb's edge.

Seeing the two bots striding nearer, anxiety gripped Salvador, but he remained in place. Running would do no good. The bots would drop him with a blast of high voltage before he got twenty steps away.

He recalled the times he had witnessed security incidents on the streets. Fleeing would prove futile in a technate that maintained surveillance everywhere, with even the devices in a home regulated and networked into the system.

Taking notice of the approaching bots, the few people out on the sidewalk nearby hurried along, clearing a wide berth around Jade and Salvador. Nobody had any desire to remain in the vicinity of the imposing security bots, who only emerged from the drones ferrying them about if a security incident loomed.

Fear shrouded the presence of a security bot. Everyone sought distance, just in case the thing scanned something unfavorable through a citizen's ID.

"Sir, stay in place, and do not try to flee," the first bot addressed Jade in a deep, commanding tone. "Your ID does not scan, and it appears that you do not possess one to begin with. Not having a functioning ID is in direct violation of Technate law, and under the authority of Technate Six you will be taken into custody."

"And what if I don't want to comply?" Jade replied, looking unruffled, smiling at the two bots. His voice also remained calm, exhibiting no trace of unease.

Salvador could not believe the man's demeanor, and worried that Jade's mind had gone askew.

"You will comply, whether you choose to cooperate, or we force you," the bot replied. "It is in your best interest to comply."

"What great choices you offer me," Jade replied with a hint of amusement. "How can I pass those wonderful options up? But you forgot another option ... one that I find a little better to my liking. What if I don't cooperate ... and you can't force me? What then? Have you thought that through, all-knowing machine?"

The bot that had spoken answered through action, bringing up a stunner to incapacitate Jade. The air crackled, but the loosed charges passed through empty space. As had happened in the park, Jade vanished, nowhere to be seen.

Salvador looked up to the pair of bots towering over him, feeling abandoned and awaiting their verdict upon him. The second bot had its stunner raised but had not triggered the device or aimed it toward him.

He kept his feet planted firmly in place, not wanting to give the thing a reason to stun him. Salvador said nothing, knowing the things could not be pleaded with, or appealed to using reason.

With Jade gone, the bots could not ignore him. Dread filled Salvador, alongside a heavy feeling of resignation. Any security monitor in the area had recorded him in the company of Jade.

At the very least he knew that he would be taken in for questions. Knowing as little about Jade that he did, he doubted that any interrogation would go well.

His nose wrinkled a few seconds later, picking up the pungent scent of burnt electronics. To his surprise, the bots did not move or make a sound in the aftermath of Jade's sudden disappearance.

After a few more moments passed, and they continued to remain inert, it dawned on Salvador that the bots had met the same fate as the drone in the park. Jade had done something to render the bots inoperable. The thick stench of burned circuitry reinforced his suspicions.

Taking a deep breath, he took a cautious step away from the bots, half-expecting to hear one of the metallic things bark a command at him. When the bots continued to remain silent, he took another step, and then a third. In less than a minute, he found that he had traveled half a block with no sign of pursuit or alarm.

Even if inexplicable, Salvador did not question his good fortune. He continued onward to his home without hindrance, his heart beating fast the entire way.

Once back home inside his mother's apartment, his breathing began returning to normal. He remained confounded, having no idea of how or why he had been able to walk free, but once again had witnessed Jade exercise total mastery over the technate's security apparatus.

The thought that something more powerful than the pervasive security structure existed in his world, and that he enjoyed favor from the one who wielded that power, gave Salvador a high degree of satisfaction. He thought back to the two menacing security bots, rendered immobile and useless through whatever method that Jade had employed.

A small worry nagged at him, regarding the visual surveillance that would show him walking away from the bots. Then again, nothing had happened in the wake of the park incident, where he knew the eyes of visual surveillance also kept up a ceaseless watch.

Somehow, he had gone unnoticed.

With a little luck, the current incident would go the same way.

Walking back to his bedroom, Salvador had a smile resting upon his face. Greatly relieved, and still feeling a rush of excitement, he wondered when he would next encounter Jade.

He did not think he would have to wait long. Even if Salvador did not understand everything yet, Jade believed that he had some kind of gift or ability.

Having seen what Jade could do, evading security with ease and displaying power over the technology, Salvador gave the mysterious figure the benefit of the doubt. At the very least, it made his own life much more buoyant at a time when he had felt terribly isolated.

Once in his bedroom, Salvador took a deep breath and let the silence of his surroundings take hold for a moment. Using a voice command, he brought the ambience in the room to a low level, enough to see by, while still casting a subdued atmosphere.

For the time being, he turned his thoughts away from Jade, the talk of Primordials and Transcendence, and the implications of having a role to play in all of it. He looked forward to just being a teenager, and enjoying an escape for a short while, having had more than his fill of real world encounters for one day.

Pulling out a pair of sensory gloves and the helmet that encompassed his head, he readied to venture into digital realms. An hour or two of gaming within a high-grade VR world would provide exactly what he needed at the moment.

When he returned to it, the world with all of its problems and revelations would still be there.

Jaelynn

Jaelynn did not find herself surprised in the least when a summons arrived to have her identification implant checked the next day. The figure displayed in her glasses instructed Jaelynn to proceed at once to a security center located near her family's apartment.

Though nervous, she did her best to remain calm during the process. From what she gathered from the security officer inspecting her implant, a malfunction had been detected the previous evening for a few minutes; roughly the amount of time that the little fae had visited in her bedroom.

Nothing wrong could be found with her implant, though as a precaution the security officer extracted the current one and replaced it with a brand new implant. Jaelynn feigned ignorance the entire time, though inside she found great pleasure at the idea the authorities had been thwarted.

Nevertheless, it chilled her that they were so quick to call her in for an examination of the implant device. It told her they did not want a fifteen-year-old girl to go unmonitored for even a full day.

There remained no doubt in her mind that those in power desired a climate of absolute control. Not a single individual could exist detached from their system, not even a girl living with her family in a little apartment within a teeming mass of tenements; housing so many thousands and thousands of others without wealth or influence.

The realization did not intimidate her in the least. Instead, it girded her resolve, and reinforced the idea that anything opposing the prevailing order had true moral authority guiding it.

Jaelynn knew the path she had to take, even if she remained uncertain of the best way to walk it. The recognition girded her demeanor, and she displayed a pleasant expression to everyone she interacted with in the security center.

When she walked from the place and started back home, not a single bot or officer had an inkling of the thoughts she harbored inside.

Haven

Haven looked at her surroundings, recognizing that she stood in the public park located near her father's apartment. Strangely, even though broad daylight reigned over the area, not a single person could be seen within the expansive tract.

Usually, the place was filled with activity, with all kinds of people taking enjoyment of one of the few larger patches of grass and trees accessible to the public.

Stepping across the soft grass, Haven listened to the sounds of the wind brushing through the boughs of an oak tree close by. Bright sunlight sparkled off a pond's surface, a short distance ahead.

She found the solitude and tranquility delightful.

Haven smiled wide, though nobody could witness her happiness. Wondering where everyone had gone, she continued to gaze around the park.

Movement drew her eyes toward the grass. She saw the edge of a large shadow drifting across the ground. The shadow grew larger, in moments swallowing the stretch of grass that she stood upon.

Raising her eyes, Haven watched in fascination as a massive flying object drifted over the treetops.

The lower part of the vessel looked like the body of an ancient sailing ship, fashioned of overlapping timber stakes. An extensive network of roping, connected to a huge, oblong balloon, held onto the ship-like portion.

A large cabin at the stern of the vessel had sets of steps flanking it, running from a railed platform above down to the main deck. The prow of the ship featured a golden lion in mid-roar, standing tall and gleaming in the sunlight.

The elaborate vessel descended toward the open stretch of ground, setting down close to the pond's edge.

Haven guessed the object to be some manner of airship, though it resembled nothing that she had ever seen in her physical world before. Only the words of old stories and a few gaming environments held anything as fantastical as the flying craft alighting upon the ground.

As incredible as the ship's appearance was, her eyes were drawn toward the front of it. At the bow stood the man whose apartment she had so recently visited. A broad smile shone upon his face, as the hull settled upon the ground.

"I would bet that you didn't expect to see me here," he called to her, in an amiable fashion.

"The Artist?" she asked, amazed at the development. She shook her head. "I know I'm dreaming."

"Yes, you are, but you have to think about what dreaming really is," he replied, grinning. The Artist gestured to her with a flare of energetic vigor. "Now don't just stand there! Come on over and climb aboard! Let's go for a ride. No better time than now!"

A feeling of excitement ran through her at the invitation. The Artist lowered a rope ladder over the side, the grin never leaving his face.

There were no restrictions in a dream, and ultimately nothing to fear. Striding quickly to the base of the ship, she reached for the rope ladder, and then paused.

"If I'm dreaming, couldn't I just fly aboard?" she asked The Artist, grinning and looking upward. "Why do I need a ladder?"

Leaning over the side, the Artist laughed. "You sure could. Why not do that?"

Imagining the act within her mind, she jumped into the air. Instead of coming back down in the pull of gravity, she drifted toward the Artist. A stab of panic went through her when she started to carry over the decking.

"Keep calm, and just alight," the Artist told her, in a reassuring tone.

His voice giving her something to focus on, she slowed, and dipped downward, until her feet touched the planks. Coming to rest on the deck, she turned and looked to the Artist.

"Dreams are not always the most stable for running or flying, are they?" the Artist remarked, shaking his head. "I can still remember long ago when I'd try to run in a nightmare. It always felt like my body was immersed in water. No matter how hard I tried, I could barely move."

Haven could relate, having experienced many of the same kinds of nightmares. From slogging forward to flying at dizzying speeds, motion could not be predicted in the realms of dreams.

"Well, let's get your first lesson out of the way," the Artist said, giving her a wink. "This might not make much sense to you now, but just humor me, and listen. We are in the Shade at the moment, the place where most dreams are experienced. We're not going to stay here. I'd like to show you a place with a little more endurance to its forms, shapes, and environments. A place no less real than the world you live in."

"I like the dream version of you," Haven replied, pleased with what her mind had conjured up while her body slumbered. The Artist carried the same personality she had witnessed at his apartment, though he beckoned to something even more fantastical than the images of the old world adorning his apartment wall.

"I'm just the same version of me that you met at the apartment," the Artist replied, adding another wink. "But I'll let you sort all of that out in time. Let's be on our way!"

It appeared as if the airship responded to his thoughts. Lifting from the ground moments later, they began ascending toward the smooth blue skies.

Haven looked over the side of the vessel and watched the park shrinking away below her. Then, the entirety of Technate Six lay sprawled beneath, the huge metropolis dwindling before her eyes as they continued rising above the dense grid of sectors.

The place that always seemed so confining, like a prison that she could never escape, grew ever more distant. Reduced by the moment into something small and abstract, the technate no longer carried the power over her that it did in her waking life.

"So, you are my dream guide then," Haven said, laughing, turning toward the Artist. "I like what you are doing already, taking me out of there. No argument here."

"I am a Navigator," he replied, with a lively look to his eyes. "Guiding is something I am very capable of. All I need is an idea of where we are going."

"And where are we going then, Navigator?" she asked, playfully.

"You are about to see, Haven," he replied. "I believe a fair wind is about to carry us onward, to the next level."

Before he had finished his words, a strong gust caught the airship. Haven felt the powerful lurch as they soared rapidly upward. In the blink of an eye, they were in the midst of a starry night sky.

She found the sudden change from day to night to be disconcerting for a moment, but the magnificence of what she found herself surrounded with pushed all anxieties from her mind. In every direction she looked, a host of radiant stars ornamented a great vastness. The sense of depth appeared like nothing she had ever gazed into before.

The airship cruised gently through the darkness, though she felt no wind. Her hair rested on her shoulders, without the slightest jostle of a breeze.

"Go ahead, look over the side," the Artist invited her, nodding toward the edge of the airship.

Walking to the edge, Haven leaned outward, and peered down. For a moment, she felt dizzy, peering into limitless depths filled with celestial lights. There was no land to be found anywhere; not a single trace of the world that they had left behind.

"Are we ... are we in space?" she asked tentatively, finding the concept hard to believe as she spoke the words. She had to remind herself again that they were in a dream.

Nobody could survive in the open, in outer space.

"Of a sort," the Artist replied with a coy grin. He gestured with a nod of his head toward the other side of the airship. "But we have a destination. Somewhere I know that you have never been before."

She followed his glance and saw that they were approaching a great planet. Haven could tell at once that the huge orb was not her own world. The outlines of the landmasses visible on its surface were very different in shape. Even more incredibly, the shapes appeared to be moving, right before her eyes.

Space operated much differently from the science that she knew, as the airship reached the outlying boundaries of the planet in just a few moments. Instead of the harrowing process incurred by a space vessel entering the atmosphere of her world, the airship glided smoothly into a thick mass of slowly drifting clouds.

Enveloped in the clouds, Haven felt the cool, soft touch of the misty vapors on her skin. After being shrouded in the billowing mass for about a minute, they broke out of the clouds, emerging into the open over a dazzling, spectacular scene.

Haven stared in wonder at a series of floating islands, staggered in a magnificent array reaching from the highest clouds down toward the surface of the planet far, far below. Overwhelming her senses, the scale and vividness of the scene took her breath away.

The islands themselves brimmed with lush greenery and an abundance of color in the many kinds of foliage thriving upon them. Even more incredible, majestic waterfalls descended from the higher islands, connecting to pools on the hovering swathes of land beneath them.

The water sparkled and shined with a crystalline quality, cascading through the series of islands all the way downward.

"Beautiful, isn't it?" the Artist asked her. "It still gives me a thrill, whenever I come back here after some time spent away."

"It is absolutely magical," she replied, keeping her gaze upon the extraordinary vision. "Just incredible."

"A good way to describe it," the Artist said. He chuckled. "This place would probably give the scientists of your world quite a few fits. Realms of consciousness do not operate under the same rules as your physical world does."

"Clearly, they don't," Haven agreed merrily. "But I don't mind that at all. I can live with this. Very easily."

The airship lowered through the midst of the islands and waterfalls until the surface of a vast ocean lay exposed to view. Glittering turquoise waters flowed in gentle, rolling waves, a harmonious rhythm of motion that captivated Haven for several moments.

On her side of the airship, the waters headed toward an immaculately white beach, forming the edge of a landmass reaching to the far horizon.

A number of birds darted and glided about in a kaleidoscopic, graceful exhibition of aerial acrobatics over the sparkling waters. The birds had feathers of resplendent hues; of green, yellow, red, silver, blue, gold, and several other vivid colors.

Haven gazed upon the scene in a rapt silence, awed by the majestic vision spread before her eyes. At a loss for words, she could only stand witness, the sheer magnitude of what she beheld making it difficult to even try getting her mind around all of it.

"Welcome to my world," the Artist told her, after several moments had passed. "My little getaway in the universes and realms of existence."

"Your ... world?" she asked, after a long pause, unsure of his meaning. She continued looking outward, unable to take her eyes away from the stunning view.

"My very own place, on the first of many levels reaching all the way up to the Source, which transcends all," the Artist answered. "This is not a physical place, in the way that you know it. But it can reflect physical properties, and it is much more permanent in nature than the Shade. In other words, what you see before you is not a dream. It is a reality."

Haven had no words to respond with, finding the concept staggering. Her mind a swirl of thoughts, she continued taking in the abundance of incredible sights.

The airship glided in the direction of the landmass, just a few hundred feet above the water. When they neared the white shoreline, an elegant manse came into view, set farther back from the sands.

"My house," the Artist remarked.

Glistening ponds and richly-cultivated gardens bursting with colors surrounded the stately edifice. Astonished at the sight of such an incredible habitation, she could not believe that anyone could have a place so beautiful.

Before she could take in every aspect of the manse, she espied some movement in the front lawn. Focusing upon a quartet of cats tumbling about the ground, she laughed, enjoying every moment of their antics.

Bounding across the emerald lawn, the cats took turns chasing each other. Watching the little creatures playing, her spirits lifted higher.

The airship lowered and gently set down on the front lawn, not far from the façade of the two-story manse.

A broad set of steps led up to a sheltered entrance supported by seven exquisitely carved pillars; each one exhibiting representations of intertwining vines adorned with an abundance of flowers. An elegant double-door of dark wood ornamented with golden handles and banding served as the main portal.

Tall bay windows protruded from several places on both levels of the grand structure, the entire edifice crowned with a crenellated rooftop. Many more large windows looked out upon the front lawn and ocean beyond.

Haven could only imagine the incredible views from within the manse. She imagined the interior to be bright and lively, containing magnificent hallways showered in light streaming through the extensive array of windows.

"If it is not entirely like a physical world, does this place still operate like a dream?" she asked the Artist, glancing toward him.

"Find out," he invited, smiling wide. "I don't think you'll be disappointed."

Concentrating on flying again, she found herself levitating, and then gliding across the deck, continuing beyond the side of the vessel. She angled toward the ground and sensed her feet sinking into the lawn's soft surface a few moments later.

"Just wait until you explore the ocean ... without having to use any kind of breathing gear," the Artist said, drifting down from the airship to stand at her side.

She looked back towards the ocean, thinking upon the implications of what the Artist had just said. "Wow! Really?

Under the water? Not having to breathe?"

"It is still a realm of consciousness, even though it reflects a lot of physical properties," the Artist said. He added with a chuckle, "Did you really think you could breathe in outer space, if this was like your world?"

"It's all just amazing," she responded, thinking of many possibilities in exploring the incredible world surrounding her. With so many limitations removed, she could barely imagine the kinds of perspectives and sensations afforded to her within the Artist's world.

"How do you do?" interjected a friendly, higher-pitched voice. "Welcome to our home."

Haven looked back around, but nobody could be seen, other than herself and the Artist. Yet there was no mistaking that she had heard a voice. She turned to the Artist with a puzzled expression.

"She doesn't know, does she?" the voice came again, with a strong undercurrent of amusement within it.

The Artist laughed heartily. "No, she doesn't. This is going to be a fun revelation."

"Who in the world are you talking to?" Haven asked him, growing more perplexed by the second.

"Who else is here, but myself and Chesiree?" the Artist replied, grinning. "I think the answer should be obvious to you. I didn't say anything, so that just leaves him."

Haven looked downward and saw one of the cats that she had seen playing on the lawn. The gray tabby with white about its paws like little socks stared up at her with golden, green-flecked eyes.

A brownish patch of fur around the cat's nose graced the white streak running between his eyes, making it look as if the little fellow had been nosing around in a bowl of chocolate.

"You?" she asked the cat, with her eyebrows raised and a

grin on her face. She found it difficult to believe that she had just addressed a cat.

"Who else do you see around here?" responded the amiable voice, carrying a stronger trace of amusement.

As a child, she had always imagined that cats and dogs could talk. But as all things went, the mundane became firmly imposed on her as she grew up.

Even the ability to imagine the possibility of animals talking got tamped down over the years. Only within gaming environments did the like happen, and she knew none of that had any real basis to begin with.

"Really?" she responded excitedly, looking back to the Artist. "He speaks?"

"Chesiree does indeed speak, and there are more than a few times I've found him to be a bit too verbose," the Artist replied, chuckling. "He'll talk your ear off sometimes."

"You just can't admit to my great wisdom," Chesiree said to the Artist.

"Oh yes, that's it, exactly," the Artist replied with an air of sarcasm, laughing. "Doesn't have anything to do with the fact that you can't seem to enjoy silence very often. Maybe going back to just purrs, meows and a few chirrups would be preferable after all."

"So you say," Chesiree replied, appearing to be in good humor. "I rather think I have a lot to offer, from discussing wonderful compositions of music to pondering the dynamics of timelessness."

"Do you have problems with overly talkative cats?" the Artist asked Haven, laughing.

"I can't say I do," she replied, also laughing, but still in a state of wonder at the development.

"And to think I get a huge dose of this, with all the cats around here," the Artist said, shaking his head.

"You stink!" another high-toned voice interjected, just a second before a burly brown and white cat tackled Chesiree from the side. Both of the cats went tumbling into a swirling mass of fur, squeals, and batting paws.

"Oh my, the unending argument resumes between those two," the Artist remarked, loosing a bemused sigh. After watching the cats go at each other with gusto for a few moments, he said calmly. "Now boys, we've got a new guest here. Behave yourselves. Show some composure and class, if you think you can handle that."

The two cats stopped their mock battle, and looked back to the Artist, their ears perked high. Disentangling, they turned to face Haven, sitting back on their haunches.

The second cat had obvious tabby features but was thicker of fur. Not quite as long of body as his companion, the second cat had a flatter facial profile. With one eye slightly cocked in comparison to the other, sparks of liveliness danced within the cat's gaze.

"This is Harrison," the Artist introduced. "Another of my close companions here."

"Nice to meet you," Harrison said to Haven. "I am sorry for the interruption. Chesiree greeted you so that he could get off easy. He knows he stinks."

Chesiree turned to look at his feline friend. "You stink!"

"No, you stink!" Harrison responded.

"No ... you stink!" Chesiree fired back.

Haven chortled as she watched their ludicrous banter accelerate. It still seemed surreal listening to a cat speak, much less two going back and forth at each other in a spirited manner, over a ridiculous topic.

"Believe me, they can hurl that accusation at each other all day long," the Artist laughed, shaking his head again. "They never seem to tire of it. I don't see the fascination, but these two seem to love it."

"Because he stinks," Harrison said matter-of-factly, looking back to the Artist and Haven. "He stinks, and he needs to accept that."

"No, he stinks," Chesiree piped up, as firm as a higher-pitched voice could sound.

"Would you believe that they are the best of friends?" the Artist asked, with a grin. "As close as you can get."

"Kind of like brothers," Haven said. "I've known a couple families who have had two boys."

"Hey, don't forget about me," a third higher-pitched voice interrupted, belonging to another cat trundling up to them. "I would like to meet our new guest."

The newcomer a coat of grayish-blue, with silvery tips that gave its fur a shimmering effect in the light. A tiny white patch marked the center of the cat's chest. Burly of body, the cat had an expressive face, staring at her with beautiful green eyes. A shorter, thick tail flicked back and forth.

"Oh Dewey, don't be ridiculous, you know you could never be forgotten," the Artist said. He looked to Haven. "Yes, this is Dewey,

"I want to meet her too," yet a fourth voice called.

Proud of bearing, the fourth cat had longer fur of a creme hue, with cute tufts about the ears and face, and a bushy tail. Lithe in movement and leaner in body than the other three, the cat looked to Haven with a golden pair of eyes.

"A true queen you are, Carmel," The Artist said.

Carmel sauntered forward and rubbed her body against Dewey as she passed him, both of the cats emitting loud purrs. Coming to a stop in front of Haven, she sat back on her haunches.

"Welcome and glad to meet you," Carmel greeted.

"Glad to meet you, Carmel, " Haven replied. She looked around at the other cats. "Glad to meet all of you. This is all so amazing."

"You can understand us better now, once you are outside of your world," Carmel said.

"Makes it easier for them to request something to eat," the Artist said, laughing. "Believe me, even if it is not a necessary thing in a world like this, I've found cats to have even greater appetites."

He leaned over and stroked Dewey from the back of the cat's head down his back, drawing a satisfied purr.

"I'll never turn down something good to eat," Dewey said. "It is quite pleasant!"

"Your round body testifies well enough to that," the Artist said.

"We choose our forms here, no matter how much we eat," Dewey replied. "You know that."

"Yes, yes, I'm well-aware of that," the Artist said. "You can eat as much as you want here. None go hungry in the realms leading to the Source."

"Oh, the fish ... the fish ... so delightful," Carmel said.

"Now you are making me hungry," Harrison said. "I love fish."

"Then why don't you go get some fish, you'll stink even more," Chesiree said to Harrison.

"Never as much as you stink," riposted Harrison.

Leaping at each other, both cats went rolling in a flurry of fur and batting paws. Haven laughed again, knowing the ruckus to be all in good fun.

The Artist shook his head. "Harrison! Chesiree! Plenty of time for that later, you little rapscallions. That's enough. I don't think Haven is interested hearing in your witty debate about which one of you stinks more."

The two cats disentangled and padded over.

"They all may not have been related by blood long ago, but

they sure are related now, no doubt about that," the Artist said. He looked toward the quartet of cats. "You've met Haven now, so go have some fun, and thank you again for keeping an eye on things around here for me."

"You are welcome," Carmel responded to the Artist. She turned toward Haven. "Nice to meet you. Hope you enjoy your visit here, and I hope you return to see us in the future."

"Yes, it is wonderful to meet you and please let us know if you need anything while you are here," Dewey said. "We're always glad to help."

"Yes, we are, and I hope to see you more here too," Chesiree said. "It is a wonderful place to enjoy."

"I'm glad to meet you too, and like Dewey said, let us know if you need something," Harrison said. He then added, in a cheerful tone. "Maybe some kind of mask, to help you around Chesiree, since he stinks!"

"Hey! You stink!" Chesiree replied to Harrison.

"Go on now, that's enough of your silly debate," the Artist interrupted them.

The two cats needed little further encouragement to continue their play. In a flash, they raced off across the lawn, bounding from sight into the trees beyond a few moments later.

Dewey turned and headed back toward the manse. Haven noticed his gait had a bit of a swagger to it.

Carmel bolted across the ground, displaying a grace of form, before leaping onto the trunk of a tall tree and scaling it in swift fashion.

"There are pets in this … dimension?" Haven asked, watching Dewey surmount the wide steps in the manse's facade. The door opened at the cat's approach.

"Oh, they are something much more," the Artist said. "They've all been to the Source, you see. And they chose to become Wards. I'm lucky to have them as friends too."

"Wards?" Haven asked.

"Protectors, guardians, that kind of thing," the Artist replied. "Don't let their cute appearances fool you. They keep an eye on this world and watch my back, too. Sometimes they go and help me when I am out and about."

"They seem like quite a handful," Haven said, laughing again, as she thought of Harrison and Chesiree's inane repartee.

"They are that too," the Artist said, chuckling and rolling his eyes. "And don't forget, there are a few more of them, staying here. You haven't met the whole bunch yet. Quite a clowder, let me tell you."

"I'm looking forward to meeting them all, everything here is just so incredible," Haven said. She gestured toward the manse. "I can only imagine what it's like inside that place."

"It's not shabby, I've tailored it to my liking," the Artist commented. "But our first visit here is nearly up. I don't want to keep you away from your world for too long."

A look of disappointment crossed her face. "I have to go back now?"

"No need to fly all the way back home. You are dreaming, you know," the Artist said. "It's just that we navigated a little further."

"But you just said this was not part of a dream," Haven replied, confused at his words.

"This world, and the level of existence we are on ... no, that's not part of a dream," he said. "But as for you, it is best to say that you are dreaming. You'll understand more in time. But that's a way of explaining it for now."

"So, there's more to it," she said.

"Perhaps much more," he said with a smile and knowing wink. "Maybe you just don't understand the nature of dreams entirely. But that's a discovery for later."

"Then I could dream myself into my world, and go

someplace where my body isn't lying asleep," she said, running the idea through her head, laughing and intending the words as a jest.

"You are getting a little closer," he replied, with a grin. "But for now, it is time for you to wake up, back in your own room."

"I really don't want to leave," she said, looking at the beautiful surroundings.

"I know you don't, but it's time to wake up where you are," he replied. "To confirm all of this is easy enough. Just come find me and remember as much as you can of this journey. Think about all of this as soon as you awake. Your physical body will then retain more."

Before she could reply, the amazing world around her began to fade. A falling sensation came over her. Haven's eyes fluttered open, and she found herself buried underneath the covers within the shadows of her bedroom.

She blinked her eyes, thinking of the astounding visions still fresh in her mind. Knowing that memories of dreams departed fast, she adhered to the Artist's words and replayed as much as she could of the incredible voyage within her mind; over and over again.

Before she had finished, an alarm beep sounded from the Home Assistant, indicating morning's arrival and the start of a new day. Looking toward her window shade, the sun's light outlining the edges, she smiled to herself.

Even if everything had just been a dream, it had been a wonderful one; taking her far away from a world that held her and so many others down.

Jaelynn

"This is my incredible mentor, and esteemed professor, Dr. Jurgen Swedenborg," Gabriel announced, gesturing to the older man seated behind a large oaken desk.

The man had made the most of his tenement dwelling, converting one of the rooms into what Jaelynn guessed to be a study. She had not been able to believe her eyes when she first walked into the room.

Lined with shelves packed with physical books, the space appeared to be a place from another age entirely. Jaelynn could not believe one man had assembled so many artifacts in one location.

No gadgetry could be seen, such as sensors to things like a holographics unit. The air itself carried a musty scent, though one she did not find unfavorable.

A few beautiful, framed images had been mounted on the wall. Jaelynn had examined one, depicting what looked to be a small house fashioned of timber, smoke rising from a chimney, sitting near a lakeside surrounded by towering, forested mountains.

The surface of the image had a texture to it, and Jaelynn realized she beheld an original painting, like the kinds kept in historical museums.

The chairs in the room, from the one Dr. Swedenborg sat in, to one set in a corner of the room, had high backs that curved around on each side. Spacious and padded, the black leather-surfaced chairs looked to offer great comfort to whoever sat in them.

A small wooden table with a circular top had been placed next to the chair in the corner. Beneath a lamp that Jaelynn deemed to be an antique, a couple of books had been stacked. She wanted to examine them, but held back the urge, wanting to be sure her first encounter with Dr. Swedenborg went as smooth as possible.

Bringing another unique aspect to the meeting, Gabriel had informed her through his handwritten method that Dr. Swedenborg had somehow shielded his apartment. Anyone inside could speak openly, without fear of surveillance.

"Perhaps you are my mentor, in many ways, young fellow," Dr. Swedenborg replied. "You are a strong young spirit, quite a rarity these days. We could do with a few more that had your fire."

A moment later, the narrow-faced man's green-hued eyes widened and sparkled with merriment. Grinning through a short-cropped, silvery beard, he covered his mouth in a gesture of having said something scandalous.

"Oops! I said the forbidden word that would vex my esteemed colleagues of the sciences ... at least those who belong to the Grand Cult of Matter," Dr.Swedenborg stated, with an air of flamboyance. "They are always so utterly confounded by such concepts, when all sorts of evidence is there to be examined and considered."

"What word is that?" Jaelynn asked, concentrating to refrain from laughing at the man's dramatic style and formal way of speaking.

"Why spirit, of course, since such a thing does not exist," Dr. Swedenborg said, with an obviously feigned somber demeanor. Like a sun emerging from behind clouds, his jovial smile returned a moment later. "Or so the Grand Cult of Matter tells us."

Jaelynn laughed, finding the professor to be more than a little odd, but undeniably engaging. "But, aren't you a scientist?"

"Wholeheartedly," Dr. Swedenborg replied. "It is my passion in life. But I am a blasphemer, a great heretic in their eyes. Ah, those self-made gods, the men and women of high genius who have bestowed immortality on the chosen few with Ascension. What a fool I am to suggest that they have succeeded in nothing more than a grand deception ... and most tragic folly."

Jaelynn could sense the great distaste the professor held towards those involved with Ascension. For her part, she had deep regret that there was no way she could afford Ascension for her ailing mother.

His coarse attitude towards Ascension troubled her, but she nonetheless took a quick liking to him. A twinkling in his eyes reflected the warm smile displayed on his face. The youthful air about him in no way aligned with his apparent age.

"Who are these self-made gods?" she asked him, curious.

"Why, the high priests of the Global Council-approved science, as it were," he remarked, chuckling. "Always claiming the possession of knowledge that they do not have, to make conclusions about things they are woefully ignorant of."

"What do you mean?" Jaelynn asked, puzzled.

"Long, long ago, people didn't know that these invisible things called viruses and bacteria existed," Dr. Swedenborg replied, a trace of a grin still resting on his face. "But did that mean they did not exist in those times, simply because they had not yet been proven to exist?"

"No, they always existed, of course," Jaelynn answered, unsure of where the professor was going with his discussion.

"What about all the far solar systems and planets, those which could not be seen with the naked eye," Dr. Swedenborg continued. "Did they not exist, in those older times, because they could not yet be proven. Or did they exist, and get discovered when humans developed better optics and capabilities?"

"They existed, whether we knew about them or not, I'm sure," Jaelynn said.

"Precisely," Dr. Swedenborg answered, his grin widening. "And now I intend to blaspheme the Infallible Religion. So brace yourself ... you are about to hear great heresy!

"All the tools we have for observation, measurement, and analysis, these things tell us much about the nature of physics, the laws that govern biology, the properties of chemistry, the things of matter and energy ... all that kind of territory, yes?"

Jaelynn nodded.

"But does it tell us anything about the setting of those laws in the first place?" Dr. Swedenborg said, with a wry grin. "Or of anything that could potentially change those laws, which would then change all the behavior of all those things that we have accepted as immutable fact?

"Do not be quick to dismiss mysteries, or believe the tools that we possess are adequate, or even capable, of answering all questions," Dr. Swedenborg said. "What I am about to tell you is sheer heresy to the fools of this age.

"There are things of a much greater nature to be found in life, Jaelynn, but they are things that confound the priests of this Grand Cult. Why is that? Because they are things that cannot be measured and repeated, or controlled; and which do not operate according to their expectations.

"The evidence is there, and has been experienced by countless multitudes over centuries, but the Priests of the Grand Cult choose to believe that by ignoring it all, or dismissing every claim, then it doesn't exist. It is no different than a man of long ages ago saying viruses did not exist because he could not touch or see them. But even that example is a crude one, because I am speaking of things that are not bound by the laws explored by the Grand Cult. I am speaking of things that transcend those laws and reach far beyond their understanding.

Pausing, he leaned back in his chair, and smiled.

"So, to sum it all up, I am most certainly a man of science, and my greatest interest is in matters of the spirit. One can be both, if one is humble enough to recognize how little we truly know.

"How's that for something different these days?"

When Dr. Swedenborg concluded, Jaelynn found herself at a loss for words. Never before had she encountered someone like the professor, who carried the authority of high education yet spoke in favorable terms about things deemed obsolete and relics of a long bygone age.

"I don't know much about the spirit, or anything like that," Jaelynn said. "It's used in gaming, but that's about it."

"A true journey of knowledge is a most humbling path to take, as every question answered opens up a host of further inquiries," Dr. Swedenborg said. "I do not see that as a problem but approach it with a feeling of wonder and joy. Discovery without limit!"

"You see why I love Dr. Swedenborg " Gabriel exclaimed. "He sees limitless horizons where everyone else in this technate is supposed to accept the way things are and believe that it can't be changed."

"I definitely see that," Jaelynn said. "But I don't understand what advantage the scientists could possibly gain by ignoring evidence? That doesn't make much sense to me."

"What advantage?" Dr. Swedenborg replied. "To accept, or even honestly investigate such evidence, would be to threaten their whole paradigm. They've built a system, and it serves a great purpose for them. The crux of the matter in this day and age is that morality has become something you can define any way you want to, using any measure you would like.

"Things I would suggest are vile and wicked can be argued as logical and efficient in their eyes ... a public need, something for the Greater Good, and taking on a guise of morality.

"Evidence toward anything beyond their paradigm undermines their power and authority ... so they simply choose to ignore it, and, even worse, suppress it. That is not a journey of understanding. It is moral and intellectual bankruptcy. A genuine and mature intellect must always be open to new information. Do not believe everything these High Priests of Oblivion tell you.

"But isn't it true that they only deal in facts," Jaelynn said, thinking of every science class she had ever taken.

"So sure?" Dr. Swedenborg grinned. "Yes, of course, you must be correct, since they proclaim they are people of science. It would be easier to accept, if so many of their positions didn't depend on beliefs."

"Beliefs?" Jaelynn asked, fast becoming confused again.

"It's that nasty, sticky part of what they do not know," Dr. Swedenborg said. "Listen carefully to their statements if you bring up something from the old world, like the possibility of a soul or spirit. Watch them recoil ... which is sometimes entertaining, I admit ... and then watch them make statements that would require them to be in possession of all knowledge in the universe to make."

"But there is no such thing as souls or spirits, those are just silly beliefs of the past," Jaelynn said. "They've said they've proven it."

"So sure? Be careful of the knowledge you claim to have," Dr. Swedenborg said. His face and tone grew somber, with no trace of jest, the change unsettling Jaelynn a little. "Do you have all knowledge in the universe?"

"No, of course not," she replied, uncomfortable.

"Then isn't it impossible to make such a claim with certainty?" Dr. Swedenborg said.

"It would be impossible," Jaelynn said. "I'd have to know everything, including what's not been discovered yet."

"You are spot on," Dr. Swedenborg replied, with a grin.

"Never thought you would hear a scientist talking like this, did you?" Gabriel asked her.

Jaelynn forced a smile, though the discomfort within persisted. "No, I didn't."

A broad smile returned to Dr. Swedenborg's face. "It's okay, Jaelynn. I'm just passionate about a few things, and that passion comes to the surface once in a while. I don't want to get our friendship off on the wrong foot here."

"Oh, you haven't, I just don't quite know how to respond," Jaelynn replied. "I haven't thought about this subject too much."

"I'm sure we will talk more," Dr. Swedenborg said. "Just let me leave you with one bit of advice. Don't jump into Ascension. You'll end up doing nothing more than making an artificially intelligent simulation of yourself, based on a copy of what's stored in your physical brain.

"What's supposedly transferred won't be you anymore. Not really."

"Won't be me?" Jaelynn asked. "Isn't it a transfer of consciousness and all that to a better body?"

"These paragons of all knowledge have placed the proverbial cart before the horse," Dr. Swedenborg replied. "It may be an incredibly convincing simulation, and even might fool some of your friends or family into thinking that what remains is still you. But it isn't you. The real you will no longer exist ... in this world at least."

Jaelynn could not believe what she was hearing. All of her hopes to save her mother hinged upon finding a way to secure

Ascension for her.

Talk had been spreading that it would become less expensive and more available to the greater public in the next few years. Even though the early predications of that broader availability and lower cost had come and gone, she had not given up hope. In Jaelynn's view, her mother needed to endure for a little time longer, and then she could be restored to youthfulness in mind and body.

Ascension promised an end to aging and disease. Like most citizens of Technate Six, Jaelynn found it horrid that only those of the greatest means could access it.

Now, she stood before an erudite man who challenged all of that thinking.

The confidence and clarity with which Dr. Swedenborg spoke deeply bothered her. She could not deny that his words made sense, and even tapped into some of the fears she harbored about Ascension; the possibility that its claims would turn out to be false.

Confusion, strong emotions, and hopes swirling inside her, Jaelynn began to tear up. She could not stop a few tears from escaping and trickling down her cheeks.

It was hard enough not being able to see a way to afford Ascension. But it was quite another to hear a man so highly respected by Gabriel say that Ascension was a falsehood.

Gabriel slid his arm around Jaelynn and hugged her to him. He said to Dr. Swedenborg, "She's dreamed of finding a way to get Ascension for her mother, who's been sick."

"I'm so sorry, I did not mean to cause you any pain," Dr. Swedenborg said, his mood shifting at once into a compassionate demeanor. His voice lowered. "I get ahead of myself, sometimes. I truly apologize."

When Jaelynn glanced up toward the professor. His eyes had softened to the point their surfaces had a light glistening to them. She knew in her heart that he had not intended to distress her.

"I'll be okay," Jaelynn said, blinking back a couple of tears. "It's just that it's the only way I can see to keep my mother safe. I don't want to think there's no hope. Ascension offers the only hope there is."

Anger flowed in her next words, and more tears streamed down her face. "Only wealthy people can get it. The rest of us are just supposed to die and go into nothing. It's just not fair that those born wealthy have the only hope!"

"I didn't say there was no hope for you," Dr. Swedenborg said in a gentle tone, looking genuinely pained at her rising distress. "I just said that those fools in the Northern Sector definitely don't offer it."

"What do you mean? What else is there?" Jaelynn countered, an emptiness growing inside.

Dr. Swedenborg pursed his lips and took a deep breath. He looked to be struggling with some interior thoughts.

"If you would be willing, come back with Gabriel in about a week," Dr. Swedenborg said. "I do not have anything here that can give you or your family members immortality in this world. But I will do what I can to show you something that may give you some comfort."

Jaelynn nodded. If only for Gabriel, she wanted to return to show that she bore no ill will towards the professor.

"I'd like that," she said.

"Good," Dr. Swedenborg replied. With an energetic flare, he continued. "With that settled, I say we adjourn to the next room and enjoy some tea. I have procured some excellent varieties, and you might wish to sample more than one before we conclude this visit."

"I don't know much about tea," Jaelynn said, as Dr. Swedenborg stood up. Taller than Gabriel, he looked to be a couple inches over six feet in height.

"Then you will know a little more about tea when you go back home today," Dr. Swedenborg replied, smiling. He chuckled. "Learning can bring with it an indulgence in taste and refreshment."

"Believe me, he always has something good to eat or drink here," Gabriel said.

"I'm relieved to know I haven't failed in that area," Dr. Swedenborg replied to Gabriel. He walked past them. "Now follow me, and we'll explore the world of tea for a bit. Just wait until you are old enough to explore the world of wine, that's a fun one too!"

Following Gabriel out the door, Jaelynn put aside her worries. She smiled to herself, looking forward to experiencing the world of tea.

Salvador

Drones of all sizes pockmarked the bright blue skies. Salvador hated the way the flying objects sullied his view of the horizons beyond the city. But the aircraft could not be avoided, cruising at a slow, purposeful speed over the city; electric eyes ever dutiful, watchful and omnipresent.

Standing on the roof of his apartment building, he looked out over the drab swathe of streets and buildings that constituted most of the world he knew. The view never failed to conjure up a feeling of insignificance within him.

"Thought I might catch you up here."

The familiar voice brought him about at once. Jade stood a few paces away, dressed in much the same manner as Salvador had seen him the last time.

"Jade," Salvador said, smiling. "You caught me by surprise."

"I tend to do that a lot," Jade replied, with a laugh. Turning his head, he gazed off in the distance. "Those drones really are annoying. I'd bring a storm down on all of them, if I wasn't worried about invoking whatever the Primordials have in place around here.

"I'm sure I've annoyed them with the incident involving their drone, and the one with their two security bots. The Primordials do have their ways, ones that can make things delicate, to say the least."

"Lots of bots and security personnel," Salvador replied, thinking of what might happen. "We'd get swarmed real fast."

"Are you so sure that's all?" Jade asked, with a smirk. He then shifted the course of the conversation. "Let me ask, have you given much thought to what we spoke about before?"

"Makes little sense, to be honest," Salvador said. "But yes, I've thought about what you talked about ... the Primordials, the Source, and all of that."

Salvador looked about, a little nervous, eyeing the drones and wondering if his words had just been recorded.

"You are safe," Jade said with a reassuring air. "Look a little closer here."

Looking down, at the rooftop, Salvador noticed a soft blue glow, not unlike the one that he had seen in the coffee shop, before Jade had disabled the two security robots.

"This power is far beyond their science, don't worry," Jade continued. "So, do you have any questions about anything? I figured I would ask you that first, before we proceed."

Salvador nodded, though he wondered at what Jade was about. "I'm interested in knowing about time, in terms of the Kairos you mentioned."

"An entire age, seeming like a moment, and a moment experienced like a vast age," Jade commented with a wistful air. "Such is the way of things with Kairos, the champion of the Source. One need not be limited to a road of past, present and future, but rather all of them intertwined. Ends can be beginnings, and beginnings can be ends. Or ... no beginning or end. I find I like that the best."

Salvador shook his head and laughed. "Oh wow ... I can't begin to get my head around that."

Jade winked. "I'll let you in on a secret ... I can't get my head around it entirely myself."

"It sounds completely overwhelming," Salvador said.

"But overwhelmingly wonderful, once you have experienced it," Jade said. "You'll never fear death again."

Awe and wonder reflected in Jade's eyes, telling Salvador that he spoke of something profound and magnificent. Yet another side remained to the equation being discussed.

"But you struggle against the Primordials at all times, if I'm hearing you right," Salvador said. "They are threatening everything, aren't they?"

Jade's face shadowed over with a stern expression. He nodded.

"Think of a bird with a broken wing, left to suffer, vulnerable to predators," Jade said. "Those of the Primordials would show the bird no mercy. They would not spare it from being torn apart. They would tell you that is the way of things. It is just nature taking its course.

"But along comes a man or woman, who choose to take that same bird in, protect it and help it heal. One day that bird soars into the sky once more.

"In their action, the man or woman has shown another way. They have fought for life against death. They have shown mercy against that which is pitiless. They have given you a view of another world, one that defies the way of the Primordials."

Jade paused and stared at Salvador. "What I have to say next will not be easy to hear."

"Go ahead," Salvador invited.

"Your ailing mother waits now for help," Jade said. "To the powers that be here, she is a statistic. A cost. A unit. What they mean, when they say all are equal in their eyes, is that everyone is interchangeable, replaceable, and ultimately expendable."

"I know they like to control us, that's pretty obvious," Salvador said.

"You need to see how they view you, and what is at stake," Jade said. "Stand near me, and do not fear what you see."

Salvador walked a few paces closer to Jade, wondering what the man intended to do.

The air shimmered, taking on a glassy sheen that distorted Salvador's view, until nothing more could be seen of the rooftop. Everything came back into focus moments later.

A gasp escaped Salvador, finding himself down on the street level in front of the tenement. Turning around, he saw no sign of Jade.

Steeling himself, he took in his surroundings. A shocking change had come over the crowded street.

Salvador did not know if he viewed people or robots. All of the figures around him were humanoid in appearance, though they had no distinguishing features to tell one apart from the next.

From their feet to their heads, the figures were identical to each other in every way. Exactly the same in height, width of shoulder, length of arm and leg, thickness of body, and without any trace of gender, the beings were composed of a dull blue substance.

They had no hair, clothes, or even expression to their faces. To Salvador, they looked like so many mannequins come to life, all created from the same mold.

Walking the same length of stride, and carrying the same posture, they moved up and down the street at the same pace.

Though none of the figures had reacted to his presence among them, Salvador had never experienced the kind of horror that he did looking upon the surreal, homogenous crowds around him.

Every last feature and characteristic Salvador had violated the pervading unity of the figures. A threat loomed, fueling a rising panic within him. He suspected that once they took notice of him, the figures, or whatever governed them, would take action against him at once.

"This is a true society of equals," Jade's voice sounded within Salvador's ears, somber and low in tone. "Look upon this and remember it well. This is what people look like to the Primordials, and to its vile champion, Chronos. Never forget this."

The scene changed in an instant.

Blinking his eyes, and jarred from the sudden shift, Salvador looked upon the street as he had known it before. Everything around him appeared restored to its original state; from the traffic on the streets to the drones hovering overhead.

Not one of the blue figures could be seen, but a part of him sensed their essence in the listless faces on the people walking up and down the sidewalk. The recognition unsettled him.

The shimmering effect ensued once more, and Salvador found himself back on the rooftop with Jade.

"A useful demonstration, one that will help you gain some understanding of what is at stake," Jade said.

"That ... was intense," Salvador said, still rattled by the whole experience.

"It's what they would love to see, if they could have their way entirely," Jade said.

"I see why you are against them," Salvador said.

"And why you should be as well," Jade replied.

"I'm against anything like that," Salvador said.

"Good to hear," Jade said. "You have some sense in you."

"I hope so," Salvador replied.

"As for my part, I have to be going," Jade said. "But there is one more thing to demonstrate to you."

Salvador hoped whatever Jade had planned would not be as disturbing as the vision of the blue figures.

"Don't look so apprehensive," Jade said, chuckling. "Nothing like what you just saw. But I do need to get going. There are a lot of tasks these days for one such as myself."

"I'm beginning to figure I'm part of that task list," Salvador said.

Jade grinned. "Perhaps so. For right now, though, I just need you to find me."

"Where?" Salvador asked.

"Just come to the park, as soon as you are able," Jade said. "I'll be there, in the place we've talked before. Now think of your body, back in your bed, sleeping. Go back to it."

Jade's words caused Salvador to realize he stood in a dream. The awareness prompted him to recall the fact that his physical body did indeed remain back in his bed. The thought of his body triggered a response before he could reply.

Everything blurred and began to fade. Panicking, his heart sped up as the sensation of falling came over him.

Salvador's eyes snapped open. He found himself lying on his side in the middle of his bed. Sweat beaded on his forehead, and he had a light headache.

His heart beating fast, he took a few long, slow breaths to calm the rate back down.

Salvador realized it had all been a dream, but it had been one so lucid and convincing that he had interacted within it on a level beyond a VR environment. He could remember everything about it in great detail, including his conversation with Jade.

He decided to act upon Jade's last request.

Swinging his legs out of bed, he got into a sitting position, bracing his palms against the mattress. Though he wondered if he had begun to lose his mind, he girded himself to go back to the park, to see if Jade could be found there.

A question directed at the Home Assistant informed Salvador that morning had come, and the time stood at a few minutes after eleven. He had gotten to sleep in a little, for a Saturday.

Voice-activating the lamp on the nightstand by his bed, he fumbled about for some clothes. Throwing on a pair of pants and a long-sleeved shirt, he slipped into some shoes and gathered himself for a long walk to the park.

The streets, as always, were crowded, with a steady stream of bicycles, drones, and pedestrians. Salvador fell into the flow and made his way several blocks to the park. He resisted the urge to break into a jog but kept his stride brisk.

Entering the park, he headed straight for his favorite spot, making his way to the far side and working his way through the trail partially concealed in brush. A look of amazement sprouted upon his face when he reached the grove of trees and eyed Jade, standing amid the familiar cluster marking the area.

"Very well done, you were prompt in getting here," Jade said, when Salvador neared.

Leaning against the trunk of a tree, a grin rested on his face. "You are here," Salvador replied, with a hint of disbelief.

"I sure am, and it shouldn't be too much of a surprise, since I told you to meet me here," Jade said. "We were just hanging out a little while ago, I believe, showing you what a world of equals really looks like. On the rooftop of your apartment building, and then down on the street level. Lots of blue people, all identical. Yes?"

"That ... was all real," Salvador managed to reply, though his mind spun at the indisputable revelation that Jade had indeed shared his dream.

"What is real? That's a good question," Jade responded, with a laugh. "That dream you just had was real enough, wasn't it?"

"But it was a dream," Salvador said. "I awoke in my bed."

"What is a dream?" Jade asked. "Or maybe it is better to ask ... what are some dreams, and what are others?"

"How did we share the same dream?" Salvador asked, struggling to get his mind around it. "How in the world does that happen?"

"Perhaps there's much more to the story about the world and the universe than you might think, and far more than they've told you," Jade replied. He gave a casual shrug. "I'm merely helping you to open up your eyes."

"And why me?" Salvador asked. "Out of all the several million people in this Technate. Why in the world would you pick me? I'm a fifteen-year-old kid who's scores are pretty average."

"Why you?" Jade asked. "Pick you? I think you found me."

"The park?" Salvador replied. "You already know I've come here for a long time. You just happened to be here that day."

Jade shook his head. "No. It has to do with dreams. Those dreams you say aren't real. Dreams you can't remember right now."

Jade's reply confused him, but there was no denying the fact of what just happened. The man had visited him in a dream and validated more than enough elements to prove it.

"I just don't understand how it is possible," Salvador said, shaking his head.

"Am I really standing here now?" Jade asked, his grin spreading. "Or am I dreaming?"

"You are obviously real and standing right here with me," Salvador said. "This is definitely the physical world. Even have a slight soreness in my right knee to remind me of it."

"I'm real, that much is true," Jade said. "As for the rest? Are you so sure I'm not dreaming, in a manner of speaking?"

Jade's smile widened, a moment before he vanished from sight. Salvador blinked his eyes, and turned in place, but no sign could be seen of the man.

Stunned, Salvador remained rooted in place for several minutes, trying to process what he had just witnessed. When he finally willed his legs to move, and started back for home, Salvador had even more to ponder about the nature of reality.

Cayden

Discovering his mother crying in the shadows of the living room, Cayden tensed. Tears often crossed her cheeks in the silence of the room, invoked by any one of a number of the things tormenting her.

Yet something about the current instance told him she was not sorrowing over the loss of Melanie or his father.

"What's happened, mom?" Cayden asked, walking over to her side.

Through the muffled sobs, she managed to reply in a low voice. "It's nothing, Cayden. Nothing important at all."

"Did something happen today?" Cayden pressed, becoming more alarmed. Knowing better than to accept her words, he slid his arm around her shoulders and sought to comfort her. "You can tell me, mom. It's okay. Just tell me."

"Nothing you can do, Cayden. Nothing I can do. And it's really silly, anyway," she replied, leaning her head wearily into Cayden's chest. "It's just the way things are these days."

"I'm sure it isn't silly, mom ... just tell me, you'll feel better," Cayden said.

Working to keep the anxiety building inside from showing on his face, he knew that her answer would not be a welcome one.

After a few moments of silence, she replied. "I just wanted to go out and treat myself to dinner, out in a restaurant. Just that. That's all that happened."

"Why didn't you?" Cayden asked, a little perplexed.

"I wasn't thinking," she told him. "I was standing at an intersection. There were no vehicles at all. I crossed before the walking light came on. I should have known better. The scanner read and fined me. The fines have gotten larger."

Purported to be for the safety of the public, the strict enforcement of pedestrian crossings looked like just another excuse to pilfer credits from the populace to Cayden's eyes. With cameras enabled with facial recognition and implanted identification chips, the enforcement took place at once. The deduction of the fine came out of a citizen's account instantly, no different than the fines assessed for everything else.

"It's such ... such a little thing," she continued, choking up. "Really, it is. It just was one thing too much, today."

"I'm really sorry, mom," Cayden said, embracing her tighter.

"I ... just can't catch a break, ever," she said through a new wave of tears. "I just wanted to go to a restaurant and can't even do that without something bad happening."

A spark of anger took flame. Cayden's mother lived a life devoid of luxurious things, and what little she could have mattered to him. A senseless regulation took away her one chance at enjoying something in a day to day life that saw few joys or respites.

"I knew better, it was the law, I deserved the fine," she said, after a few moments had passed. "Not disputing that. Just upset I got so careless, I guess."

"No, you didn't deserve a fine," Cayden replied in a firmer tone. "It's a stupid law, made by stupid people, who just want a way to take more credits from people that don't have much, and who can't fight back. That's what it's all about. You are an adult, and you could tell the street was clear. There was no reason you shouldn't be able to cross it."

"Cayden ... Cayden!" his mother replied, sounding alarmed. She looked up to him with a look of distress. Gesturing with her eyes, she indicated the potential of home devices hearing what he had just said.

"I just don't like what happened to you," Cayden said, holding back a few other thoughts about the law and those who made it. "Not at all."

"That's the way it is, and if I violate the law then I have to answer for it," she said.

"I'm really, really sorry," Cayden responded, while repressing a number of angry thoughts.

"I'll be alright, I promise," his mother replied, regaining a little composure. "Just let me sit here for a little while. I'll be okay."

Cayden nodded. "I love you, mom. I don't like seeing you so upset."

"Love you, too," she replied. "More than I can say."

Cayden gave her one more hug before leaving the room. Ambling back to his bedroom, he wished that he had some kind of funds that he could use to take his mother out to dinner.

A sense of helplessness pervaded him, regarding the laws, his mother's enduring sadness, and his own lack of power to change anything.

A raw anger simmered within his heart.

Shutting his door, he did not bother to have the lights turned on. Removing his shoes and tossing them in the corner, he trudged over and slumped into his bed.

Already tired, and his heart weighing heavier, it did not take long for him to fall asleep.

Her voice came to him, before he had a complete grasp on his surroundings. "Are you ready for a Guardian, Cayden?"

Cayden smiled, elated to see her standing at his side on a lofty, windswept ledge. The high vantage afforded him a spectacular view of a crevice-riddled plain, beneath a rolling, ash-gray mass of clouds.

He knew the answer to her question at once. Cayden had suffered more than enough of frustration and feelings of powerlessness. For a moment, he thought of his mother crying, and how he could offer her nothing more than words and a hug.

It all had to end.

"Yes," Cayden responded, mustering conviction into his voice, and looking her in the eyes. "Yes ... I am."

She gave him a radiant smile. "You have taken the first step to mastering your world. I am with you now, and you are now part of something much, much greater than ever before."

Cayden smiled back, wondering what the future held. Laying her hand gently on his cheek, she caressed his face.

"Let us fly together," she invited him. "Show your faith in me."

Cayden peered out, the hot winds beating against his face and whipping his hair about. The drop beyond the cliff's edge dizzying to view, he had no desire to approach the jagged boundary any closer, much less go beyond it.

"You have to trust me, Cayden," she said. "Leap, and fly."

He looked at her for several moments, and then took a deep breath. Edging forward, he brought himself to the lip of the drop.

Heartbeat accelerating, he girded his resolve. Staring straight ahead, and trying not to look down, he jumped from the ledge.

Though every instinct within him cried out in dire alarm, he did not fall. Instead, Cayden glided forward, though what power propelled him he could not ascertain.

A vast plain spreading far and wide beneath him, Cayden could not make out any details of the landscape from the tremendous height he started from. Sinewy tendrils of black mist snaked past him.

Keeping his arms relaxed at his sides, Cayden continued forward. No physical rules governed his flight. Only an exercise of consciousness proved necessary to sustain his altitude and proceed forward.

Movement to his right drew his eyes. The Guardian pulled up alongside him, keeping pace without difficulty. She smiled again.

"Was that so difficult?" she asked. "You must learn to give me your trust in all things. Then you will be able to do so much more."

"Will I ever be able to do this in my world?" he asked, curious. A pit forming in his stomach, he gazed down, peering into the maw of a deep gorge.

"You are going to be able to do far more than you realize," she said. "As long as you place your full trust in me, and you accept my guidance."

"Can I ask you your name, or what I'm supposed to call you?" Cayden asked.

"Names do not matter to a Guardian, for our cause is everything," she replied. "But if it helps you, you may call me Lilithian."

"What is this place, Lilithian?" he asked, trying out the name for the first time. It rolled smooth off of his tongue, sounding graceful and strong.

"Just one of many realms," Lilithian replied.

Cayden waited for her to continue, but she did not offer anything more in the way of explanation.

"Are you ready for your first lesson?" she asked. "I think you'll enjoy this one."

His environs pitch black, Cayden could not see a thing through the dense mists shrouding him. Unable to tell if anything loomed ahead, he began to get nervous, unable to hear a sound.

Then, as if within his head, he heard his Guardian with perfect clarity. "Part the mists. Imagine sending a wave of energy that can push them away. Envision it coming from within you."

Focusing on her voice, he took initiative, doing as Lilithian instructed.

A pulse of energy radiated outward from Cayden. The black mists reeled back, pushed by the wave of power generated from within Cayden.

The skyline of a large metropolis beckoned ahead. It looked nothing like Technate Six, having a lot of variance in the kinds of buildings he could see.

Not far from Cayden, a drone held airborne with several rotors hovered.

"Slow down," Lilithian said.

Cayden did as she told him to do, coming to a hover himself. The drone then began moving, heading in their direction.

"Imagine the energy again, coming from inside you, and direct it at that drone," Lilithian said. "Imagine it being consumed in a wave of blistering heat. Imagine it falling."

Nodding, Cayden eyed the drone. He envisioned generating another wave of energy and having it envelop the incoming drone. His body tingled all over, and something passed from him.

A moment later, the drone ceased its approach, shook, and then plunged downward. Cayden watched it descend, until it crashed into the ground far below.

"Well done," Lilithian said, hovering at his side. "Now you will see that this can be done in your world. Return, and find something that angers you. You will hear from me then. Think of your body now ... back in your world."

Reminded of his physical form, Cayden's vision clouded over. When he opened them again, his gaze filled with the sight of his bedroom ceiling.

Remembering Lilithian's directive at once, Cayden wasted no time in getting out of bed. Throwing on his shoes, he headed out of the apartment and continued down to the street level. Turning left, he started off along the sidewalk.

He wished that he could take to flight and soar across the technate, but Cayden doubted that possible in his own world. He missed the Guardian already. She made him feel stronger and more capable with her presence alone.

With so much to occupy his thoughts, he found it strange that he perceived the world around him so differently. Somehow, everything appeared less imposing, and a sense of impermanence filled the air.

After agonizing for as long as he could remember about how nothing changed, or ever would change, the realization surprised Cayden greatly. Instead of feeling like a victim, he saw a path to becoming a master.

Slowing toward the end of the block, he came to a stop. Looking at the police vehicle rolling past him for a moment, he swept his eyes around, taking in the cameras and other electronics mounted everywhere.

Around him, a number of other people waited near the curb for the pedestrian light to change so that they could cross the street.

A few seconds later, the street stood entirely clear, with nothing coming in his direction either way. Yet nobody moved even a step. As if one mass, the people waited, with their eyes fixed on the crossing light.

If any of them stepped forward a moment too soon, they would incur the same punishment that his mother had. A scanner would read their position, access their ID's, and fine their accounts on the spot.

Even so, they were all perfectly capable of judging for themselves that crossing the street would be safe at that time. All of the people surrounding Cayden grown adults, a single little light held them in place; like a herd of children.

He thought of his mother, sitting in the darkness of her living room crying and prevented from having a simple dinner out of the apartment because she had dared to use common sense. Her tear-stained face and the echoes of her sobs ran through his mind.

All of the thoughts about his mother and the sheep-like people around him spurred his blood to running a little faster, a surge of anger rising within. Eyeing the people around him, Cayden did not consider himself to be among their number.

To him, they stood as a group of adults shunning logic and willfully intimidated. He wished that he could teach them all a lesson, from the cowed group huddled at the edge of the curb, to the authorities with their arsenal of scanners, vehicles and monitors.

"Go ahead, Cayden. I am still with you, and the power is still within you," Lilithian's voice sounded inside his head. "Remember how you parted the darkness. Remember how you brought the drone down. Let a wave loose, and witness what happens."

A smirk threatened to arise on his lips, but he held the expression at bay. He thought it best to give no indication of his exercise of will; whether the attempt worked in his world or not.

He thought of how he had felt in the other realm, steeped in the black mists. All of his focus centered upon gathering and loosing a pulse of energy. The tingling sensation that he had experienced before returned, all over his body.

With a single thought, he sent an emanation radiating through the street. Whether a trick of his eye or not, he thought he caught a brief shimmer in the air as it happened. There were no mists to push back this time, but the wave of energy had a powerful, and immediate, effect.

At once, the lights went out everywhere, for about a block's distance. The police vehicle, now farther down the road, rolled to a stop.

A few startled cries erupted as a small surveillance drone clanged loudly into the middle of the street, parts of it scattering all over the place as it broke apart. Though they still rested in place where they had been mounted, Cayden knew in his heart that all of the cameras in the vicinity had been rendered useless.

The burst of energy that he had generated and set loose had destroyed the circuitry governing all of the devices, from surveillance devices to the police drones. Every last tool put in place by the highest authorities had become impotent from a single electromagnetic pulse; summoned at the command of Cayden's mind.

Seeing the stalled police vehicle and the lights out, the people along the streets took on immediate looks of anxiety and confusion. Voices carrying an air of panic soon filled the air, but Cayden stood calm in the burgeoning disarray.

He harbored a little disgust at their nervous reactions. To him, it appeared that they wished for the lights and drones to return; as if unable to contemplate going about life without the presence of the controlling apparatus.

He had given them a microcosm of being free, and yet he saw significant apprehension in the faces around him. Managing to keep his face still, Cayden left the adults milling about.

Strolling across the street, he had no fear of being fined or identified. Once on the opposite side, he turned and crossed again.

At his return, a few of the adults began to cross the street themselves, taking cautious steps. Cayden paid them little attention, basking in the joy of what he had just accomplished.

Continuing back to his mother's apartment, he walked a little taller, finding his stride much more steady and confident.

Nothing had happened on his part to bring any guilt or regret. Nobody had died, and the equipment of an oppressive technate comprised the largest amount of damage.

Cayden had no illusions about what he had done. Everything that had been damaged or destroyed would be replaced soon enough.

Nevertheless, a wonderful feeling filled him. For once, Cayden did not feel so helpless or powerless in the face of everything in his life. Lilithian had helped in empowering him to take charge of his circumstances; if only for those few moments at the curbside.

A strange notion came to him, when Cayden reached the doors of the tenement building. He thought of Technate Six Council Representative Lane Margolis, and how smug the man had looked while talking about policies that would bring hardship to thousands upon thousands.

He remembered what the Guardian had told him about people like Lane Margolis, who were said to have undergone Ascension. If the politician had embraced Ascension, and had truly transferred himself into an artificial body, then he stood highly vulnerable in the face of someone with abilities like Cayden's.

With a mere thought, Cayden could bring an end to the man, no different than a light going out on the street, or a surveillance drone falling from the sky. The power that Cayden had just demonstrated would not affect anyone living in the tenements. It would only target the highest among the elite class; the types who sequestered themselves away from the greater populace, behind the towering barriers of the Northern Sector.

Cayden laughed again, thinking of how any of those who had undergone Ascension did not realize how lucky they were that day. If any of them had been standing on the city street with him just minutes before, they would have seen their privilege and wealth come to an abrupt end.

Thinking of how his mother and so many others lived almost made him change course and take a stroll toward the Northern Sector.

After thinking upon the tantalizing idea for a moment, he decided to continue home, having done enough for one day.

***

Though startled, Cayden played ignorant less than an hour later when a pair of technate security officers showed up at his apartment. His mother became fearful at once, speaking in deferential tones to the officers as they entered the apartment and ushered Cayden into the living room.

To his relief, they quickly dispelled his initial fears that they had somehow identified him as the cause of the anomaly on the street. His mother became eased when the officers made it clear that Cayden had not committed any infractions.

Without any delay, they indicated that an unexpected malfunction had resulted in many ID's becoming inoperable and that Cayden's had been one of those affected. They merely wished to remove his ID and replace it with a new one. There were no threats of interrogations, and he did not even have to leave the apartment with them.

A mild hassle, Cayden cooperated with the officers as they executed the procedure right in his living room. He felt a little pinch at the extraction of the damaged ID, but the new implant went in painlessly. When finished, the officers closed up the case with the implanting and extracting tools and left the apartment.

His mother went to the kitchen as soon as the front door shut. A minute later, he could hear the rattle of ice cubes and liquid being poured into a glass.

The excess costs she paid every month for the amount of alcohol that she consumed were the one penalty she embraced without protest. Knowing well-enough that she would not stop with one glass, and not wanting to stay around, he went back to his bedroom.

Sitting on his bed and looking at the spot where the implant resided, Cayden grinned to himself. He had been so focused on the cameras, police vehicles, and other larger devices that he had forgotten all about the IDs. Though nanoscale, they were still electronic in nature, and the energy wave had clearly fried all the ones within range.

He imagined that a bunch of them going out at once had instigated a panic among the authorities. The thought of their discomfort brought him great pleasure, but it also demonstrated what a threat his ability could be.

Cayden knew that he had to be careful in how he exercised a power like that. If the powers in charge of the technate had any inkling of what he could do, they would sweep him up in an instant.

The range of his effort had covered an entire technate block, and he wondered whether the ability could be strengthened further. He mused over the idea of growing the range to the point where he could send a massive pulse of energy across the entire technate.

In a single stroke, he could bring down the most elite and break the shackles on the masses. Everything they depended on in their technology-driven imprisonment of the majority would be neutralized.

Cayden laughed aloud. Just days ago, he had limped home, bruised and battered from being pummeled by one of his peers. Now, he found himself pondering the act of shutting the entire technate down.

The idea of it thrilled him.

Haven

Heart beating fast, Haven knocked on the door to the Artist's apartment. She braced herself. Everything hinged upon the next few moments.

The difference between a doorway opening to something incredible and grave disappointment loomed right in front of her.

She heard muffled footsteps, with someone approaching the door from the other side. The door began pulling back.

Relief flooded over her. The opened doorway revealed the Artist.

A grin on his face, the Artist's eyes carried a lively gleam.

"I had begun to wonder when I might be seeing you again," he said, looking greatly amused.

"I … I just … " she started to say, before she found herself entangled within a horde of thoughts, trying to figure out the best way to ask the Artist about the incredible dream.

"It's not all that hard. I told you to come see me, though you might be a little disappointed that neither Harrison nor Chesiree are here, and nor are Dewey and Carmel," the Artist said. He added, after a moment's pause. "Nor is the airship. No grand homes, either. No floating islands with big waterfalls. It's just me and this little apartment."

"Wow!" Haven exclaimed, feeling a rush of excitement. Laughing, she shook her head, before taking a deep breath. Her mind raced to grapple with the confirmation in the Artist's words. "So, the whole thing was real, after all. Truly real! In its entirety, a real experience!"

"What is reality anyway?" the Artist asked her, grinning. "A single dream may go through many changes, but when you think about it, this entire world we're in right now has nothing of permanence in it.

"The world changes with every moment. If you could see over the span of an age, you would know that nothing of this world truly lasts. Not the greatest mountain, or the largest ocean. It is always changing. Just like a dream."

"I never thought about that," Haven said.

"So ... why are we standing here, when you can come in, sit down, and have one of those soft drinks you seemed to like so much?" the Artist asked, stepping back to allow her entrance into the apartment.

"That sounds great," Haven said. "I'll take you up on the offer."

She walked by him in a giddy state, finding her eyes drawn at once to the framed art displayed on the wall. Hearing the door being shut behind, she gazed upon the art for a second time.

After experiencing the dream, the possibilities depicted in the images sprang to greater life. If her airship journey had truly shown her new realities, then the wondrous vistas, mountains, shores and lakes she saw depicted on the wall could all be experienced in person.

Visions of floating, lush islands, connected by cascades of sparkling waterfalls, passed through her mind as she continued down the hall and into the living room. Taking a seat on the couch, she waited as the Artist proceeded into his kitchen. He returned a couple minutes later with a glass full of the cherry-flavored soft drink.

Taking a sip, she closed her eyes for a second, savoring the flavors bursting within her mouth. "I wish so badly I had this back at my apartment."

"I'll have to send you home with what you need to make it yourself," the Artist said, taking a seat on another couch.

Haven looked over to him and smiled. "Well, I got the answer I was hoping for."

"Which is?" he asked, a curious expression on his face.

"The dream," Haven said. Right after the words left her lips, she paused, and corrected herself. "Or whatever it was."

"The experience you had ... that's what you mean," the Artist said.

"I really hope it isn't the last," Haven said with a wistful air.

"I have a strong suspicion it isn't, to put it mildly," the Artist replied, chuckling.

"You think so?" she asked, smiling.

"Far, far from it, in fact," he replied.

She took another long draught of the soft drink, relishing every moment of the sweet taste in her mouth. Nutrition regulations would never allow her to purchase something like the liquid in the cup.

"So, if it isn't the last time, then what's this all about?" she asked. "I doubt all of this is without some kind of purpose."

"There's the big question," the Artist said. He shook his head slowly, the levity in his expression fading. "Times, they are changing fast ... and they're getting a lot tougher."

"Well, that's certainly great news," Haven replied, in a sarcastic tone. "Just what I wanted to hear at seventeen years old."

"Things are as they are," the Artist said. "I'm not just talking about your technate, either. Primordials have a strong hold on your entire world now. It's a chokehold, really. And they are seeking always to push higher, to reach into other worlds, and do the same thing to them."

"Primordials?" Haven asked, her brow furrowing. "What are they?"

"The essence of the great struggle," the Artist replied. "Here's how I look at it ... you might refer to the Primordials as the takers, the parasites of the planes of existence.

"On the other hand, the Transcendents are the generators, and the creators. The Transcendents build and grow. Each and every one of them embraces what it means to be free. The Primordials consume with a hunger that can never be sated. A vicious urge to control dwells within them. They cannot tolerate even the existence of something that does not submit to their will."

"You are a Transcendent, then," Haven said, looking him in the eye "Obviously."

"I'm glad that much is clear to you," the Artist replied, with a light grin. "The alternative would be unthinkable to me."

"So how does this all apply to me?" Haven asked, not sure if she really wanted to know the answer.

"It's a lot to take in, I'll grant you that," the Artist said. "I've had much longer than you've been alive to work through a lot of this.

"Unfortunately, you are getting the crash course right now, and I'm sorry about that. But, basically, you have what it takes to resist the Primordials. And we need some resistance to take shape in this world, very desperately. The line must be drawn here. It is far past the time to roll them back down to the depths they came from."

Haven saw a glint of anger in his eyes at the mention of the Primordials.

"It is a lot to take in," she replied, after an extended silence. She took another sip of the soft drink. "But how can I deal with any of this? I don't know what Primordials really are, or how to even identify one."

"You aren't able to see them just yet, but you can feel their presence," the Artist said. "Around people ... and, worse, sometimes, inside of them."

"Even more encouraging," Haven said. "So, whatever this invisible thing is, it can get inside a person. Then what do you advise I look for?"

"Look for the negative, heavier energy, it's a big indicator," the Artist said. "You can't look at it in a sense of logic, because the Primordials are defined by some things that don't seem to make any sense at all. So often, they seek power for power's sake alone, not a means to any end. The power is the goal.

"The same with control. They have to control everything about you, even if it really brings them nothing in return. The control is its own end. Worst of all, they are always seeking a semblance of consent from those they enslave. There's much to talk about there, but never forget that they desire the appearance of consent."

"And the Transcendents? What of them?" she asked.

"Free will ... you will find that always with us," the Artist said. "That includes the freedom to make mistakes, too. We desire each individual to flourish and become the highest and best version of themselves. The realization of your greatest potential.

"A person must find that path on their own, without coercion or control. We do not initiate violence or coercion against others ... or gain their compliance with the threat of those things. A Primoridal wants the appearance of consent, but a threat of punishment awaits those who do not wish to choose what they want."

"I wish things were more like the way you describe the Transcendents," Haven said, finding a natural attraction to that way of thinking. To her, the path of a Transcendent simply sounded right. "I'm curious, what is a Transcendent working toward?"

"We are all working our way to what you may call the Source ... the eternal essence of life itself," the Artist said. "I know that sounds very strange to you, but that is the truth of it."

"Sounds a lot like a religion of the old world," Haven said.

"It's not a religion ... it's nothing you have to choose to believe in," the Artist said. "It does not depend on where you were born, or how you were raised. It is simply what is. You can't really put the essence of the Source into words but let me try to explain it to you this way."

The pitch of his voice changed, becoming lower and softer. The Artist had a faraway look in his eyes, and the trace of a smile on his lips.

"It is the spark in the eyes of two people who love each other. It is the arm of a friend around your shoulder, when you feel alone. It is the peace at heart you feel when you are doing something that you have a passion for. It is the whisper of the wonder of life when you are gazing upon a vision of astounding beauty. It is that voice inside that tells you to get up and keeping moving forward, when the world tells you to stay down."

The Artist became quiet for several moments, looking as if he were contemplating something. Then, he raised his eyes back up, meeting those of Haven.

"I could give you many, many more examples," he said. "But those are a few of the ways I would describe it."

Haven found herself speechless. The beauty reflected in the examples pointed toward something tremendous and mysterious.

She could understand why the Artist believed that words were inadequate to convey the nature of the Source. He spoke of something that went far beyond the world itself, and perhaps even the entire universe.

"So where does that put everything?" The Artist asked. "And what is your place in all of this? Those are two of the questions at the forefront of your mind ... am I right?"

"To say the least," she replied, not knowing where to start with the questions flooding her mind.

"I imagine it is all a little overwhelming," the Artist said. "Believe it or not, it was once for me, too."

"It is overwhelming," Haven confirmed.

"Just always keep in mind what I said, in that the Primordials are about power. They feed off heavier, darker energies," the Artist said, his grin receding back into a somber expression.

"You keep speaking of energies. What do you mean?" Haven asked. "That's something I really don't get."

"The real you isn't just a bunch of matter and chemical reactions, ruled by algorithms, though there are some who want you to think that is so," the Artist replied. "Your true consciousness is an energy ... an energy that involves your personality, your dreams, everything that governs your body and focus. Do you understand what I mean by that?"

Haven thought about it for a few moments and nodded. "It's the driving force ... of all I do. If I am not conscious, I just remain in place."

"Exactly," the Artist said. "And that's why the Primordials hunger for such energy when it is in a certain state. Feeding off you gives them strength."

"We are being fed upon?" she asked, unnerved at the idea of something unknown and invisible feeding on her.

"When people are subdued, and no longer pursue the things of their dreams and ambitions, they sink into a place where their energies darken and become more dense," the Artist replied. "In a way of looking at it, they become something that the Primordials can feed upon. The more a person is fed upon, the more the part of them that can lift them beyond the reach of the Primordials weakens. They continue to sink, continue to be fed upon, and the course is difficult to reverse. It is a vicious cycle."

"And this is why the Primordials are trying to advance into new worlds?" Haven asked.

The Artist nodded. "They will never have their fill. They seek to consume everything, at a level of madness, even if that leads to their own destruction. Feeding off the essences of life is their addiction."

"And I'm guessing these things are everywhere," Haven said.

The Artist looked to the left and right, and then up toward the ceiling. "I don't see anything in here."

"I mean out there, in the technate," Haven said, though she sensed a hint of something deeper within the Artist's words. She finished off the glass of the cherry soft drink and set it down on the low, glass-surfaced table in front of her.

"You may not want to really see what's happening out there," the Artist said.

Haven cast a glance toward the window giving a view of the outside. "I'd rather see these things than have them remain invisible to me."

"A wise choice," the Artist said.

"How in the world am I going to be able to deal with these things, even if I can see them?" Haven asked, increasingly perplexed.

"Become a Navigator," the Artist said. "It's what I am. It's what you can become. You have what it takes."

"A Navigator?" she asked.

"I could be dreaming right now, and the body you see here is nothing more than my manifestation of my dream-self ... right here in this apartment," the Artist said.

"That would be something," Haven said. "If I could believe it."

"Not asking you to believe it, I'm inviting you to know it," the Artist replied, with a knowing smile.

"So you are saying you could be dreaming, and I'm a part of

your dream," Haven said, fascinated by the idea.

A smile bloomed on the Artist's face. "Like I said, maybe I am dreaming right now. Just be sure to lock the door on your way out, and I'll catch up again with you soon!"

He cast her a grin and wink, tipping his hat towards her. The words confused her, but before she could give them any further thought her breath caught in her throat.

The Artist faded from sight.

One moment he had been sitting on the couch talking with her. In the next, his features blurred, became translucent, and then ebbed from sight.

Haven found it hard believe her eyes, even though she still sat on the Artist's couch, in his apartment. She knew she was wide-awake and well-rested.

At first, she thought of holographics, but knew that no holographic system could pour a physical soft drink and give it to her. She stared at the glass in her hand, almost empty of its contents.

She did not have long to contemplate the phenomenon. Haven heard the door to the apartment opening, causing her to sit up straight.

Light footsteps approached, and a moment later a tall, dark-haired woman of about thirty years of age walked into the living room. She had a calm look on her face and showed no sign of surprise at seeing Haven on the couch.

Her hazel eyes sparkled with a buoyant liveliness that reflected in her smile. She came to a stop and looked upon Haven.

"A new friend of his, I would guess," the woman stated, matter-of-factly. "I am Serena. You could say this is my apartment, actually ... though I wouldn't blame you for thinking it's an art gallery."

"I ... didn't know," Haven said, nerves jostled. She didn't know where to begin. "He ... was just here. I swear."

"Who was here?" Serena asked. Then, after a pause, she chuckled. "Just kidding with you. Pulled a disappearing act, did he? I remember the first time I witnessed it. I thought I had to be high on something potent from the streets of Sector Nine."

"I can't explain it," Haven said, still trying to gather her composure at the woman's presence.

"He lives somewhere in this world, but Navigators rarely reveal the place where their bodily self is located," Serena explained. "Navigators can dream themselves into any world, including this one."

"Like being two places in the world at once," Haven observed.

"It is," Serena agreed, smiling.

"And you?" Haven asked. "Are you a Navigator, too? Like him?"

"No, it's not for me, I have a different path than him, but I have come to really like that guy," Serena replied. "I definitely want to do everything I can to help him, or we are all in a lot of trouble. It requires all types, though. Navigators aren't the only ones needed in this fight."

"Then he was dreaming the entire time, when I was here during the hardware delivery?" Haven asked, thinking back to the first day that she had met him.

"Every time he's here in this apartment, he's in a dream of his own," Serena said, nodding.

"But he got me this soft drink," Haven said, indicating the drink in his hand. "He wasn't just an image. He was physical in every way."

"Just like you are within a dream, when you interact with those environments," Serena said. "You pick up objects in them, yes?"

"Yes, I do," Haven replied, working to grasp the concept. "So, he can dream himself here, and it's like he's here in person."

"That's a pretty good way of saying it," Serena answered.

The revelation put Haven's mind to the edge of spinning. The idea that she had interacted with someone as a part of their own personal dream boggled her.

"Don't worry, you are real enough, if that's what you are worried about," Serena said, laughing, looking at the expression on Haven's face. "Yes, it does call everything you know into question, but that's not a bad thing."

"I don't even know where to begin," Haven said, exasperated.

"I'm guessing he sees that you are Navigator material," Serena replied. "He doesn't visit with people casually, especially nowadays, when everything in this world is on the brink of a final disaster."

"He did talk to me about possibly becoming a Navigator, even if I still don't really know what those are," Haven said.

"I'm sure he'll explain more in time," Serena said. "Knowing him as I do, he'll probably do it in a creative way, too. He's never been known for being overly subtle."

"Tell me about it," Haven said, thinking of the magnificent world and ornate dwelling he had taken her to. "Likes cats, too, apparently."

Serena laughed. "He's got quite a clowder living in the home he's fashioned for himself in a higher realm, and all of them are full of mischief. Chesiree and Harrison never tire of chasing after each other. And Dewey is such a smart cat."

"Was that his true body? When he took me there?" Haven asked, curious.

"Not if he was taking you into higher realms," Serena said. "There are ways a physical being can go into other realms of existence, but Navigators operate in states of consciousness."

"Such a mystery ... Navigators ... other realms ... and all of this," Haven remarked, a sigh escaping her.

"Navigators are a mystery to me, too, in many ways," Serena replied. "Then again, I'm sure a lot about me is a mystery to him, too."

"So, there are other kinds of things, in addition to Navigators?" Haven asked, the mystery of it all deepening in her mind.

"Oh yes," Serena replied, a smile spreading on her face. "We all have our roles in this fight. But Navigators are vital. Right now, it is enough for you to focus on what a Navigator is and does."

"What does a Navigator do?" Haven asked, wondering what the Artist saw her becoming.

"A Navigator is an ultimate dreamer," Serena explained. "A person who masters the realm of dreams to a level where they can travel planes of existence, worlds in the universe, and the dream realms. The dream of the Navigator encompasses all of that."

"He does have a name other than the Artist, yes?" Haven asked.

Serena laughed. "Yes, yes, he does, and I will give it to you, so that you have proof you met me the next time you see him. His name is Christopher Brendan."

Haven grinned. "At least I finally have a surprise for him."

"Christopher needs surprises, every now and then," Serena replied, laughing again.

"Thank you for sharing that with me," Haven said.

"You are quite welcome," Serena replied.

"This is a lot to take in, you know," Haven said. "Only a matter of days ago I thought the technate held everything in my existence."

"And so it is for most living in this technate," Serena replied. "It's why there is a constant hunger for escape, though the paths most take escape nothing."

"VR worlds, substances, I'm guessing," Haven said.

Serena nodded. "Well-laid traps, set in place by a formidable enemy."

"An enemy that has something to do with the ways things are in the modern day," Haven responded.

"Very much so," Serena said. "But you have enough to think about for now. Go and get some rest. A journey is taking a step at a time, a day at a time. You need not have everything figured out right now."

"That's a relief," Haven said, laughing.

"For myself as well," Serena replied, grinning.

Haven edged forward, preparing to get to her feet. "I suppose I should be going. I do have a lot to process. You probably had been wanting to relax in your home, and here you found me, a stranger sitting right in the middle of your living room."

"Don't think of it like that," Serena said. "It is always good to make a new friend."

"I'm pretty sure nobody I know would take finding a new person in their living room nearly as well as you have," Haven said, laughing.

"You have a point," Serena said, laughing. "Then again, we all have our roles."

"I'd best let you get some downtime, you've already been more than generous with your time," Haven said.

"Downtime is good," Serena said. "I am needing to make some dinner, though. Been a long day for me, and I built up an appetite. If you would like to stay, I'd love for you to join me for it. I don't get too much company here beyond Christopher."

"And I bet he just shows up out of thin air?"

"He gives me the courtesy of knocking on my door, in most instances," Serena said. "He only shows up inside unannounced when there's an emergency."

"That sounds a little easier to deal with," Haven said.

"I do appreciate his courtesy, that's for sure," Serena said. "So how about dinner? I could use the company."

"That would be great," Haven said. "Thank you."

"Give me a little time to get settled and organize everything, and make yourself at home," Serena said.

"Thank you, very much," Haven said.

"Navigators and Voyagers alike shouldn't starve themselves," Serena replied with a wink, before heading into her kitchen.

Haven had no reply at the mention of Voyagers, wondering what new revelations would be forthcoming. Knowing the things Christopher had demonstrated, she could not help thinking about the wonders Serena might be harboring.

Sitting back in the couch, Haven let out a sigh. Knowing all the answers would not be given at once, she had to restrain her impatience.

Before long, the apartment filled with a pleasant aroma. Provoking a watering in her mouth, the scent tugged at her own appetite.

Though she wanted to press Serena for more answers, she sensed that enough had been covered for one day. A good dinner would have to suffice for the time being. In light of the delicious soft drink, Haven suspected the food would be magnificent.

Above all, though, she had gained a chance to develop another new friend. That alone filled her with gratitude.

Smiling to herself, she looked forward to her next interaction with the Artist, Christopher Brendan.

Jaelynn

After seeing Gabriel in such a buoyant mood around Dr. Swedenborg, his current disposition made Jaelynn uneasy. With his lips pressed tight and jaws taut, he glowered in silence from where he sat across from her in the booth.

The cafe had a light crowd at the present moment, affording them a small degree of privacy.

"Another one, just removed them outright from the VR channels," Gabriel said, shaking his head.

"Nothing can be done about it," Jaelynn said.

"Any show close to making any sense is shut down," Gabriel said. He grinned, but no joy could be found in the expression.

"I hadn't seen that one yet," Jaelynn said.

"Nobody in this technate can live without subsidies. Nobody can do anything, anymore, unless you are in the Northern Sector," Gabriel said, the anger building in his voice. "Want to start any kind of organization or venture? A wall of permits, mandates, regulations, and even if you get by all that, they'll just shut you down without recourse if you don't fit their narrative."

"Gabriel," Jaelynn said, her voice filling with apprehension. She raised her eyes in a gesture toward the sensors engaged in surveillance of the cafe.

The same as those on the streets outside, the sensors collected audio and visual information, in addition to scanning the implanted identification tags of every patron and employee in the cafe. Government mandate had extended surveillance to the interior of businesses, citing that there stood a public interest, since anyone from the general population could access a business site.

"Yeah, I know, I know" Gabriel said irritably, glaring toward the sensors. Sarcasm flowed through his words, adding, "Keeping us safe, right?"

"Let me get another coffee," Jaelynn said, hoping that a few moments to himself would help Gabriel calm his frustration.

Standing up, she slipped on her MR glasses and made her way over to the counter. Making her choice, and relieved to know she still had authorization for one more refill, she awaited the automated system to process her request and deliver a full cup of hot coffee. Just as her credits and balance were listed on the projection before her eyes, everything went blank.

A few muttered curses and audible sighs emitted from the patrons around her. Everyone knew what was coming. Turning, and looking out the broad windows into the street, she watched everything but the security drones roll to a halt.

A few seconds later, the lights went out.

Everything would be shutting down across the technate, save for the security infrastructure. From personal devices to public utilities, everything would grind to a halt.

Called a Reminder, the planned instances occurred a few times a year.

The technate government stated that the purpose of the periodic shutdowns was to remind the populace of everything made possible with the stability of the Greater Good Doctrine. To her eyes, the incidents were stark reminders of the power of the government to shut everything down if it wished to.

She took her glasses off, not wanting to see the VR broadcast that would be taking over all accessible channels. She had viewed and listened to the forthcoming explanation enough times already.

Giving a shrug, she returned to the booth, sitting down with Gabriel to wait out the Reminder. As she expected, a dark scowl covered his face.

"Lovely, isn't it?" he remarked. "Just letting the sheep know who's in charge."

"Not everything is shut down, you know that," Jaelynn said hurriedly, knowing that the security apparatus never ceased its watch.

Gabriel clenched his fists, staring out the windows. A police drone cruised by the civilian vehicles idle in the middle of the road. He closed his eyes for a moment, his chest heaving with a deep breath.

"Would love to see those all roll to a halt, and all their cameras go dark, and maybe then we could go beyond the walls of this prison and live where we want to," Gabriel said in a wistful air. "I read about a really nasty place called hell in the religions of the old histories. I can say, without a doubt ... to hell with all of them."

"That's enough, Gabriel," Jaelynn said, an edge to her voice. "Stop it."

He looked back to her, gazing into her eyes for a moment, and then nodded. "Okay, I know. I'm sorry. I get carried away sometimes. But all of this is just wrong. Very wrong. And I'm not about to take meds just to cover that up."

Jaelynn looked at the faces around her and did not need to ask a single person to know that everyone in the cafe felt the same way that Gabriel did. Only fear kept everyone else silent and compliant; and fear was something he seemed to have much less of than other people.

Then again, most people availed themselves of the medications provided by the Technate Health Service, especially Balancers.

Jaelynn could not understand how he put fear aside without the use of medications like Balancers. A threat loomed at all times, to each and every person in the technate.

In an instant, the government could take away all her credits, and even her identity. It could bring the entire technate to a standstill, just like it was doing now. She wished things were otherwise, but reality could not be ignored or denied.

Looking out to the street, she saw the delivery vehicles begin rolling again, a moment before the lights came back on in the cafe. A few claps and exclamations of relief emitted from the other patrons.

"Let's try this again," Jaelynn announced, standing up to go make another attempt to get coffee. She slipped on her MR glasses.

"The high masters aren't known for doing back to back Reminders, I think you should be good this time," Gabriel quipped.

"Let's hope that stays so," she said, sharing his ire, but not his lack of fear. Giving him a smile, she turned to walk back to the service counter.

Cayden

Unseen and unheard, Cayden followed the two men strolling along the lakeshore. He found it difficult to focus on them, and not keep gazing at his surroundings.

A lake sparkling in sunlight spread to Cayden's right. To his left, nestled among some high trees, stood what looked to be a large residence fashioned out of timber.

Rising two stories in height, the facade held many large windows, indicating more rooms inside than Cayden had ever imagined a home being able to have. A railed balcony ran along the entire length of the second level.

A winding roadway led from the structure and disappeared into the hills ringing the area. Set near the house, a pair of vehicles had been parked. Both were luxury models, of the type that only those from the Northern Sector traveled in.

Though dressed in casual attire, the two men had a formal air about them. Both looked to be in their thirties, and not a speck of gray marred their dark hair.

Water lapped gently at the shoreline, as the two men conversed.

"We can give you extraction rights in a fifty-thousand-acre zone," the man to the left stated.

"Can I have a place like this?" the other asked, his words spoken with a far eastern accent.

"If you wish. I'd say you'll need some kind of residence for an ongoing project," the other man replied, with a laugh.

"Nothing as tranquil as this in my sector, back in Technate 29," the second man said.

Anger surging within, Cayden thought about how almost no one in his technate could choose to reside in even one acre. Fifty-thousand acres being casually allocated, the space being discussed covered more land than had been used to stuff a multitude of tenements and living quarters for thousands upon thousands in the confines of Technate Six.

The only way those such as Cayden could experience an area such as the one around him was through virtual worlds, holographics, or a trip to a public nature zone; the latter a rare opportunity for most.

"I will make certain your surroundings are like mine are here," the first man said.

"I would say we have a deal then," other man replied, extending his hand, a cheerful look blooming on his face.

The other man shook his hand firmly in response, smiling broadly. "That is great to hear. I will see that all details are taken care of, and I welcome you as a neighbor! And now, for a little celebration ... I have a couple of the latest models here. I think you'll find them extraordinary."

As if on cue, a couple of tall female figures walked from the front of the timber edifice. Both had short skirts, and tops that hugged the contours of their bodies.

Stunning long-legged beauties, the pair had flawless symmetry. They continued down from the home and made their way to the shore. They passed within a few strides of Cayden.

Looking into their eyes, Cayden knew at once the figures were entertainment bots, and not genuine women.

Both stepped over to the man with the far eastern accent, placing their hands on his shoulders and caressing him.

Looking between the two, he said to his companion, "You sure know how to celebrate the completion of a deal."

"Indeed, I do," the other man replied, with a broad grin.

Having had enough of the spectacle, Cayden willed himself back to the high overlook where Lilithian awaited him.

"Different rules for different people," his Guardian said, when he stood at her side once more. "Though it will not be classified as private property, the man you saw will soon have over fifty thousand acres of land to do with as he wishes."

"While the rest of us are all crammed into tall buildings," Cayden remarked.

"But it's all for the Greater Good, is it not?" she replied, with the trace of a smile.

"Yeah, much greater for them, and not good for most of us," Cayden replied, irritated.

"I wonder what would happen if their technology became crippled," she said.

Cayden noticed the intensity in her gaze.

"I imagine everything would unravel very fast," he answered.

"Yes, indeed it would," she said. "It would be much more than a Reminder, wouldn't it?"

Haven

Life did not stop its incessant march, even if new worlds beckoned. Haven still had to attend to her work duties, though she could not keep her mind from thoughts of Navigators, Serena, and new horizons.

Thankfully, the day's itinerary promised to be much more interesting than usual. A wide gulf separated the two types of destinations on the list.

The delivery vehicle first took Haven and Carlos deep into the poorest section of the technate, Sector Six; dubbed the Gray Sector by those who lived within it, and those familiar with it.

The nickname fit the sector's atmosphere well. Most of the inhabitants there dwelled within high subsidy apartments, the size of which made the small residences like Haven lived in seem palatial in comparison.

She could only imagine how many of the tiny dwellings were stuffed into the lofty towers they passed by. The looks on the faces of pedestrians ranged from brooding to hostile. With nary a smile to be found anywhere, the air itself seemed to carry a denser quality in that part of the technate.

The number of security drones in the air and rolling through the streets had increased significantly since her last visit to the area. Looking around the streets, Haven could not help but feel lucky that she did not call the Gray Sector her home.

The delivery vehicle pulled to a stop at the curb before the hundred-story tenement serving as their next destination. Stepping out of the vehicle, Haven craned her neck and gazed upward, noticing that even the overcast sky above had a drab gray hue.

She turned to help Carlos, while the delivery bot unloaded itself, with a new modular sleeping unit already mounted upon it. With Haven at the lead and Carlos at the back, they accompanied the bot through the front entrance of the tenement.

Using a larger capacity freight elevator, Haven and Carlos took the modular sleeping unit up to the fortieth floor. The apartment they sought rested about midway down the hallway.

They were welcomed at the door by a short, older woman, who Haven judged to be in her mid-sixties.

"Come in, please do come in," the woman invited them, offering a polite smile. "My name is Margaret. My husband and I have been looking forward to the bed replacement very much. It took a while for technate approval of a new one. Glad that wait is over. He'll be glad when he gets back this afternoon. He's at the bar right now. This early in the month, he hasn't used up all his alcohol credits."

Margaret rolled her eyes on the last remark. She then pressed to the side to allow them entrance, holding the door open. Haven stepped into the dwelling with Carlos and the delivery bot just behind her.

The narrow, rectangular space would only take a few strides to cross in its entirety. Haven kept her face straight, but inside she recoiled at the idea of two adults living within the tiny space.

A little bathroom, where a toilet and stand up shower occupied the same square space, with only a curtain to pull over for privacy, could be seen at the back. The next small section contained a sink, fabricator unit, and a few kitchen elements. The walls contained shelving alcoves for storage, continuing the pattern of utilizing every last smidgen of space.

The bed panel lowered from the wall to the left. When raised, a panel with a flat surface, serving as a dinner table, could be lowered from the right side of the room. The interior space miniscule, Haven continued wondering how two people could live every day within such a cramped place, without being driven to madness.

Loud voices from the floor below and music from the floor above converged in the little room. Haven could only imagine how things could get, when more people were in their residences.

"At least it is quiet on this side," Margaret said, gesturing to the wall on Haven's right. "Not occupied at the moment. Probably won't be for a little while longer, if we're lucky."

Embarrassment flooded Haven, realizing that the woman had caught her attention on the adjacent floors. She mustered a friendly smile, though her eyes carried a hint of sadness.

"All the same, I miss the lady who had been there the most," Margaret continued. "She qualified for Elected Transition with the Federal Health Services and chose that option."

The news cast an even darker pall over the moment. Elected Transition applied to situations where a person facing an illness leading to death untreated could choose to avoid treatment altogether.

Drugs to give comfort were supplied to the person, allowing the affliction to take its course. If drugs proved ineffective for pain, the person in Elected Transition could choose to avail themselves of assistance to accelerate the process; even to the point of immediacy.

Among the elderly, the number of individuals choosing Elected Transition had increased considerably over recent years. Haven had seen more than one relative decide to depart the world through that route.

Individuals choosing that route were praised for thinking of others, and not being a burden on resources and energy. But Haven had never seen Elected Transition in a good light. Every instinct within her told her that it reflected something deeply wrong.

"I'm sorry to hear that," Haven said, in a low voice.

The woman shrugged. The sarcasm in her voice could not be missed as she said, "I'm so surprised she chose not to fight the cancer, even if the odds of beating it were slim. Who in their right mind would want to miss all this opulence and excitement most of us experience every day?"

The laugh that followed sounded far more bittersweet than humorous. Haven mustered a polite laugh along with the woman but found herself at a loss for any other response.

"Maybe if we lived in the Northern Sector we would have a life worth fighting for," the woman continued, after a moment. She displayed a forced-looking smile. "But there I go again. Just an old lady complaining, when you young ones have your whole lives ahead of you."

Looking at the apartment, and hearing about the choice of the lady's neighbor regarding Elected Transition, did nothing to buoy Haven's hopes about growing old in the technate. If she ever found herself living in such a situation, she had to admit that Elected Transition might not sound so bad, after all.

Then again, that kind of thinking likely reflected what the ruling authorities desired when it came to the elderly populace. Their expiration deemed another contribution to the Greater Good, additional resources and energy could be allocated to more productive, and efficient, uses.

Taking her mind from the dismaying thoughts, she put her attention to finishing the job at hand. Working alongside Carlos, they first removed the old bed panel, dispatching the bot to take it out for disposal before installing the new unit.

A modular system offered no major hurdles, and the task went smooth enough. Before an hour had passed, they were finished with the installation. After exchanging pleasantries with Margaret, they proceeded back down to the street level.

A melancholic feeling pervaded Haven when she and Carlos stepped back into daylight. At least the clouds had started to break up, allowing pools of sunlight through. Haven rubbed her right elbow as they walked, having bumped it hard when fitting the new bed panel into the wall slot.

"Collect another bruise?" Carlos asked.

"We'll see how much of one by tomorrow," Haven replied. "And there's still time for another today. Maybe more than one."

Carlos grimaced. "We should have worked much slower."

"Things are what they are," Haven said, feeling the light throb in her arm.

"So, what's next?" Carlos asked, they neared the vehicle. Ahead of them the bot switched from wheels to legs, and climbed aboard, into the open cargo bay. "You can mark that one down as finished."

"A day of extremes, but this one should be much less sore on the eyes," Haven answered. "You aren't going to believe it, but the next delivery is going to take place in the Northern Sector."

Carlos stared at her. "You are kidding, right?"

Haven grinned at the look on her friend's face. "Not in the least. Check the itinerary yourself."

"You know me, I just get in and go wherever it takes us," Carlos said. "But this is a surprise. Never been to the Northern Sector."

"Well, we're about to go," Haven said. "I'd expect to be treated like an outsider, which we are to them, but we're going to have an opportunity to see how the luckiest ones among us live."

In a wistful tone, Carlos remarked, "Ah, the lottery of life.

You gotta love it."

"I really have no love for it at all," Haven replied with a sour edge. "Makes a big difference who you are born to in today's world."

"Do you know who we are going to see? Anyone famous or important?" Carlos asked.

"They're all important, or they wouldn't live there," Haven quipped.

"That's true," Carlos said. "But do you know much about who it will be?"

"Let's find out as we ride," Haven said.

The two got into the vehicle and slipped their MR glasses on. Before the delivery vehicle had pulled from the curb they both stood together facing Walter in the virtual replication of his office.

"You two were quick with the first stop," Walter said. "Impressive."

"Not an uplifting place to be, probably motivated us to get done much faster," Haven said. "But it did go very smooth. Client was really nice."

"It's why they call it the Grey Sector, a depressing place for sure," Walter commented. "With all the unrest in the air, its probably even more suffocating to be living there these days."

"Saw a lot more security this time, that's for sure," Carlos said.

"I see you are en route to the second location," Walter said.

"We are," Haven said. "And while we are riding, we figured we'd ask you about who it is we're seeing. Carlos is curious."

"I don't know much," Walter replied. "But as far as I know, you will be going to the home of a major corporate executive, who along with his wife have recently undergone Ascension."

"Never met anyone who has Ascended before," Carlos said. "Just heard about it."

"I've always been curious myself about what someone who's Ascended is like in person," Walter said. "You two let me know. But don't forget, the days don't get younger, and you know how the regulations are. I still want to get this delivery done on time. Even without penalties, margins are razor tight."

"No worries," Haven replied with a smile. "How often do we let you down?"

"You have me there, the two of you are hard workers," Walter said. "A rarity. I'm a very lucky guy."

"Thank you, Walter. We will get this done on time, don't worry. Be checking back with you soon," Haven said, before exiting the virtual environment.

The streets of the technate came back into focus around her, outside the vehicle's windows. Easing back into her seat, Haven found it hard to believe she would be inside the Northern Sector that very day.

She wondered what the storied area would be like. She had never been inside that section of the technate, but plenty of talk and speculation took place in the social circles she participated in.

Rumors made many outlandish claims, but it could not be denied that all of the biggest celebrities, highest-ranking politicians, and heads of the most powerful corporations residing in the technate lived within the Northern Sector. Every person from Technate Six who had undergone Ascension came from that area. It could not be denied that the Northern Sector carried an elite connotation for solid reasons.

Haven had to admit that she shared Walter's curiosity about those who had Ascended. With so much talk in the public about Ascension, and what it involved, to have a chance to meet someone who had undergone the mystery-laden process interested her to a great degree.

Passing out of the Grey Sector, they entered the outskirts of

Sector Seven. Though still filled with tenements, Sector Seven had a much lighter air to it. Most of the people on bicycles or walking still had leaden expressions, but the decrease in security apparatus and cleaner streets took much of the tension out of the views meeting Haven's eyes.

Sector Eight proved to be about the same as Sector Seven, and Haven grew restless by the time they reached its outer boundary. When Sector Nine, the vaunted Northern Sector, loomed, the stark contrast with the other sectors gripped Haven's attention at once.

Sectioned off by a towering wall, the Northern Sector featured multiple layers of security. Upon reaching the outermost gate, their vehicle pulled aside for a full inspection.

A pair of security troopers clad in body armor directed Haven and Carlos out of the vehicle, while a small, hovering bot entered it.

Haven and Carlos were then made to pass through an encompassing body scanner, while their purpose for traveling in the Northern Sector was verified again.

While going through the process, Haven mused that it seemed like they were crossing the border from one realm into another. The heavy security being applied made her feel like a foreigner; and an unwelcome one at that.

Thinking about the analogy, she found that it appeared increasingly fitting. The world they entered in the Northern Sector was about as far removed as it could get from the world she woke up in each and every day.

Though lots of rhetoric bandied about regarding the equality of the people in the eyes of the law, the harsh truth could not be denied. The people of the Northern Sector lived under one set of rules; and everyone else another.

She did not imagine many of those residing in the Northern Sector ever felt inclined to choose Elected Transition, like the old woman's neighbor had. Rather, these were the people who had access to Ascension, and the tremendous life-extension that came along with it.

Once cleared and inspected, they were allowed to proceed onward. Beyond the wall, exquisite sights found nowhere else in Technate Six greeted Haven's eyes.

The first thing striking Haven about the Northern Sector was the abundance of open space, featuring lavish beds of colorful flowers and well-manicured lawns of a rich green hue. Beautiful, flowering trees dotted the grounds, adding to the captivating aesthetic.

Tucked away within the scenery, magnificent edifices marked the residences of those dwelling in the Northern Sector. Each one different from the other in their architecture, the variety on display astonished Haven.

It did not pass Haven unnoticed that the skies held little clutter in the way of aerial drones. At most, she espied a couple, spread far apart and high in elevation. A bit of envy welled up within her with the thought that those in the Northern Sector got to enjoy unsullied skies during their days.

A few kilometers into the sprawling landscape of the Northern Sector, the delivery vehicle turned from the main roadway. A narrow, winding road led through a grove of trees, and then past a fenced in swathe of ground that held several grazing horses.

Haven eyed the sleek, muscular animals with a sense of wonder. Savoring the opportunity to see real horses from such a close proximity, she wished they could stop right there, and get out of the vehicle. She knew that to be frivolous thinking, as the vehicle would not veer from its course, no matter what Haven wanted.

A little farther down the road, the vehicle pulled into a broad, circular driveway, fronting the entryway to an ornate, three-level structure. Three large, shining golden domes crowned the ivory-white building.

Haven eyed an outer, railed walkway lining the uppermost floor, running the length of the facade and disappearing around the ends. Everything about the stately place held a bright sheen, from the surface of crystal-clear windows to the walls themselves.

She could not believe that someone called the opulent building their private home. The delivery vehicle rolled to a stop at the base of the steps leading to the entrance.

The side bay opened and the bot got out, holding the sealed crate they were scheduled to deliver. Haven and Carlos disembarked from the vehicle and approached the steps.

She could not stop from gawking at the place while they climbed the marble steps.

A tall, exquisitely handsome man with an olive hue of skin greeted them at the entrance. He wore a dark brown business suit, ending in a shiny pair of shoes, of a matching color.

His curly black locks touched the edge of the snow-white shirt lying underneath the suit jacket, the former bisected with a golden-hued tie. Everything about him reflected the polished air of the entire place.

"Welcome to the Creassan Estate, I am Sebastian, the Estate Manager," the man introduced himself, in a formal, polite manner. "Mrs. Creassan has been expecting you. If you would follow me."

The double doors behind him opened wide, making no sound. Turning, he led them into the massive home.

Once inside the doors, Haven could not help staring at the great, multi-tiered chandelier, suspended over an atrium rising three stories in height, and encompassed within one of the golden domes. Beyond the atrium, to the right and left, two staircases flanking a grand archway circled up to reach second and third levels. Sebastian guided them through the atrium, across a floor of marble.

The cavernous atrium covered about as much space as Haven's family had for their entire apartment. She found her gaze drawn toward the archway itself, the facing of which held some manner of inscription, in lettering she did not recognize.

Beyond the archway, they continued through the midst of a living room like no other she had seen. Passing through the large space seemed like walking through another world.

Plush-looking couches, low profile, glass-top tables, ornate lamps, deep blue carpeting and statuary filled the space, much of it contained inside a sunken area a few steps down. The walls held an unbroken view of spectacular mountain peaks, cradling a lake whose still surface carried a perfect reflection of the majestic summits looming beyond.

The air carried a bounty of floral scents and the sounds of chirping birds. It seemed to Haven that she could step right out of the living room and onto the shore of the lake, though she knew the crystal-clear vision masked the walls of the room.

Sebastian then came to a stop. "Wait here for a moment, I shall return with Mrs. Creassan. Make yourselves comfortable."

Walking across the room, he exited through double doors on the far side.

"And how does all of this align with the Greater Good?" she whispered to Carlos, catching him looking around the ornate interior.

"I ... don't know," Carlos answered, after a few moments drifted by. His widened eyes reflected astonishment at the opulent surroundings.

She could not blame him for the reaction. The idea that anyone in the technate lived within such splendor staggered her. Nobody in her sector had any path to acquire the means to live in such a manner, save for the rare individual who became an athletic star or entertainment celebrity.

The doors on the other side of the room opened once more,

and Sebastian looked to them with a smile.

"If you would follow me," he said.

Haven and Carlos walked across the room, followed by the delivery bot. The doors led onto a covered, marble-surfaced landing.

Beyond the sheltered landing, the surface of a large pool in the shape of a crescent sparkled in the sun's rays. An arched walkway of stone crossed over the pool at its broadest point, bisecting the water in the direct center.

Set within an expanse of bright green moss, a pair of small, circular ponds glimmered on the other side of the pool.

A woman standing on the short bridge turned toward them, when they emerged onto the landing.

"Mrs. Creassan," Sebastian said in a low voice, bringing the group to a halt.

The woman strode toward them with a graceful step.

Haven's first impression was that she had never seen a more flawless appearance in her entire life. A brilliant white smile complimented facial features in perfect symmetry. Stunning jade eyes took in the sight of Haven and her co-worker.

The woman's lustrous black hair had been cropped in a style ending a little below her chin, with longer lengths at the forefront sweeping to shorter ones in the back. The silken sheen of her locks enhanced by the sun's golden touch, not a single hair appeared to be out of order.

She wore a low-cut, white blouse with a short skirt of a matching hue. Golden bracelets decorated her arms, and a diamond pendant hung from a necklace fashioned from thin, platinum links. Black leather sandal-shoes with lacing winding midway up her calves ornamented her feet.

Her skin exhibited no blemishes, looking smooth and youthful, even more vibrant than Haven's at just seventeen years of age. Tall and shapely, her body exhibited flowing, supple tones;

appearing as if she had been sculpted from clay with the hands of a masterful artist.

Haven had not seen one person living in her sector who could rival the woman's astounding beauty. For his part, Carlos stood speechless, the wide-eyed look remaining.

"Welcome to my home," the woman greeted them with a polite air, her voice melodious in tone. "What are your names?"

Having never met an individual who had undergone Ascension, Haven found herself at the edge of stupefied at her first encounter. Gathering her composure, she offered her hand in greeting.

"I'm Haven...and this is Carlos," she replied to the woman.

"You may call me Athena," the woman said, taking Haven's hand in a firm grip and flashing a dazzling smile. "It is a good day to be outside. May I have Sebastian get the both of you some beverages?"

"No thank you, we are fine, but I appreciate it very much," Haven answered, though she could only imagine what a place like Athena's had in the way of beverages and food.

"I'm sure you have a schedule to keep, but I want your visit to my home to be a pleasant one," Athena said. "Besides, I enjoy the company, with my husband gone on business."

"What...does your husband do?" Carlos ventured. He quickly added, "If you don't mind me asking."

"I don't mind at all," she replied. "He is an executive with Draco Systems. With them being the company that provides the software governing the identification chips we all wear, you can imagine the demands on his time."

The way she spoke carried a distinctive air of pride regarding her husband's firm.

To Haven, the explanation was unnecessary. Like anyone who lived in the technate, she knew about Draco Systems, one of the largest global-scale corporations.

Holding her tongue, she wanted to relay the thought perched on the forefront of her mind. Working for the company that made the operation of everyone's electronic shackles and ceaseless watchers possible represented nothing to be proud of.

Haven knew the Artist would have had something profound to say on the matter, but for her part she remained quiet.

As if catching her restraint, the woman fixed her with an intent gaze, and asked, "Something trouble you?"

Haven caught the change in the woman's look and knew the question had not been asked out of any concern for her well-being. She recognized it as a probe for a trace of defiance or discontent.

Mustering a polite smile, she replied. "No, I just look serious when I'm thinking. And I was thinking about how extensive a challenge it is to keep a system running that involves every single person in the technate. It's really hard to get your mind around it all."

The woman appeared to be placated with the response. Her expression eased, the look in her eyes softened, and a smile grew upon her lips. "I know exactly what you mean. My head hurts if I try to think about it long enough. Much has been achieved in population reduction worldwide these past few decades, but there are still well over 3 billion organized under this system."

Haven kept her expression pleasant, though she recoiled inside. She knew the reduction celebrated by Athena only concerned the kind of people who did not live in the Northern Sector; namely people like Haven, Carlos, and their families and friends.

"That is a lot of hardware too, running across seven continents," Carlos said. "Maintenance must be constant."

"Only six have full infrastructure, there's next to nothing to be concerned with in Antarctica," Athena said. She turned her gaze toward the crate being carried by the delivery bot. "I suppose I should be attentive to the reason you are here."

Walking over to the side of the case, she placed her hands on the latches. In response to her touch and attuned to her ID, the latches clicked open.

Athena raised the lid. From her vantage, Haven could not tell what lay within the dark crate.

Smiling, Athena looked back to Haven and Carlos. "Everything appears in good order here. A successful delivery. Convey my satisfaction with your service."

"I will, and thank you," Haven replied, nodding.

Looking to the bot, she instructed it, "Place the crate in Study Room One, to the right of main desk."

At her words, the bot set into motion, heading back into the house. Needing no guide, it would interface with whatever kind of Home Assistant Athena utilized and acquire the layout of the house.

"That will take a few minutes," Athena said. "Come with me and let me get you each a drink before you have to depart."

Striding past, she led them back inside, where they turned to the right and went through another set of doors into a lavish dining hall. Seats for at least twenty lined the long table, with another beautiful, multi-tiered crystal chandelier suspended above the center of the room.

Fashioned of wood, each of the chairs had carved floral designs on their backsides and tops, with velvet cushioning covering the seats. Gleaming sets of silver utensils and shining plates filled the table surface, arranged in perfect order for each place setting.

Haven had trouble believing her eyes.

"Is that real silver?" she asked, looking at the forks, knives, and spoons.

"It is indeed," Athena said.

Nobody that Haven knew owned so much as one object of

silver, much less an entire array of dining utensils. She could not begin to imagine the kind of meals hosted within such an environment.

Beyond the dining area they entered a kitchen that could house several of the size found in the average technate apartment. A large granite-topped counter stood in the open, and an arsenal of finely-crafted wooden cabinets and drawers lined the walls, along with multiple refrigerators, sinks, and a few different types of ovens.

"Prepare them a fresh glass of orange juice," Athena instructed Sebastian.

Walking over to one of the cabinets, he retrieved a pair of long-stemmed crystal glasses, and proceeded to one of the refrigerators. Clicking one of the beverage levers in its facing, he filled the glasses with juice, and then returned.

After a sip, Carlos exclaimed, "So fresh!"

Athena smiled. "As fresh as it gets"

Haven took a sip and savored the taste, far superior to the kind of juice she could access back in her sector.

"It is wonderful," Haven remarked.

Continuing to look around the immense kitchen, Haven took another drink of the juice while awaiting the return of the delivery bot.

"It would take me awhile just to learn where everything is, in a kitchen like this," she said, with an air of good humor.

"That's what I pay my chef Maurice for," Athena replied. "He knows every last centimeter of this kitchen, and how to use it at a high level."

Haven did not know how to respond, finding it incredible that a person could hire someone to just be a personal cook, within their own private home. People like Haven could not pay anyone, even if they wanted to, with the transfer of credits being so tightly regulated.

After finishing his glass of juice, Carlos asked, "May I use the bathroom?"

"It is through that door, to the right," Sebastian replied, pointing to another doorway across the kitchen.

Carlos excused himself, leaving Haven alone in the kitchen with Athena and Sebastian.

"We shouldn't be much longer, I don't want to disrupt your day," Haven said, hoping the bot would return soon.

"You are not disrupting anything," Athena replied. "I'm taking the day to relax, and I enjoy meeting new people. It is no trouble at all. If you do not mind me asking, what are your other deliveries like?"

"Some go very well, others can be a little more difficult, but I wouldn't say we've had any bad ones recently," Haven said.

"Do you meet some interesting people?" Athena asked.

Haven heard the probing undercurrent in the question.

"Often we do," Haven said with a casual air.

"I imagine dealing with so many people, you find yourself taking a liking to some and not to others," Athena replied.

Haven nodded, sensing the continuance of the subtle probe. "Just depends on how hospitable they are. You are one of our favorite kind of stops."

"I'm sure this sector is interesting enough, but surely you make some fascinating new friends in other sectors," Athena said.

Looking down at the juice in her hand, a nagging thought tugged at Haven. She wondered why a person of the Northern Sector would bother to spend so much time with a pair of teenagers from the general population.

A reason existed, and Haven suspected it aligned with the unease in her heart regarding Athena's curiosity about the kind of individuals Haven encountered.

Taking another sip from her glass, Haven looked back to Athena, and found the woman staring at her. They held each other's eyes for a moment, and Haven had a tightening in her gut.

For an instant, the woman's eyes appeared to be pure black, without a speck of anything human to be found within the icy gaze.

Haven looked over to Sebastian, but his eyes appeared as they did before. When she looked back to Athena, the woman's eyes had returned to their previous state.

"Is something the matter?" Athena asked, her stare continuing to bore into Haven.

"No ... I'm okay," she answered, the growing weight of the other's gaze bringing her further anxiety.

Carlos came back into the kitchen, his return bringing a welcome distraction. He looked over to Haven. "It's probably time we get headed back. Bot's done and on its way back to the truck."

Never had Haven been so relieved to be at the end of a delivery.

Mustering a polite smile, she said to Athena, "Thank you very much for the juice."

"Yeah, thank you very much for that," Carlos added.

"You are both welcome," Athena replied. A cold glint reflected in her eyes when she looked to Haven. "Perhaps I will see you all again, sometime soon. It has been good making your acquaintances."

Haven nodded and replied, "It has been good making yours as well."

"It has been a great visit," Carlos said.

Sebastian took them from the kitchen and showed them out of the house. The return trip went smooth enough, though they had to stop for another thorough inspection before leaving the Northern Sector.

While enduring the inspection, Haven watched a few luxury vehicles passing through the gateway. She observed that none of them were made to endure the kind of scrutiny that she and Carlos had been subjected to.

The people of the Northern Sector lived under a much different set of rules than everyone else dwelling in Technate Six.

Despite the prevalent beauty and luxuriousness inside the walls of the Northern Sector, Haven found herself glad to leave the place behind. Beneath the veneer of the Northern Sector's abundance, something rotten and menacing lurked; and Haven had gained a hint of the disease in the look within Athena's eyes.

Her heart told the truth of it. The delivery's location, and meeting Athena, had not been random incidents. Haven would have to take every step forward with great care.

Jaelynn

"I have zero interest in going to the game," Gabriel declared, looking irritable.

Over a hundred and twenty thousand people would be packed into the stadium at the center of the technate. Many more times that number would watch the game from the comfort of their homes, using VR or holographics.

Jaelynn had little interest in football, but professional games were a spectacular event to witness live. At the very least, it represented something different to do, instead of sitting around and doing nothing.

"It was just a suggestion," Jaelynn said, reading his expression and not wanting to aggravate him any further.

"I know, it's all there is to do," Gabriel said. "That, or holographics, or VR gaming."

"Seems like it," Jaelynn remarked.

He sat up and gave a shrug. "But who can really blame anyone? Why bother? Try to do anything, and you'll run into a hundred hurdles ... and that's if you are very lucky to begin with."

"Then what do you want to do?" she asked, wanting to change the subject.

He eased closer to Jaelynn, reaching out and pulling her

closer. Leaning forward he gave her a soft kiss on the lips. He parted their lips long enough to whisper, "Something real? Like kissing you?"

Smiling, she pressed her lips against his, and kissed him deeply. Without warning, the door to Gabriel's bedroom banged opened, startling both of them.

Encased head to foot in black body armor, faces hidden behind dark visors, a pair of security troopers tromped into the room.

Squaring their bodies toward Gabriel, both took up positions before him.

"Gabriel Adamson," the first trooper addressed in a deep voice. "You are to be apprehended and taken into Rehabilitation, for multiple violations of the Greater Good Doctrine. Come with us."

"Move aside," the other trooper told Jaelynn in a brusque manner.

"For what?" Gabriel asked the pair of troopers, a quizzical look on his face. "What violations?"

The troopers gave him no time to discuss the matter. Stepping forward, they bound his hands behind his back and stood him upright, ignoring his continued protests and questions.

Stunned at the development, Jaelynn finally mustered the courage to speak to the troopers. They had propped Gabriel into a standing position and were about to take him from the room.

"Where are you taking him?" she asked.

"He will first be taken for a psychological evaluation, and then it will be determined where he is assigned in Rehabilitation," one of the troopers answered in a cold manner. "I would advise you not to get into the same trouble as him."

"What trouble? What did I do?" Gabriel asked. "You can at least tell me that."

The troopers did not answer his questions. In silence, they

forced him to move forward, and exited the room.

More troopers were in the apartment when Jaelynn finally walked out of Gabriel's room, following several paces behind.

She found the rest of Gabriel's family huddled together in the living room, facing three armored law enforcement agents. Tears streamed down the face of Gabriel's mother, her eyes glistening with fear when she looked to Jaelynn.

The guards had weapons in hand and at the ready, the posture nothing out of the ordinary under the system put in place to protect officer safety. For men of larger stature, who prided themselves on toughness, Jaelynn wondered why they needed weapons and twice the numbers of the apartment's inhabitants to subdue a peaceful family; and detain a teenage boy.

She knew the answer to her own question. The display of force made a statement to everyone witnessing it; the Technate wielded overwhelming power and could never be resisted.

Jaelynn walked over and waited patiently, while one of the officers spoke briefly with Gabriel's parents. He informed them of the fines they would incur from their credits, effective immediately, for having a dependent that had been detained.

Watching the proceedings, Jaelynn remembered how Gabriel often mentioned how law enforcement had become little more than a revenue generator for the Technate. Every violation, whether administered by a robot, human, or other device, came with a cost; one that could not be protested or challenged, deducted in an instant from the account of the hapless individual who had run afoul of Technate statutes and regulations.

Everything that followed seemed enveloped in a deep haze. Watching the security officers lead Gabriel away, tears of frustration trickled down her cheeks. Prevented from following him by the three officers remaining in the living room, she glared at the invaders.

The officers maintained their place for a few minutes more,

until the rest of the family and Jaelynn were at last allowed to go about their own business. The officers trod out of the apartment, leaving a frightened and bewildered family in their wake.

Jaelynn knew where she needed to go. Expressing her sympathies to the shaken Adamson family, and giving Gabriel's mother an extended hug, she took her leave and exited the apartment.

Setting out from the tenement, Jaelynn focused on the bare minimum in her surroundings, making her way directly to Dr. Swedenborg's apartment. Masses of dark gray filled the skies, heralding rain, though no drops had fallen as of yet. A chill pervaded the air, the starker atmosphere proving fitting to her dampened mood.

Indistinct faces, cameras, drones and vehicles swirled into a fogged blur. Her thoughts far away, she could not have described much at all about how she got to Dr. Swedenborg's door when she finally arrived there.

"Come in, come in," he said, gesturing for her to enter, a look of concern coming to his face the moment he laid eyes upon her.

Sitting her down in a high-backed felt chair within his living room, he left her just long enough to get some tea. Handing a cup over to her, he took a seat in another chair close by.

"What happened? It's Gabriel, isn't it?" he asked in a low voice, leaning toward her.

Jaelynn nodded, her eyes tearing up at the mention of his name. "Security officers busted right into his room while I was there. They arrested him. Didn't even tell us why."

"He's clever, but all it takes is one slip up to run afoul of their system," Dr. Swedenborg said, frowning at her news.

"I ... I can't say it," Jaelynn said, thinking of the mandated sensors installed in residences.

"Remember, we can speak freely here," Dr. Swedenborg said

in a gentle air. "Don't forget, their eyes are blind and their ears deaf within these walls."

She nodded. "I forgot about that. Just nervous. It all scared me a lot."

"I imagine so, when a bunch of militarized entities invade the sanctity of a home," Dr. Swedenborg replied. "But there's nothing to fear, in my home. Tell me, what do you think happened that got them to do this?"

"He ... he stood against them," she said, still anxious, despite the man's assurances. "And they knew about him, somehow."

"I know he opposes everything they are ... we talked often, as you know," Dr. Swedenborg said. "Like I said, it only takes a few slip ups to land someone in their claws."

"What is going to happen to him?" Jaelynn asked, not sure if she wanted to know the answers.

"They will look to brainwash him. Get him conformed to their ... *Greater Good Doctrine*," Dr. Swedenborg said, speaking the last three words with an air of distaste.

"Nothing I can do about that, I can't even reach him if I wanted to," Jaelynn said.

"Are you so sure about that?" he asked, a curious look in his eyes.

His response evoked memories of the glowing Faerie, Sendinian, and the fantastical night that had opened her mind to tremendous possibilities. The Faerie had been in her dream, and then appeared to Jaelynn in her room while she was fully awake.

"Aha, so you do know something of other planes of existence," the old man declared, with a gleam of triumph in his eyes. "I can see it in your face. It's hard to hide it from your eyes, when you are thinking about those realms."

"It's all ... kind of hard to explain," she said.

"Understandable, it's not every day you find out that not everything is under the suffocating thumb of the Technate, or

Global Council," Dr. Swedenborg said. "They'd like to control everything, but they don't. Far, far from it."

"I know what I saw, but I can't say who was in control of what I went through and experienced," she said.

"Who's ever in control of anything?" he replied, looking amused. "I would say it would be pretty fascinating if the authorities suddenly lost control of some things, and the people gained control of others ... now wouldn't it?"

Jaelynn nodded, though she did not understand exactly what Dr. Swedenborg meant. A cryptic air surrounded his words, just like the mystery surrounding the nature of the projects Gabriel had been engaged in.

"So, find a way ... a way to help Gabriel ... and a way to help everyone locked within this glorified prison," Dr. Swedenborg said. Nothing in his face or tone of voice gave the slightest indication of jest.

"If I can, I will," she responded, meaning every word to the core of her heart.

"Perhaps you should sleep on it, tonight," Dr. Swedenborg said, the enigmatic air returning. "I have a strong inclination that doors are about to open for you, as they once opened for me, before any of this Technate nightmare had been set in place."

"Before the Technate?" Jaelynn asked, her curiosity piqued.

"I remember when the world just had cities ... and towns big and small... and even smaller communities, all across this land," Dr. Swedenborg said. He glanced away for a moment, and a trace of a smile came to his face, though the look held a degree of sadness to it. "Far from a perfect world, but a much better one without question. A world without technates."

"How ... old are you?" Jaelynn asked, hoping she did not offend him with the question.

"Perhaps a little older than you might think," Dr. Swedenborg replied, with a grin that told her he did not mind the inquiry.

"How much of the old world did you see?" Jaelynn asked, a multitude of questions forming in her mind.

"Enough to see the final stages, before this mess that everyone is in today took hold," Dr. Swedenborg said.

"Seeing all of that, and how things came to be ... that couldn't have been easy," Jaelynn observed. "I mean, you saw the entire world change."

"I did, and not for the better," Dr. Swedenborg said.

"What was that like?" Jaelynn asked. "It's said the majority of the population demanded the Greater Good Doctrine, to fix a world in chaos."

"That's one way of describing it," Dr. Swedenborg said.

"How would you describe it, then?" she asked.

"Howling mobs baying for the system that would soon cage all but the most powerful," Dr. Swedenborg said, shaking his head. "The hysteria in those short-sighted fools astonished me at the time, and it led me to take a deeper look."

"What did you find?" Jaelynn asked.

"Much more than I ever could have imagined," Dr. Swednborg said, looking somber. "I found answers and had even more questions. But I know my instincts were not wrong about what the powerful were herding everyone else toward in those days."

"Was that when doors opened for you?" Jaelynn asked.

"Yes, but it made it all the harder watching that final stage run its course," Dr. Swedenborg said. "Because I knew what lurked behind it all. Watching it proclaim victory made me sick to the core of my soul."

"What lurked behind it all?"

"That's a lot to take in at once, but the ones who are in control of the Technate, and the Global Council, are a good place to start," Dr. Swedenborg said. "They knew what they were doing. They were methodical, bringing their vision in slowly, over many decades. Doing it in gradual steps kept the masses blinded."

"What about the normal people?" Jaelynn asked. "What did they think of it all? Didn't anyone see what the powerful ones were doing?"

"No, the powerful played the masses like puppets, at every turn, especially when the realization of their vision drew close," Dr. Swedenborg said. "They divided them, they kept them immersed in mindless entertainment, they steered the things they focused on using the media they controlled ... and they guided the very education of their children. Sometimes what is not taught is more instructive about reality than what is taught. Divided, distracted, unaware and conditioned, the masses proved quite easy to control when the final blows came.

"The public became vicious toward anyone speaking out against the things that were happening. In an example of true madness, they served the purpose of those who enslaved them."

"Did anyone at all object? I thought life was difficult in those days for most people," Jaelynn said. "At least that's what they always tell us."

"Oh, it was a difficult time," Dr. Swedenborg said. "Crime rising, infrastructure crumbling, substances being abused everywhere, families fracturing apart, and most struggling to meet the costs of living. The masses did object to many things, shouting and railing, marching and sometimes even rioting. Yet they dutifully got in line and gave consent to the elites who orchestrated the path that brought all those terrible things upon them. Even worse, they were so blinded they condemned and persecuted anyone who tried to expose and resist those cunning elites.

"The masses devoured promises of security and feared the freedom they gave up for those empty promises. In the end, they had neither of those things. Anyone with a shred of wit can see that today."

"Kind of ironic, since they always talk about everyone having freedom today," Jaelynn said.

"Up is down, down is up, good is called evil, and evil good," Dr. Swedenborg said. "They also claim we live in a society of tolerance, but what they fail to clarify is that they just mean tolerance for those who fully agree with them. They're quite the intolerant lot toward anyone with another point of view. You could see that coming clear enough in the final stage."

"But even if we aren't free, aren't we at least safe in today's world?" Jaelynn asked.

"Are you really safe when every aspect of your life has been removed from your control?" Dr. Swedenborg asked, his gaze piercing. "Are you safe when disagreement with something, or someone, is deemed hate or incitement? When you can no longer call insanity, insanity? When you can no longer say up is up, and down is down? When you can no longer dispute a claim that two plus two equals five? That's really where we are today."

"I guess we aren't safe, not at all," Jaelynn said, recognizing for the first time just how unprotected the main populace was.

"And if you are not safe, what then?" Dr. Swedenborg questioned. "What should anyone do when they are not safe?'

"Try and protect themselves," Jaelynn said.

"That's what Gabriel and others have been doing," Dr. Swedenborg said. "Protecting oneself is a natural right. One of the most fundamental natural rights."

"And you?" she asked.

"I am no different from them, but I understand much more of the nature of the adversary we face," Dr. Swedenborg replied.

"Its nature?" Jaelynn asked.

"You have just begun to explore the nature of things," Dr. Swedenborg said. "I could see in your eyes that you are just beginning to perceive realities different than anything you knew before.

"That's not an easy road to travel, and I do not wish to add to your burden, but time grows short and danger looms. You will have to tell me what you have experienced, and I will do my utmost to help you on this journey."

"You are going to be my navigator then?" Jaelynn asked.

The old professor nodded and gave a slight grin. "Navigator ... a most appropriate word to use."

"I know I need some help with everything that's been happening recently," Jaelynn said.

"Then let us begin with what has happened to you," Dr. Swedenborg said. "And we'll go from there."

Jaelynn proceeded to relate her experiences with the Faerie, Sendinian, beginning with the strange dream and ending with the manifestation of the little entity within her bedroom. Dr. Swedenborg exhibited an intent look while listening to her account, showing no sign of surprise or disbelief.

"You've found favor with beings of the Transcendent, something we will discuss more in detail later," Dr. Swedenborg said when she had concluded. "That Faerie chose you."

"Why favor me?" Jaelynn asked, voicing the most obvious question to come into her mind. "I haven't done anything extraordinary. My grades are just above average. I'm not great at athletics or music. I'm not even one of the few girls my age with a job. Why would I be chosen for anything?"

"Why not?" Dr. Swedenborg said, a merry glint in his eyes. "Just because you haven't done anything that you think is extraordinary yet, does not mean you don't have the potential to do many extraordinary things. Everyone is capable of great acts, but most douse the fires of potential in torrents of doubts and fear."

"What can I do, then?" Jaelynn said. "I'm not from the Northern Sector. I don't have any influence or power like they do. I'm like countless others my age in this technate. I get up and live my life under a system that isn't going to change anytime soon. Tell me, what else is there to do?"

"Explore reality," Dr. Swedenborg said, in a matter-of-fact tone. "And see where that leads you. You might surprise yourself."

"Explore reality?" she asked, confused at the meaning of the question.

"The greatest trick played on the masses lies in the fact that their immersion into virtual reality turns them farther away from discovering the nature of reality itself," Dr. Swedenborg said. "You have a chance to see what exists under the surface, and what exists beyond the horizon."

Jaelynn could not help harboring a tinge of fear at the thought. She pursed her lips, growing tense.

A gentle smile came to Dr. Swedenborg's face. "It is daunting, I understand. But it is also a cause for celebration. You have a chance to see that the universe is so much more than they've ever told you before."

"Sounds overwhelming," Jaelynn replied.

"Isn't life already overwhelming, at times?" Dr. Swedenborg asked.

She nodded, thinking of the many days where she had seen herself trapped in a futile situation; unable to help her family, or achieve anything she wanted.

"Life's road is not easy to travel," Dr. Swedenborg said. "Especially at your age, when you are just beginning your path. It requires courage and willpower, and you have both within you."

"I don't even know where to begin, or what to do next," Jaelynn replied, a little nervous laughter escaping her.

"Learn more about the nature of reality, and then free Gabriel," Dr. Swedenborg said, without a speck of jest.

Jaelynn's eyes widened. "Free him? How in the world can that be done?"

"Find out what is possible, and then act," Dr. Swedenborg

answered.

She had no response for Dr. Swedenborg. Her thoughts a jumble, she took a deep breath, letting it out in slow fashion.

"I think we've covered quite enough ground for one day," Dr. Swedenborg said. "You have a lot to process. But before we conclude for the day, let me give you a token to reflect upon."

Reaching onto his desk, he picked up a small, clear square case and opened it. He took up a round, silver object displayed within. Holding it in his palm, he looked upon it for a moment, then raised his eyes to Jaelynn.

"Here, catch," he said, with a smile.

From where he sat, he tossed the object toward Jaelynn. Startled, she recovered fast enough to catch it in her right hand, on its downward arc.

Made of metal, the round piece had raised images depicted on both of its surfaces. The side profile of a man with an unusual hairstyle occupied one side, while the other displayed a building with what looked to be facade of several columns, with a small dome at the center of its roof.

"What is this?" Jaelynn asked, turning the object over again to look at the man, wondering who he was.

"In another time, if you worked for that coin and earned it, you could keep it," Dr. Swedenborg said. "You could give it to whomever you wished. You could trade it for something you wanted, without anyone recording what you traded for, or whom you traded with. If you chose to do so, you could save that and add more to it over time, to purchase what you wished. If you wanted to, you could even flick it into a pool of water and make a wish. It was not something that vanished at the beginning of the month, under someone else's control."

Looking at the inscriptions upon the object, Jaelynn asked, "Is this ... some kind of credit from the old world?"

"Not credits, but money, that you owned, that was yours to

do with as you chose," Dr. Swedenborg said. "I've kept that coin on my desk for a long while and found that it has come to be a symbol of what was taken from most of us by those in power."

"You could use it for anything?" Jaelynn said, thinking of the various allocations and categories of credits she had to deal with in making any transactions.

Dr. Swedenborg nodded. "If that coin was yours, then it remained yours to do with as you wished. You truly could use it for anything, save it, give it away, whatever you liked."

"Wow," Jaelynn said, staring at the shiny surface in amazement. "I wish credits worked like that."

"So would most under the yoke of this loathsome system," Dr. Swedenborg said. "But when the masses gave the very means of transaction over to elites who could control, monitor, tax, and even freeze their accounts at the touch of a button, they removed one of the final obstacles to subjugating the full populace. No person could live outside their system ... even if one chose to live feral in the wilderness, they did so in transgression of the new order, on lands the Global Council of Technates claimed full dominion over."

"And here we are," Jaelynn said, mustering a smile despite the ill feeling she had concerning everything described by Dr. Swedenborg. She could not dispute anything he had said about the modern world.

"Yes, here we are," Dr. Swedenborg said. "So keep that coin, think upon what it means, and begin to explore reality."

Dr. Swedenborg said nothing more about the matter, and their conversation turned to other things. He gave her some advice toward gaining a visitation with Gabriel and told her what to expect in the process. Though none of what he said about Gabriel's current predicament encouraged her much, Jaelynn appreciated the information.

About an hour later, she left Dr. Swedenborg's residence. Her mind taken up in a plethora of thoughts about the conversation with Dr. Swedenborg, Jaelynn's surroundings barely registered on her walk back home.

Once she had returned to her apartment, she paused to talk with her mother for a few minutes, before taking a shower and changing into her bedclothes.

Shutting her door and turning the lights off, she lay down on her mattress and eased under the covers. In a few minutes, her eyelids growing heavy, Jaelynn began to drift into slumber.

Thoughts of Sendinian lingered upon her mind when she fell into the arms of sleep.

Haven

A bright, cloudless day reigned over the technate, yet a storm coalesced upon the streets. Haven could see the tension brewing out the side windows of the delivery vehicle, as they made their way into one of the poorest sectors of the technate.

Not a word spoken within the vehicle, the attention of both herself and Carlos remained glued to the scenes taking place just outside.

People teemed on the sidewalks, and many had begun walking into the streets. Faces filled with anger met Haven's eyes.

Many in the swelling crowd were shouting, though what they said could not be deciphered inside the vehicle.

"I think we'd better pull over, until this passes," Haven said. "I don't like the looks of it at all."

"I think so too," Carlos replied, casting Haven a glance that showed his unease. "Never seen anything like this before. So many out in the streets."

Haven gave the vehicle the command to park. It responded at once, rolling over to a smooth halt along the curb.

Above them, immense tenements loomed; all of the buildings in their view well over two hundred stories in height.

Sector Six held the highest density of populace within the

technate, and also happened to be the one with the heaviest degree of support in subsidies.

Haven knew the dangers of Sector Six. With so few jobs available, Sector Six harbored an environment fertile for crime and many other kinds of abuses.

The unrest she now viewed stood very different from the usual crime in the area, which thrived in the shadows. The activity growing outside the vehicle's windows was transpiring in broad daylight and involved a sizeable multitude.

"Let's try to see what's happening," Haven said.

"Be careful," Carlos said. "We don't want to get caught up in this."

"No, we don't," Haven agreed.

With another voice command, the windows on the vehicle lowered just enough to let in the noises from outside.

Security drones were trying to edge through the throngs on the streets. Loud, authoritative voices sounded from the speakers mounted upon them.

Orders to disperse were repeated again and again, yet nobody heeded the directives.

From the curses, shouts and waves of chants, Haven figured out the reason for the growing protest quickly enough. Openly voicing their displeasure, the people most affected by the recent austerity cuts in subsidies gave vent to their anger and resentment.

Dread took root in the pit of her stomach. She knew the people had no authority from the government to gather in the streets. Every one of the individuals in the streets brazenly transgressed a host of technate regulations.

A response would be forthcoming from the authorities, and it would not be gentle. The best that could be done given the congestion in the streets was to hunker down and let everything run its course.

Within minutes, the orders to disperse began blaring from

the skies above. Pressing against the side windows and looking upward, Haven could see the shapes of several large security drones, hovering over the streets at lower altitudes.

Despite the presence of numerous aerial drones, the people in the streets continued with their protest. Many shook their fists and made obscene gestures at the drones, cursing at the top of their lungs in a raw display of defiance.

Like the outbreak of a hellish rain, the drones above and those on the ground loosed swarms of tranquilizing drones. The people targeted with the small, dart-like drones could not get away; no matter which way they tried running.

Coordinating with each other so that none targeted the same individual, the little darts homed in upon the implanted ID's of the people they selected. Locked on their targets, the darts moved like little missiles, adjusting their course at every attempt to dodge them.

Cries and screams broke out everywhere on the streets. People began falling to the ground in droves. In a few chaotic minutes, the massive protest came to an end.

An eerie silence fell over the area. To Haven's eyes, it looked as if hundreds upon hundreds of people were just sleeping on the ground.

A cold, clammy sensation passed over her in the aftermath, as a horde of security bots and other support drones entered the area and began taking away the unconscious people. Drone after drone loaded up with human cargo. New vehicles pulled in at a steady rate, the ones filled to capacity departing for their designated detainment facilities.

The bots paid the idle delivery vehicle by the curb no attention. Haven and Carlos had not taken part in the street demonstration. She had acted as expected of her by the authorities, in parking the vehicle, and did not trigger any kind of response from the security drones.

During the collection of the protestors, one of the security bots patrolling the ground approached the vehicle, sparking anxiety in Haven.

The hulking robotic thing loomed over the side where Haven sat. She looked up into its expressionless face, awaiting the bot's pronouncement.

Haven said nothing, knowing there was nothing she could tell it. The bot had already identified her, Carlos, and the vehicle, including their itinerary.

Mandated by regulation, the delivery vehicle had filed its destination and purpose to the technate's security network at the day's outset. Up to the moment it parked at the curb, the vehicle's every move had been recorded and stored in the technate's system.

"You may proceed with your delivery to unit two-thousand forty-five, in building four hundred thirty two of Sector Six," the bot announced, in the deep, resonant tone common to security devices. "You have authorization to travel, and your destination area is not a zone under a lock down."

Haven nodded to the bot. Without another word, the bot turned and strode away.

She commanded the vehicle to continue onward, to its target destination. Lurching into motion, the vehicle pulled away from the curb and headed at a slow speed down the road.

Breathing out in great relief, and glad to be free of the bot's presence, Haven was eager to get out of the zone under lockdown.

Easing back into the seat of the vehicle, she thought about what she had just witnessed. People steeped in misery and frustration had been shown once more that they could not defy the power that governed their lives every day.

Haven imagined that if she could see the Primordials, they would be salivating at the kinds of energies that would increase in the wake of the government's response. A harvest of frustration, despair and hopelessness would create a feast for the vile things.

A sense of despair dwelled within her own heart, even if she had awareness of what fed upon those energies. She did not see how anything could resist the heavy-handed control in place.

A multitude had been rendered inert in a handful of moments. The failure of the large mass of people would serve as its own deterrent toward those who had not taken part.

The thought made her angry. She wanted nothing more than to find a way to fight back against a system that weighed people down. She saw the evil behind every drone, bot, and surveillance camera much more clearly.

Any icy tingle passed through her, as she recalled the cold, black eyes of Athena staring at her in the kitchen during her visit to the Northern Sector.

The delivery vehicle pulled up at their intended destination. Haven got out and mustered a smile when catching Carlos' eyes, but a deep-seeded restlessness plagued her.

Haven knew that getting through the rest of the day would be a challenge; at least until she could make her way to Serena's apartment. Haven could only hope that the Artist would be dreaming and happen to be there.

Feeling ill-prepared, Haven sensed a growing threat in the air.

Cayden

Taking off his gaming helmet, Cayden walked across his room and peered out the window. Far below, and a good distance down the street, he could see a cluster of drones hovering above streets filled with ground vehicles and security bots.

He watched the security frenzy with great interest. Something major had happened. Cayden wondered what he had missed, but when he wore the gaming helmet no outside sounds could reach him.

Whatever had occurred, the event had concluded, or at least was under control. Nothing new streamed in the direction of the activity, while larger transport vehicles rolled down the street, heading away from the concentrated area.

The flexing of that kind of power could not have been over one individual, or even a handful. With the IDs implanted in everyone, a person could not run and hide. The ID would lead security elements right to them, with precise tracking.

Living on the border of Sector Six carried its own range of problems, namely that authorities seemed to allow a little more leeway in the poorest area of the city, with regard to violence and crime. Cayden knew it to be the reason he suffered beatings that no teenager growing up in the Northern Sector would have had to endure, beyond the first.

With all of the high technology used to cage the technate, Cayden wondered why the authorities allowed Sector Six to brim with crime, but he had no answers. What he did know concerned the reality that the place brooded and seethed with a darkened mood of its own.

As densely populated as his own Sector was, and lacking in opportunities, Cayden's own situation stood far, far better than the unfortunates living in the most heavily subsidized region. With virtually no employment, and living at the whims of the technate's authorities, the people of Sector Six lived in an atmosphere that cultivated a dangerous underground.

The lives of most people in Sector Six remained caught between the upper jaws of the authorities and the lower jaws of the streets. Desperation and resentment led to occasional eruptions, and Cayden suspected an outburst of unrest behind the high security presence he now viewed.

Cayden frowned, and a malaise of resentment came over him. The image of Dante flowed through his mind, embodying both halves of the jaws crushing the people between them.

Staring at the flock of drones in the air, anger spiraled within him, the longer he thought about everything. The security drones represented the forces stacked against him on a daily basis.

Anger becoming rage, Cayden chose to bring them down.

Centering his focus and putting all his concentration into the act, he loosed another wave of energy. He did not stop to think of whether it would be strong enough, or even have the range to reach the security cordon.

His answer came in the form of the drones' lights shutting off, as they fell in a metallic hail from the skies. The vehicles on the ground also came to a stop. Gazing upon the inert vehicles, Cayden knew the security bots in the same zone had stopped in their tracks.

Though feeling a rush from the act, Cayden braced himself on the window's sill. Extreme dizziness filled his head, and his body sagged from weakness, to the point that he would have slumped to the ground had he not grabbed the sill.

At first alarmed, Cayden fought off the tendrils of panic that sprouted at the sudden change within him. His action had sapped his energies, little different than the aftermath of extended physical exertion.

Remaining in place, he focused on his breathing, drawing some traction in his unsteady legs and gathering his thoughts. His head spinning, he lurched away from the window and tumbled into his bed. Rolling onto his back, he adjusted his head on the pillow.

Shutting his eyes and succumbing to the weariness pervading both mind and body, it took little time to fall asleep.

"It is time you learned a little more, Cayden," the Guardian's voice carried to him.

Though he could see her features, he found himself surrounded by a deep gloom. He could see no sources of light, despite being able to recognize the look of irritation simmering within the Guardian's blue eyes.

Seeing her displeasure, Cayden did not know what to say, and remained silent.

"That was reckless," Lilithian said.

Salvador

66 "Somebody did something ... and that somebody definitely wasn't me," Jade remarked, looking far more serious than Salvador would have guessed.

He thought that Jade would have been much more pleased in demeanor. A moment before, Salvador had suspected that the man had been involved somehow with the major upheaval that had just taken place in Sector Six.

A spontaneous protest on the streets in response to the austerity cuts in subsidies had been suppressed with great force. In the aftermath, an unknown technical malfunction had occurred.

The unexplained phenomenon resulted in drones falling from the skies, and all bots and vehicles on the ground becoming inert.

A riot had quickly germinated on the streets of Sector Six in the wake of the breakdown, requiring a massive response on the part of the technate to quell the fires of unrest. Before the responding security elements ended the second wave of upheaval, the people of Sector Six had poured into the streets of neighboring sectors.

The news of the extensive security malfunction could not

easily be spun or suppressed. Even the best technology could not offset word of mouth from direct eyewitnesses.

Images of shattered aerial drones on the streets of Sector Six girded the verbal accounts for a time, before the authorities had all video and images of the fallen drones scrubbed from the online networks.

Questions to technate authorities about the extensive malfunctions went maddeningly unanswered. No explanation had been offered through the official media channels; all of which carried an ambiguous statement about a large technical failure.

The extensive breakdown of the security apparatus was unprecedented. To Salvador's ears, all of it sounded like a highly-magnified version of what Jade had done to the aerial drone in the park, and the security bots in front of the cafe.

The fact that Salvador encountered Jade only a day after the incident had taken place drove his suspicions further. Not feeling like gaming in virtual worlds and wanting to escape the concrete jungle that he lived in every day, Salvador had gone to the park in his sector, to spend some time in the company of trees and grass.

Walking across a wide lawn toward his favorite, semi-secluded spot, he had found Jade strolling along the edge of the park's small lake. With his height, wide-brimmed hat, and dark clothing, the man stood out from the park's usual patrons.

Approaching him, Salvador had taken note of his pensive expression at once. Jade had acted as if he had expected to see Salvador, but the denial of involvement with the previous day's incident in Sector Six came as an unexpected surprise.

A flare of amusement came to the other man's face as he continued. "I can't say I didn't derive some personal satisfaction, thinking about the panic of the authorities when their precious gear failed to do their bidding. The looks on their faces must have been priceless when their fancy drones began dropping like flies."

"But if it wasn't you, then who could it have been?" Salvador asked, a moment later. "Do you know?"

The look of amusement faded from Jade's face. "That part is a bit troubling. I don't know, and that's what worries me. I only know that I would not have done something like that, nor would any of my friends. So, I can guarantee that it didn't come from anyone who is a Transcendent."

Though the mention of friends intrigued Salvador, another question burned brighter. "Why wouldn't you have don't that? Wouldn't that free everyone by shutting off their main control system?"

Jade looked reflective, pausing a few moments before answering. "It's about timing, and what kind of storms you set loose. Just because you can do something, and, on the surface, it might even seem the right thing to do immediately, doesn't mean you should. You always have to think of the consequences."

Salvador shook his head. "I don't get it. If you knock out their system, the chains are off. The consequences are that they lose control and people are free. Isn't that what you want?"

Jade smiled. "I like the spirit you have. Fiery indeed. Yes, breaking the chains they have placed on people is what I want, but the situation is more complicated."

"Then tell me how it's complicated, I don't understand," Salvador said.

"I know you don't have much experience with the wilderness, being cooped up in this technate your whole life, but I think this example explains it best," Jade began. "If you set a fire out in the middle of a dry forest, one plagued by a long drought, an inferno will erupt that spreads fast and out of control. It will rage with terrible ferocity, until it burns itself out.

"That's what would happen if you just shut down Sector Six, with nothing to channel the fires that would erupt afterward. It would be a destructive human inferno that would have to run its course. You saw a hint of that yesterday, as people spilled out of Sector Six into the surrounding areas. The veil between civility and chaos both thin and fragile."

Salvador's brow furrowed. "You leave the people suffocating endlessly? With all the crime there? Nothing to hope for? Just leave them trapped? I really don't get it, Jade. I know that isn't right."

"I didn't say not to ever shut it down," Jade responded. "It should be shut down, but an idea has to be there to channel the forces that would surely be loosed.

"I'm not talking about replacing one method of control for another. I'm talking about making sure there is a beacon for people to look to ... something to give them some pause in the heat of their emotions."

"What kind of idea is that?" Salvador asked.

"Something that can point them away from the Primordials and toward a path of Transcendence," Jade answered. "They've lived in the morass of the Primordials for so long it will not be easy to get many to see the path in the other direction. Some find security in their enslavement. Those will be the hardest of all to reach."

"Nobody wants to live like they do in Sector Six," Salvador said. "I'm sure few really want to live like they do in my sector, no matter how many times they tell us how great we have it nowadays."

"There are many other chains present in Sector Six that you have to keep in mind," Jade said. "From the substances that so many have turned to, to the crime that others profit from, and the power they derive from it.

"Then there are those who have surrendered themselves to the system as it is. They are resigned to letting it take care of them, because they are frightened of a world that does not make them promises of security and safety. You could open the doors to their cells, and they would choose to remain within them."

Salvador frowned listening to Jade's disheartening words. He found it hard to believe that anyone would want to continue living in the dismal environs of Sector Six, if given an alternative.

Though he could not understand what would drive a person to willingly remain in that condition, he knew that Jade's words resonated with truth. No matter how unhappy people seemed to be in his own sector, there were never any significant efforts to change the prevailing order.

Salvador figured that most people did nothing because they felt utterly powerless in the face of a pervasive control system. The removal of that barrier being the primary hindrance to the people making their own choices stood as the reason that he believed that an immediate shutdown would be the best path of liberation.

Yet the more that he thought about what Jade told him, the more he saw that things were not as clear cut as he initially thought.

"I can see by the look on your face that you believe at least some of what I'm saying," Jade said. He paused for a second, before adding, "And that you are having a hard time with the rest of it."

"Is mind reading another of your capabilities?" retorted Salvador, a tingle of unease rippling through him at the thought.

"No, I just understand how all of this might sound to you right now," Jade replied, with no trace of being patronizing.

Salvador shrugged. "I just don't see how anyone really wants all of this. Not just in Sector Six. Only the people in the Northern Sector probably don't want anything to change."

"And on many levels you are right," Jade said, nodding. "Just don't underestimate the power of fear and what it does to people. Fear is part of the Primordials' way. It is woven into the essence of Chronos, who mesmerizes so many into thinking that everything is just one, linear, inevitable and finite path. A beginning sliding to an unavoidable end in oblivion. The people who embrace that idea will do everything they can to scrape and hold their place on that steep slope."

"And others?" Salvador asked, not telling Jade that he had always believed life held a long descent into the finality of non-existence.

"Many know deep down that all of this ... the way people are living, the control, the surveillance ... is very wrong," Jade said. "When you've walked in darkness for so very long, sometimes you need a light to shine, to reveal another direction to choose."

"That makes sense," Salvador said.

"And that's what those such as myself are about," Jade said. "Yes, we want to be able to shut all of this down. This ... technate ... offends everything about the potential of each and every person. But we want to see a light shining for others to look to, so it doesn't become an uncontrollable fire of destruction."

Salvador took Jade's words in, sensing the great concern in the man. He could not deny that things had been spiraling out of control fast when the technology had broken down. People had lashed out, rather than remain focused and in control of themselves.

"So what about that event and who caused it?" Salvador asked.

"Whoever caused that breakdown is strong. Very strong," Jade said, looking away, across the glimmering lake. "They either did not know their own strength, or they are committed to a darker purpose. They set off a wildfire, as you saw. Imagine that spreading over the entire technate. That was no undertaking by any Transcendent. That, I am sure of."

Thinking upon it in that light, Salvador saw Jade's reasoning in a much clearer fashion. The eruption in Sector Six had been an outpouring of anger and resentment, with nothing of substance lying beyond it.

"So what are you going to do? Can you find out who did it?" Salvador inquired.

"We have to find out," Jade replied firmly, turning back to him. "Our situation is delicate enough. The Primordials are on the verge of consuming this world and the level it exists in. A great conflagration without anything to channel it would only hasten that calamity."

"Then it's important to put a beacon in place, just in case everything gets shut down again," Salvador said, thinking on the dilemma.

Jade nodded. "You're right. And that's the challenge. Because we don't know who did this, or how it came about, we have no way of knowing when it might happen again. It could happen in a week, or a day, or even an hour from now. If it happens on a much bigger scale, the consequences would be terrible."

"I wish I could help in the search," Salvador said.

Jade stared toward him, a somber look on his face. "I have to get you to a place where you can."

"Meaning?" Salvador responded, his voice carrying an edge of anxiety.

"It means that I don't have the time I would have liked to have, to introduce you to everything," Jade said. "It means that you have to make difficult choices much sooner than I anticipated."

"What do I have to do?" Salvador asked, not liking the sound of it.

"I have to show you how to become a Navigator, in a short amount of time," Jade replied. "We are going to need as many as we can get in the time to come."

Salvador could not shake the unease swirling within him. Much of what Jade had said made sense, and yet so much about it all still confused him.

"Life moves forward, whether we are ready or not," Jade

continued.

Salvador nodded, looking Jade in the eyes. "Believe me, I know."

Jaelynn

Voices raised in excitement and alarm surrounded Jaelynn. Trying to discern what caused all the commotion, she looked around with a little difficulty, the glare of a midday sun forcing her to squint.

The ground shaking, a loud boom filled the air. Flinching from the sound and looking to the left, her eyes fell upon the smoking ruin of an aerial security drone.

It was only the beginning of an unfurling scene of chaos.

Vehicles spun out of control, slamming into buildings, and other airborne drones plummeted to destruction on the ground. Several more explosions breaking out, Jaelynn stayed rooted in place, having no idea where to run with the maelstrom encompassing her.

Hisses, pops, and bursts of sparks erupted from the mounted surveillance sensors, up and down the street. The technate's extensive security apparatus unraveling everywhere she cast her gaze, Jaelynn could hardly believe her eyes.

Soon after, the streets began filling up with people. Men, women, and children alike poured from the residential towers onto the streets.

Looks of shock and amazement could be seen everywhere.

The swelling crowd milled about, talking in voices sounding anxious and fearful.

Then, a strange phenomenon occurred. Everywhere she turned, Jaelynn saw Gabriel moving throughout the crowd.

It looked as if he had been cloned and replicated a thousand times over. Wherever he passed, people ceased their conversations, and the looks of confusion faded from their faces.

Stepping into the street and moving together, a trickle became a stream, and then turned into a river, as the populace flowed along the thoroughfare. All headed in the direction of the Northern Sector, walking tall, thousands upon thousands strong.

Before Jaelynn could make any sense of it, the scene faded. She found herself standing at the edge of a broad meadow, on the cusp of twilight.

Winds rustling the knee-high grasses, the air's cool touch caressed her face. A tranquil silence reigned, easing Jaelynn's nerves.

"What life were you meant for?" came a familiar voice.

Sendinian hovered to her right at shoulder level, the faerie's light radiant and beautiful set against the violet hue of the gloaming.

"What do you mean?" Jaelynn asked.

"Maybe it would be better if I showed you," Sendinan replied.

The glow about the faerie surged, until it encompassed both Sendinian and Jaelynn. The light filled Jaelynn's vision until nothing could be seen of the meadow.

A new scene came into focus.

A majestic ocean reached to the horizons before her eyes. Soft white sands beneath her feet, Jaelynn stood at the edge of a beach.

The iridescent surface of the water contained hues unlike anything that Jaelynn had viewed in her life, including the most fantastical VR worlds she had explored. Like cascades of radiant crystals, waves crashed upon the beach, washing across the sands.

The skies had an ethereal, glimmering quality to them, with varying shades of blue shifting within the dynamic firmament.

Despite the great abundance of light, no sun could be found within the cloudless sky. Nevertheless, an embrace of comforting warmth, with the gentle touch of a mild, early summer day, cradled Jaelynn.

"Beautiful, isn't it?" Sendinian said.

"This is breathtaking," Jaelynn said, gazing in wonder. "What is this place?"

"Faraway," Sendinian replied.

Jaelynn could not take her eyes from the stunning vision. "This is the most magnificent dream I have ever had."

"A dream?" Sendinian replied. A merry laugh came from the faerie. "What you see before you is no dream."

Smiling, Jaelynn said, "I wish that were true."

"It is true," Sendinian responded, firm of tone.

Glancing toward the faerie, Jaelynn was about to make an argument when she noticed a young, dark-skinned man walking barefoot along the beach toward them. Standing about her height, his sleeves and pants had been rolled up, exposing a shapely musculature.

Drawing near, his face shined with a bright smile, and a kind look rested within his light brown eyes.

"Hello Jaelynn," he greeted. He looked toward the faerie. "And hello to you, Sendinian."

"Hello Jonathan," the faerie replied, beaming with a look of happiness.

"Have we met before?" Jaelynn asked, sensing something familiar about the man.

"Not in person," he replied. "But I've wanted to meet you, for a very long time."

His response confused her a little. "Why is that?"

"I would rather we had grown up together," he said, and for a moment a wistful look came into his eyes.

"I ... I don't understand," Jaelynn said, trying not to be impolite, but finding herself increasingly perplexed.

"I'm your brother," he stated, looking her in the eyes.

Her brow furrowing, Jaelynn did not know how to respond. She had no brothers, or even sisters. From the day she had been born, she had been an only child.

"I never left the womb of our mother," Jonathan said. "She had a miscarriage, about two years before you were born."

"She has never said a single word about it to me," Jaelynn said, in a state of disbelief.

"It is a heavy burden she carries with our father in silence," Jonathan said. "If you speak my name to her, you will see that what I say is true."

Jaelynn looked from Sendinian to Jonathan, shaking her head. "This is crazy. I know mother would have told me about something like this."

"Just ask her," Jonathan said, in a gentle manner. "I don't want to upset you, but you deserve to know."

"You will find that what he says is true," Sendinian added. "It will prove to you that this is no dream."

The revelation unsettled Jaelynn, but nothing about the faerie or Jonathan hinted of an ill intent. Her mind swimming, she did not know how to respond.

"When you see mother, ask her," Jonathan said in a low voice. "Her eyes will tell you what you need to know."

"Do what Jonathan says, and you will know the truth of it," Sendinian said. "It is now time for you to return to your world, but you and Jonathan will see each other again."

Jaelynn looked toward Jonathan, seeing the reflections of her mother and father within his face. His gaze brimmed with both joy and sadness.

"When you know the truth, tell mother I love her," he told her, the words conveying a sense of regret and pain. "I always have, and I wish that things could have taken a different course. Thank her for bringing me into life."

Jaelynn did not know what to say, but she could not let such a request go unanswered. She nodded to the young man. "I will."

The faerie began to glow brighter, the radiance expanding until it enveloped Jaelynn and filled her vision. When the light dissipated, she found herself lying back in her bed.

Heart pounding in her chest, Jaelynn sat up, looking at her surroundings. Sendinian was nowhere to be found.

"Some dream," Jaelynn said aloud, the sound of her voice calming.

Getting out of her bed, Jaelynn made her way to the kitchen and fixed herself a cup of water. Her breathing settled, returning to a normal rate, and she took a long drink of the cool liquid.

"Can't sleep either?" her mother's voice interjected.

Jaelynn walked to the edge of the kitchen. In the shadows of the living room, her mother sat reclined in her usual chair. Dressed in her bedclothes, she had a weary expression on her face.

"Not at the moment," Jaelynn answered. "Is everything okay?"

Her mother smiled. "Things are okay. No worse than before at least."

"I need ... to ask you about something," Jaelynn said, with an air of hesitation.

Her mother nodded. "Sure, but come in here, and sit with me."

Jaelynn stepped forward, taking a seat on the couch at the end nearest her mother's chair. She continued to hesitate, worrying about the effect her question might have on her mother.

"Go ahead, you know you can ask me anything, Jaelynn," her mother prompted in a gentle voice. Eyes narrowing, she asked, "Are you okay?"

Jaelynn nodded. "I'm fine, mom. I just have to ask you a question that might be difficult ... and I know you are going through a lot of stress at the moment."

A deeper look of concern came over her mother's face. "Nothing's wrong? Are you sure?"

"Nothing is wrong, I just need to know something, and it may seem like a strange question" Jaelynn said.

"Go ahead, ask me," her mother encouraged.

Looking her mother in the eyes, Jaelynn took a deep breath. "Did I have a brother named Jonathan ... a brother that wasn't born? A miscarriage? About two years before I was born?"

Her mother's look in response to Jaelynn's questions confirmed everything, beyond a flicker of a doubt. She did not give an answer at first.

Her eyes filled with tears that began trickling down her cheeks a few moments later. Every single tear testified to the words that followed.

"Yes ... and how ... how do you know that?" she asked in a low voice, beginning to tremble. "How could you know that?"

Jaelynn got up and moved close to her mother. Wrapping her arms about her, she replied, "I had a very powerful dream. One that seemed so real. A dream where I met him, in the appearance of a young man."

"I ... don't know how ... this is possible," her mother whispered, choking back heaving sobs.

"You could have told me," Jaelynn said. "You did not need to carry this by yourself."

Mother and daughter holding onto each other, her mother buried her face into Jaelynn's shoulder for a minute. At last, she looked up into Jaelynn's face, with tear-stained cheeks.

"It was a great burden ... one that only your father and I should carry," she said.

"Jonathan is a part of this family," Jaelynn said. "What happened was not your fault, or dad's."

"I know ... I know," she replied, a fresh wave of tears welling up. "But no matter what my mind says ... a void has been in my heart since that day."

Jaelynn could not imagine the pain carried deep inside her mother for so many years. Her words had opened the wound once more, but it had to be done. She hoped that bringing the matter into the open could somehow lead to healing.

Thought still wrestling with the avalanche of revelations about life and reality itself, Jaelynn wished she could comfort her mother that Jonathan's life had not come to an end. She wanted so badly to convey how vibrant and healthy he looked.

"It'll be okay, it is good that I know too," Jaelynn said. "I want to hold my brother in my heart."

Like a ray of sun breaking through storm clouds, a smile came to her mother's face. "I am glad that you feel that way. I can't describe how hard it was to get through that time."

"You had to be strong, mom," Jaelynn said. "You and dad both."

"I didn't feel strong, and I still don't," she replied. "I feel so beaten down."

"You've been strong, through so much," Jaelynn said, thinking of the present trials her mother endured. She realized she had come to a deeper understanding of her mother, allowing her to see everything in a much clearer light. "I'm sorry I didn't know this before. I would have wanted to be there for you, as you've always been there for me."

"Oh Jaelynn," she exclaimed, hugging her daughter tight. "I'm just a worn down, older woman who wishes she could make sure her daughter's life would be a better one than she had. And I know I can't do that. I can't give you the life you deserve to have."

"You've done everything you can, and it's up to me to do my part, too," Jaelynn said. "I can honor everything you've given me by choosing the right path for myself."

"What have I given you? Credits can't be given, and the technate assigned me this tiny apartment," her mother replied. "There's so little I can give, the way everything is."

"You give me love, you encourage me to believe in myself, and you encourage me to think," Jaelynn said. "Those three things make all the difference in the world, more than you might know."

"Thank you," her mother said. She looked downward. "These days, I often think I'm such a failure."

"As does about everyone living in this technate, if they're honest with themselves," Jaelynn said, stopping herself from going farther to explain that the sense of helplessness and apathy had come about by design.

"Sure seems that way," her mother said, looking back up. "Hard to feel confident about anything."

"Maybe things will change," Jaelynn said. "But you've got much more strength that you realize, mom. Hold strong."

"I'll do my best," she said.

"It's all any of us can do," Jaelynn replied, thinking of Gabriel, Dr. Swedenborg, Sendinian, Jonathan, and her parents. Then she remembered a promise. "And one more thing ... something I promised to pass along."

"Yes?" her mother asked.

"Jonathan said to tell you that he loves you, and to thank you for bringing him into life," Jaelynn said.

Her mother's eyes gleamed with fresh tears, but sorrow did not hold full dominion in the look she gave Jaelynn. A smile came to her face.

"If you see him again, tell him I've always loved him," she

said. "Tell him it is my honor to be his mother, and one of the two greatest gifts I have received in life."

Jaelynn nodded, and hugged her mother tight once more. Thinking of what had been lost, and what could have been, tears welled up in her eyes.

Like Jonathan, she wished things could have taken a different path.

Jaelynn

Looking across at Gabriel, sitting in the chair opposite her, Jaelynn stifled her dismay. His face carried no distinct expression, but his eyes conveyed a host of unpleasant things to her.

"I'm going through my therapy," he said in a leaden voice. "They've got me back on regular medication, a full array of Balancers, and it seems I'm making some progress."

His eyes gave the lie to any claims of making progress. Deep within his gaze, Jaelynn could see a raw anger boiling within him.

"Any word of how much longer you will have here in Rehabilitation?" she asked.

"Nothing definite, just whenever they deem me ready and fit to return home," Gabriel said.

She nodded. "I'm looking forward to that day. I've missed you a lot, and I know your family has been missing you."

"I've missed you," Gabriel said, with an air of sadness. "Very much."

Jaelynn smiled, though she had to blink back a few tears. "Hopefully it won't be much longer."

"Let's hope," he replied, his expression showing that he did not have much confidence in being released anytime soon. "Be sure to let everyone know I'm okay. I'm not allowed access to the social networks yet."

"I keep everyone updated on how you are doing," Jaelynn assured him.

The door to the room opened. Clad in the gray uniform of a Rehabilitation Center staff member, a young woman looked in.

"Time is about up for visitation," she said.

"Thank you," Gabriel replied to her. He looked back to Jaelynn. "Looks like I have to get back to my treatment."

Standing up, he walked over and embraced Jaelynn.

"See you as soon as I can," Jaelynn said, giving him a kiss.

"I'll be thinking of you until then," Gabriel said.

"And I you," she replied.

Gabriel looked back to her as he exited the room with the woman from the staff. Jaelynn stood in place, holding his eyes with her own until the door closed shut behind him.

Taking a deep breath, she gathered herself for a moment and then left the room by way of a door on the opposite side. Making her way through the crowded lobby, containing others waiting to visit friends and loved ones in Rehabilitation, Jaelynn collected her thoughts.

Her mood dampened from being in the Rehabilitation center, she put her mind to the promise she had just made Gabriel. She first thought of Dr. Swedenborg.

He would want to know how Gabriel fared, and Jaelynn needed the refuge that the man's place offered her. With so many things rolling through her mind, a chance to speak openly would be a welcome oasis in a desert of worries and concerns.

Spying an open seat near the center's front doors, she headed over to it and sat down. Putting on her MR glasses, she reached out to Dr. Swedenborg, wanting to see if he was home and would be open for a visit.

Instead of Dr. Swedenborg's image, the avatar of a beautiful young woman appeared in response to her outreach. Jaelynn braced herself, knowing at once that something was amiss.

"I regret to inform you that Dr. Swedenborg has been apprehended by technate law enforcement officers due to several violations of the Hate and Incitement section of the Greater Good Doctrine," the woman announced to Jaelynn in a formal tone.

The news stunned her.

"He's been apprehended?" Jaelynn replied, the words more of a statement of disbelief than a question to the avatar.

"Yes," the woman answered. "He is to serve an incarceration period of one year, followed by an undetermined period of Rehabilitation."

Jaelynn wanted to ask more questions about the situation with Dr. Swedenborg but knew further inquiries would not give her any real answers. Even worse, asking more questions could invite scrutiny upon her from the authorities. One small misstep could land her in the same predicament as Gabriel.

"Thank you for letting me know," Jaelynn told the avatar.

"You are welcome," the avatar replied in a polite manner, before fading from sight.

Removing herself from the virtual environment, Jaelynn sat still for a moment, adjusting to the shock of the terrible news. The weight of the development bore down upon her. Another person she needed in her world had been taken away.

Rising to her feet, she made her way toward the exit.

Registering her ID, the door clicked open at her approach. Jaelynn walked through and eyed the robotic attendant standing on the other side.

"Finished with your visit, Jaelynn?" the human-looking bot asked her in a pleasant manner. "I hope it was a good one for you."

"I am finished, and it was good," she answered, with as much politeness as she could muster. Reeling inside, she had no desire to engage in conversation with a bot.

"Don't forget that you can have visitations with Gabriel in a simulated environment, accessing them from the comfort of your home," the robot informed her in a pleasant tone. "You may wish to take advantage of that option."

"I'm aware of it," Jaelynn responded, holding back a few choice words she would have rather given the bot. "I just wanted to see him in person this time. Maybe I'll make use of that next time."

"Let us know how we can be of help, we are here to serve the citizens of Technate Six," the robot said. "Have a nice day."

"Thank you," Jaelynn replied, relieved at the conclusion of the interaction. She did not think she could keep up a polite facade for much longer.

Continuing past the robot, Jaelynn left the entrance behind. She came to a stop at the edge of the sidewalk running in front of the building.

Looking down the crowded street, a frown shadowed her face. Despair threatened to take hold of her.

With Gabriel locked up in the Rehabilitation Center behind her, and Dr. Swedenborg taken into custody, and no idea of how to reach Sendinian, an overwhelming situation faced Jaelynn. Her world had emptied of the main two individuals she now relied on for help. Only a non-human entity who she could not reach at will remained.

Heading away from the Rehabilitation Center, she concentrated on taking one step at a time, making her way down the sidewalk. The noise of the streets blending together, Jaelynn focused on nothing in particular beyond reaching her apartment.

The sidewalk could well have been made of fragile, cracking ice. The thinnest of barriers stood between holding up and drowning in freezing waters of despair.

Holding the pressing waves of negative emotions at bay, Jaelynn willed herself forward, the steps adding up. Eventually, she reached the tenement with the apartment she called home.

Though she had ridden the elevator by herself up to her floor countless times, the upward climb had never seemed as slow or lonesome as it did now. Her steps down the hall to her apartment door heavy and ponderous, she took a deep breath before entering.

Walking into her bedroom, Jaelynn headed over to the nightstand at her bedside and picked up the small, silver coin lying upon it; the one that Dr. Swedenborg had given her. Gazing upon its shiny surface, she thought of the kind-hearted older man, and what he had shared with her.

Sendinian and Dr. Swedenborg had opened her eyes to new possibilities and ways of looking at the world itself. Seeds of hope had sprouted within her, bathing in the sunlight of incredible revelations about the nature of reality itself.

Jaelynn had not anticipated seeing everything fall under the gray skies of uncertainty so soon. Ill-prepared, and on her own, she could not see a path through the fog brought on by the terrible developments.

A wave of fear gripped Jaelynn, a part of her wondering when the authorities would come for her. To her eyes, in light of her associations with Dr. Swedenborg and Gabriel, it stood only a matter of time. Technate authorities could not fail to know her close relationship with Gabriel, and her visits with Dr. Swedenborg.

Closing her palm about the metal coin, she squeezed it tight, and closed her eyes, a couple of tears escaping down her cheeks. Kicking her shoes off, she lay down upon the bed.

Drifting off to sleep, and still clutching the coin in her hand, she tried not to think about the myriad of worries and fears plaguing her. It took some time for fatigue to prevail over the storm within her mind, but at last it overcame her, mercifully taking her into the depths of unconsciousness.

Salvador

"What kind of dream is this?" Salvador exclaimed, captivated by the magical scenery spread before his eyes.

Jade stood close at Salvador's right side. "Pay close attention and let me know what you think of all of this."

Night reigned over the incredible vision, and no less than three moons could be seen in the cloudless, starry skies above. All of them shone bright and full, though not even one of the orbs was needed to see for a fair distance.

A wonder world filled with phosphorescent glows of a variety of blue shades reached to the far horizons.

Strange, colossal tree-like growths, set well apart from each other, loomed over a sea of waist-high grasses.

With trunks so broad it would take many people with outstretched arms to wrap around, the tree-like growths each rose a few hundred meters. A network of branches radiating from the trunk near the top supported a circular swathe of foliage resembling the shape of a mushroom.

From the base of the trunk to the apex high above, the tree-like growths gave off a light blue glow, the latter brightest on the branches supporting the canopy of foliage.

Shimmering whenever a breeze passed through, the grasses covering the ground level had a deeper blue color to the glow about them.

Small blue-green lights hovered, drifted, and darted through the air. Flying at levels just above the tips of the grass sea and reaching up to heights near the undersides of the foliage atop the tree-like structures, the lights numbered in the thousands.

A few of the lights ventured close enough that Salvador could see what they were.

"What in the world?" he whispered, eyes widening in surprise and amazement.

"I suppose you can name them, if you'd like to," Jade said.

The creatures looked to be a hybrid kind of entity, combining features of a bird, insect, and a humanoid.

Elongated in body, each of the creatures had six appendages. The front pair ended in tiny, human-like hands, while the rear sets resembled those of an insect.

Translucent and filled with a network of brighter-glowing filaments, three pairs of wings sprouted from their segmented bodies.

The heads of the creatures had a lengthy profile, with deep-set eyes of a crystalline appearance. Beyond a pair of nostril slits, a long, curving beak extended outward, ending in a sharp point.

Though many passed close enough that Salvador could have reached forth and snatched one out of the air, the little entities paid no heed to him or Jade.

"I can't think of any name that would sum these things up in the right way," Salvador said, fascinated. "Do they not see us here?"

"We're just observers, unseen and of no disturbance to their environment," Jade replied.

"Might be a good thing, those little beaks look like they could hurt more than a bee's sting," Salvador replied.

"Very much so," Jade said, laughing.

"What a dream world this is!" Salvador said.

"Dream is not the right word to apply to all of this," Jade answered.

"I don't get it," Salvador said, glancing at Jade.

Jade gave him a wink. "Keep watching."

A few moments later, sharper chittering filled the air.

The sprawling multitude of little flying creatures had a swift reaction to the swelling noise. Most descending into the swaying grasses, others headed fast toward the foliage canopies atop the tree-like structures.

A cluster of much larger flying creatures came into view, speeding down from the upper heights toward the sea of grass. Like everything else in the area, the incoming creatures had a solid glow about them, theirs being of a turquoise hue.

Broad of wing, the newcomers lowered pairs of long legs ending in wide, protracted sets of claws. Steadying out their flight near the top of the grasses, the creatures dipped their claws and raked through the deep blue stalks.

Within moments, one lifted back up, a wriggling, caterpillar-like creature clutched tight within its claws.

One after another, others among the flock of predators lurched back toward the skies with similar prey ensnared.

A couple of them flew to within a handful of paces from the place where Salvador and Jade stood. Like the little entities, neither showed any reaction to their presence. Nevertheless, Salvador had a wave of anxiety pass over him as he gained a better view of their appearance.

Opening their long jaws, lined with sharp, needle-like teeth, the predators continued to give off the strange, higher-pitched sounds.

Not all of the hunters took their prey along with them. Right after snatching one of the caterpillar-like things, one flung its victim into the air. Snapping it out of the air using its jaws, the predator gobbled down its catch entirely within seconds.

The wave of predators left the area, all having been successful in procuring a meal from the sea of grass. Salvador watched them climbing back into the skies, their forms dwindling lights until they finally passed out of sight.

Not long after the larger predators had passed through, the smaller entities reemerged, taking to flight and filling the air once more.

Explosions of light broke out above, surrounding each of the foliage canopies atop the towering trunks. Resembling massive bursts of sparks, of a hue so light blue they could almost be deemed white, innumerable points of light radiated outward from each of the tree-like growths and began spreading.

The six-winged creatures hastened into the midst of the expanding clouds of light, spurring the latter into even faster movement. Within a short time, the entire area teemed with a dazzling mixture of flying lights.

For every one of the beaked entities, there were hundreds of the new ones, and after a short while the frenzy of movement died down. Salvador eyed a few of the beaked ones carrying off prey of their own, descending into the grasses. Soon, only the tiny entities remained in the air, their numbers so great it seemed as if a glowing mist had draped over the grass sea in every direction.

The masses of tiny entities encompassing Salvador slowed in their movements, and he finally gained a good look at them.

Each had round heads with large, bulbous eyes. Short and stocky of body in proportion to their wings, they drew into a hover, as if in expectation.

What they awaited did not take long to manifest.

All throughout the grasses, a brilliant host of blooms unfurled, a breathtaking sight that mesmerized Salvador at once. Opening to the skies, the petals of each blooming surrounded a gleaming, sparkling core spheroid in form.

Alighting on the center of the vibrant flowers, the tiny creatures crawled around the surface. Pulsing and turning a deeper shade of blue, they exhibited a noticeable expansion in body.

After a few moments, the flowers themselves began to surge in luminance, taking on lighter shades of blue.

Watching the changes, Salvador could see a symbiotic relationship between the creatures and the flowers not too different from that of bees in his own world.

Taking flight and having twice the luminance of their kind that had not yet attended to a flower, the creatures headed back toward the tree-like structures they had come from.

After a while, the activity began to settle. A few of the tinier creatures still roved the grasses and sought out flowers, but for the most part the environment quieted. Even the flowers began to close up and lower into the grasses.

"Wow," Salvador exclaimed, looking out over the tranquil scene, the grasses swaying gently in the light breezes. "Just incredible."

"It always is for me too, even though I've witnessed this several times," Jade said.

"Probably good they couldn't see us," Salvador said. "That's one swarm you couldn't escape. Their numbers are mind-blowing to think about."

"No, we couldn't escape something like that," Jade replied, grinning. "Also, be glad your physical body was not here, or you would have found you could not breathe the air in this world."

"We caught them at feeding time, that's definite," Salvador said, grinning. Then he paused, thinking about the words Jade had used. "This world?"

"Correct, this world," Jade said. "Not another plane of existence. This is on your plane of existence."

"So where is this place, or world?" Salvador asked.

"A part of your own universe," Jade stated. "A Navigator can go into the worlds of the subconscious, realms of different states of existence, and realms within the same state of existence."

"I'm on another entire planet right now?" Salvador questioned. "One that a spaceship could reach?"

Jade nodded. "Yes, though they don't have the kind of technology capable of reaching this distance in any reasonable amount of time."

"So we are exploring a world that spaceships would take ridiculously long to reach," Salvador responded.

"That's exactly right," Jade said. "It's important for you to understand all aspects of a Navigator, and what's possible in traveling the paths of reality."

"I don't know where to begin," Salvador replied, astounded.

"Once I didn't know where to begin either, it's perfectly okay to feel like that," Jade said, giving him a smile.

"I sure hope it all makes more sense, or my brain is going to explode," Salvador said, grinning, though his words were not entirely in jest.

"It will," Jade replied in a reassuring manner. "Just takes a little time."

"Okay, then what's next on my crash course?" Salvador asked.

"This is enough to process for now, even on a crash course," Jade said. "Take a break for the moment. I intend to demonstrate to you the kind of power that a Navigator can wield in various realms of reality, and I also want to show you why all the effort, sacrifice, and trials are worth it. One visit to Faraway will make that clear to you. Faraway is a place that must be experienced for you to understand."

"Can we go there now?" Salvador asked, sensing something very unique about the place, just from the tone Jade had when speaking of it. "To Faraway."

"Very shortly," Jade said. "For now, think about what you've just seen. Wake up in your body, back in your bedroom."

The mention of his physical body catalyzed Salvador's return. No matter how much he wished to keep viewing it, the spectacular world blurred and faded out of sight. Everything ebbed to black, and then he opened his eyes, seeing the familiar surroundings of his bedroom.

His mind swirling with the astonishing experience he had undergone, Salvador lay quietly, thinking about the notion that he had just been somewhere in the farther reaches of the universe. The notion staggering to his mind, he pondered what Jade had told him.

A Navigator could travel realities of all kinds, including the subconscious, other planes of existence, and even within the universe where Salvador lived in a physical sense. The idea beckoned with infinite possibilities.

He wondered about the things Jade would be showing him in the near future; the abilities of a Navigator, and a mysterious place called Faraway.

Salvador wished he had not been made to return to his bedroom. The continuation of his journey could not come a moment too soon.

Jaelynn

A radiant burst of light to the right of Jaelynn announced the arrival of Sendinian. The winged figure hovered at about eye level, gazing upon her.

"Hello again," Jaelynn greeted the faerie, relieved to see the small creature. "I am so glad to see you."

A dream version of Technate Six surrounded them. The streets teemed with bicycles and wheeled drones, and the sidewalks held a dense, steady flow of pedestrians. In many respects, the scene bore no difference from the reality Jaelynn experienced on a daily basis in her physical life.

"You are deeply worried," Sendinian asked, drifting a little closer. "And frightened. What has happened?"

"The technate authorities took Gabriel away, and they've also got a friend of ours, Dr. Swedenborg, in custody," Jaelynn informed Sendinian.

"I am sorry to hear this," Sendinian replied with a somber air. "Many have been taken by those serving the Primordials."

"Can anything be done to help them?" Jaelynn asked, hoping the faerie had some answers.

"Not just yet," Sendinian said, a frown shadowing her face. "I wish I could say something to comfort you."

"I feel so helpless," Jaelynn said, a veil of sadness coming over her at the open admission. "I'm without anyone I can go to, in my world. I've never felt so alone."

"I've known the scourge of loneliness, many times," Sendinan replied in a low voice, in a tone brimming with sympathy.

"And now that I know about all of this," Jaelynn said, gesturing around, "So much under the surface and beyond ... I find myself more lost than ever."

"Don't give despair any sustenance," Sendinian told her. Fluttering her wings, she moved closer to Jaelynn, taking a position an arm's length from her face. Staring into her eyes, the faerie continued, "Despair is one of the things that drives so many into the clutches of the Primordials. It clouds judgment, agitates, and leads to reckless choices."

Jaelynn nodded. "I know. I can see that. But I can't help feeling what I feel."

"No, you cannot," Sendinian said. "But you must use your will to master that storm inside. It is not easy."

"It was all I could do to walk home, from where they're holding Gabriel," Jaelynn said. "It took all I had in me just to walk down the street."

"But you did walk," Sendinian responded.

"Where do I go from here?" Jaelynn asked. "How can I find you when I need to?"

"There is much to learn," Sendinian answered. "Gaining a greater understanding of other realities is a place we can start."

The light surrounding the faerie swelled. Before Jaelynn could reply, the scene of the technate street around her faded, and a much different vision took shape.

Another street, in a different kind of place, lay before her eyes. Each with square plots of ground in front of them, houses lined both sides of the thoroughfare.

An unbroken mass of gray clouds crawled across the skies.

Cold winds swept past, throwing scraps of trash down the street and sending a shiver through Jaelynn.

Weeds and brush had overtaken the ground, and every house in view had numerous signs of disrepair and neglect. From broken windows, to faded, chipped paint, to missing roof tiles, the edifices had decayed far from what they once had been.

Alone, or in small clusters, a number of people began emerging from the various houses and making their way toward the newcomers. All had a forlorn, haunted look about them, rife with elements of fear and anxiety.

Watching the people trudging toward them, a look of concern crossed Jaelynn's face.

"What's wrong with them?" Jaelynn asked in a low voice, shuddering as another rush of icy wind blew over her.

"Something feeds upon them, and is consuming this world," Sendinian replied, her voice conveying great sadness.

"I do not like the look of this place," Jaelynn stated. "Not one bit."

"There is much to dislike about what is happening here," Sendinian replied

"Who are they?" Jaelynn asked, looking upon the despondent faces drawing steadily closer to them.

"Some who have not found their way to better horizons," Sendinian said. "Some who have a much longer road to take."

From the people to the environment, Jaelynn suspected everything to be an echo, or shadow, of something much greater. Like a wilting flower, the entire atmosphere had the appearance of decline and decay.

"See what this place is a shadow of," Sendinian said, as if perceiving Jaelynn's thoughts.

In an instant, Jaelynn looked upon houses in fresh coats of paint, with all of their roof tiles and windows in good order. Front lawns of lustrous, green grass trimmed low hosted a variety of colorful flowers in orderly arrangements.

The merry laughter of children playing carried across sunlit air, beneath blue skies dotted with puffy white clouds. Windows down and music playing from within, a vehicle rolled past them on the street.

A girl no older than Jaelynn appeared to be operating the vehicle. She talked and laughed with another girl riding in the seat next to her. Both looked to be carefree and enjoying themselves to a great degree.

Sleek and graceful, a gray cat bounded across a couple lawns. Wagging its tail, a large brown dog behind a fence in back of one of the houses barked at the racing cat.

Everywhere Jaelynn looked, she could see everything that was absent from the previous state she had witnessed. Confidence and a robust vigor for life reflected in the surroundings; in stark contrast to the drab, miserable appearance the place had held moments earlier.

Jaelynn found her spirits lifting. Savoring the touch of the sun's warm rays, a smile bloomed upon her face.

The scene vanished in abrupt fashion, returning to its former state. Jaelynn flinched at the jarring shift, and then took a step back, seeing dour faces all around her; now within just a few short paces.

"The echo of that world is yet cradled within their minds," Sendinian said in a low voice. "They all hold on to that vision. It is up to them to choose to bring that state of being back, and reject the downward slide they now find themselves in. It is merely a matter of willpower. Mastery over the mind, as I have told you before."

"Who are you?" one of the women asked, squinting, and sounding nervous.

Those closest to the faerie also squinted or shielded their eyes.

"So much light," a man exclaimed, looking pained. "A light I wish I could bear."

"A light all of you can choose to have," Sendinian replied. "One that will give you comfort, and strengthen you, even if it is difficult to look upon now."

"Nothing can be done here," another woman said in a forlorn manner.

"Everything can be done here," Sendinian replied in a gentle tone. "Make this world what all of you remember, deep inside, and then you will reach higher."

"It is becoming harder to remember," a man said, his creased face reflecting a deep weariness.

"All of that seems like just a dream now," yet another woman said, a wistful look in her eyes.

"A dream passes in the night, and a physical life passes over a handful of years," Sendinian said. "Where time holds no dominion, both are the same."

"We can change this?" a man asked, a glint of hope underlying his words.

"Yes, if you choose to act," Sendinian said. "You must not wait for others to make the change. That is what brought you and all gathered here into this state to begin with."

Spreading her arms, and with a focused look, Sendinian turned her attention toward one of the houses. The unkempt mass of uncut grass and sprawling weeds began peeling back and shrinking.

Jaelynn watched the changes in a state of wonderment, and many gasps and exclamations of surprise came from the assembled group of people.

Beyond the front lawn, the house began to change. Patches of missing paint filled in, and then all the color took on a richer, more vibrant hue. A shutter that had fallen lifted itself from the ground, rising and then taking its place along a window that now had a full, unbroken pane.

Tiles began fitting themselves into place until a complete roof had been restored. Trash and other debris around the house began collecting itself into a pile, before vanishing from sight.

A few moments later, a house much like the ones Jaelynn had witnessed in the other vision of the street now stood before her. Sharing the astonishment of the other people, she gazed in astonishment upon the handiwork of Sendinian.

"This is a realm of existence based upon thought forms," Sendinian told Jaelynn in a low voice, meant for her ears alone. "They must realize that, and then they can change all of this.

"But in a way it is no different from your own world. What the mind determines sets the course for the changes made. A refusal to exercise the mind brings decay and decline to your world, as much as the will to act can build a place where each and every soul can flourish. They all must grasp that lesson, before they can reach for the higher realms and begin the journey to a true home."

"So ... these people were all once living in my world?" Jaelynn said, coming to a profound realization.

"Yes, many years ago," Sendinian replied. "Long before the time of technates and the Global Council."

In slow fashion, smiles began emerging on the faces around Jaelynn. The changes in expression dropped years from the people's faces, replacing the veneer of weariness with a vibrant, youthful energy.

"I remember very clearly now," one of the men said, looking back to Sendinian and Jaelynn with a beaming expression.

"Thank you," a woman said, turning to look back to the faerie. "It's been so long, I had all but forgotten. Thank you so much!"

"Now that you have your memories rekindled, see to reclaiming this place," Sendinian told the gathering. "It will restore your hearts to where you can see to other, far greater horizons."

All of the others nodded, and an excited murmur ran throughout the group. A few exchanged tight embraces, and a sense of relief permeated the air.

The sight gladdened Jaelynn, and she smiled at the faerie. "This is wonderful!"

"It is just a start, and it took great energy for me to do this," Sendinian replied. "This realm has long been steeped in decay and is yet in the hold of the Primordials."

"Where are they?" Jaelynn asked.

"They may make their presence known, but we have lit a fire within these people, and given them a weapon to resist," Sendinian said. "It is all we can do for them, in this state of existence. The rest will be up to them."

The winds then began to die down, and a pensive stillness took hold over the area. Something about the shift provoked a deep unease within Jaelynn, and she began to look about for the source of it.

"You feel it, too," Sendinian said, also looking around.

"Yes," Jaelynn said, nodding, the discomfort continuing to rise inside her.

The crowd in the street appeared oblivious to whatever Jaelynn and Sendinian sensed. They had begun to move closer to the transformed house, remaining enthralled in the change that had taken place.

"I think they have taken notice, and they are not pleased," Sendinian said.

Jaelynn knew the faerie was not referring to the people.

A raspy, hissing sound drew Jaelynn's attention. Faint at first, it began increasing in volume.

"Do not run," Sendinian said, in a firm manner.

"What is happening?" Jaelynn asked.

Before the faerie could answer Jaelynn, a harrowing scene unfolded fast before her eyes.

Rising from every shadow, crevice and nook, dark shapes streamed into view. Serpentine, wraith-like, or in other forms, the entities spread outward, some keeping low to the ground and others lifting higher into the air.

At the shadow beings' appearance, the joyful mood encompassing the people from the houses shattered apart. The men and women scattered in all directions, crying out and screaming in terror.

Running for the houses, they scrambled up porches and threw doors open, hurrying inside the dwellings. Slamming the doors shut behind them, they left Sendinian and Jaelynn alone to face the growing mass of shadows.

"Something is wrong, for there are far too many of them for the state this realm is in," Sendinian said, in a tone of alarm.

Jaelynn remained at Sendinian's side, her own fear spiraling fast, but unsure of what to do. The ethereal creatures kept pouring into the air, forming vast flocks of living darkness above the houses.

"Primordials," Jaelynn said under her breath.

"Yes," confirmed Sendinian.

A few of the Primordials began trickling toward the faerie and Jaelynn. Converging from all over, the Primordials soon became a flood, surrounding the two figures in a swirling mass of darkness.

The light around Sendinian expanded, taking on a great radiance that the shadow entities recoiled from. The luminance encompassed both Jaelynn and Sendinian, taking the shape of a large sphere.

An intense look of concentration on her face, Sendinian glared at the masses of shadows teeming at the edges of the light. The entities pressed in on all sides, but they would not transgress the boundary of the sphere.

"I cannot hold them back for much longer," Sendinian exclaimed. "This is beyond the power I can exercise."

"What can I do?" Jaelynn asked, scared, but wanting to help the faerie.

"Leave this place," Sendinian told her.

"I cannot leave you," Jaelynn replied, panicking.

"Think upon your body, sleeping back in your bed, and wake up, Jaelynn! Go to your physical body!" Sendinian cried out, arms wide and palms open. Her face an image of strain, the bubble of light she had generated still held the shadows at bay.

To Jaelynn's horror, the light began to dim, allowing the mass of shadows to encroach closer.

"Go Jaelynn, think of your body, now!" Sendinian called, urgent and insistent.

Sendinian's words triggered thoughts in Jaelynn of her body lying in slumber. At once, she found herself snapped out of the scene, the cyclone-like mass of dark entities replaced with the quiet of her bedroom.

Jaelynn sat up quickly, breathing fast. Tears came to her eyes, and she began to cry, overwhelmed from everything that had just transpired.

Fearing for Sendinian, she thought of her last image of the little faerie. Face contorted in exertion, the winged creature held back a great multitude of living darkness.

The shadows no longer pressed in around Jaelynn, but an even heavier feeling of loneliness now shrouded her. She had lost Gabriel and Dr. Swedenborg, and she had no way of knowing the fate of Sendinian.

Jaelynn feared the worst, suspecting her world reduced even further. Curling up and hugging her knees to her body, she sobbed, wondering how she could ever find help with the fantastical kinds of things revealed to her.

Haven

Haven made her way to Serena's apartment in the latter part of the afternoon. Her mind a jumble of thoughts and worries, she hoped the Artist would be present.

Serena greeted her at the door with a smile. Stepping back, she gestured for Haven to enter.

"Haven, come on in," Serena invited. "Christopher is not here at the moment, if that's who you are looking for."

"I'm really needing to talk with him," Haven replied, stepping into the apartment.

Serena shut the door behind them and led Haven to the living room. So many things consumed Haven's mind that she paid little more than a glance to the artwork lining the walls of the hallway.

Taking leave for a moment, Serena went to the kitchen, returning a few minutes later with a couple glasses. She handed one over to Haven, who had taken a seat on one of the couches.

Haven took a sip from the cup and discovered that it held a sweet orange soft drink.

"Your face alone tells me you are filled with concerns," Serena said, sitting down on a couch opposite her.

"A lot has happened in a short time," Haven said.

"Care to tell me about it?" Serena asked.

With nobody else to confide in, Haven took advantage of the offer, telling Serena about everything that had happened. She described the visit to the Northern Sector and the encounter with Athena. Then, she proceeded to relate her account of the street protest and subsequent security crackdown.

"I don't know what it is, but I can't shake the feeling there's something in common, between what I saw in the Northern Sector and what happened out on the street," Haven stated.

"Two entirely different worlds, the Northern Sector and the rest of the technate," Serena commented.

"There's a threat in the air, though," Haven said. "I just know it. And the thing I saw in that woman's eyes ... I could not help thinking Athena suspected something about me. I was lucky when Carlos came back. I don't think I could have held up for much longer under that stare she gave me. I'm sure the black eyes were just a trick of my imagination."

"Or maybe not," Serena replied, without a trace of jest. "It might be that you are having your first encounters with the true nature of things in the world."

"Then I'm woefully unprepared," Haven said, a tinge of despair underlying her words.

"I think the Artist will need to help you accelerate your path," Serena said. "He is good about that, with his personal style of doing things."

"Accelerate?" Haven asked.

"Open your eyes to even greater things than what you've experienced so far," Serena said.

"I'd just like to ask him a few questions," Haven said. "Do you know any way of reaching Christopher?"

"Navigators are not the easiest of individuals to find," Serena replied. "At least when it comes to their physical selves. But I have my ways."

Serena called for the time from her residence's Home Assistant.

"A little more than two hours to twilight," Serena commented, after getting the answer.

"You expect Christopher back then?" Haven asked.

"More to do with Twilight's Passage, a Moment of Kairos, but that's something to discuss at a later time," Serena replied. "You are in need of Christopher's guidance now, in regard to your own path."

"What should I do then?" Haven asked. "Do I need to wait here?"

"No, there's no need to wait here," Serena answered. "You should go home, make yourself comfortable, and go to sleep at dusk. Christopher will find you then. In the meantime, it will be fun for me to find him, given the number of times he surprises me here."

"I'm going to have a lot of questions for you one day, you know," Haven replied, with a smile. "Twilight's Passage. Moments of Kairos. You've got my curiosity, that's for sure."

"You'll get the answers soon enough," Serena replied, grinning.

Serena got up and took the now-empty cup from Haven's hand.

"You just need to keep your mind on the world of Navigators, and look forward to a grand experience, this very night," she announced. "An experience that will give you some needed relief from all the stress you have been going through."

"Now, you've really got my curiosity," Haven said, rising to her feet. "But I like the sound of getting some relief from stress."

"Every Navigator needs to learn the way to a place ... Faraway," Serena replied, with a wink.

Cayden

liding through wave after wave of dense black mists, Cayden forged his way deeper into the storm-filled realm. His Guardian Lilithian had not guided him there, and he had no idea of her whereabouts.

This night, he had chosen to travel wherever his inclinations took him. Giving himself over to the heavier sensation pervading him, he had passed through several regions until he reached the one he now explored.

Each of the places Cayden had seen prior to his arrival in the current one harbored foreboding appearances, with increasingly violent atmospheres. The stark scenes both fascinated and terrified him.

More than once he had espied movements in the desolate landscapes he had set his eyes upon, but he kept sinking into new realms before he could ascertain much in the way of details.

At last, the downward pull within him had come to an end. Flying along the underbelly of a black cloud mass that cloaked the skies in every direction, he eyed the barren terrain below.

Far below him, an enormous pit gaped, surrounded on all sides with towering rock walls. At the bottom of the pit, he could see figures moving about.

Descending from the churning skies, he alighted at the edge of the pit. From the closer vantage, he could see that the walls lining the pit could not be scaled in a physical sense. The smooth obsidian facing would not allow for so much as a single fingertip to gain hold.

Turning his attention toward the bottom of the pit, he made out the distant forms of what looked to be many hundreds of figures moving around. To his eyes, they looked to be people, all appearing trapped, with no openings of any kind to be seen along the pit's sides.

Lucid, and knowing that he was not in a physical state, he took courage that the normal laws of nature did not govern in such a place. Staring downward, Cayden thought about investigating the strange sight further.

Looking around, but could see nothing more than an endless, flat plain spreading in every direction from the area of the pit. A sulfuric taint to the hot air currents sweeping across the plain, Cayden wrinkled his nose.

The longer he remained at the edge of the pit, the greater his curiosity rose concerning the throngs at the base of it. After a short while, he decided to explore further.

Lifting from the ground, he lowered into the pit. Controlled, and slow, he managed his descent with care, eyeing some open patches of ground to land on.

Angling to the left, he continued with his descent until at last he touched down on the parched, dusty soil covering the bottom of the pit. He peered at the mobs of figures shuffling across the ground.

The beings all had human appearances, though their rheumy, pale eyes, emaciated bodies and ash-gray skin tones related more to something dead than living. Aside from their faces, the corpse-like beings had little else to distinguish them.

All of the entities had a listless, dreary look about them.

One turned its head in Cayden's direction. Their eyes met, and recognition sparked in him at once.

Gazing upon the unmistakable face of Lane Margolis, Cayden's breathing quickened.

The figure oriented toward Cayden and started toward him, emitting a low moan. Others in the vicinity slowed at the sound, and they began looking around.

Becoming more astonished by the moment, Cayden found that he recognized more than one of them. Many of the beings he identified were figures of fame and influence in his world. Several other faces he had seen at the party where he and Lilithian had walked among the guests incognito.

The being resembling Lane Margolis drew closer, the moan rising and sharpening into a shrill wail. Lifting its bony arms, it reached toward Cayden.

Others began to break out in moans and howls, adding to the growing, eerie chorus filling the air. An air of dread accompanied the groundswell of activity focusing on Cayden.

A circle of grasping, groaning figures closed in on him with slow steps. Not wanting to discover whether or not the beings could affect him in a non-physical state, Cayden deemed it time to depart.

Thinking of the mountain where he had begun his exploration into other realms, he lifted off the ground. Out of the reach of the figures in the pit, he headed skyward, the pitiful entities below shrieking and howling at his escape.

His environment shifted, the transition between realms blurring his vision for a moment.

Lilithian awaited when Cayden arrived on the mountainside.

A humorless look on her face, she fixed him with a piercing gaze.

"You don't understand the dangers of what you have just done," she told him in an angry tone. "You took far too great a risk."

"I just wanted to take a look around," Cayden said.

"It is a dangerous wilderness," she replied. "You are not immune to harm in other planes."

"I'm sorry," he said with an air of contrition.

"Do not be reckless," Lilithian said. "Where did you go?"

"Several places," Cayden replied.

Cayden thought of the final realm he had explored, recalling the figures who looked like people from his own world.

"I saw all these people I've seen before, at the bottom of a great pit in the last place I went," he continued. "One of them was the Technate Representative ... Margolis. Looked exactly like him. Saw lots of people I recognized. Famous people, and a few from that formal party we walked through. But they all seemed crazy ... really out of their minds. Before I left they had started to crowd in around me."

"You tread on very dangerous ground there," Lilithian said. "You are lucky you are standing here."

"What were they?" Cayden asked. "They couldn't be the people they looked like, because those people are living now in my world."

"Nothing you are ready for right now," she replied in a curt manner. "Don't ever try that again. Do you understand me?"

Cayden nodded, hating the fact that he had angered her. "I'm really sorry. I just got curious."

"That's what I'm here for," Lilithian said. "I am your Guardian."

"Understood," Cayden said, looking down, unable to meet her eyes and endure the weight of her gaze.

"You need to start associating with others who have discovered other planes of existence," Lilithian said, her tone less irate.

Cayden nodded. "I would like that, but how would I find

anyone like that?"

"There is a girl your age, who lives near you, who has also been opened up to these realms," the Guardian said. "It would be a very good idea to try make friends with her."

Curiosity piqued, he asked, "How do I find her?"

"Why don't I show you," Lilithian replied.

The high mountainside view changed into a ground-level one of a technate street. His Guardian remained standing at his side, on the sidewalk.

"Is this real, or a dream?" he asked, looking around at the familiar environment.

"A dream," she replied.

An attractive girl with a darker complexion of skin, of about his age and dressed in a casual manner, walked along the sidewalk.

"Is that her?" he asked.

The Guardian nodded.

"And you say she lives near me?"

"Yes, not far at all," Lilithian replied. "She has lost those who had been helping her, and needs guidance. I know she would like to meet another in her world, of her age, who could understand what she is going through."

"I would like that too," Cayden said, watching the girl continue onward.

"Then think of her, when you are in a dream, and desire to find her," Lilithian said. "Make it your only thought. If she is also dreaming, you will find her. Then you can introduce yourself."

"What then?" Cayden asked, suspecting there was more to all of it.

"Bring her to me," Lilithian said. "She has met me before and will recognize me. I will bring her a Guardian of her own."

It all sounded easy enough to Cayden, and the prospect of a new friend in his world who shared his journey into other realms and planes of existence would be more than welcome.

"I can do that," he replied to Lilithian.

A trace of a smile came to her lips, though the glint in her eyes remained serious. "That's what I hoped to hear."

Jaelynn

Not even her favorite virtual environment, hand-gliding through vistas of beautiful mountain scenery, could ease her mind from the thoughts plaguing her without respite.

Many days had passed since the vision of the Primordials, and several dreams had been entered, with no sign of Sendinian. Jaelynn had become lucid in more than one of the dreams, and had called out for the faerie, to no avail.

Going about her lessons, or walking about the streets, Jaelynn could not shake the restlessness growing inside her. Her mind raced to the point she found it difficult to sleep.

Making things worse, she had gained a keener understanding of her own world, in a way that gave her no consolations.

Most faces of those she viewed out in public reminded her of the beleaguered people in the world of gray skies and decaying structures. Without digital avatars to mask their appearances, the looks in the eyes of men and women alike resembled the kinds of despondent gazes she had beheld at Sendinian's side; before the host of dark entities had burst into view.

She recalled the faerie's words about thoughts leading to action, and the refusal to exercise thought bringing about decay. The decay she witnessed on the streets of Technate Six had a more interior quality to it, but it did have outward reflections; in the unanimity of the tenements, drones and security bots, and many other things so pervasive in her world.

Though more than a thousand people moved along the streets within eyesight, Jaelynn could not remember a time she had felt so alone.

Her world had been confusing enough prior to all the revelations of other realms, and the ability to explore them. In little time at all, she had lost everyone who could give her any degree of support or answers.

Gazing down the street, she wondered if anyone else on the street silently harbored the kind of knowledge that she how held. Jaelynn had no way of reaching out to find such a person.

Under an umbrella of constant surveillance, even inside virtual realms, she could not openly search for such an individual. One might come to her, as Sendinian had done, but she could not be guaranteed of that happening.

As things stood, she would have to find a way to learn more about the realms she had been exposed to. She longed to be back at the beach talking with Sendinian and her brother, though she had no idea of how to get back to the beautiful place.

Risks would have to be taken, and the thought frightened her. Yet the realities she had been awakened to could not be ignored.

Around her, wheeled vehicles rolled to a stop. A number of curses sounded from many people nearby, and a great number of individuals walking along the streets came to a stop.

Jaelynn kept walking and did not bother to put on her MR glasses. The Reminder would come to an end soon enough.

She looked about. Looks of tension and anxiety spread fast on the faces of the pedestrians.

Jaelynn could now see the Reminder's true nature. The Technate that claimed to provide for everything could also take everything away; in a single moment.

The demonstration of power could not be delayed, avoided, or ignored. The flying security drones and bots on the ground displayed the precision of that power; an overwhelming power that could shut down just one person's world, if it chose to.

Not a single transaction could take place until The Reminder came to an end, nor could anyone access a virtual world, or other kind of network. Clothes could not be washed, nothing could be made in a fabricator, music could not be listened to, and no interactions could take place beyond those of a face to face nature.

Jaelynn surmised that most people could not function, and would not know how to handle themselves, if the Reminder extended throughout an entire day.

She eyed the numerous bicycles that had come to a stop. The riders remained in place, adhering to the regulations demanding them to halt during a Reminder, lest they incur fines to their accounts.

Monitors built into the bicycles informed the security apparatus whether or not the riders complied. None of the riders would dare move forward until the small blinking red lights on their handlebars changed to green.

Though the Reminder lasted less than a minute, the atmosphere brimmed with agitation and anxiety when it finally came to an end. Vehicles rolled forward once more, riders lurched into motion on their bicycles, and many put their MR glasses back on.

Jaelynn comforted herself with the knowledge that while the Technate could be brought to a halt during a Reminder, those governing it had no such control over the new realms she could now explore.

Wishing she could take Gabriel from the Rehabilitation Center and leave at once for one of those worlds, she longed for a place where her words and movements would not be watched, recorded, and tracked.

Having had enough of the Technate for the time being, she turned back for her family's apartment. The walk back took only about ten minutes.

Jaelynn set her mind on finding a good distraction. When she reached her bedroom, she donned her VR helmet, checking in on the latest updates involving space exploration.

Taking in the spectacular views provided by the bots and vessels involved in the unmanned missions, Jaelynn tried to occupy her mind with other kinds of thoughts. She wondered what space exploration was like decades before, when men and women operated spacecraft and worked inside space stations orbiting the world.

Many virtual environments featured spacecraft and alien planets, but the gaming plots did not reflect the way things stood in the modern day. Humans did not go on space missions anymore.

Jaelynn had heard that the entertainment of the old world was rife with stories featuring humans exploring the wonders of space in person. She imagined the people living in those times had envisioned such a grandiose future, but reality had turned out very different.

Bots did not have to eat, breath air, or sleep, and much more efficient exploration vessels could be designed when a living crew did not have to be accounted for. A bot did not need a suit to go outside a vessel in space, nor did it need one for setting foot on other planets with different atmospheres. A bot could handle extremes of pressure, heat and cold.

The last missions involving humans conducting exploratory work in space had come to an end many years before. Though the changes made logical sense, the recognition of it saddened Jaelynn.

After a short while, even a virtual exploration of the images captured from the world's space missions failed to distract her mind. Logging out of her VR helmet, she took it off and put it back on the shelf in its usual place.

Thinking of her brother, Sendinian, and the resplendent ocean she had witnessed, she lay down on her bed and shut her eyes. After a little time had passed, she finally slipped into unconsciousness.

The streets and buildings of an older metropolis enveloped Jaelynn. Standing on a sidewalk, she looked toward a wide edifice of great height, rising far above a long, semicircular building complex that had the look of an outer wall. Eyeing the dark skyscraper for a moment, she wondered as to its nature and purpose.

Gray blanketed the skies above, and the colors in her surroundings had a dull and faded appearance.

Many people walked along the streets, and a nervous energy filled the air. Vehicles traversed the road, all of them under the control of human drivers.

Nobody smiled, and a majority had irritable expressions. All had a hurried, rushed air about their movements.

A few of them glanced at Jaelynn but did not break stride as they continued at brisk gaits along the sidewalks.

Making her way through the pedestrian flow, Jaelynn found her way to an alcove in the facade of a building. Once free of the bustle, she took a moment to collect her thoughts.

Realizing she stood within a dream, a stream of clarity rushed into her mind. Lucid, and conscious of her state, Jaelynn turned her mind toward her brother, and the tremendous world she had met him in.

She thought of the ocean, with its pure white sand and crystalline waters, desiring to stand in that place once more.

For a brief moment, Jaelynn's vision began to blur, but her focus came back. To her disappointment, she remained in place beneath the gray skies.

She then tried to fly, as she had done so many times before through the years within dreams. Lifting from the ground, she rose a few meters into the air, before sinking back downward.

The failed attempt troubled her, but she tried again. Once more, she began to rise, but did not get as far as the first time before lowering back to the ground. It seemed as if the environment itself dragged her down.

"What in the hell do you think you're doing?"

In the wake of her two failed attempts, the caustic question jarred her. Looking up, she met the slate gray eyes of a narrow-faced man with a long nose. Dressed in a suit and tie, his clothes hung a little loose on his lean frame.

"Trying to get out of here," she answered.

"Wish I could too, but you can't just fly out of here, that's just ridiculous," he said, in a derisive tone. "Things are the way they are. You can't change it. Best you just deal with it and move on."

Shaking his head and making a disgusted face, he turned and headed onward.

The interruption weighed further upon her. Jaelynn just wanted to get out of the dreary place. Setting her mind to leaving the place, with no formal idea of a destination, the scene blurred out.

This time, when vision returned to her, a change had occurred. Dismayed, she looked upon another metropolis, this one shrouded in a menacing darkness.

Like the bones of some long-dead, huge beast, buildings of great height jutted toward the billowing clouds drifting far above. Gusts of wind howled through the edifices. No matter where Jaelynn turned her eyes, no sign of a living thing could be seen.

In a strange sense, the dismal scene reflected the emptiness she felt deep inside. Despite the recognition, she did not want to stay a moment longer.

Once more, she set her mind to the act of flight and reaching a vibrant realm. Though a faint tugging sensation rippled through her for a moment, her feet did not leave the ground.

She stayed rooted in place.

At that moment, she espied movements all around her. Coming from buildings and out from alleyways and side streets, a large number of figures shuffled into view.

With movements slow and ponderous, the men and women had severe, emaciated appearances, the clothing on their bony forms in a tattered, soot-covered condition. Sunken eyes casting dull gazes in Jaelynn's direction, they began moving toward her.

None of them spoke so much as a single word, and their leaden expressions gave no sign of their intent. In their dark world, she seemed like a beacon, continuing to draw more of the figures from the buildings and toward her; though what attracted them in such a powerful way she could not tell.

For a moment, Jaelynn wondered if she remained in a dream, or stood within another kind of realm. Where her brother had been in realm of a lively, vibrant nature, it stood to reason that other realms could have an opposite kind of nature; such as the malignant atmosphere she now beheld.

The multitude shambled toward Jaelynn, though they still had a lot of ground to cover to reach her.

A lone figure drew her eyes toward the left. Cleaving through the disheveled throngs, the woman's strides conveyed purpose.

Dark-haired and clad in flowing attire, the woman had an appearance of strength and vitality. She did not suffer any obstructions, shoving aside any who blocked her path.

Breaking into the forefront of the horde, she fixed her ice-blue eyes on Jaelynn.

"This place is not for you," the woman announced, when

she had come within a few paces of Jaelynn.

"Who are you?" Jaelynn asked.

"Someone you need in your world," the woman announced. "I can see this is not your realm."

Behind the enigmatic woman, the denizens of the dark metropolis had come to a halt. They continued to linger and stare but made no move to come any closer to Jaelynn.

It seemed to Jaelynn that the woman's mere presence held them at bay.

"No, it's not my realm at all," Jaelynn replied, grateful for the woman's appearance as she eyed the swelling, disheveled ranks well beyond her. "I just wanted to find my way out of another place and ended up here instead. I didn't choose this place."

The hint of a smile played about the woman's face. "Lost your navigator?"

Jaelynn's expression did not hide her surprise at hearing the particular word, drawing a full grin from the woman.

"I don't have any navigator," Jaelynn answered. "It's just me."

"You've lost your guides then?" the woman asked.

Jaelynn nodded. "Everyone who knows about these places."

"And you can't utter a word about it in the world you are from, or you will be hauled in," the woman said. "I know about that world, with its technates."

"Are you a Navigator?" Jaelynn asked.

"I am a Guardian," the woman replied. "And it looks like you could use one."

The idea of a protector appealed to Jaelynn. She hoped the woman did not turn out to be the figment of a dream or a figure bound to another realm.

"I could use some help," Jaelynn admitted.

"I have helped others, of about your age, who live in your world, and I can help you," the woman said. "You merely have to consent to letting me help you."

The way things stood, Jaelynn had little to lose.

"I need some help," she told the woman.

"I know you do not like to be alone," the woman said. "I will bring someone to you, who is also of your world, so you will have someone there who understands what you are going through in terms of the revelations you have had."

"That would be wonderful," Jaelynn responded, doubting that Gabriel or Dr. Swedenborg would be released anytime soon.

"For now, do not try to seek other realms," the woman said. "In your state of mind, and not knowing how to travel other realms, that can be very dangerous."

Jaelynn could not dispute the woman's warning. She had tried to find her own way about, only to find herself in a grim, hectic metropolis, and then an even gloomier, dismal realm. She did not doubt she could end up in even worse places.

With no viable options, she would have to take a few chances, and she decided to place some trust in the woman.

"I understand, I won't try to travel about on my own," Jaelynn said.

"That is best for now," the woman replied. "You will not have to wait long before you have a new friend who shares the kind of knowledge that you have. Go back now, to your body, and keep your eyes open."

Fading out from the drab realm, Jaelynn's last image was of the woman's smile. Blinking her eyes and opening them, she stretched, and then sat up on her bed.

Though she had no idea of when the woman's introduction to another of her age group would happen, the notion of making another friend who understood what she was going through brought some comfort to her distressed mind.

She did not know what to make of the woman just yet. A part of her wished she could ask Dr. Swedenborg or Sendinian about what a Guardian was, but there was nothing that could be done. Both of them had been removed from her, and were inaccessible, as far as she knew.

Quite simply, chances would have to be taken, even if that meant a little risk.

Haven

Despite its ample size, the airship had no difficulties lowering itself through the towering, concrete forest of tenements. Aware that she was in a dream, Haven savored the surge of excitement at seeing the familiar vessel.

The Artist peered over the side, smiling down at her. "I heard you missed me. Serena was pretty emphatic that I visit you soon ... as in immediately."

"Took you long enough," Haven exclaimed, laughing, though relieved to see his face. "I've gone through a bit since I last saw you."

"That's what Serena told me," the Artist replied. The airship slowed, coming to a stop a short distance above the ground. "You know it isn't necessary to bring this all the way down. I didn't even need to come this far."

Haven shook her head and laughed again. "Fine then, be that way ... Christopher Brendan!"

She laughed at the look of surprise that arose on his face when she mentioned the name revealed to her by Serena.

"And here I was, so content being called the Artist," he

replied, with an air of good humor. "Now I hesitate to ask what else Serena has told you. She is up to mischief indeed!"

"At least I got to surprise you, for once!" Haven declared in a merry fashion. "Don't worry, I still like calling you the Artist. Hold on there, I'm on my way up!"

Putting her focus into the act, Haven lifted from the sidewalk and soared up toward the airship. She arced over the side of the vessel and came to stand on the upper deck, alongside the Artist.

A smile beamed on her face as she looked down and saw Harrison, Chesiree, Dewey, and Carmel looking back at her. Seated on their haunches, the cats had their ears perked up and cocked toward her.

"Well hello, my friends!" she greeted the feline quartet.

"Hello, Haven," Chesiree replied in his high-pitched voice. "I thought we'd come along for the ride on this trip."

"Don't you guys watch over the Artist's place?" she asked the cats, grinning.

"It will be fine, there's a few more of us there ... we wanted to go along with you on this particular journey," Harrison said.

"What they really mean is that they wanted to go with you ... and they also wanted to go where we are going," the Artist said, smiling at the cats. "It's a trip they didn't want to pass up."

"Not one to miss for sure," Carmel added.

"Then let's not delay a moment longer," the Artist stated.

As he spoke, the airship lifted back upward, heading toward the skies. An adventure beckoning, Haven walked over to the side of the vessel, giving her attention to the view of the Technate falling away beneath her.

"So then, I take it that we are not going back to where your estate is," Haven remarked, intrigued, and wondering what the Artist was up to.

The Artist shook his head, and he gave her a smile and a wink. "No, we are going somewhere much, much more wonderful than that."

Given what Serena had hinted at, his statement did not come as a total surprise, but the notion staggered her nonetheless. Thinking of the dazzling sights she had beheld in his personal world, Haven could not imagine anything being more wonderful, much less to a significant degree.

The airship rising fast, the sky above kept brightening. Haven finally could not bear the tremendous radiance and had to shut her eyes.

"No need to keep your eyes closed," the Artist said, a few moments later. "Open them and take a look."

Tentatively, she did as he instructed.

Haven's eyes filled with a kaleidoscopic wonder. Colors of all hues, including some she had never witnessed before, poured into her eyes.

A buoyant energy flowed throughout her. Haven's body felt lighter than air itself. A feeling of peace, like nothing she had ever experienced, permeated her entire being.

A tremendous vista spread before her, of a rolling landscape with a brilliant horizon. Haven gasped, looking upon shapes familiar yet entirely new.

Flowers gleamed like gemstones, and grasses swayed in a graceful rhythm, emitting a subtle radiance. Glittering streams of silver, emerald and sapphire meandered through the beautiful landscape, crossed at points with exquisitely-fashioned bridges, that looked to be formed out of pure crystal.

As spectacular as the landscape was, an even more breathtaking vision loomed ahead. Spires soaring to tremendous heights formed the tines of a spellbinding metropolis' crown.

Buildings with gleaming surfaces, some metallic, others ebony, ivory, and other solid hues, spread in a radiating elegance from the loftiest heights at the metropolis' center to the lowest points on its outskirts.

The metropolis presented no eyesore to the majestic panorama. If anything, the metropolis formed the centerpiece of a grander, spectacular vision.

Each and every building carried its own identity, exhibiting a broad range of architectural styles. Haven could at best describe the array of designs as ranging from classical to futuristic.

"What ... is this place?" she whispered in a low, dreamy voice, gazing at everything in a state of sheer awe.

"Welcome to Faraway, young Haven," the Artist exclaimed, his voice brimming with merriment. "And what you feel is what I feel, each and every time I come here."

"It ... it is all so beautiful," Haven said, looking at the grand bridges spanning silvery channels running through the metropolis' midst.

Haven could see the distant forms of people, strolling along golden boulevards, standing on bridges and balconies, and walking along other places in the great cityscape. After spending a lifetime living among towering, blocky tenements, she could not imagine living amid such tremendous splendor and beauty. Not even the Northern Sector had anything that could begin to compare to just a single blade of grass in the wondrous world she gazed upon.

"People ... live here?" she asked, amazed. Looking down, she gazed upon a pair of individuals in a small boat of the purest white, drifting along the glassy surface of a lake whose clear waters revealed a forest of colorful, coral-like formations beneath. "Who are they?"

"All sorts," the Artist replied. "And this is the residence for many beings. It is also a borderland."

"A borderland?" she asked. "For what?"

"Realms that even I cannot enter," the Artist said, his tone carrying a trace of regret.

"What realms are those?" she asked.

"Places that make this one look like your technate appears in relation to here," he said.

Looking upon the grandeur all around her, she found his statement hard to believe.

"Where are we going to land?" Chesiree asked, brushing up against the leg of the Artist.

"I have the perfect spot," the Artist replied, casting Haven a sideways wink.

The vessel continued forward, though it began to drift toward the right of the metropolis' heart.

Ahead, an emerald lake drew into view, and soon the airship glided over its lustrous surface. Spaced well-apart from each other, set along the shores of the lake, a variety of edifices could be seen.

A few rivaled the majesty of the Artist's manse, back in his own realm. Others had the appearances of simple, one-story cabins; rustic and nestled into the part of the shore area they occupied.

The airship shifted course, heading toward a small inlet. A two-story, gable-ended edifice of timber, surrounded by a sizeable grove of towering pine trees, rested near the edge of the shore.

The closer the airship drew toward the structure, the more Haven could perceive a light, golden glow that filled the windows and limned the edges of the building.

"What place is that?" Haven asked, eyeing the cozy-looking edifice.

"A home, like all the other structures you see around the lake," the Artist said. "Those who live in them have their preference in style."

"These are all homes?" Haven said, astounded at the thought.

"Each and every one," the Artist replied.

The airship slowed, coming to a stop a short distance above the treetops.

"Go down to the shore, near that house," the Artist told her.
"Aren't you coming?" Haven asked him.
"We will be following soon, but there is someone you need to meet here," the Artist said, smiling. "Go ahead ... this is a special moment meant for you alone."

Perceiving a gentle compassionate air about the Artist, Haven stared at him for a moment, her curiosity rising at his words. She wondered who it was that she needed to meet in such an incredible place, but she could think of no one.

"Go ahead," the Artist encouraged her. "Down there, by the shore."

Haven disembarked, levitating up, gliding outward, and then descending to the ground. Alighting upon the shore, she became startled for a moment, seeing a young woman with lustrous golden hair, just a few paces from where she had landed.

The woman looked toward her with a calm demeanor, showing no surprise at Haven's close presence.

Haven hesitated, recognizing something familiar about her. The woman had bright blue eyes, and the smile she cast told Haven she was no stranger.

"Maybe a little shift in appearance would help you?" she asked, with a glint of merriment in her eyes.

Haven froze at the sound of the voice, as the form of the woman shimmered and transformed. Short, silvery gray locks replaced the golden ones, and her frame now held more weight; revealing a rather plump, elderly woman of about eighty years of age.

Her thoughts a jumble, Haven could not speak at first. Finally, she managed to collect herself enough to say, "Grandma?"

"I was wondering when you might recognize me, Haven," her grandmother replied with a laugh, the smile on her face spreading wider. Walking forward, she spread her arms wide.

Exhilarated, Haven stepped forward to meet her. She threw

her arms around her grandmother, who had died when she was just eleven years old.

An illness had taken her grandmother, which had been Haven's first introduction to death. Never did Haven think she would ever see her grandmother again; save for dreams and the memories she could hold onto.

Tears burst from Haven's eyes. Her mind wrestled with what seemed impossible only scant moments before.

Everything rushed back to the times she spent as a child with her grandmother. From the laughs they shared, to the final days in the medical facility, where the doctors ceased to treat her ailment and instead aided her comfort in dying.

Even though she had been eleven, Haven could not believe they had stopped trying to fight the disease ravaging her beloved grandmother. Everyone around Haven had patronized her with comments about how her grandmother had 'lived a good long life', and that the medical professionals had 'decided that her time had come to go'.

Their words had only served to make her tears of sorrow sting even hotter.

Grandmother and granddaughter embraced on the shoreline for an extended time. Haven could not let go, unwilling to relinquish the unexpected miracle.

"Don't worry, I'm not going to vanish, if that's what you're worried about, Haven," her grandmother said, laughing. She eased back and looked past Haven's shoulder. "Thank you for bringing her here."

"You are most welcome," the Artist replied, from behind Haven.

Haven cast a quick glance back, and saw that he now stood on the shore, a short distance away. She looked back to her grandmother, nervous to take her eyes off her, finding that she did not entirely trust the promise not to disappear. "How ... how is this happening?"

"Like I said, things are as they are," the Artist said. "And your grandmother, the elegant Desiree Hamilton that you see before you, wanted to see you again. I merely wished to accommodate this kind-hearted lady."

"But ... but ...," Haven said, hesitant, not wanting to voice the words on her tongue aloud.

"But I died?" Desiree asked. She shook her head, grinning. "Is that what you wanted to say? Maybe in the way you define it. I just left the cocoon and became the butterfly ... that's all."

"I ... don't know what to say," Haven said. Ingrained in her mind, death represented absolute finality. What she saw before her contradicted everything that had been told to her, all of her life.

"Came as a bit of a surprise to me too, to be honest," Desiree continued, laughing again. "One moment I'm frail and sick, and in the next I'm better than I ever was. Not something you expect, to be sure, Haven."

Tears continued to stream down Haven's cheeks. She struggled with the powerful emotions flowing through her; so many things she thought she knew upended in a handful of moments.

Looking toward the Artist, Haven said with a grin, "There's a purpose to this, too. You aren't doing this just to be nice. I know you a little better than that."

The words sounded a little like an accusation, but they carried truth. She had no doubts the Artist had arranged the meeting between a girl and her grandmother for a decided purpose.

"I figured this would be a most wonderful way to show you the true nature of things," the Artist said, with a smile and a shrug. "I think you are capable of figuring out quite a lot from this reunion."

"Then ... we don't really die?" Haven asked, hardly believing that she asked such a question.

It flew in the face of all she had been taught of the foolishness and superstitions of the old world. Then again, she realized the Artist had not asked her to believe anything.

She had been shown things, as they were.

"Do I look dead to you Haven?" Desiree asked, laughing heartily. "Never felt more alive, to tell you the truth. No weariness. Not a single ache. Boundless energy. And I look upon things with more wonder and excitement than I ever did as a child. I'm quite alive, I'm happy to report."

"Do you live here?" Haven asked her grandmother, eyeing the cozy-looking home beyond her.

"No, I'm just visiting this place," she answered. "I came here from some places beyond the borders of Faraway. I do enjoy coming to Faraway, and I've enjoyed our visits within your dreams."

Haven's eyes spread wider. "Our visits? In my dreams?"

She thought of the multitude of times she had dreamed of her grandmother over the years. Many had been lucid, appearing so real she had awoken with tears of joy coming from her eyes.

"Not all of your dreams about me really had me in them, but more than a few of them did," Desiree answered. "You probably didn't remember many of them when you woke up. Just the way dreams work when we are in a physical form."

"You really visited me in dreams," Haven said, astounded at the revelation.

"I can do that, just like anyone from the places beyond Faraway," Desiree said, nodding. "Dreams are a nice crossroads for all of us. Just like you don't forget us when we pass onward ... we don't forget you, either. I've missed you, Haven, very much so."

"This ... is quite a lot to take in," Haven said, looking between her grandmother and the Artist, a new batch of tears rolling from her eyes.

"I'm sure it all does come as a big surprise ... as it would to anyone being suffocated in a world infested with the Primordials," the Artist said, his demeanor growing more somber for a moment. "Theirs is a road to oblivion, and they want everyone to travel along it with them."

"Such a terrible scourge," Desiree commented, shaking her head, a sad look in her eyes.

"I'm not taking that road," Haven replied, resolute.

"That brings me more joy than I can possibly express," her grandmother responded, smiling again.

"And I'm here to help you on better roads," the Artist stated.

"Thank you," Haven said. "I will make sure I stay on them."

"That's all I ask," the Artist said.

"Well, enough of dour subjects like Primordials for the moment," Desiree said, looking to the other two with a smile. "I'm sure my granddaughter has a few questions about Faraway."

"Okay, here's one I have ... whose house is that, if it's not your residence here?" Haven asked, curious about the place where they had landed.

"A friend of mine. A very good friend who you will meet in time," the Artist answered.

"More surprises," Haven retorted, grinning at him, but unsure if she could handle anything more of a substantial nature at the moment.

"One thing at a time, Haven," the Artist replied with a smile, as if he had read her mind.

Haven broke into full laughter, filled with gratitude. "I owe you, you strange man. I really do."

"And I have to say I am in his debt myself, for arranging this wonderful moment," her grandmother added. She fixed her eyes on Haven. "I knew we'd see each other again. I had just not expected it in this way."

"She's going to make a great Navigator," the Artist said to Desiree.

"I have no doubts of that, she is a very strong young woman," Desiree replied, an undercurrent of pride in her tone.

"I still have a lot to learn about all of this," Haven said.

"We all have a lot to learn," her grandmother responded. "Learning and discovery are among the richest gifts we receive, on any level of existence."

"The more one learns, the more there is to discover," the Artist said, nodding.

Haven's grandmother looked downward, and her eyes sparkled with light from within. A look of joy blossomed on her face.

"You have brought some more guests, I see," she declared.

Dewey, Chesiree, Harrison, and Carmel padded forward, curling around the woman's legs. The air filled with the low rumble of purrs.

Leaning over, she stroked their fur and scratched each of them behind the ears, eliciting even stronger purrs from the cats.

"You are a most delightful bunch!" she stated.

"You'll think that, until you live with them for a little while," the Artist quipped, chuckling, and casting Haven a wink. "They can be quite a handful."

"Hey now, we can hear you, you know," Dewey retorted to the Artist. "We're right here!"

Haven and her grandmother laughed.

"We choose to stay with you ... we can go back with her, you know," Harrison stated, looking up to Desiree.

"You'd miss me far too much," the Artist said. "Admit it."

"Yes, I suppose we would," Harrison replied in a playful tone, before closing his eyes as Desiree ruffled the fur on the back of his head.

After greeting Desiree for a little while, the cats began to eye the cabin and surrounding area.

"Not even a change in realms can stymie the curiosity of a cat," Desiree observed, grinning wide.

"Go on, I know you all want to play and explore," the Artist said to the quartet, making a shooing motion with his hands.

The cats looked to the Artist for a moment, and then bounded off in the direction of the cabin. Carmel leaped onto the trunk of a towering pine near the cabin and began scaling it. In mere seconds she was lost to sight within its upper branches.

"It never gets old, watching them," the Artist remarked.

"They are a lively bunch," Haven said.

"Good traveling companions, I'll bet," Desiree said.

"That they are," the Artist said, and Haven could sense the genuine appreciation in her friend toward the cats.

"This is all so wonderful," Haven commented, continuing to watch the cats dart about the cabin. "I wish I could stay here a long while."

"One day you can, but that time isn't here yet," Desiree replied. "You have a life to live, in the world we once shared."

"I know, grandma," Haven said in a lower voice, unable to dismiss having a pang of disappointment at the thought of returning to her own world.

"Everything here is so amazing ... I wish I could explore it all," Haven said, looking in the direction of the great city.

From where they stood, the highest spires could be seen on the horizon, glittering with light.

"I will take you there, but not on this visit," the Artist said. "First things first. This is a good step we are taking now."

"I didn't want to go there right now," Haven said, smiling at her grandmother. "I want to visit with my grandma for as long as I can."

"We've got a little time yet," the Artist said. "The two of you should visit, while I keep an eye on those four ruffians."

He glanced toward the cats. Shaking his head and laughing, he strode away from the shoreline toward them, leaving Haven and Desiree to themselves.

"Let's walk along the lakeside," Desiree said, taking Haven's hand and taking a step forward. "There is so much to catch up on."

Many hours could have passed, but Haven lost all sense of time as she strolled along the water's edge with her grandmother. They spoke at length of times they had shared together, in addition to a number of things that had transpired since Desiree had entered another state of existence.

Haven had so many questions for her grandmother, and so much she thought she had forgotten about her childhood years resurfaced the longer they talked. All of her worries ebbed, a carefree sensation taking over that she wished could last forever.

At some point, Haven looked up and recognized that they were nearing the home where they had started. The Artist, with the four cats gathered close around him, waited for them with a smile on his face.

"Time to go back," he said in a gentle manner, when they drew close. "But come to see me when you wake up, just so you know all of this is as it appears. I know it's a lot to process, but this is a very special visit ... your first time in Faraway."

"Thank you for this wonderful gift," Desiree said to the Artist. "Few of us who have gone onward get such a chance."

"My pleasure, and my honor," the Artist replied, extending a graceful bow to her.

Haven looked to her grandmother, a tinge of worry pulling at her. "Will I really see you again?"

Desiree smiled. "What do you think?"

Grinning, and looking into her grandmother's eyes, so full of life, peace, and joy, Haven knew the answer. She nodded. "Yes,

I will."

"Yes, you will," her grandmother confirmed. Her smile broadened. "Come here, and give me a hug before you go, Haven."

Desiree spread her arms wide, and Haven stepped forward, reaching out to her. The two hugged each other tight.

"I love you, Haven, and know in your heart that love goes onward," Desiree said.

"I love you, grandma," Haven said, her eyes glistening over once more.

"Til the next time, Haven," Desiree said in a gentle tone, her image and the surroundings beginning to fade from Haven's sight.

Drifting out of awareness, her vision clouding over, Haven's experience in the fantastical realm drew to an end. A few moments later, her eyes fluttered open, back in the dim ambience of her bedroom.

She found her cheeks tear-stained, but that discovery came as little surprise. It would have been hard to believe they would not be, after the powerful surges of emotions she had just experienced.

Swinging her legs around, and setting her feet on the soft carpet, Haven took several long, slow breaths. Having gone to bed as one person, she had awoken a different one.

The seed of something grand and wonderful had taken root deep within her. Haven knew that she had the strength and the willpower to take on the Primordial cancer embedded so thoroughly within her world.

When she rose up, she stood as a young woman with a new fire kindled inside. The world no longer seemed so daunting, and its bevy of threats and intimidation rang much more hollow.

The technate and all of its power no longer held a sense of finality. Something far greater existed, a reality transcending everything in her world.

Thinking of her grandmother's smiling face and loving gaze invoked a wellspring of peace and joy within Haven. What had seemed impossible only a day ago now had become part of her own reality.

Love did survive and go onward; into far better realms where shadow and sorrow held no dominion.

Taking a shower and getting changed into a fresh set of clothes, Haven headed out of the apartment less than thirty minutes later. During her visit to Faraway she had been given one remaining task, and she refused to delay a moment longer in seeing to it.

Walking into the streets of the technate, she looked at a security drone rolling by on the street. She grinned at the object, knowing the power of such things over her inner self had diminished greatly, in the span of a single night.

The experience of Faraway had freed her, in a deep, fundamental way.

More than ever before, the world around her no longer represented everything about reality. If anything, as she gazed upon drones and other vehicles rolling down the streets in the shadow of lofty tenements, all watched over by a multitude of sensors, the entire scene had an air of the illusory about it.

Continuing down the sidewalk, the realization stunned her. Never had she imagined looking upon a world that others might describe as mere dreams to be reality, all the while regarding the one she had always viewed as solid reality to be nothing more than a grand illusion.

After visiting with her grandmother in Faraway, Haven knew that the world around her was not her destination; but only a step on a far more incredible road.

A smile still rested on her face the moment she entered the building where Serena's apartment was located. Riding the elevator upward, no doubt existed in Haven's heart; the Artist would be there.

Striding down the hallway, she rapped upon the door without delay. The door opened a few moments later, revealing the Artist within the frame, a joyous smile on his face.

Serena stood at his right shoulder, just behind him, looking every bit as happy.

"You've been to Faraway, and it is now time to become a Navigator, dear Haven," he said, stepping forward and giving her a warm embrace. "Are you ready for the grand adventure?"

"I am," she replied with determination, returning the hug. "Thank you, Christopher Brendan ... for everything."

Clarity bloomed within her heart. A new, wondrous horizon called to her, inviting Haven on the greatest of adventures.

Jaelynn

Sitting on the rail, his back to the river, the boy eyed Jaelynn with a relaxed expression. Making her way across the bridge, she approached the place he occupied.

Sitting directly underneath one of the streetlights set at even intervals along the walkway, he had made no effort to conceal himself. In a pool of light, he kept his eyes fixed toward Jaelynn, watching her stride closer to him.

Medium-length dark hair framed a face with angular features. He did not look to be tall, but his body carried a gangly appearance, having not yet grown and matured into its fullness.

While not striking in appearance, the boy was not unattractive either. Jaelynn estimated him to be about her age, with at most a year's difference between them.

A few people walked on the opposite side of the street, and a handful of drone vehicles trundled along the roadway. Even if there had been nobody in sight, Jaelynn doubted that she would have been nervous.

The boy looked friendly enough. Jaelynn had long since learned to discern the nature of a gaze and expression, and nothing she saw within the boy's face put her on the defensive.

Catching her eyes, he smiled at her. "Hey, how are you? I

think you live near me, I've seen you around before."

"Doing fine," she replied, reaching the place where he sat astride the rail.

She slowed down, deciding against continuing onward at his mention of seeing her before. Jaelynn searched her mind but could not place the boy in any particular encounter. She only knew that he was not a member of Gabriel's circle of friends.

"Looks like we're both out and about late tonight," the boy said, grinning.

"I'm just taking a walk and getting away from my apartment for a while," she replied, with a polite smile. "What about you?"

"I'm just taking it easy. Not much for anyone to aspire to in this technate," the boy said, a grim edge to his words. "Probably am supposed to take more Balancer meds when I think like that, but I like knowing what my thoughts really are."

Jaelynn nodded. "I know what you mean. Believe me, I do. I'd rather do without taking those meds myself."

The boy looked around, watching more traffic pass by. She followed his gaze to where it settled upon on a cluster of people walking on the other side of the street.

"Every single move we make, recorded and watched," he said, frowning. "Nowhere you can get away from it in this technate."

"No, there isn't anywhere to run to," Jaelynn said, with the air of a sigh.

"All we get is this crap," the boy said, looking up at the streetlight, where the eye of a security sensor stared back toward them. "Anyone who tries to do anything about it, they just round up."

"You don't have to tell me about that, I've seen way too much of it," Jaelynn said, bitterness rising like bile inside her. Images of Gabriel and Dr. Swedenborg flashed through her mind, speeding the anger running through her body.

"Be nice to upend it all, wouldn't it?" the boy asked. "Shut the whole thing down, turn it off like a switch."

Jaelynn came to the brink of voicing her agreement, but she stopped at the cusp of saying the words. She looked up at the sensor on the streetlight, knowing images were not the only thing the unit recorded.

"I wish that life could be better," Jaelynn said, keeping her words general in nature.

"What if I told you the whole thing could be turned off, like a switch," the boy said. A grin spread across his face, and a glint came to his eyes.

"I would be careful about," she said, hoping he caught her sense of warning. She cast a glance up at the sensor, intending for him to catch the gesture.

A look of concentration came over the boy's face. He looked off down the street, and his body tensed, hands gripping onto the rails tightly.

For an instant, it appeared to Jaelynn as if the air shimmered. She felt a tingle pass over her body.

A moment later, the lights across the bridge went out. Seconds later, the scent of something burning wafted over her.

The bridge now spanned a river lit only by starlight. She knew the security sensor on the streetlight had been blinded and rendered deaf.

Looking back toward the boy, she asked. "What just happened?"

The triumphant smile on his face answered her question well enough. She knew Gabriel and Dr. Swedenborg would have been elated with what had just transpired.

"And I can do that in our world too," the boy stated, grinning wider.

"Our world? This is our world," Jaelynn responded, a little confused.

"This is a dream, but it is a very good one, I have to say," the boy said. "You know dreams aren't as they appear to be. We both know that."

The boy's words triggered lucidity in Jaelynn. She remembered lying down in her bed and realized that she stood within a dream.

The boy's words were correct in more than one way. Dreams were not what they appeared to be. She had learned that lesson well enough already.

"Who are you?" she asked the boy, finding herself much more curious about his identity.

"Cayden," the boy answered. "I'd like to ask you one favor. Come to this bridge tomorrow, in our world. You'll find me there. It will be all the proof you need that this was more than just a dream."

"And if you are real?" Jaelynn asked.

"I need friends in my world who are dealing with the bigger picture, too," Cayden responded.

"I need a friend like that, too," Jaelynn admitted, thinking of the enigmatic woman she had encountered in the dusky world.

"Then come find me tomorrow," Cayden said.

With another grin, he hopped down from the rail. He started down the sidewalk, going a few strides before looking back over his shoulder.

"Don't forget, this bridge, tomorrow," he said. After a moment, he added, "Lots to look forward to ... we can do our part to bring all of this crashing down."

"I won't forget," Jaelynn replied, finding his invitation more than compelling. Seeing the power of the technate come crashing down sounded wonderful to her ears.

Smiling at the thought of having Gabriel and Dr. Swedenborg freed again, she watched Cayden walk down the street.

Salvador

S tanding on the roof of the tenement, over a hundred and fifty stories in the air, Salvador looked outward, gazing toward the dark cloud masses rolling toward the city. The gusting winds lashed against his face, an icy chill deepening within the air surrounding him.

Jade stood at his right side, casting a piercing stare toward the oncoming storm front. A grim expression shone on his face, enhancing the intensity within his eyes.

Salvador turned to look at Jade and said, "The weather was supposed to be clear today, tomorrow, and, they said, the day after. Not supposed to be a hint of rain."

"You did your homework well," Jade replied, the trace of a grin playing about his lips. "I know this development has more than a few observers scratching their heads about right now."

"Hey, you said to be sure to take a look at the official reports," Salvador responded. "I did listen, and I did take a look."

Jade nodded. "I did tell you to do that, so this demonstration would be a little more clear to you."

"Couldn't be clearer than all of that," Salvador said, nodding and gesturing toward the formations of thunderheads in the distance. It would not be long before the blackening, vaporous masses enveloped the entire technate.

"I didn't think you'd miss it," Jade said, an inkling of humor dancing about his words and within his eyes.

"Kind of hard to miss a gigantic storm front rolling right toward you," Salvador said, laughing as another gust of cold wind blasted against him.

Jade's wide-brimmed hat did not move in the slightest, despite the buffeting, high winds. The lack of any effect served as a telltale sign of the fact that everything around him carried the essence of a dream.

For Salvador, the very same things held the nature of a physical reality. Yet the man standing next to him wielded a tremendous power over that reality; to a degree that he had been able to summon a massive storm into bright, clear skies.

Salvador thought back to his first encounter with Jade in the park, and the sudden change in weather that had brewed in the skies above them. He could not deny what had happened then, or the phenomenon now manifesting before his eyes.

"Navigator and storm master," Salvador commented with an air of respect, watching pulses of lightning ripple through the cloud-filled horizon.

"Just a Navigator," Jade replied. "But Navigators are not all the same. We each have our strengths, and our weaknesses. We're still human."

"And if I become one, then what do you think my strength is?" Salvador asked.

"Discovery is the fun part," Jade said, chuckling. "It might be something along the lines of what I have. Or it might be something entirely different. I guess we'll find out."

"How long does it take?" Salvador asked, impatient to learn if he had any abilities like that of Jade.

"I can't give you an answer to that, but we do need to get you started on your journey," Jade said. "Go back to your room and go to sleep. Rejoin me, then."

Salvador walked back to the roof access hatch, the winds beating against him with greater ferocity. Before climbing down the ladder, he looked back.

Jade had already turned his attention to the oncoming storm. The rain beginning to fall, he stretched his arms out wide, as if welcoming every single drop.

Thunder boomed and shook the building, a wave of lightning filling the skies with a brilliant, white radiance.

Salvador climbed down the steps and shut the hatch behind him. The blue glow lingered just above him, reminding him that Jade's power had allowed him to access the roof without triggering technate security elements.

He had come to trust that power, and knew he could handle more, but still could not shed having a little anxiety regarding the unknown.

Salvador proceeded back to his apartment, and then continued into his bedroom. Changing into some bedclothes, he commanded the Home Assistant to dim the lights and drape his windows.

A storm raging outside, he lay down on his bed and stared toward the ceiling, wondering what Jade intended for him next. Though difficult, he emptied his mind as best he could, knowing the answers would come with sleep.

The winds, rain, and peals of thunder lulled him into a relaxed state. At last, his eyelids grew heavy, and then he drifted off, ready to experience new horizons.

Jaelynn

Jaelynn looked around the virtual environment, which took the form of an elaborate dance club filled with patrons both real and generated. A series of platforms and catwalks spanned the multi-level interior. Pulsating rhythms boomed throughout the vast space.

Sitting on a plush couch within an alcove, she eyed the other three figures nearby. Of the trio, only one shared the same reality as her.

In the physical world, Roxy was a slender girl of sixteen, with long, straight brown hair. Within the digital realm, she changed her appearances on a regular basis.

Currently, Roxy had taken the form of a tall, athletic-looking woman of about thirty, with piercing blue eyes. Not once had Jaelynn seen Roxy assume her true physical appearance within the virtual realms.

The other two were digital constructs.

One had the name of Murak, taking the form of a dark-haired male of medium height in his early twenties. His olive-toned skin had not a speck of blemish, and he wore a collared shirt, slacks, and well-shined dress shoes. Murak carried himself with a refined air that matched his polished appearance.

Sitting next to him, the other had the name of Zania, and appeared as a woman of about twenty. She had pink and blue hair of a neon brilliance that no natural dye could mimic. Clad in a black leather jacket, t-shirt, jeans, and an assortment of accessories, Zania's rougher look fit well with her vivacious demeanor.

Both Murak and Zania could be found with Roxy wherever she roved in the digital realms. Had Jaelynn not known otherwise, she would have deemed them to be the avatars of real humans.

Roxy spoke of them as if they were real friends, in every way, and sometimes Jaelynn found herself forgetting their true natures. It proved an easy slip, given that she interacted with them no differently than she did with Roxy in the virtual atmospheres.

Looking up, Roxy exclaimed, "Yay! Looks like Veronica is finally here. Been waiting on her for some time now. Be back in a sec!"

She got up to her feet.

"I'll go with you," Murak said, collecting himself and standing up. "I've missed seeing her."

"I'll stay," Zania stated. "She wants to see me, she knows where to find me."

The other two vanished from sight a moment later, reappearing on a higher level where a woman standing on the edge of a balcony reacted to their presence with a broad smile.

"You seem distracted tonight, Jaelynn," Zania remarked, looking toward Jaelynn. "What's up?"

"Just a lot on my head," Jaelynn replied. She mustered a grin. "Nothing I can't handle."

"I am sure it hasn't been easy on you with Gabriel in Rehabilitation," Zania said, a concerned look on her face.

Jaelynn worked to keep her composure steady. She had said nothing about the matter to Roxy, and certainly not a word of it to Zania.

The fact that the AI-driven avatar knew of her predicament did not seem out of line with what she had discovered about the reality of the world. Any digital creation was merely a manifestation of the greater system; connected to networks in every way, and able to access everything within them.

In a way of looking at it, underneath the facade of an individual being, Zania was nothing more than an extension of the same power that had monitored and then apprehended Gabriel.

"And also your friend, Dr. Swedenborg, that had to be awful too, I'm very sorry," Zania continued, in a convincing tone of sympathy.

Though alarmed by the comment, Jaelynn forced a smile upon her face. "It has been a difficult time. I never expected all of that to happen with people I know."

"You never saw them do anything that they got in trouble for?" Zania asked, in a casual tone that did not fool Jaelynn.

Treading on thinner ice, Jaelynn knew she had to choose her next words very carefully. The digital construct before her had become an interrogator, in the guise of a social companion.

"No, never talked about anything serious with Dr. Swedenborg ... and Gabriel has been a great boyfriend to me," Jaelynn answered. "All of this hit me by total surprise. I just don't know why they needed to be taken in. The worst part of it all is not having any answers."

"I imagine so," Zania said, staring intently. "But what about you? You were in both of their circles. Aren't you worried?"

"Not really," Jaelynn replied, mimicking confidence and veiling her unease. "I know I'll be okay ... all they have to do is analyze what they've got filed from the sensors."

Jaelynn thought of the use of writing on physical paper with Gabriel, and Dr. Swedenborg's claim that his apartment had a shield of privacy. She could only hope that both elements protected her enough to get her through any security analysis.

Only time would tell if she had evaded the notice of the system but listening to Zania she doubted it. The digital being's line of questioning was anything but casual.

Zania nodded. "True, or you would have been taken in, too."

"It is now eight pm," the voice of Jaelynn's Home Assistant sounded crisp and clear in her ears, providing the alarm she had asked for.

The notice came as a great relief to Jaelynn. She did not want to make one misstep with Zania.

"Well, it looks like I have to get back to a few things at the apartment," Jaelynn said, smiling at Zania. "Tell Roxy and Murak bye for me when they come back."

"I will," Zania said, returning the smile. "I'm sure I'll see you soon enough. Try to behave if you can."

"I'll do my best ... see you later!" Jaelynn said in a friendly manner, before exiting the virtual environment.

Taking off her VR helmet, Jaelynn kept still a few seconds, her bedroom coming back into focus. The pounding drumbeats and flashing lights replaced abruptly with silence and a low-ambience jarred her for a moment.

Thinking about what had just happened, Jaelynn realized she could never look at the world in the same way again. Understanding the nature of the system governing life in Technate Six, she had gained a new perspective on the things transpiring within the virtual realms.

The extent of the technate's reach had become even more clear. Sensors in the physical world were not the only monitors of individuals across the various sectors. Some eyes of the technate took the form of companions and confidants; able to glean thoughts and feelings in unguarded moments.

Heightened wariness had spared Jaelynn. In earlier days,

she might well have said something to Zania that would have led to a stint in Rehabilitation.

Taking a deep breath, and grateful for her increased level of caution, Jaelynn got up and put on her shoes. The time had come to take a walk to a particular bridge.

Cayden

angling his legs, Cayden sat on the rail, in about the same place he had been in the dream-rendered version of the location. The streetlight watched over him with its surveillance apparatus, and far beneath the broad river flowed in a star-glittered procession.

Cayden wondered if the girl would show up. Thinking back upon the dream realm encounter, Cayden still found it surprising how confident he had been in his interaction with her.

Things had changed to a great degree since the times before meeting the Guardian, Lilithian. In the past, when around girls who were his peers, Cayden never would have exhibited the kind of confident demeanor that he had presented to the auburn-haired girl.

He had not been self-conscious or intimidated. His thoughts had not been clouded, and no awkwardness haunted his conversation with her.

Tapping into his inner strength with the help of the Guardian had opened up so much more for Cayden. He could not thank Lilithian enough for saving him from the timid, fearful person that he had been.

Looking up and smiling, Cayden beheld the dark-skinned

girl approaching on his side of the bridge. She walked alone, giving a wide berth between her and the next pedestrian.

"I was hoping you would show up here," he said, when she drew near.

"Hi Cayden," she replied. "See? I didn't forget your name. I knew you would be here."

"Maybe it's time I learn your name," Cayden said, with a grin. "I forgot to ask you, the last time we talked."

"I'm Jaelynn," she said extending her hand.

He grinned wider, shaking her hand. "I suspect we have more than a few things in common. I think we're going to be good friends."

"I think we are, too," she responded, a smile spreading upon her face.

Glancing up toward the sensor on the light pole close by, and giving Jaelynn a pointed look, he said, "So much to talk about. Maybe a quieter place to visit would be better?"

"Not a lot of quiet places in this crowded technate," Jaelynn replied, with an expression that told him she understood what he meant.

"Then maybe we should just hang out for a little while, not worry about anything too important, and catch back up in a better location," he said, his true meaning conveyed in his tone.

She nodded, a look of understanding in her eyes. "Sounds like a plan to me."

"How far do you live from here?" he asked.

"Just a couple of blocks," she answered, pointing back. "In that direction."

"You aren't too far from me then," he said, gesturing to an area located just to the right of where she had indicated. He got down from the railing and arched his back, stretching. "What would you like to do?"

"Get one of those nice homes in the Northern Sector?" she

responded, laughing. "That would be so great."

"Wouldn't we all want one of those?" he replied, chuckling. "Trade in an apartment for one of the big residences I've heard they all have in there."

"Would be nice," Jaelynn said. "But since that's not an option at the moment, how about we get some coffee or maybe a bite to eat?"

"Sounds good to me, I haven't used up too many credits this month yet," Cayden said, hopping down from the railing.

"I'm not wiped out yet myself," Jaelynn said, matching his side as they crossed the bridge. "Just wish credits carried over."

"Well, you know what they say about stockpiling leading to inequality, like in the old world," Cayden said. "But it sure would be nice."

"Well, we're all equally managed now, that's for sure," Jaelynn said.

"Except for the Northern Sector," Cayden said.

"The word equal has a different definition there I think," Jaelynn retorted, laughing.

Cayden found himself taking a great liking to Jaelynn. Though her words remained guarded, he sensed a kindred nature in her.

She was not the type to swallow every spoonful of propaganda fed by the technate. Like him, she embraced her own mind.

The next couple of hours confirmed his initial thoughts. Over a coffee and a long walk, Cayden learned a lot about her.

She harbored fears but had not succumbed to them. It was clear she needed a friend just like him, and he intended to be that for her.

He did not like hearing about what had happened to her boyfriend, and an older friend; a doctor that had been incarcerated. The absence of the two had clearly left a void in her world; one that he could help her endure.

Cayden needed a friend like Jaelynn as well. Finally, he had someone his own age that could relate to him on many levels.

By the time their visit came to an end, and the two parted ways to return to their respective apartments, a new friendship had taken root. Though Cayden wished the visit could have continued for a little while longer, he would be seeing Jaelynn soon enough; within other realms of existence.

The thought brought a smile to his face. For the first time in his heart, Cayden recognized in that moment that the world no longer had him caged and at its mercy.

Salvador

Salvador gawked about in a state of sheer astonishment. Everywhere he turned, spellbinding sights flooded his widened eyes.

No two buildings alike, and every single one of them a beautiful work of art, a surreal metropolis surrounded him.

Elaborate constructs soared toward skies of shimmering hues. Spaced well apart, the buildings were separated by tracts of ground filled with an abundance of foliage and trees.

Placed all throughout the various grounds, magnificent floral displays had been cultivated, containing many colors Salvador had never seen before.

"Welcome to Faraway, a way station at the edge of even grander realms," Jade commented, gazing upon everything with a look of serenity on his face. He turned to look toward Salvador.

"Grander realms? Than this?" Salvador asked, in disbelief.

"Very much so," Jade replied, looking amused at Salvador's reaction.

"I can't believe what I'm seeing here," Salvador said. The sights far surpassed any virtual environment he had explored.

The inhabitants of the metropolis looked human enough, though they had a much different air about them than the citizens of Technate Six.

Without exception, all had youthful, joyful appearances. Carefree laughter carried along the gentle breezes, the touch of the latter refreshing in a way Salvador could not compare to anything in his physical world.

"I really don't know what to say," Salvador said, looking down on a fountain whose waters had the hue and luster of sapphires.

"Sometimes it's best to say nothing, and just take in the experience," Jade said. "How does it feel standing at the edge of forever?"

"Indescribable," Salvador replied.

Savoring every moment, Salvador placed his hands on the gleaming, golden rail before him. A breeze flowed over him, brushing soft against his skin, giving off a low, melodious sound.

"Incredible," Salvador said, listening to the wind's gentle music.

"You will find music all throughout Faraway," Jade said. "This is a place of harmony, where corruption has no place."

Salvador glanced back at the spacious lounge behind him. Suited for reclining, a group of chaises and low couches faced toward the view of the metropolis. Accompanied by a number of exquisite crystal glasses, several decanters stood on an ornate table.

The decanters themselves looked to be fashioned of the substance of jewels, one of them ruby, another sapphire, and another emerald. Salvador could only imagine what kind of liquids they contained.

"Nobody goes hungry or thirsty here, I bet," Salvador remarked.

"Food and drink is not needed here, but it can be enjoyed," Jade replied. "The finest tastes you have ever experienced."

"So you eat just because you want to," Salvador said.

"With no chance of indigestion, gaining weight, or getting sick," Jade said, nodding.

"Now that sounds like my kind of nutrition," Salvador said.

"Go ahead, try out one of those," Jade said, indicating the decanters.

Salvador walked over to the table, marveling at the vessels displayed upon it. Each cup distinct, the designs had a flowing, graceful motif, with vines and flowers reaching up to gird a basin serving as the main liquid receptacle.

Reaching out, Salvador picked up the emerald decanter. The touch of its surface smooth, the decanter contained a light green liquid brimming with tiny sparkles. He poured a small amount in one of the glasses.

Setting the decanter back down, he picked the glass up and raised it to his lips. A bouquet of pleasant aromas enveloping his olfactory senses, the scents gave him the first hint that he was about to taste something beyond anything he had ever had.

Tilting the glass, he sipped.

Blinking his widening eyes, he stared at the glass as the sweet flavor burst within his mouth. He had never tasted anything so delectable in all of his life.

"Wow!" Salvador exclaimed, looking back to Jade.

"It is incredible, isn't it?" Jade replied, smiling.

Salvador eagerly drank down the rest of the cup's contents, before pouring himself another glass.

"Just enjoy the taste, no need to rush," Jade commented, laughing.

Salvador spent a little time sampling all of the beverages on the table. All had different tastes, with different profiles of fruit and degrees of sweetness, but all of the liquids engaged his tastes so powerfully that he could not say if he found any one of them better than another.

"Just wait until you try the food around here," Jade told him, when he had finished trying all of the decanters.

"Can we?" Salvador asked.

Jade smiled. "Not on this trip. We've got a little work to accomplish."

"I suppose so," Salvador said. "Sorry if I got a little greedy."

Jade laughed heartily. "No worry about greed where there is no shortage of anything. You were just enjoying yourself, not a bad thing at all."

"No, I guess not," Salvador replied, smiling. "So I'm guessing people live here. Who are they?"

"They do, and there are many like us who visit," Jade said. "As far as those who dwell here, you've known a few of them before."

"I have?" Salvador asked.

"You have," a third voice interjected.

Salvador turned about, seeing a slender, dark-haired young man with a thick beard walking up from behind the chaises and couches. A warm smile on his face, the man had something very familiar about him.

"Who does he make you think of?" Jade asked, with a grin.

Salvador looked into the other man's dark eyes. Only one person came to mind. "He is several years older than the one I think of ... but he reminds me of a friend I had when I was younger ... about ten or eleven."

"A friend named Asher, perhaps?" the young man asked.

"Yes," Salvador answered.

"Did he look more like ... this?" the young man asked, his smile becoming wider as he began to shimmer.

The man's form changed right before Salvador's eyes, becoming that of a boy Salvador recognized at once.

"Asher?" Salvador asked, astonished.

"I am he," the boy answered in a voice unmistakable.

"Is ... this real?" Salvador asked in disbelief, glancing for a moment toward Jade, though not wanting to take his eyes off Asher for even an instant.

Jade laughed. "It is as real as real can possibly get, my young friend."

"I am as alive as you," Asher said, a joyful look on his face.

"But, it cannot be," Salvador said, recalling the terrible accident that had claimed his friend at the construction site of a tenement. "Death is final."

"Let me explain it to you in another way," Jade said. "Energy is never destroyed. It changes forms. The energy that is Asher moved onward, to take forms in higher planes when released from the physical body."

"I want to believe this," Salvador said, wrestling with a number of emotions as he began to allow himself to consider the idea put forth by Jade.

"There is no need to believe it, when you know it," Asher said.

Continuing forward, Asher came to stand in front of Salvador. Reaching out, he grabbed Salvador's upper right arm, giving it a light squeeze.

"I am no illusion," Asher said. "How about another friend of yours?"

A small dog trundled out from behind the couch, wagging its plumed tail. The dog's thick coat of golden-brown and white fur had a luxuriant sheen. Triangular ears perked up, the little creature's short muzzle looked to be exhibiting a smile; an expression Salvador knew so very well.

Astonished, Salvador could not say a word.

The last time he had seen the dog, the little fellow had been old and frail, straining to breath on a countertop inside a technate center for animals. Salvador had gone home without Rocky on that horrid day.

The dog represented Salvador's first encounter with death,

at the age of nine. He could remember the agony he experienced when the finality of death was explained to him. He had been told to hold onto memories, the only thing that could last beyond death.

No amount of memories could stave off the unbearable emptiness within Salvador's home in the aftermath of Rocky's death.

Salvador had stayed with Rocky to the very end, the dog looking straight into his eyes until the last breath. Whether a construct of his imagination or not, Salvador had never been able to forget seeing the light going out of the dog's eyes, when the final breath expired.

He never had another dog in his home after that traumatic experience, but it was not because of the mounting technate regulations toward the keeping of animals. Salvador did not ever want to feel as helpless and powerless as he did when seeing the old dog slip away.

The dog standing before him was no memory, but rather a living, vibrant being. No trace of advanced age or frailty could be found on the little dog. Young once more, Rocky trotted up to him with a confident strut.

"Hi Salvador, I've missed you, very much so," a new voice said.

Salvador's eyes widened, for the voice seemed to have come from the dog.

"Here you can understand my words, in your mind," the voice continued, gentle and kind in tone.

Salvador fell to his knees, petting and stroking Rocky's soft fur. Learning over, he put his head to the dog's forehead. Like a dam finally giving way, tears began to fall from his eyes.

"You've always been ... in my heart," Salvador said to Rocky, voice choking up with emotion.

"I know, as you've been in mine," Rocky said, raising his

head up and licking Salvador on the face.

"I ... can't believe it," Salvador muttered, overwhelmed with emotion.

"Nothing to believe, just something to know," Rocky replied, with a trace of amusement, echoing what Asher had just told him moments before.

"I've missed you so much," Salvador said, scooping the dog up and hugging Rocky to him.

Rocky licked him again on the face. "I've missed you as well."

Holding onto the dog, he talked for a long while with Asher, Rocky, and Jade. Both Rocky and Asher dwelled in the realms beyond Faraway, though both had come back at the behest of Jade, to help Salvador understand the nature of the higher realms.

Salvador wondered how he had been able to reach out to them, since Jade had mentioned he could not go beyond Faraway himself. Keeping his curiosity to himself, Salvador focused on staying in the moment and enjoying the incredible reunion with two dear individuals he had once thought were gone forever from his life.

Finally, Jade brought the visit to an end, indicating that he needed to take Salvador onward.

Though not wanting the visit to end, Salvador understood. Saying goodbye to both Asher and Rocky so soon after reuniting proved difficult, but he found a little comfort in the idea that he could see them again.

Asher summed it up well when he told Salvador, "No need for a goodbye ... How about a 'til we meet again'?"

"I like the sound of that," Salvador replied. "Then til we meet again, it is!"

Asher and Rocky then departed, leaving Salvador with Jade on the landing.

"It's hard for me to accept what just happened," Salvador

remarked, his gaze lingering in the direction where the other two had gone.

"You've had a lifetime of being told what you just saw is all folly," Jade commented. "By those who could only claim such absolutes if they possessed all knowledge."

Salvador looked back to Jade and smiled. "I guess I'm just going to have to accept this aspect of reality."

"I'm sure it's such a disappointment," Jade replied, chuckling.

"I hope I see them both again soon," Salvador responded, a wistful edge to his voice.

"You will, but I have more to show you on this visit," Jade said.

"In Faraway?" Salvador asked.

Jade shook his head.

"Not here ... I need to show you what is happening elsewhere, in other realms," Jade said, his tone growing somber. "I have to warn you ahead of time that this excursion won't be pleasant in nature."

Salvador frowned at the news, not wanting to leave the magical place encompassing him. "Now?"

"You'll be able to come back here, don't worry," Jade said. "But you won't fully appreciate Faraway, or what Navigators are fighting for, unless you open your eyes to some other kinds of realities ... even if they are difficult to witness. You must be aware of the lower realms, as much as the higher ones."

Looking around, Salvador's gaze soaked up the lavish scenery with all of its impressive forms and hues. He hoped it would not be long before he could return to Faraway and behold its wonders again.

Jade walked over to stand at Salvador's side, and everything blurred and dimmed, at last becoming pitch black. Vision returned to him a few moments later.

Drab, gray surroundings met Salvador's eyes, the vision a

stark contrast to the wonders he had just experienced. Masses of clouds, like vast formations of ash, rolled across the upper skies.

The cold chill within the winds carried a sharp bite, and a scent like the mix of rotten eggs and decaying flesh permeated the air.

Old buildings in advanced states of disrepair loomed all around him. Some had collapsed into piles of rubble, and mounds of rubbish littered the streets all over.

Here and there, fires burned within niches and alcoves. The thin flames appeared fragile, as if they were on the verge of flicking out at any moment.

The light given off from the flames had a strange quality to it. To Salvador's eyes, it looked as if the shadows pressed in, keeping the light contained, and suppressing its radiance.

Despite the dusky environs, Salvador could see a far distance.

His mood dampened swiftly. Feelings of dread and despair took root and grew the longer he gazed upon the dismal scene.

"Walk with me," Jade said, in a somber tone.

Not wanting to be left alone for an instant, Salvador kept close to Jade as he led him toward the nearest fire. After a few paces, Salvador took notice of a small group of individuals huddled near the wispy flames.

Dressed in little more than rags, the men and women looked haggard and emaciated. Weathered, dirty faces creased with wrinkles turned to peer at Jade and Salvador as they approached.

"Who are you?" one of the men asked, in a confrontational manner that was much more of a challenge than an outright question.

"Just travelers," Jade answered in an even tone.

Salvador took confidence from Jade's unruffled composure, though his anxiety kept increasing.

"You aren't from this cursed place," a woman said. She eyed Salvador, squinting a little. "Neither of you."

"No, we're not," Jade told her.

The looks on the faces of the group around the fire ranged from disbelief, to sadness, to fear, and even to anger.

"Come here to deceive us, did you?" another man asked, his eyes glinting with raw hostility.

"If you came here from another place, then there's a way out of here?" a woman asked in a plaintive voice, looking to Jade. Tears welled up within her eyes.

"Shut up!" the irritable man yelled at her.

Paying no attention to the man, Jade did not raise his voice when he responded to the woman. "There is a way out of here, but you have to find the light within you and let it grow."

Glaring at Jade, the contentious man rose to his feet and clenched his dirt-encrusted fists. Jade had no change in his composure, simply turning to look at the man with a solemn expression.

Suddenly, the fire died down further, and the shadows deepened before Salvador's eyes. Looking away from Jade, fear replaced anger in the eyes of the man standing, and some of the others looked terrified.

"Please, take us with you!" the woman who had asked about a way out pleaded, terror brimming within her eyes.

"I cannot, in the condition you are in now, but this does not have to remain permanent," Jade said to the woman, sorrow thick within his voice. He turned toward Salvador. "Look around you now, and do not forget what you see."

Salvador looked away from the fire and the people around it to take in the dimming environment. Panic surged and raced throughout him at the sight meeting his eyes.

Dark, snake-like shapes slithered through the air and along the ground. Ghostly-wraiths glided about and hovered, their skeletal, humanoid faces leering at the group around the fire.

A wave of nausea passed through Salvador. He did not

have to ask Jade what the things were. Every instinct within him declared their identity.

Primordials.

The host of creatures appeared far more intent on Jade and Salvador than they did the bedraggled figures. Watching the eyes of the men and women, he soon realized they could not see the shadow-entities.

A monstrosity flew out of the shadows. Head resembling a flaring cobra, the entity had broad, bat-like wings and an elongated set of appendages ending in curving talons.

Unlike with the shadow-entities, the group around the fire could see the grisly newcomer.

Screaming and crying out, the cluster of men and women abandoned the fire in great haste, scrambling to get away from the area. The monster sped forward, into the group's midst, taking up one of the men before he had gotten five strides.

Salvador recognized the man as the one who had clenched his fists in anger toward Jade.

Crying out, the hapless victim flailed and thrashed to no avail. His bestial captor flapped its broad wings, lifting higher, and soon melting into the shadows of the upper heights of the surrounding buildings.

Circling around Jade and Salvador, the horde of shadow-creatures remained behind, paying no heed to the fleeing people. Though having a tremendous advantage in numbers, the dark creatures held back.

Salvador knew the reason centered on Jade.

"It's time for us to leave this place, I've had enough of these cowardly Primordials," Jade said, scowling at the dark entities, as if daring them to attack. "Think of the park, and the place where I first met you."

Setting his mind on the spot mentioned by Jade, and closing his eyes, Salvador concentrated. Blocking out the horrific visions around him, he thought of the old oak tree and the soft grass, along with the other trees marking the place that had become his personal refuge.

A moment later, Salvador found himself standing a few paces from the oak tree. Moonlight cast soft shadows across the ground. Between a few patches of clouds, a starry sky glittered above.

Relieved at the familiar sight, Salvador looked around for Jade, finding his friend and guide a couple paces to the right.

"This is like Faraway compared to that place," Salvador exclaimed, giving a light shudder at the thought of the terrible realm they had left behind.

"You've gotten your first look at Primordials, the ones those people could not see," Jade said. "And now that you have beheld them, you can see them."

Unsure of whether that ability could be deemed a blessing or a curse, Salvador asked, "In my world? Here?"

Jade nodded.

"What exactly are they?" Salvador queried. "It looked like there were several different kinds."

"Manifestations of the basest negative energy," Jade said. "They cannot enter any realm or reality unless they have negative energy to feed upon. It's why they are gaining a powerful hold over your world. They feast upon a world such as this."

"But they could never enter a place like Faraway," Salvador said, the remembrance of the incredible place having a soothing effect on his rattled mind.

A grim expression rose on Jade's face. "It would be possible. A little fear in one place, a touch of hate in another, and a shred of despair in yet another can open doorways and give them something to clutch onto. It's how your world has become so infested."

"It's like a disease, spreading from one place to another,"

Salvador observed.

"Precisely," Jade said. "An infection of the worst kind."

"What about that last thing, the one that the other people could see?" Salvador asked, a pang of fear accompanying the memory of the cobra-headed beast. The scream of its pitiful victim echoed within his mind.

"That place is a creation of those who dwell within it, including the people like you saw," Jade answered.

"They made a place like that?" Salvador asked, astonished. "Willingly? I find that so hard to believe."

"The environment reflects their nature, and others like them gravitate to it, adding to its reality and giving birth to new horrors," Jade said. "Their thoughts darken and give everything around them greater solidity."

"But you told that woman it wasn't permanent," Salvador said, perplexed.

"Individuals can leave such a place, but only when their nature can no longer abide in that kind of realm. Then, they are in a state that can dwell in a light-filled plane of existence," Jade explained. "It is often a slow process, though sometimes it can be aided to go faster."

"Maybe what you told that woman will help her," Salvador said.

Jade nodded. "That is always my intent; and my desire."

Salvador thought of the haunted looks on the faces of the people he had seen. "I would like to be able to help people like that, too."

"Another reason you are suited to be a Navigator," Jade replied. "But always remember, those you seek to help must choose their own path, using their own willpower. No amount of help you can offer can take them from a darker realm. In the end, it is always up to them."

Salvador nodded. "Such a terrible place."

"What I showed you is far from the worst," Jade replied.

"Far from the worst?" Salvador asked.

"There are planes of existence you are far from ready to set your eyes upon," Jade said in a grim tone. "The levels in the outermost darkness."

Salvador took in the words with a heavier heart. It stood to reason that if there were places beyond Faraway even more magnificent, then there had to be places of an opposing nature. He did not want to think of what such an awful place would be like.

Jaelynn

"We can talk openly here," Cayden said.

Pedestrian traffic flowed around them, but Jaelynn had no worries. Knowing the two of them stood within a dreamscape, like the ones she had encountered Sendinian within, she could relax her guard.

"Agreed," she replied, at ease.

"So, we both know a little more about the world and its nature, I'm guessing," Cayden said.

"You can say that ... for certain," Jaelynn said, rolling her eyes.

"It's pretty clear both of us aren't happy at all with the way things are," Cayden said. "And not just us ... many more out there are as upset as we are. Am I wrong?"

"Not at all," Jaelynn said, the faces of Gabriel, Dr. Swedenborg, and Sendinian coming into her mind. "I'm so tired of seeing people I care about treated so badly. All over. From family to friends."

"I'm thinking you didn't just stumble into all of this," Cayden said. "Like me, you probably got a little help, from at least one person."

"A little," Jaelynn said, hesitant, not wanting to divulge too much yet.

"I have a Guardian," Cayden stated. "At least that's what she calls herself. She opened my eyes to new realities."

"What's a Guardian?" Jaelynn asked.

"Not a hundred percent sure," Cayden said. "My Guardian has helped me more than anyone ever has. I understand the way the world works a lot better, and she's helping me to develop the things I need to make changes in it. Big changes."

His description of a Guardian sounded a lot like what Dr. Swedenborg had been talking about. Jaelynn decided she could share a little more with Cayden.

"I had someone similar in my life, but he got swept up by the authorities," Jaelynn said. "He was incarcerated, under the Hate and Incitement codes."

"They don't want any of us getting empowered," Cayden said. A smile then broke out on his face. "But they haven't stopped me. Want to see a little demonstration? I don't want it to scare you, though."

"Sure," Jaelynn said, curiosity overriding any trepidation she had.

"Come with me, for a few moments," he said, his smile widening. "I'll show you what's possible."

The scene shifted, and Jaelynn saw that they now stood near one of the Technate's several incarceration centers. She knew the stout-looking rectangular building looming in front of them was just the tip of a mountain.

Beneath it, a labyrinthine complex extended far underground. Holding thousands of inmates, incarceration centers were familiar places to a great proportion of the technate's adult populace.

Most of those apprehended had stays of just a few days for minor violations of the extensive legal codes brought about with the Greater Good Doctrine. Others had lengthier imprisonment terms, measured in months, years, and even some of a permanent status.

Authorities in the technate often spoke of how so much crime had been eradicated in the modern age. If that were so, Jaelynn wondered why there stood a need for so many incarcerations; with the overwhelming majority of violations being of a non-violent nature.

Transgression of the Hate and Incitement codes resulted in a huge number of incarcerations. For many, like Dr. Swedenborg, the mere act of holding a dissenting opinion violated those codes. Jaelynn knew the law did not remove differing views from the hearts of people; but it did suppress them.

"You don't like these places much, either," Cayden stated, looking toward her. "I can see it in your eyes."

A deep scowl on her face, Jaelynn replied, "No, I don't. Or Rehabilitation Centers, either. I hate them both."

"Well, get ready to smile, then" Cayden declared, flashing a smile of his own, and turning his attention toward the huge structure before them.

Brow furrowing, he closed his eyes, taking on an appearance of intense concentration. Jaelynn's skin tingled all over a few seconds later, and she sensed something taking place within the air around them.

The tingling on her skin intensified.

No figment of her imagination, she knew the sensation derived from whatever Cayden had engaged in. Then, he opened his eyes. Jaelynn flinched at the solid black surfaces revealed beneath his eyelids.

An enormous pulse of energy ran through Jaelynn, sparking momentary fear. Then, the sense of energy vanished, and she no longer felt the tingling along her skin.

The air filling with a noxious, burning scent, several loud noises erupted around her. Looking around, she took in the sight of several ground vehicles that had just crashed, and a few airborne drones that had fallen to the ground.

A number of voices drew her attention back toward the front of the incarceration center. Several figures had emerged from the doors of the facility, a few dressed in the uniforms of security elements, and many others in the tell-tale, bright orange jumpsuits of prisoners.

All of them had looks of bewilderment.

None seemed to take notice of either Jaelynn or Cayden, even though they stood right before the growing throng. They looked around at the crashed vehicles and drones, and the sense of confusion permeated the atmosphere.

Others continued to emerge, with an increasing number wearing the jumpsuits. A few of the freed prisoners began to laugh and shout, exuberant at the unexpected change in their fortunes.

Most of the prisoners remained peaceful, milling about the street, but several began turning their attention to those who wore security uniforms. The latter grouped together, wherever they could. From their movements and looks of frustration, Jaelynn could tell that the security officers could not access any network through MR glasses or ocular implants.

"Security robots have been put out of commission, in addition to all their weapons," Cayden remarked, watching the developments. "The glasses and implants have been fried too, as the human security officers are finding out now."

To her relief, Cayden's eyes had returned to a normal state. She could see that he took great pleasure in the scene unfolding before them, and she could not deny that she shared in that elation; seeing the extensive apparatus of the authorities rendered powerless.

More prisoners emerged, and the number who exhibited hostile demeanors continued to build. It did not take long for the few in security uniforms to become surrounded.

The aggressive prisoners began to taunt and shove the trapped security personnel. It did not take long before punches and kicks were visited upon the terrified-looking security officers.

The initial outbreak of violence escalated rapidly.

Swarmed and taken to the ground, the encircled security officers stood no chance. When the brutal beatings came to an end, and the prisoners began to disperse, Jaelynn could not tell if the still forms lying on the ground were unconscious or dead.

"No ... oh no," Jaelynn said, eyes wide in shock and horrified at the sight.

"Things like that are going to happen, when chains are broken," Cayden replied in a low voice, with no sign of distress on his face. "It's unfortunate, but only a few of those freed were involved. You can't condemn the rest of the freed prisoners, who didn't deserve to be locked up."

Looking at his face, Jaelynn could not tell if he approved of the harsh assaults or not, and the lack of clarity disturbed her.

"You can't possibly support what they did to those officers," she said. "Those officers didn't deserve that at all."

Cayden looked back to her, and she caught a spark of irritation in his eyes. "I didn't intend that. I didn't want that. But you better understand that if you bring it all crashing down, it's going to be messier than you think."

Jaelynn looked back at the inert bodies, feeling sorrowful for the men and women who had suffered. She could not deny that Cayden was right. An overhaul of a system such as the one they lived in could not possibly go smooth.

Turning her attention to the prisoners, she saw that most of them continued to stand around the front of the building. A few of them walked away, but she wondered how far any of them could really get, wearing the distinctive jumpsuits.

The response to the release of the prisoners did not take long to manifest. Aerial drones began to appear in the sky, circling and hovering about, and a large number of armored ground vehicles rumbled into sight.

A horde of security robots marched in the wake of the vehicles and began to hem in the massive throng of prisoners. Many began to shout and curse, but in moments the multitude found itself being pressed into a dense mass.

Loud crackles accompanied the stunning of those who tried to resist. Robots began to secure the places where officers had been assaulted, creating channels accessed by medical teams.

For the majority of the prisoners, everything had been for naught. Soon they would be returned to the cells that they had started the day in, with nothing gained.

"Let's go," Cayden said, his words carrying a simmering anger. He glared at the fast-growing security presence. "I can't do anything more for them today. But one day ... one day."

The scene blurred and shifted. Jaelynn stood on the edge of a great precipice, a pit forming in her stomach when she looked downward.

"That wasn't a dream, was it?" Jaelynn asked.

"No, and you'll be able to verify it all when you get back," Cayden said.

"So those people, the security officers, really got hurt, or died," she said.

"We can't control everything that happens," Cayden responded. "But don't you want that system to come to an end? Do you think it's right that so many are held in prison? The Rehabilitation Centers are a kind of prison. They just medicate and brainwash you."

Thinking of Gabriel and Dr. Swedenborg, she nodded. "I know. I just wish there was a way to do it without people getting hurt."

"We can free everyone, not just in the incarceration centers,"

Cayden said, the anger leaving his voice and replaced with excitement. "Your friends, everyone. I'm getting stronger, but if we get a few more involved, like you, we can cover the entire technate. Give everyone a chance at something new, and better."

Jaelynn did not know what to say at first. Gabriel also wanted to free everyone in the Technate, but his goal seemed impossible. Witnessing Cayden's demonstration of power, the goal no longer seemed out of reach.

She wished she could speak with Gabriel about what had just happened, to see if he would have done the same thing as Cayden. Most of the prisoners did not deserve incarceration, but a few were dangerous threats. Yet she did not see any other way around the situation, if the system could be overcome.

"Look, I wish it could all be easier," Cayden said. "But it's not going to be easy. It's going to get rough in the time ahead. But in the end, we bring down the greatest prison of them all, the technate itself."

Jaelynn had no argument. Wanting to live in a world where everything she did was not measured, monitored, and controlled by various boards of authority, she found that she could not walk away from Cayden.

"So, are you in with me?" he asked.

"You really didn't intend to see those security officers hurt?" she asked.

"No," Cayden said. "I just want everyone to have a chance to be free ... your friends to everyone not lucky enough to be in the Northern Sector."

After an extended pause, Jaelynn nodded. "I am with you. But I don't know a lot about what I am doing in all of this. Or even why all of this has happened to me so fast."

"There's help for all of that, and those who can give you that help are here," Cayden said, looking away.

She followed his eyes, seeing a pair of figures in dark attire drifting through the air toward them.

Jaelynn's eyes widened, recognizing one of the incoming figures. The last time she had seen the woman with the piercing blue eyes had been in the depths of a horrid dream. Surrounded by an encroaching horde of listless, starved-looking people, Jaelynn had seen the woman as a liberator.

Her companion to the left was another woman, with long locks of dark hair and an olive complexion to her skin.

The pair alighted on the ground a few paces in front of Cayden and Jaelynn.

The blue-eyed woman smiled at Cayden, and looked to Jaelynn, saying, "It is good he found you."

"This is my Guardian, the one I told you about," Cayden said, with an air of pride. "Lilithian."

"She has seen me before," the woman said to Cayden. "I helped her out of a recent predicament she had gotten herself into."

Jaelynn looked to the woman. "Thank you again for doing that for me. I was more than overwhelmed when you showed up."

"It's not a good idea to explore any realm you wander into by yourself," the woman replied, the look on her face showing that the words were meant for Cayden as much as Jaelynn.

The other woman then spoke, "I am sure a lot of things are overwhelming when you find out what lies beyond the world you live in."

"Definitely," Jaelynn agreed. "I'm trying my best to figure it all out, and not doing a great job at getting answers."

"It is a difficult time, but we will try to help you, as much as we can," Lilithian said. "I understand you have had some who was important to you, in your world, taken from you?"

Jaelynn nodded. "My boyfriend ... and a man who I thought would be a teacher, and mentor."

She left out Sendinian, unsure of how to classify the little ethereal being.

"Misfortune comes upon many, and most often without warning," Lilithian said. "But we can help you."

"We can guide you, and give you protection," the dark-eyed woman added.

Looking at each of the tall women, Jaelynn marveled at the strong presence both of them conveyed. In the prime of health, and flawless in appearance, they carried themselves with a supreme level of confidence.

She envied the intimidating pair, a part of her hungering to be able to carry herself in the same way.

"You don't want to go forward alone," Cayden said. "There's way too much out there. It's best to have a guide, and they'll help you."

"What do I have to do?" Jaelynn asked, doubting that anything would come without a price.

"Accept a Guardian for yourself, nothing more," the dark-eyed woman said. "Accept one who can act as your mentor and teacher."

"You'll learn how to handle all of this, and develop abilities you never thought you had," Lilithian said.

"This is all so much to think about," Jaelynn said, apprehensive and looking between the faces of the others.

"It is a lot to take in," the dark-eyed woman said. "Take some time to think upon everything, and when you are ready, return to us."

"Wake up now, and see for yourself that Cayden spoke true," Lilithian said, her gaze boring into Jaelynn's eyes. "Put your mind to your body, sleeping in your bedroom. Think only of your physical body and wake up."

The remembrance of her sleeping form, back in her bedroom, snapped Jaelynn from the scene on the high ledge.

Sitting up in her bed, she had a distinct heaviness permeating her body.

Rubbing her eyes, she let her breathing settle.

Slipping the covers off, she walked out to the kitchen, intending to get a drink and collect her thoughts. Coming to a stop in the living room, she took notice of her mother, sitting in her favorite chair.

"Hey mom," Jaelynn greeted in a low voice. "You are still up?"

"Aren't I always?" her mother answered in a tired-sounding voice, with a grin that reflected more than a little sadness. "Have you been asleep?"

"Yes, for a while," Jaelynn answered. "Just a little thirsty. Probably going to go back to bed after I get a drink."

"You probably didn't hear what happened earlier tonight, then," her mother said. "Not the usual news you get these days."

"About what?" Jaelynn asked, tensing up a little, bracing for the words she suspected would be coming from the lips of her mother.

"One of the incarceration centers had a complete malfunction, and all the prisoners were let loose," she answered. "Right onto the street. Imagine how dangerous that had to be. A couple thousand prisoners … let out all at once."

"Really?" Jaelynn responded, feigning surprise. She thought of what she had seen, and a cold chill passed through her. "How did that happen?"

"They are claiming a major technical problem," her mother answered. "But it must have been a big one. And very unprecedented. Said even the backup systems failed. Many of the staff were assaulted in the aftermath, and a couple even died."

"I'm sorry to hear that," Jaelynn replied, dismayed at the news of the deaths.

"They're investigating how it all happened, but they're

giving no final answers as of yet," her mother responded. "I doubt they'll give us the full story."

Jaelynn doubted the official explanation would come anywhere near the truth of it; that an unseen sixteen-year-old boy had crippled the entire system running the incarceration center, wielding an unknown power.

The public and the government of the technate could not begin to handle the implications of something like that.

"Just glad they got it all under control quickly," her mother continued. "Most of the ones released were probably harmless, but there were some really dangerous ones among them."

"I imagine so," Jaelynn replied.

"What if things like that start happening more often," her mother asked, a trace of fear in her eyes.

Jaelynn could see something more reflected in her mother's face. Belief in a system deemed unshakable, and something to be depended upon, had been shattered.

Having been conditioned not to think of any alternatives, the idea of new possibilities would be more frightening to someone such as her mother, who had lived much longer under the system. While Jaelynn had not known anything different her entire life, neither was she a full adult participant in society.

Her own mind prepared for changes in her own life, and as a result she realized she was in a better condition for a major transformation of the prevailing order. In light of the revelation, Jaelynn harbored a new level of sympathy toward her mother.

"Whatever happens, we stay together, mom," Jaelynn said, walking over and giving her a hug. "Family above everything."

"That's right, Jaelynn, family stays together ... whatever comes our way," her mother answered, squeezing her tight.

Jaelynn held onto her mother for several moments. She took in the familiar scents of her hair and favorite perfume; scents she had known since her earliest recollections of childhood. They had a calming effect on her, just as they had back when she had first learned to walk.

She wished she could take her mother by the hand and whisk her away to the surreal oceanfront where Sendinian had taken her, to meet Brandon and gain the comfort of knowing other realms of existence did indeed exist. As things stood, she had been stymied from returning herself, the last time she had attempted it.

Without the intervention from the enigmatic blue-eyed woman named Lilithian, Jaelynn wondered what would have happened when the denizens of that dreary realm reached the place where she had been standing. She did not imagine it would have been anything good.

Releasing her embrace, she looked into her mother's eyes. "What do you say we both get some rest now. Come with me. Let's get you to bed, too."

Raising back up, she extended her hand. Her mother grasped it, and Jaelynn helped her get out of the chair.

Walking with slow and careful steps, she held onto her mother's hand and led her back to her bedroom. Helping her into bed, Jaelynn pulled the covers over her body. Leaning over, she kissed her mother on the forehead, and gently pulled the top cover a little higher.

"Love you, mom," she said.

"Love you too, Jaelynn," her mother replied, eyelids already looking heavy.

"Sweet dreams," Jaelynn said, walking to the doorway.

She paused and looked back, a smile coming to her face. Jaelynn thought of the vast multitude of times her mother had stood at a doorway and looked upon her, after tucking her in for the night.

All cares and concerns fled her mind. For a moment, she had the same pure, uplifting feeling inside that she had experienced standing on the edge of the extraordinary shore, meeting her brother for the first time.

The moment reflected a great truth Jaelynn had spoken to her mother in the living room. In a world with so many trials, disappointments, and illusions, family could rise above everything.

Haven

"Go ahead," the Artist invited. "Pick one, let your mind clear, and concentrate upon it, to the exclusion of all else."

"Any of them?" Haven asked, smiling, looking at the array of magnificent scenes displayed along the wall in the hallway.

"Any one you want," the Artist confirmed. "I'll catch up with you, in whichever one you choose."

Haven turned toward one of the first paintings she had noticed upon her first visit to the apartment. Her eyes set upon the vehicle traveling down the winding road on a bright summer day.

Letting go of her worries, she let the vision fill her mind.

A vivid countryside of rolling hills just outside the open window to her right, a strong pull resonated in Haven's stomach, as the vehicle hugged a bend at a high speed. Hair flowing free in the wind, she smiled at the pleasant sensation.

Looking around, she found The Artist next to her. Holding onto a wheel in the other seat, he pressed down with his right leg on something down on the floorboard.

In that moment, she saw a contrast between the Artist and the surroundings. The appearances of everything aside from him had the quality of the painting, as if the artwork had come to life and they had entered it.

Glancing down, she saw that her body held a look of full realism, while the seat, dashboard, and door retained the texture and look of the painting.

"Wow!" she exclaimed. "This is amazing!"

"This is one way to experience artwork," the Artist said, with a broad grin. "Immerse right into it."

"I wonder how close this feels to what vehicles were like, when people drove them," Haven said, a look of wonder spreading on her face.

"This is what a car was like, long ago," the Artist said. He laughed and gave her a wink. "Ready to see what this Camaro can do?"

"Sure!" she replied, excitedly.

Reaching down, he gripped a shaft to his right and shifted it, doing something with his left leg at the same time. The car responded at once, surging in speed, a throaty roar erupting from the engine.

The road racing beneath them, the car continued to accelerate. Haven found the experience exhilarating, her hair now whipping about in the winds coursing through the open window.

The Artist drove for a long while, taking the car up and down hills, around bends, and hurtling down straight segments. Haven savored every single moment, from the thrill of the high speed to the visual splendor all around her.

At long last, the Artist slowed the car down, looked over toward Haven, and grinned. "We'll go back now. Next time, I'll show you how to drive one of these."

"I'd love to!" exclaimed Haven.

"You'll pick it up quick," the Artist replied.

A few moments later, Haven stood in the hallway, catching

her breath and looking back at the painting. It looked as it did before.

"That was beyond incredible!" Haven stated.

The Artist looked around at the wall. "You've got quite a few more of my works to explore here."

Looking at all of the incredible paintings, the notion delighted her.

"Dreams, other levels of existence, and even dreaming myself into my own world," Haven said. "Seems there are no limits to what you can imagine."

"Now you are getting it," the Artist said, a knowing grin on his face.

"Reality is so much more than I ever imagined!" Haven exclaimed.

"And you've only just begun exploring it," The Artist said, giving her warm smile. "It is a journey without end or boundary. The farther you go into it, you will find that more opens up to you."

"Kind of hard to get your mind around," Haven replied. "But it sounds so wonderful."

"It most certainly is," the Artist replied, nodding. "I see you growing by leaps and bounds as you become a Navigator."

"I'm ready to do whatever it takes," Haven said, her tone full of conviction.

"Patience, my young friend," the Artist said, laughing. "It doesn't all happen overnight."

"I didn't think it would," Haven said. "I'm just eager to take the next steps."

"And you will take a new step every day," the Artist said.

Walking into the hallway, Serena joined them.

"It's about time for her to learn a little more about Voyagers as well," Serena said, giving the Artist a wink.

"Voyagers?" Haven asked. "I've heard that word mentioned

here before."

"There's a lot more for you to discover," the Artist said. "There are many others who fight alongside us, to roll back the darkness ... and it's time to begin learning of these others."

"Many others," Serena said, smiling. For a moment, her eyes filled with a brilliant white light, a luminance that at once conveyed healing, strength, and love.

Haven looked back at Serena in a state of awe.

"Be seeing you soon," the Artist said. "Now go awake from your nap and relax for a bit. That part of life is important, too."

***

Eyes fluttering open, Haven took in the sight of her bedroom, basking in the array of invigorating feelings rippling throughout her.

Rays of sunlight peeked around the edges of the window shade, piercing the gloom.

Morning beckoned. A new day had arrived.

Waking up into a world of existence that no longer held limits, a smile brimming with joy and tranquility bloomed upon Haven's face.

Jaelynn

After donning her MR glasses, Jaelynn looked up Takeshi, finding him hanging out in one of the countless virtual social environments available to the mass public. In an instant, she shifted into his avatar's location; a sun-bathed beach of white sands sloping into waters of an exquisite turquoise hue.

Once she would have found the beachfront scene captivating, but the sight paled in comparison to the one where she had been introduced to her brother. The environment in the virtual construct did not begin to approach the kinds of hues, qualities of light and other sensations she had experienced in a realm of intrinsic reality.

She could not put one fact far from her thoughts. Though elaborate, and encompassing every detail possible, the views around her remained at their core a digital fabrication. A virtual environment could only simulate; it could never truly be.

A short distance from the beach, Takeshi and several others skimmed along the rolling waves on colorful, jet-powered watercraft. His avatar in the virtual environment reflected his real appearance, though her glasses would have identified him easily enough.

Making her way over to a dock jutting from the shore,

Jaelynn walked toward the far end of it, waving at Takeshi. It took her a few moments to gain his attention. Seeing her at last, he veered away from his companions and made his way to the dock's side.

"Hey Takeshi, sorry to interrupt!" Jaelynn called out, as he pulled alongside her, turning the engine of his watercraft off.

Flashing her a smile, he replied, "It's all good. I've wasted way too much time today out here."

"Looks like a lot of fun though," Jaelynn said, eyeing the sleek gold and black watercraft bobbing in the water.

"I'd like to try the real thing someday," Takeshi said, stepping onto the dock. Drops of water glistened on his skin and trickled down from his wet hair, but in the virtual environment he gained a dry appearance in just a few moments. "So, what's up?"

"Wanted to see if I could come over and visit," Jaelynn said. "Just to talk for a little while. Not been the easiest of times on my end."

"I'm home right now," Takeshi said, nodding. "And I understand. It's not been the best of times for me, either."

"Really wanted to see you in person," Jaelynn said, not wanting to give any more information within a virtual environment that had even more surveillance in it than the real world outside of it. "Hope that isn't too much of a problem."

"Not a problem at all," Takeshi said. He gave her a smile. "I'll be looking out for you, and I really look forward to seeing you."

"See you shortly then," Jaelynn said, smiling back, before phasing out of the virtual environment.

Jaelynn put on her shoes and headed out of her apartment. Melding into the flow of pedestrian traffic, she kept a brisk pace, a multitude of thoughts weighing on her mind.

She wondered how much she could share with Takeshi about everything that had transpired in recent days. Doubting he knew anything of the other levels of reality she had been exposed to, Jaelynn suspected he still continued forward with whatever he and Gabriel had been constructing.

Greeting her at the door to his apartment, Takeshi extended her a warm smile. "Hey Jaelynn, come on in!"

"Thanks," she replied, following him back to his bedroom.

When they were inside and the door was shut behind, she said, "Sorry again about interrupting you on the jet skis. That really did look fun."

"You spared me from wasting more time in there, that's all," he replied with a laugh. "Distractions are more tempting these days."

Jaelynn then made a gesture that mimicked the act of writing something, giving Takeshi a knowing look. His expression growing serious, he nodded.

Turning, he walked over to the nightstand by his bed and retrieved a piece of paper and a pen from the top drawer.

"Been to see Gabriel at all?" Jaelynn asked, keeping her voice casual. She folded the paper and began to write upon it.

"Got to see him just yesterday, in fact," Takeshi said. "Hope they let him go soon. Hate seeing him in there."

"Me too," Jaelynn said. She handed the paper over to him.

'Be very careful. They arrested Dr. Swedenborg. And another friend of mine was taken. Something is really wrong,' she had written. She omitted the fact that the friend mentioned happened to be a faerie, taken in another level of reality.

'I'm keeping quiet. Just hope Gabriel hasn't changed much when they release him,' Takeshi replied in writing, a look of concern on his face.

'I don't think he'll change much,' she wrote back. *'But whatever you two were doing, be very careful.'*

He cast a glance to the side. Following his eyes, she saw a small dark box, similar to the one in Gabriel's room, sitting on the floor.

'*We were about finished,*' he wrote. '*I've done some more work since they took Gabriel to Rehabilitation.*'

'*I'm guessing there are a few others involved,*' she wrote back.

'*I know of a few. Probably many more I don't know,*' Takeshi replied on the paper.

'*So curious about what this all is about,*' she responded. '*Gabriel didn't want to tell me until he knew if it really worked.*'

Takeshi chuckled, writing back, '*That sounds just like him.*'

About to reply, she saw the levity fading from his face. He gestured for Jaelynn to give him the sheet of paper back. She returned it without a response.

An anxious look in his eyes, he stared at her for a few moments. Pursing his lips, he fixed his eyes on the paper and took a deep breath. He wrote a large number of words down and returned the paper to her.

'*What we are building is a way to give us an oasis of freedom. A place where ideas can be shared without intimidation or threat. A place where dissent does not get you apprehended or punished in other ways.*'

She read the words and looked back to the small box, wondering what form the vision described by Takeshi took. Gabriel had never gone into great detail about the project, but his eyes had always lit up with excitement whenever he referred to it in some manner.

Now, she was beginning to understand the magnitude of what they had been engaged in doing.

'*But there are probably a ton of laws you are breaking doing this,*' Jaelynn wrote.

'*Laws made by people who want to suffocate ninety-nine-point nine percent of the population*' Takeshi responded.

'*I don't want to see you taken in by them*' she wrote. '*They know you are a friend of Gabriel's. They know who all our friends are and where we go.'*

'I'll be okay. And this project will be okay. We've got help.' Takeshi wrote.

'I'm glad to hear that. That's all I needed to say. Wanted to be sure you'll be okay.' Jaelynn wrote back, keeping the sadness welling up inside from showing on her face.

Jaelynn could not say if she would be okay. At the moment, she had no one to help her. Unlike Takeshi, she stood alone; except for one offer.

In that moment, Jaelynn knew what she had to do.

Takeshi took the paper and burned it to ash in the same vessel she had seen him use when she had visited with Gabriel.

"So what do you say we go try out some jet skis?" he asked. "Easy as putting on a helmet right here."

"I would love to, but I have some things I need to take care of," Jaelynn said. "I really wanted to check in on you, while we are all waiting for Gabriel to be returned to us. I promised Gabriel I'd keep an eye on his friends."

"Thank you, Jaelynn," Takeshi said, smiling. "I'm so glad he found you, and I'm lucky to have you as a friend of mine, too."

"I'm lucky to have you as a friend," Jaelynn replied. "Thanks again for letting me come over."

"Anytime," he said, with an air of sincerity.

"Take care of yourself, and stay out of trouble," she said in a lighthearted manner, before exiting.

Leaving Takeshi's apartment, Jaelynn set her sights on returning to her apartment and going to bed, but not for the purpose of sleep. She had to find Cayden or one of the two mysterious women she had encountered on the high precipice.

Having come to know far too much about the true nature of reality, she could not go back to the ways things had been before. Neither could she go forward without some manner of tutelage and guidance.

She made her decision.

Like Cayden, she needed someone in her unfamiliar and daunting new world.

Jaelynn chose to accept the offer to have a Guardian.

Cayden

"No more displays like that," the Guardian said in a stern voice. Unrelenting in its intensity, her gaze bored into him. "Not until you are ready to do what needs to be done."

"I just wanted to show her what is possible," Cayden said, unable to meet her eyes. "She's got two friends locked up, one in Rehabilitation, and another in an incarceration center. I figured she'd like to see how quick people can be freed."

"You made your point and don't need to do it again," the Guardian replied in a curt manner. "It may have been useful to you, but for all the people let out of the incarceration center, it was a total waste."

"I don't understand," Cayden replied.

"They were all set free for a few minutes and then rounded back up and returned to their cells," the Guardian replied. "They gained absolutely nothing. Nothing changed for them."

"I wasn't strong enough to do more when the drones and bots came," Cayden said.

"And even if you had halted all of that, the prisoners would not have gotten much farther," the Guardian replied. "They would have been apprehended again, whether in another street or sector."

The lightning-riddled cloud masses above them appeared to mirror her anger, surging in brightness with every flashing wave. Around them, cold winds whistled through the ruins of tall buildings.

They stood within a large square, the middle of which contained a colossal statue of a being clad in flowing robes. Cayden could not tell from its misshapen head whether the being was even human or not, much less male or female.

Looking at the dismal surroundings, Cayden wondered why every environment he had visited or explored, with or without the Guardian, had such foreboding atmospheres. Many times, he had set his mind on reaching a place with sunshine and clear skies, but every attempt had seen him land in yet another gray, dusky environment.

He could not refrain from asking her about it.

"Are there any worlds outside the one I live in where it's not so harsh?" Cayden asked.

The Guardian stared at him for a moment, but her expression and eyes gave him no hint of whatever she was thinking.

"There are many such places, but now is a time for you to become strong and grow into the fullness of what you are capable of," she said. "Then you will do what you need to do in your world, and after that you will understand everything."

The answer did not satisfy him, but he was not about to press her about the matter. He looked back toward the statue.

Other Guardians manifested out of the shadows, each of them accompanied by a boy or girl of roughly the same age as Cayden. Within moments, at least fifty Guardians stood within the open square.

The boys and girls looked to each other, some of them wide-eyed and curious, and others more calm and settled. Looking from face to face, Cayden did not recognize any of the others; save for one.

Across the square from him, Jaelynn stood with the Guardian that she had been introduced to when Cayden had last seen her. When she caught Cayden's eyes, she mustered a smile, though he could tell she was in a nervous state.

The sight of someone else familiar to him relieved some of the tension that had been building inside Cayden. He wanted to go talk with Jaelynn, but the formality of the assembly prevented him from doing anything more than returning her smile.

They held each other's gaze a few more moments. Then, Jaelynn shifted her attention away, looking toward the center of the open plaza, a stunned expression manifesting on her face.

Cayden followed her gaze.

Eyes widening, Cayden stared in astonishment. The massive statue had begun to move.

The robes on the figure took on a vaporous quality, resembling a continuous, downward flow of dark mist. Expanding in size, the humanoid entity gazed upon those gathered with large, protruding eyes of pitch black.

A powerful energy radiated from the towering being. A strong pressure weighed upon Cayden, all over, and an extreme sensation of heaviness permeated his body.

Cayden did not think he could move a single step forward, even if he wanted to. Neither could he take his eyes off the hulking figure. His will sapped, he could do no more than remain captivated by the dark entity.

"Behold, Chronos," the voice of his Guardian sounding in his mind and carrying an unmistakable tone of reverence.

Cayden could not find his voice to reply, nor could he think of a response. Mesmerized, and awed, he remained transfixed, gazing at the entity.

The shape of the entity began to change, the humanoid figure becoming a host of narrow, tentacle-like appendages that snaked out toward the silent audience. The dark extensions differentiated between Guardians and those with them; orienting upon the latter.

In some remote part of Cayden, a spark of fear tried to ignite. But he could do little more than stare at the tendril drawing nearer to him.

Sending a cold chill through his entire body, the tip of the lengthy tendril made contact with the skin at the center of Cayden's forehead. Unable to form a thought, he remained rooted in place, helpless and vulnerable to the invading presence.

All around the plaza, the others such as Cayden and Jaelynn remained standing as the tendrils continued burrowing into their bodies, through their foreheads. The dark mass at the center of the plaza reduced in size until there was nothing more, the ends of the serpentine lengths passing into each girl and boy.

After a long while, fragments of thoughts began returning to Cayden's mind, eventually taking greater clarity and form. A wave of nausea pervading him, dizzy and light-headed, Cayden struggled to remain upright.

Casting his gaze about, he searched for Jaelynn on the opposite side of the plaza. When he found her, he saw a look of disorientation on her face.

Unable to make any sense out of what had just happened, he turned his eyes to the Guardian at his side. "What happened to me?"

"You are stronger now," his Guardian replied.

"I feel sick," he responded, wishing he could just lie down for a bit of time.

"Now you are ready to do what needs to be done," his Guardian announced. "As are all the others who have been gathered here."

"What needs to be done?" he asked, the queasiness inside continuing to worsen.

"Bring your world into a better order," she said. "It's what you desired, is it not?"

Cayden wrestled with his thoughts, unable to recall the things that had bothered him prior to the phenomenon involving the statue. Stymied and frustrated, he looked downward with a dejected expression.

"Put your mind to the task at hand," his Guardian continued.

"What's inside me?" he asked, fearful, and about to begin gagging.

Anger brimmed within her eyes. "You must stop thinking of yourself. A greater need is at hand. The world you live in remains exposed to those who would set it back to primitive ways, after so many years of progress."

Cayden wondered who she spoke of, but had a difficult time focusing on the matter. He could not define what she meant in terms of primitive ways, or progress.

Finding it much easier to accept her claims as truth, he nodded. "I will try to stop thinking of myself."

Seeing the smile spreading across Lilithian's face at his answer, Cayden gave no thought to what he had just said.

"Chronos dwells within you now," Lilithian said. "Go back to your world, and your body, in the knowledge that you have taken a great stride. Soon you will return to me, and then you will take even more strides."

Cayden did not want to think of taking any more strides. He could think of nothing else but the sense of illness pervading him. Disoriented in the manner of an advanced fever, and ready to heave at any moment with the rising nausea inside, he thought only of returning to his bedroom.

When Cayden thought of his physical body and the bed awaiting him, the dark, urban environment around him faded from sight. Awakening in his bed, he made no effort to get up.

The severity of whatever had come over him in the other realm echoed within his physical body. Weighed down with an extreme grogginess, and contending with a burgeoning headache, he groaned.

Keeping the lights off, he curled up into a ball, sweat beading his forehead and his stomach uneasy. For the first time in a long while, tears of frustration came to his eyes.

He understood nothing of what had just happened, only that something had invaded his very being. A part of him feared what would come of it, and he also worried about his new friend Jaelynn.

Something had taken root deep within him, and he had no idea what would come of it. So invigorated over the powers he had been unlocking in recent days, Cayden despaired, wondering if all the empowerment he had enjoyed would prove to be fleeting.

Having tasted such a great degree of power, he could not go back to what he had been before.

From the shadows of his troubled mind, an inner voice whispered.

It told Cayden that he had not gone through everything for no reason. The silken voice soothed his distress, telling him that greater things lay just ahead; things far beyond what he had experienced since encountering Lilithian.

He determined to trust the voice, a tether to hold onto and stop his reeling mind from going adrift. Lilithian had not led him astray so far. Perhaps whatever had happened within the other realm's plaza would prove to be a great stride forward.

The headache and feelings of heaviness began to recede, along with the queasiness in his stomach. In a few moments, he straightened out on the bed, clarity returning to his mind and steadiness to his limbs.

Getting out of bed, he contended with a little restlessness. Thinking of Jaelynn, he determined to contact her and see how she fared.

They both shared a path with many others, heading toward

a destiny far greater than enduring a faceless existence as one of millions passing their days under the control of a technate.

Jaelynn

Jaelynn returned to waking consciousness. Rolling out of bed, she stumbled to the bathroom, getting there just in time to throw up. It had been a long while since she had been so sick.

Her skin covered in a clammy sweat, she shivered, thinking about everything that had just happened. She could remember the awful moment the tendril from the dark being had reached her.

Wondering what it all signified, Jaelynn feared that something terrible had taken place.

Turning her thoughts to Gabriel and Dr. Swedenborg, she knew she could not go back. She had to find a way to help them, and to understand the new worlds that had opened up to her.

A clear thought emerged from the turbulence in her mind. Like a new voice inside, it promised that she would not be at the mercy of the technate. Rather, she would rise above its power; as long as she continued on the new road she found herself on.

Jaelynn steadied herself, the wave of nausea passing. She would find a way to help Gabriel and Dr. Swedenborg. In the meantime, she would learn as much as she could from her new Guardian and make certain that she no longer stood helpless or powerless.

She remembered that she had a friend on the same journey as her. Thinking of Cayden, she stood up, setting her mind on reaching out to him.

There was much to discuss, and even more to look toward.

Salvador

Blinking his eyes, Salvador waited for a few moments to allow the room to come back into focus.

Breathing deep, Salvador weighed whether to get out of bed and see what his new sight brought him or continue to sleep through until dawn.

Not wanting to delay the inevitable, he roused himself from the bed. After donning a new shirt and pants, he made his way to the living room.

Freezing in place, he espied some movement near the holographic unit. The slender form unmistakable, one of the same, snake-like shadow creatures that he had seen within the decaying metropolis now drifted about the object.

The dark thing reacted to his presence, parting from the holographic unit and floating across the living room to draw within an arm's length. Salvador stayed in place, reminding himself that he had lived for years in a world where such things existed; the only difference now being that he could see them.

Abruptly, the serpentine form jerked backward, and retreated to coil about the holographic unit. Defensive, and maybe even afraid, the thing oriented toward him and kept still.

After watching the creature for a little longer, Salvador

stepped away, making his way to the front door of the apartment. Continuing out the door and down the hallway outside, he encountered another of the snake-like things in the elevator, but like the other it recoiled fast from him.

The elevator door opened on the ground floor and Salvador headed out into the streets. The overcast skies and a light rain enhanced the troubling discovery meeting his eyes.

Everywhere he looked, dark forms drifted about. Whether snake-like, wraith-like, or even other shapes, the entities roved the air from the ground level up to the heights of the tenements. Many of the entities shadowed pedestrians on the street in a close manner, a few of the shadow beings even appearing to be attached to a person.

Looking up and down the street, Salvador's heart sank. Hundreds upon hundreds of the entities glided and flew about, without any sign of hindrance.

Walking along the street, Salvador took note of more than one of the things backing away quick when he drew close to them. After a little more time had passed, he began to notice a few other people like him, who also appeared to be shunned by the entities.

Looking at those particular individuals with great interest, he wondered if they might be Navigators, or whether something else explained the defensive behavior of the shadow-things. Trying to approach the select individuals was not an option. Salvador dared not inquire out in the open where his words could be picked up by surveillance, and because he could not make any assumptions about other people in the technate. At the moment, he could only observe and reflect.

In a similar fashion, Salvador focused on instances where larger concentrations of the entities had gathered around something.

Security bots and drones all had several of the entities following them. A great multitude, like a black cloud, swirled about an incarceration center. Salvador imagined that anything around the technate's security apparatus feasted upon an abundance of darker, negative energies.

After having more than enough of viewing the shadow-entities in the streets, Salvador returned to his apartment with a suspicion tugging at his mind. Making his way back to his bedroom, he ignored the primordial still lingering about the holographic unit in his living room. Once in his room he shut the door behind him.

Placing his VR helmet on, he sought out one of the club-like environments many of his peers spent so many hours socializing within. He chose to present himself in the form of his favorite avatar; a tall, dark-haired man of about twenty-five, with broad shoulders and a narrow waist.

Strolling over to a railing providing an overlook of the virtual club's main dance floor, he took in a broad view of the place. Gazing out over a throng of avatars, some representing real individuals, and others of a purely digital origin, he confirmed his suspicion.

Virtual environments were not immune to the presence of the shadow entities.

Dark shapes coiled and floated about many of the patrons, while paying no heed to others. The latter did not cause the kind of defensive reactions that Salvador did, along with a few others he had witnessed out on the streets of the technate. The entities showed no response of any kind when such an individual came close.

Though Salvador had no way of confirming it, he speculated that the Primordials focused on the avatars of living individuals while having no interest in avatars that were artificially intelligent constructs. If true, the observation raised a very interesting issue. The Primordials had a way of differentiating between the digital representations of real individuals and those that were merely artificial creations of the system itself.

Salvador pondered the full implications. The VR realm, where conscious individuals experienced, explored, and interacted, was just as vulnerable to the Primordials as a dream world, another planet in the universe, or a realm in another state of existence.

It sickened Salvador that Primordials could infect any place that a human could experience and spread a malignant disease that extinguished the best aspects about life. He fought back the despair threatening to overcome him at the railing's edge, knowing that the loss of hope reflected the core nature of the Primordials.

Continuing with his silent observation, Salvador watched the shadowy forms flow throughout the dense crowd. A part of him wished he could turn the ability to see the Primordials off.

He could not help noticing and focusing upon the dark entities. Those unable to see the things would probably find his seemingly random shifts in attention a sign of madness.

Unless Jade had another answer, Salvador would have to learn to consign the Primordials to the periphery of his attention when going about a typical day in the technate. He did not doubt it would take some time and training to condition himself.

A wraith-like entity drifted near him, darting aside when it had come within a few paces. Watching the fast reaction of the Primordial, Salvador thought of something else that he had to be careful of.

Others, like Jade, who could see the entities, could tell something of Salvador's nature from the shadow entities' distinct responses to him.

"Want to dance?" inquired a beautiful girl with long locks that were a blend of silver and black. Swaying to the steady beat of the music, she flashed him a playful smile.

Salvador returned the expression, knowing from an icon

displaying in his field of view that she was an avatar governed by AI. As much as the illusion of having such a beauty interested in him appealed, he had other intents.

"Some other time, but I appreciate it," he replied in a polite tone.

"No problem, next time it is then," she replied in an amiable manner, moving onward.

Salvador had seen enough of the Primordials' infection for one evening. Opting out of the VR environment, he took his helmet off and set it down, allowing himself a moment to adjust to the quiet and calm of his bedroom.

Lying down on his bed, he called for the Home Assistant to turn the lights off. With so much on his mind, it took some time for him to fall asleep, but at last he found himself walking within a dream.

Looking around, he eyed another version of Technate Six, staring at a wall of dizzying height looming before him. Behind Salvador, a host of tenements and other buildings marked the other sectors.

Salvador knew he stood at the cusp of the Northern Sector, though the wall marking its boundary rose much higher in his dream than it did in the physical world.

In a dream, no wall could stop him, nor could the limits of the physical world hold him. Willing himself upward, he took to flight, with one destination fixed in his mind.

Racing up the height of the wall, he soared into the skies above, his eyes filling with a blinding light. His vision returned a moment later, a host of vibrant colors flooding his eyes.

The majestic landscape he had viewed once before spread beneath him. Sapphire and emerald streams sparkled, meandering through fields abounding with stunning floral displays.

All of the despair and anxiety that had crept into his heart when observing the Primordials fled, replaced with a lighthearted joy that soon had him laughing aloud. Slowing his speed, Salvador continued forward, savoring all the sights.

A few people walking through the fields turned their faces upward as he passed overhead. Smiling and laughing, they waved to Salvador, and he waved back to them.

None of them appeared to be a stranger. Sensing a connection to each and every one, he knew he shared something with them on a deeper level.

Flying toward the great city on the horizon, he oriented upon the spire rising from the top of the most prominent edifice within the incredible metropolis. Its high point looked to be touching the shimmering sky.

Nearing the crystalline structure, Salvador espied a narrow circular platform ringing the spire just beneath the uppermost point. A lone figure stood there, looking toward him.

Salvador smiled in recognition, alighting on the platform next to Jade.

"Well done, you made it to Faraway on your own," Jade said. "That is a stride in itself."

"How did you know I would come here, now?" Salvador asked, surprised, but not in any way distressed. "I could have just stayed awake for a while, or just gone to sleep without any intent of going anywhere."

"I may have been tipped off by a Voyager," Jade said, chuckling.

"A Voyager?" Salvador asked. "I know I have so much to learn."

"Anyone with a shred of wisdom recognizes there is so much to learn," Jade said, grinning. "So you are on the right path."

Salvador looked out over the metropolis with its wonders of architecture, beautiful parks, and dazzling waterways. Standing there at the top of the highest spire, he found it hard to believe it had all started in his favorite spot in the park, back in Technate

Six.

"I intend to stay on the right path," Salvador said, the enormity of it all striking him. "But thank you for taking me far away from where I was. This is far more than I could ever have hoped for, before I met you."

"I could only give you some guidance and insight," Jade said. "It was up to you to choose to embrace new possibilities and look to new horizons ... as it is for every person, no matter if they are in the physical world or another plane of existence."

Salvador looked back to Jade. Gratitude filled him, but so did the burning flame of a more personal mission.

"I want to help as many as I can to see those possibilities," he said, looking Jade in the eyes. "And I want to encourage them to go after them, without looking back. If I have a dream now, then that's it."

"That is the dream of the Navigator, my young friend," Jade replied with a kind smile. "To help others travel far away from the reach of darkness ... to see the horizons of realms unimaginable ... and to grow into the highest state of being ... forevermore."

A fire of purpose kindled inside, and serenity filled his heart, Salvador turned his gaze toward the horizon. A radiant smile beaming on his face, Salvador knew in the truest sense that he stood at the edge of forever.

From within the magnificent light, the grandest of journeys beckoned.

About the Author

Stephen Zimmer is an award-winning author and filmmaker based out of Lexington Kentucky. His works include the Rayden Valkyrie novels and Tales (Sword and Sorcery), the Rising Dawn Saga (Cross Genre), the Fires in Eden Series (Epic Fantasy), the Hellscapes short story collections (Horror), the Chronicles of Ave short story collections (Fantasy), the Harvey and Solomon Tales (Steampunk), The Faraway Saga (YA Dystopian/Cross-Genre) and the Ragnar Stormbringer Tales (Sword and Sorcery).

Stephen's visual work includes the feature film Shadows Light, shorts films such as The Sirens and Swordbearer, and the forthcoming Rayden Valkyrie: Saga of a Lionheart TV Pilot.

Stephen is a proud Kentucky Colonel who also enjoys the realms of music, martial arts, good bourbons, and spending time with family.

Find Stephen online at:

Website: www.stephenzimmer.com

Facebook: www.facebook.com/stephenzimmer7

Twitter: @sgzimmer

Instagram: @stephenzimmer7

www.ingramcontent.com/pod-product-compliance
Lightning Source LLC
Chambersburg PA
CBHW030552020726

47494CB00005B/1584